Ties That Bind

Ties That
Bind

PHILLIP MARGOLIN

HarperLargePrint
A Division of HarperCollins*Publishers*

HarperCollins books may be purchased for educational, business, or sales promotional use. For information, please write: Special Markets Department, Harper-Collins Publishers Inc., 10 East 53rd Street, New York, NY 10022.

FIRST LARGE PRINT EDITION

Designed by Jackie McKee

Printed on acid-free paper

Library of Congress Cataloging-in-Publication Data is available upon request.

ISBN 0-06-053326-9 (Large Print)
ISBN 0-06-008324-7 (Hardcover)

03 04 05 06 07 ❖/RRD 10 9 8 7 6 5 4 3 2 1

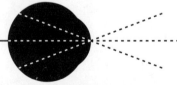

This Large Print Book carries the
Seal of Approval of N.A.V.H.

For Helen and Norman Stamm, great in-laws, thanks for raising such an excellent daughter.

Ties That
Bind

Prologue

JUNIOR
ACHIEVEMENT
December 1970

Pedro Aragon lay naked on a white sand beach in the arms of a lithe, brown-skinned woman who smelled of hibiscus. The fronds of a sheltering palm swayed to and fro above the lovers. Waves beat wildly against the shore. The moment would have been perfect had it not been for the fly buzzing in Pedro's ear.

Pedro tried to ignore the insect, but the incessant hum would not stop. He flicked a hand at it. The buzzing grew louder. Pedro opened his eyes, and the sun-kissed beach morphed into a narrow bed covered by soiled sheets. The sound of waves was replaced by the rat-a-tat-tat of rain beating on the grime-streaked windowpanes in Pedro's low-rent apartment. Gone, too, was the sweet scent of hibiscus. In its place was the musty smell of sweat, stale beer, and half-eaten pizza.

Pedro rolled on his side and stared at his droning alarm clock. For a moment, he regretted setting it. The dream had been so good. Then he remembered what might happen this evening, and he struggled out of bed. Pedro had seen too many lazy men miss their chances, and he was not going to let his slip away.

Pedro Aragon had left the slums of Mexico City for the gold-paved streets of America when he was fourteen. He was a slender boy with pearl-white teeth, dancing eyes, and a well-groomed mustache that covered lips prone to smile. It was hard to picture him hurting, let alone killing, anyone. But Pedro's easygoing mood could change without warning, bringing on brief moments of insane violence. It was this lack of predictability that made him so dangerous and caused even hard men to hesitate before challenging him.

Jesus Delgado, Portland point man for a Mexican cartel, was quick to recognize the young man's talents. Under his guidance, Pedro had become an effective member of Delgado's narcotics operation. Two months ago, Jesus had instructed his protégé to use a chainsaw to downsize a crew chief who was skimming profits. His reward was the deceased's job. Normally Pedro sold street amounts of heroin to burnouts, but tonight three college punks were looking to move some weight, and he could smell the money.

Pedro's current place of business was an abandoned house in a rundown neighborhood where people knew better than to complain to the cops—assuming that they'd talk to the cops at all. The lawn of the dilapidated house was out of control, dull gray paint was peeling from every exterior wall, and the overhang on the porch threatened to collapse. Pedro dashed through the rain and rapped on the front door. It opened instantly.

"Que pasa?" Pedro asked the armed guard.

"Business is slow."

"It'll pick up when the sun goes down."

Clyde Hopkins, a muscular cowboy with ties to Las Vegas gangsters, greeted Pedro then followed him down the hall. When they entered a small room at the back of the house, a slender man with glasses was swapping a stoned Janis Joplin wannabe a bindle of white powder for a fistful of crumpled currency. The woman rushed out without even a glance at Pedro. He knew that the entrance of the Devil himself wouldn't distract a junkie from her fix.

"Hey, Benny," Pedro said to the slender man,

who was sitting behind a rickety bridge table on which lay baggies filled with product. Behind the table stood an armed and grim-looking body-builder.

"Business is slow tonight," Benny answered, pointing to a stack of bedraggled bills bound with a rubber band. Pedro counted the day's take. It was low, but he wasn't worried. The college boys would come at ten-thirty and make everything right.

The preppies appeared right on time. Pedro watched them through the front window and laughed out loud as they got out of their wine-red Jaguar.

"Do you believe this?" he asked Clyde, who was watching over Pedro's shoulder.

"How have these boys stayed alive?" Clyde answered with a shake of his head. Driving a fancy car into this neighborhood was tantamount to carrying a sign that read PLEASE ROB ME.

Pedro judged the boys to be about his age—eighteen—but where the streets had made Pedro into a man, these three looked . . . juvenile. Yeah, soft, childlike, their well-fed faces still marred by acne; fear and want absent from their eyes. He re-

membered the way they had acted the night before at The Penthouse, Jesus Delgado's upscale
strip club, all peace signs and "groovy," larding
their conversation with high-school Spanish to
show that they were "cool"—calling Pedro
"amigo" and "bro."

The preppies were wearing a uniform as dis-
tinctive as gang colors: school blazers, chinos,
Oxford blue button-down shirts, and crew-neck
sweaters. The first boy was football-player big,
but flabby and soft, with a mop of unruly blond
hair. Still carrying his baby fat, Pedro thought.
The next one through the door was Pedro's
height—five ten—and skinny, with black horn-
rimmed glasses and limp black hair that hung to
his shoulders. He looked young, like a kid. Most
people would figure him for junior high way before they thought college. The last preppie was a
light heavyweight, rangy and strong-looking, with
a crewcut. If any of them were dangerous, it
would be number three. But Pedro did not expect danger; he expected cash, or "mucho
dinero," as the boys had put it when they explained their proposition, which involved moving
dope on their college campus. Pedro had listened
politely, knowing he couldn't lose. He'd rip them

off if their deal didn't feel right, or he'd start a pipeline into a seller's market where the consumers could pay top dollar.

"Pedro, my man!" Baby Fat said.

"Amigo," Pedro responded, initiating an elaborate handshake that he made up as he went along. **"Mi casa es su casa."**

"Right on!" Baby Fat answered enthusiastically. He beamed while the other two looked around nervously, taking in the AK-47 that rested on a table near a sagging couch, and the three hard cases who watched them from various parts of the room.

"So, we do business, no?" Pedro asked, putting on a heavy accent he'd mostly lost after four years in the States.

"Business, **si, amigo.** Lots of business."

"So, what you got for me?" Pedro asked.

"Hey, hey, that depends on what you got for us," Baby Fat answered cagily as the heads of the other two continued to swivel from one of Pedro's men to the other.

Pedro grinned. "For you I got the best shit ever. Come, I show you."

He started to turn but stopped, as the front-door guard stumbled into the room. Blood was running down the front of the guard's tie-dyed

T-shirt. Someone had slit his throat. The guard collapsed on the floor. Behind him stood a muscular black man sporting a wild Afro and holding a very large gun. The preppies' eyes went wide, and Clyde dove for the AK.

"Nah, I don't think so," the black man said, squeezing off two rounds. By the time Clyde's dead body hit the floor, the room was filled with armed and dangerous-looking men. The man who'd murdered Clyde lowered his weapon. Two of his associates moved cautiously down the hall toward the back room.

"You must be Pedro," he said calmly. Pedro did not answer. "Soon you're gonna be ex-Pedro." He chuckled. As Pedro's brain raced, trying to figure out a way to stay alive, he heard several shots and a scream from the direction of the back room. The leader grinned.

"I think my boys found your stash," he told Pedro. Then he looked at the white boys, paying attention to them for the first time. They looked terrified. Their hands were stretched high above their heads as if this were a western and the stagecoach robbers had just told them to grab some sky.

"What have we got here?" He looked over his shoulder at a man with an eye-catching scar that traced a ragged path from cheek to jaw. "Abdul, what you call those nice young boys who sing all pretty at the high school?"

"Glee club."

"Yeah, glee club." He turned back to the boys. "You all in a glee club?"

He shifted his attention back to Pedro. "Did I fuck up, Pedro? Word I had was that you're selling dope where you ain't supposed to, stealin' my customers, but I apologize if I messed up here. Was you all getting ready to sing 'Old Black Joe'?"

Pedro didn't answer.

"Yeah, that's what I thought. You motherfuckers ain't a glee club." He pointed his gun at Pedro. "I think you're a dope dealer who's dealin' dope in my territory." He shifted the gun muzzle so it pointed at the college boys. "And you're customers giving this spic motherfucker my money. Which means, you all got to die."

"Please, sir," the kid with the horn-rimmed glasses stuttered. "Can't you let us go? We won't tell anyone. I swear."

The leader looked as if he was considering the proposal.

"You swear, huh?"

"Yes, sir. We didn't know this was your territory.

We can buy our dope from you. We have plenty of money."

The black man grinned and nodded. "That sounds reasonable." He turned his head. "That sound reasonable to you, Abdul?"

"They do look like upstanding white boys," Abdul answered.

"You are upstanding, ain't you?" the leader asked.

"Yes, sir," said the kid with the glasses, nodding his head vigorously. "We all have very good grades."

"That right? Well then, Abdul, I think we can take their word that they won't tell the police that we blew away a house full of people and stole their money, don't you?"

"Definitely," Abdul said, flashing an evil smile at the boys.

"You will promise, won't you? Scout's honor?"

His light tone disappeared as he slowly raised the muzzle of his gun so it was pointing at the gold emblem that was sown on the blazer directly over the quaking boy's heart.

"I have money," the kid pleaded. "Lots of money."

As he reached behind him toward his wallet pocket, a wet stain spread across the front of the kid's chinos and a yellow puddle formed on the floor at his feet. The gang leader stared, then started to laugh. The eyes of the black invaders focused on the skinny kid's pee-stained crotch.

"You see that? He pissed himself."

They were all laughing when the kid whipped out the pistol concealed beneath his blazer and started blasting. The gangsters froze, then tried to react as the Light Heavy and Baby Fat pumped shots into them. Glass shattered, and chunks of the wall flew in all directions. Pedro dove for the AK-47. A shot blew out plaster where he'd been standing. He grabbed the gun, rolled behind a couch, and came up shooting as two men rushed out of the back room. The automatic sprayed shots across their chests, and they crumpled to the floor.

"Stop," the Light Heavy shouted, pressing the hot muzzle of his gun against Pedro's temple. "Put it down, Pedro. Be cool. I just want to be sure I don't get shot in the confusion."

Pedro weighed his chances. The gun screwed tighter into his skull, twisting the skin. He dropped his weapon.

"Okay," the Light Heavy said as he stepped back. Pedro looked around. Everyone was dead except him, the three schoolboys, and the leader of the black gang, who was gut-shot and rolling back and forth on the floor.

"Man, that was something," the kid with the horn-rimmed glasses said in an awed whisper.

"That was fucking-A great," Baby Fat agreed, "especially when you peed yourself."

"Hey, it got their attention, didn't it?" the kid asked with a grin.

Baby Fat sniffed as he waved a hand in front of his nose. "It's getting mine now."

"Screw you," the kid laughed, and he and Baby Fat traded high fives while Pedro stared in amazement. Then the kid walked over to the wounded black man, who was moaning in pain. The preppie grinned.

"Golly, I bet that hurts."

"Fuck you," the wounded man managed.

"Frankly, sir, I don't think you could get it up in your condition."

Baby Fat laughed.

"Finish him," the Light Heavy said, his voice tight. "We gotta get out of here."

"Be cool," the kid said as he circled his prey, pointing his gun at various parts of the man's anatomy while chanting, "Eeny meeny miny mo."

"Stop being a jerk," the Light Heavy told him.

"Gosh, you're no fun," the kid answered as he blew out the wounded man's kneecap, eliciting a hideous scream.

The kid laughed. "You can really hit those high notes." Then the smile left his lips and he looked the screaming man in the eyes. "Were you in your high school glee club, asshole?"

"Oh, for Christ's sake," the Light Heavy said, emptying two shots into the screaming man's head. "Now cut the shit and let's move."

Pedro tried to contain his fear. If he was going to die, he wanted to die like a man.

The Light Heavy turned to him. "Grab your dope."

Pedro wasn't sure he'd heard correctly.

"We gotta go. The cops will be here any minute."

They weren't going to kill him! Pedro's legs suddenly worked. He ran to the back room. Benny lay sprawled on the floor, a bullet hole in the center of his forehead. His bodyguard lay crumpled in a corner. Pedro tore his eyes away and stuffed his stash into a suitcase, then headed back to the front room.

"The goodies!" Baby Fat shouted.

"We got your money," the kid told Pedro. "We can still do this."

Pedro hesitated, confused.

"You owe us, amigo," Baby Fat told him. "You'd be dead if we weren't so fucking lethal."

Pedro stared at the Jaguar outside. "I don't know, man. You're gonna be hot. The cops will trace your car."

The preppies looked at each other and broke out laughing.

"Not to worry, bro," the kid assured him. "It's stolen."

Pedro thought he was beyond surprise, but these guys were from outer space. Then Baby Fat wrapped an arm around Pedro's shoulders. One look at his face told Pedro that everything that had happened here and at The Penthouse had been an act. He was suddenly more frightened than he'd been when he was facing certain death.

"We could kill you and steal your drugs," the fat boy told him in a quiet and confident tone, "but that would be short-sighted. What we want is a mutually beneficial partnership that will make us all a lot of money."

The kid shrugged. "If you're not interested, take off and Godspeed."

"What do you say, Pedro?" the Light Heavy asked. "Do you want to make some money?"

Pedro thought about the woman in his dream and the clean white beach.

"Let's go someplace and talk," he said.

Part One

THE FLASH
The Present

one

United States Senator Chester Whipple, Republican from South Carolina, a staunch soldier of God, did not drink, a fact he regretted as he paced back and forth across the front room of his Georgetown town house. It was two in the morning; his investigator, Jerry Freemont, was three hours late, and prayer alone was not calming his nerves.

The doorbell rang. Whipple rushed into the foyer, but he did not find his investigator standing on his front stoop when he opened the door. Instead, an elegantly dressed man, wearing an old school tie from Whipple's alma mater, smiled at him. The senator's visitor was of medium build and height. He wore his sandy hair slicked down; wire-rimmed glasses perched on a Roman nose. Whipple, a scholarship boy from a rural public school, disliked most of his privileged Harvard classmates, but they did not threaten him. In truth, Chester Whipple was a difficult man to frighten: He had the physical strength of a man who worked the land and the spiritual fortitude of one who never wavered in his faith.

"Senator, I apologize for the intrusion at this late hour," the man said, handing Whipple his card. It announced that J. Stanton Northwood II was a partner in a prominent D.C. firm. Later that week, Whipple would discover that the firm employed no one by that name.

"What do you want?" Whipple asked, genuinely puzzled and anxious for Northwood to leave before Jerry arrived.

Whipple's visitor looked grim. "I'm afraid that I'm the bearer of bad news. May I come in?"

Whipple hesitated, then led Northwood into the living room and motioned him into a seat. The lawyer leaned back, crossing his right leg over his left to expose freshly polished wingtips.

"It's Mr. Freemont," Northwood said. "He's not coming."

Whipple was confused. The lawyer looked solemn. "He was a fine investigator, Senator. He found the memo proving that several biotech companies contributed millions to a secret slush fund that Harold Travis is using to defeat the anti-cloning bill. Mr. Freemont also had pictorial and audio evidence that would have made a very persuasive case for criminal charges against Senator Travis and others. Unfortunately for you, he no longer has this evidence—we do."

Whipple was truly bewildered. He had no idea how Northwood knew about Jerry Freemont's assignment.

"It's all very perplexing, isn't it?" Northwood said. "You're expecting your investigator to bring you the key to your presidential nomination, and I show up instead." He dipped his head in mock sympathy. "But surely you didn't think that my principals would just stand by quietly while you put us out of business?"

The lawyer's condescension sparked Whipple's anger. He was a powerful man, feared by many, and he was not going to be patronized.

"Where is Jerry Freemont?" he demanded, rising to his full height so that he towered over the lawyer. Northwood was not fazed.

"I advise you to sit down," Whipple's visitor said. "You're in for a fairly strong shock."

"Listen, you two-bit shyster, you've got ten seconds to tell me where Jerry is before I beat it out of you."

"Let me show you," Northwood said as he pulled a snapshot out of his pocket and set it on the coffee table that separated him from the senator. "He was very brave. I want you to know that. It took several hours to convince him to tell us where he was hiding the evidence."

Whipple was stunned. The photograph showed a man, barely recognizable as Jerry Freemont, suspended in air by a length of chain that bound his wrists. It was impossible to tell where the shot had been taken, but the bare beams and peaked roof suggested a barn. Only Freemont's torso and head were visible in the shot, but the cuts and burns on his body could be seen clearly.

"Not a pretty sight," Northwood sighed. "But you need to know that my clients are very serious when they say that they will stop at nothing to achieve their ends."

Whipple could not tear his eyes from the photograph. Jerry Freemont was a tough ex–state trooper, a dear friend who had been with the senator since his first run at political office twenty years earlier. Whipple's features suffused with rage, and his muscles bunched for action. Then he froze. Northwood was pointing a gun at his heart.

"Sit," he said. Whipple hesitated for a moment.

Northwood dropped two more photographs on the coffee table. The blood drained from the senator's face.

"Your wife is a very handsome woman, and your granddaughter looks charming. She's five, isn't she?"

"What have you . . . ?"

"No, no. They're perfectly fine. If you cooperate, there will be absolutely nothing to worry about."

Whipple's hands curled into fists but he stayed where he was, seething with impotent fury.

"Please don't force me to shoot you, Senator. That wouldn't be good for you or my principals. And it certainly wouldn't save your family. If you think we'll forget about them once you're dead, you're mistaken."

Whipple felt his strength and anger drain out of him. He slumped back onto his chair.

"If you do as we say, you and your family will be safe."

"What do you want?" Whipple asked. He sounded completely defeated.

Northwood stood up. "Twenty years is a long time to be in politics, Senator. Maybe this would be a good time to retire so you can spend more time with your family. And you can do something for mankind as well by making certain that the anti-cloning bill doesn't make it out of your committee. There are some very fine companies trying to develop cures for disease through the use of cloning technology. When you think about how many sick people those companies can help I'm sure you'll see that your previous position on the bill was a mistake."

Northwood pocketed the photographs. "Do we understand each other, Senator?"

Whipple stared at the top of the coffee table. After a moment he nodded.

"I'm glad," Northwood said, sounding genuinely pleased. "Good evening."

Whipple listened to the clack of Northwood's shoes as he crossed the parquet floor of the foyer, undid the latch, and stepped outside. He heard the front door swing shut—a sound that signaled the end of a lifelong dream.

two

Amanda Jaffe stroked hard and felt her body rise as she cut through the water in the YMCA pool. This was the final fifty of a two hundred-meter workout leg, and she was going as hard as she could. For a moment, she felt like she was flying instead of swimming, then the far wall appeared and she jackknifed her body into a flip turn. Amanda came out of it perfectly and dug in for the final twenty-five meters. She was a tall woman with broad shoulders and well-muscled arms that moved her forward with grace and speed. Seconds later, she crashed against the wall and came up gasping for air.

"Not bad."

Amanda looked up, startled. A man crouched on the edge of the pool with a stopwatch in his hand. He had messy auburn hair and looked to be in his early thirties—somewhere around her age. His build marked him as a competitive swimmer. Despite his cheery grin and pleasant features, Amanda backed away from the wall to put space between them.

"Want to know your time?"

Amanda tried to ignore the sliver of fear that cut through her gut. She was still too winded to speak, so she nodded warily. When the man told her the time, Amanda couldn't believe it. She hadn't swum that fast in years.

"I'm Toby Brooks." He motioned toward the first two lanes where several men and women of various ages were churning the water. "I'm with the Masters swim team."

"Amanda Jaffe," she managed, fighting to tamp down her fear.

"Nice to meet you." Suddenly Brooks looked puzzled. Then he snapped his fingers. "Jaffe. Right!" Amanda was certain he was going to mention one of her cases. "UC Berkeley about 1993?"

Amanda's eyes widened from surprise, relieved that Brooks was not going to make her relive the recent past. "'92, but that's pretty good. How'd you know?"

"I swam for UCLA. You won the two hundred free at the Pac-10s, right?"

Amanda smiled despite herself. "You have some memory."

"My girlfriend at the time was one of the women you beat. She was really upset. You sure ruined my plans for the evening."

"Sorry," Amanda said. She felt uncomfortable with Brooks so close.

Brooks grinned. "No need to be. We weren't getting on that well, anyway. So, what happened after the Pac-10s?"

"Nationals. Then I quit. I was pretty burned out by my senior year. I stayed away from pools for about five years after I graduated."

"Me, too. I ran for a while until my joints started to ache. I just got back into competitive swimming."

Brooks stopped talking and Amanda knew he was waiting for her to continue the conversation.

"So, do you work at the Y?" she asked for something to say.

"No. I'm an investment banker."

"Oh," Amanda said, embarrassed. "I thought you were coaching the team."

"I swim on the team and help out. Our coach is

out sick today. Which reminds me. I put the clock on you for a reason. Ever thought about competing again? The Masters program is pretty low-key. We've got a good spread in our age groups—late twenties to three swimmers in their eighties. We could use someone with your experience."

"Thanks, but I have no interest in competing."

"Could have fooled me, the way you went at that last two hundred."

Amanda knew that Brooks was just trying to be friendly, but he just made her anxious. To her relief, he glanced over at the far lanes where a group of Masters swimmers had gathered along the wall. He stood up.

"Duty calls. It was nice meeting you, Amanda. Let me know if you change your mind about joining the team. We'd love to have you."

Brooks walked back to his charges. Amanda sank low in the water, leaned her head against the edge of the pool, and closed her eyes. Anyone watching would think that she was recovering from her swim, but Amanda was really fighting to keep her fear in check. She told herself that Brooks was just being friendly and that she had nothing to worry about, but she still felt anxious.

Little more than a year ago, she had almost

died solving a horrifying series of murders committed by a surgeon at St. Francis Medical Center. She had never fully recovered from the experience. Before the Cardoni case, swimming was a sure way to relax. That didn't always work now. Amanda thought about trying another hard two hundred, but she didn't have the mental or physical energy to swim another lap. The encounter with Brooks had drained her.

three

The caterers were packing up and the band had already left when Harold Travis said good-bye to the last of the guests who were not on the special-contributors list. Those four men were lounging in the den, smoking Cuban cigars and sipping 1934 Taylor Fladgate port. They were also making the acquaintance of some special ladies who were going to give them an erotic thank-you for their illegal campaign contributions to the man who would soon be the Republican nominee for president of the United States.

The fund-raiser had been held in the country-side, miles from Portland, in a seventeen-thou-sand-square-foot octagonal house; one of four owned by the chairman of the board of a California biotech company, who was in the master bedroom with a stunning Eurasian beauty. Moments after the taillights of the caterer's van faded away, Travis nodded to one of several body-guards who had moved among the guests incon-spicuously during the evening. When the guard began speaking into his cell phone, Travis crossed the lawn and lay down on a lounge chair at the edge of the swimming pool. The house lights re-flected in the dark water, floating ghostlike in the ripples caused by the breeze. It was the senator's first moment alone in hours, and he savored the quiet.

All of the party's biggest contributors were lin-ing up now that Chester Whipple was out of the race. If the newspapers had been caught off guard by his sudden withdrawal, they were stunned by the vote he'd used to block the anti-cloning bill, which he had supported with reli-gious fervor. Whipple's supporters were forced to back Travis now, if they wanted to have any in-fluence in the White House. The senator was making it easy for them. He had fought the anti-cloning bill behind the scenes, using front men to do the dirty work, and he was solidly conservative on most of the other issues Whipple's people favored.

Travis closed his eyes and imagined his victory in November. The Democrats were in disarray. They didn't even have a clear front-runner in the primaries, let alone someone who would threaten him in the general election. The presidency was his for the taking.

"They're pulling up, Senator."

Travis had been so absorbed in his thoughts that he had not heard the bodyguard approach. He followed the man to the front of the house. A black Porsche was just rounding the last turn in the long driveway. Travis grew hard with anticipation and did not notice Ally Bennett, a dark-haired woman in a short black evening dress, who also watched the arrival of the Porsche from the front door.

When the car stopped, the bodyguard opened the passenger door, and Lori Andrews, a slender blonde, got out. She looked around nervously. The heat rose in the senator's cheeks and groin, making him feel like a horny teenager who was about to get laid for the first time.

Jon Dupre, a handsome young man dressed in jeans, a tight black T-shirt, and a white silk jacket got out of the driver's side of the Porsche and walked over to Travis. Ally Bennett walked to his side and smiled at Lori.

"Special delivery as requested, Senator," Dupre said, flashing a cocky smile.

"Thank you, Jon."

When Lori saw the senator, the blood drained from her face. Andrews was frail and tiny, and looked as if she'd just recently hit puberty, even though she was a mother in her early twenties. Lori's parents were hard-nosed farmers who had kicked her out when they learned that she was pregnant. She hadn't finished high school, she was not particularly bright, and her looks were all she had going for her. Jon Dupre had taken her off the streets, cleaned her and fed her, and added her to his stable, because he knew that she would do anything to keep her daughter, Stacey, safe and warm. Fear and necessity had made her Jon's slave, but that was going to change. She knew that she and Stacey would be free soon. Until that happened, she had to do what Jon commanded, but she never dreamed that Jon would make her go with the senator again, especially after the last time.

Lori grabbed her pimp's sleeve. "Please, Jon."

"What's the matter?" asked Ally Bennett as she slipped a miniature cassette into Dupre's hand. He pocketed it quickly.

"He's the one," Lori said.

Ally looked blank for a second. Then she understood. She stepped in front of Dupre, blocking his path to the senator.

"You can't, Jon. Please," Ally begged.

"It's out of my hands," Dupre answered.

"You're a real bastard."

Dupre looked embarrassed. Before he could answer, Travis said, "Aren't you supposed to be in the den?"

Travis nodded to one of the bodyguards. "Get her out of here."

The bodyguard took hold of Ally's elbow.

"Let go of me," Ally said angrily. She tried to pull away but the guard's grip was too strong.

"I'm sorry," Ally told Lori as she was led into the house.

"I thought you were bringing your best girls," Travis snapped.

"Ally is great," Dupre assured him. "She'll be terrific."

"She'd better be," Travis said. Then he nodded to another man who had been quietly smoking in the shadows at the side of the house. The man walked into the light. He was dark-skinned, wiry, and of average height. His short-sleeved shirt showed off muscular arms covered by threatening tattoos. The man's face was flat and pockmarked; his brown eyes were lifeless. A slight mustache covered his upper lip.

"**Buenos noches,** Lori," he said in a sweet voice that belied his hard looks. "Once again, I will be your driver."

Lori's hand flew to her mouth.

"Come, **chiquita.**"

She cast a pleading look at Dupre, but he would not meet her eye.

"What about one of the other girls," he suggested to Travis, a slight quaver in his voice.

"Don't you have enough trouble without pissing me off?" the senator answered angrily before turning his back on Dupre and walking into the house.

"Manuel," Dupre said to the man who was standing next to Lori, "can't you do anything?"

"Who am I to stand in the way of true love?"

"He's a fucking psycho," Dupre said, lowering his voice so that only he, Manuel, and Lori could hear. Manuel nodded his head toward Andrews.

"She's just pussy, man. Harold is gonna be the head of the FBI, the CIA, the DEA, and a lot of other letters in the alphabet that can fuck up both of us. That's not a man you want to annoy."

Reality set in and Dupre swallowed. When he turned to Lori, he tried to look reassuring.

"I'm sorry, kid. There's nothing I can do."

Lori looked sick. Manuel took her by the arm and led her toward a waiting car. As they faded into the dark, Dupre touched the cassette through the fabric of his coat. Manuel was right. He was out on bail, and his lawyer wasn't too sure about the outcome of his case. He needed friends in high places, and there wasn't any place higher than the White House.

Harold Travis uncurled his clenched fists and noticed that they were covered in blood. How had that happened? He remembered the girl fleeing the bedroom. My, she was fast. Her little rump had been tight and her little breasts had jiggled when she jumped across the bed. He'd let her think she could get away before catching her in the living room. He remembered leaping over the couch and grabbing a fistful of hair, but the rest was a blur. Now, Andrews was sprawled on the floor, her head turned at an odd angle and surrounded by a halo of blood. What a waste.

Travis closed his eyes and took slow, deep breaths. When he opened his eyes, he felt calmer and better able to evaluate the situation. No need to get excited, he convinced himself. This was just a tragic accident. The girl must have hit her head on the baseboard and snapped her neck or some such thing. Accidents happened every day. It wasn't his fault if the girl met with an accident. The phrase itself flooded him with relief. "Met with an accident" was exactly what she'd done. The little blonde was in the living room, and an accident was in the living room, and they'd met, that's all. It had nothing to do with him.

Travis caught a glimpse of his reflection in the mirror. It startled him. Blood had turned some of his curly black chest hairs red, and there was spatter on his cheeks and forehead. What a mess.

What to do? What to do? Take a shower, of course, but what about the body? He wasn't going to risk getting caught moving it, which meant that he'd have to have Pedro Aragon's man— Manuel—take care of it. Shower first or call Manuel first, that was the question. There was the sticky problem of getting blood all over the phone, so Travis compromised. He headed for the kitchen sink. It felt good to walk naked through the house. He was in his late forties, but his body was still firm, powerful. He liked feeling strong and sexually potent.

Travis continued to consider his options as he washed his hands. Manuel had been very efficient that other time. Of course, he only had to take the girl to the hospital and threaten her a little, then pay her something extra. There hadn't been a body to dispose of, or a room to clean. And the downside of using one of Aragon's men was that Manuel would tell Pedro, and Pedro'd tell the others, but it couldn't be helped. He was certain that they would call him on the carpet, as they had before. He smiled as he remembered how they had berated him. He'd hung his head and acted contrite, but inside he'd been laughing. Let them save face, let them think that they were in charge. He was the United States senator. He was the one who would soon be the president of the United States.

four

Tim Kerrigan groped for his coffee mug without taking his eyes from his computer monitor. He took a sip and grimaced. The office coffee was vile to start with. Now it was cold. How long did it take for hot coffee to cool? The senior deputy district attorney looked at his watch and cursed. It was already seven-thirty, and his brief had to be in Judge Lerner's chambers by nine.

Patrolman Myron Tebo, with all of six weeks on the job, had arrested Claude Digby while he was standing over the battered body of Ella Morris, an eighty-five-year-old widow. The teenage burglar had confessed to the murder but yesterday, moments before court adjourned, Digby's lawyer had cross-examined Tebo about the circumstances surrounding his client's statements. It was the rookie's first time on the stand and he'd fallen apart, forcing Kerrigan to spend the previous evening in the courthouse library researching the law of criminal confessions.

Tim's wife, Cindy, had been upset when he told her he wouldn't be home for dinner. Megan, too: she was five years old and didn't understand why Daddy wanted to write a memo to a judge when he should be reading her another bedtime installment of **Alice's Adventures in Wonderland**. Tim had thought about trying to explain why his work was important, but he was too tired to make the effort. Cindy had barely spoken to him this morning when he crept out of bed at five-thirty to go downtown to finish the memo. Since six-fifteen, he had been hunting for the words that would convince a liberal judge that a flustered rookie cop's slightly altered version of the Miranda warnings should not invalidate a confession of murder.

"You busy?"

Kerrigan looked up and found Maria Lopez standing in the doorway. Crumbs from one of the doughnuts she was always munching clung to her lower lip. After a year of handling misdemeanors, the slightly overweight, bespectacled deputy DA had graduated recently to Unit D, which prosecuted sex crimes, assaults, and other felonies. Tim was the senior deputy in Unit D, which made him Maria's supervisor. The interruption annoyed Tim but he didn't let it show.

"What's up?" he asked, taking a quick look at his watch.

Maria slumped into a seat across from the senior deputy. Her suit was rumpled and her long black hair had partially slipped out of the barrette that pinned it in a bun at the back of her head. Maria's bloodshot eyes told Kerrigan that the deputy hadn't slept either.

"I'm prosecuting a guy named Jon Dupre."

"Pimping, right?"

Lopez nodded. "Compelling and promoting. The guy runs an upscale escort service."

"Drugs, too, no?"

"Cocaine and ecstasy for college kids. My case is strictly the escort service, and it depends on the testimony of one of Dupre's women, who we rolled."

Lopez shifted in her seat. She was definitely on edge.

"And?" Kerrigan prodded.

"Stan Gregaros can't find her."

"Does Stan think she split?" Kerrigan asked, concerned. Dupre wasn't the biggest fish in corruption's pond, but he wasn't a minnow, either.

"He's not sure. Lori's kid was staying with a neighbor. . . ."

"Lori?"

"Lori Andrews. She's the witness."

"Go ahead," Kerrigan said, sneaking another look at his watch.

"Andrews and the neighbor have an arrangement. The kid stays with her when Lori's working. The problem is, Lori never picked up Stacey."

"Is Andrews the type to run and leave her kid?"

Lopez shook her head. "The kid's the reason she agreed to testify. We had her on possession and sale, and she knew Children's Services would take her daughter away from her if she went to prison."

"Do you think Dupre did something to her?"

"I don't know. He could've. He's brutal if his girls get out of line."

"What happens if Stan doesn't find her?"

Lopez fidgeted and looked down. "When we indicted, we convinced Judge Robard to treat our witness as a confidential reliable informant so we wouldn't have to give Dupre her name."

"Why didn't you just put her somewhere he couldn't find her?"

Lopez reddened.

Kerrigan sat up straight. "Tell me she's not still turning tricks."

"The feds are involved. They wanted her inside to find out where Dupre kept his records."

Kerrigan calmed himself. It wasn't Maria's fault. Federal agents could be intimidating, and she was new in felonies and would want to play ball. Kerrigan remembered how important he'd felt the first time one of his cases had been big enough to involve the FBI.

"The trial starts this afternoon," Lopez continued uncomfortably. "I don't have a case without the CRI."

"Ask for a setover."

"We've asked for two already so the FBI could milk the witness. Dupre's attorney went ballistic the second time, and Judge Robard said there wouldn't be a third."

"This woman is essential?" Kerrigan asked.

Lopez nodded.

"If you pick a jury and she doesn't show, will Dupre get a Judgment of Acquittal?"

"Robard wouldn't have a choice."

"Then you have to dismiss, because Double Jeopardy attaches as soon as the jury is sworn."

"Dupre's lawyer will move for a dismissal with prejudice."

Kerrigan thought for a moment. "Robard is a hard-ass," he said. "He won't grant one. And, even if he does, the odds are that it wouldn't stand up on appeal."

Lopez balled her fists. "I really want this guy."

"You'll get him, Maria. Guys like Dupre always trip over their egos. Trust me. It's just a matter of time."

Heads turned when Tim Kerrigan pushed through the courtroom doors and took a seat on the backbench of Judge Ivan Robard's court-room—fewer than would have turned when he first joined the office four years ago, but enough to still make him feel uncomfortable. The bailiff, the court guards, and the other regulars were used to seeing Kerrigan, but some of the casual spectators cast excited glances his way and whispered to each other.

Tim saw his celebrity as a curse. It meant being constantly on display. He also thought of his looks as a curse. He was six two, tall enough to always be in plain sight, and he had wavy blond hair and green eyes that made him stand out in a crowd. More than once, he had daydreamed about walking into a courtroom unrecognized. He envied Maria Lopez. No one looked twice at her; strangers didn't stop her on the street or interrupt her meals to ask for autographs. Tim was certain that given the chance to be a celebrity, Maria would trade places with him eagerly. He would have swapped in an instant, without warning her to be careful about what she wished for.

Kerrigan had just gotten settled when Jon Dupre strutted into the courtroom in a dark, tailor-made suit, basking in the same stares that Kerrigan dreaded. He was tall, tanned, handsome, and muscular, and he walked with an easy confidence that came from growing up wealthy and pampered. A gold earring in the shape of a cross dangled from an earlobe—just one of many pieces of flashy jewelry that the light danced off as he walked.

Trailing behind Dupre was his lawyer, Oscar Baron, a short, nervous man who, rumor had it, took part of his attorney fee in the women and drugs that Dupre sold.

Lopez looked up from her case file when Dupre entered the bar of the court. The defendant ignored the deputy DA and took his seat at the defense table, but Baron paused to speak to his opponent in low tones. When the bailiff rapped his gavel, there was a broad smile on Baron's face and a grim look of defeat on Maria's.

Judge Robard entered the courtroom through a door behind the dais, and everyone stood. Most eyes turned toward the judge, but Kerrigan's stayed focused on Dupre who had been talking to a woman seated behind him in the spectators' section. Another spectator blocked Tim's view of the woman, but the man shifted slightly when he stood for the judge. Kerrigan's breath caught in his chest.

Every once in a while a man will see a woman whose beauty short-circuits his senses. This woman's raw sensuality stunned Kerrigan. Lustrous, jet-black hair framed her heart-shaped face. She had olive skin, full lips, wide brown eyes, and high cheekbones. The bailiff rapped his gavel a second time, and Kerrigan lost sight of her again when everyone sat, but he could not tear his eyes away from the spot where she'd stood.

"Nice ass, huh?" whispered Stanley Gregaros, a detective with vice who was working Dupre's case.

Kerrigan felt heat spread across his cheeks. "Who is she?"

"Ally Bennett," answered Gregaros as he slipped into the seat beside Kerrigan. "She's in Jon's stable. Calls herself Jasmine when she's working."

"She doesn't look like your typical hooker."

"None of Jon's girls do. They're all classy fillies. College kids, smart, sassy, corn-fed. Jon's clientele is rich and influential. A congressman or CEO isn't going to spend a grand or two on a crack whore."

"Call the case," Judge Robard ordered. The bailiff rattled off the case name and number as Maria Lopez stood.

"Are you ready to proceed, Miss Lopez?" the judge asked.

"The state has a problem, Your Honor. I'm asking for a setover."

"We object, Your Honor," Oscar Baron said, leaping to his feet. "This is the third time Miss Lopez has done this. The last time . . ."

The judge cut him off with a wave of his hand. He did not look happy. "What's the basis for your motion, Miss Lopez?"

"Our key witness has disappeared. We were in

contact with her as late as two days ago. The witness was under subpoena and assured us that she would appear."

"But she hasn't?"

"No, Your Honor. I talked to my trial assistant before I came to court. We sent an investigator to pick her up, but she wasn't home."

"The last time I granted your setover request I told you that I wouldn't grant another. Can you give me one good reason to change my mind?"

Lopez cast a nervous glance at Jon Dupre, who looked bored to death.

"Mr. Dupre has been out of custody since his bail hearing. He has a history of violence toward women . . ."

"This is outrageous," Oscar Baron shouted. "Mr. Dupre has always claimed that he's innocent of these groundless charges. I'm not surprised the state's witness didn't show. She's probably worried about perjury. And to suggest that my client had anything to do with her disappearance . . ."

"There's no need for speeches, Mr. Baron," Judge Robard said.

He turned back to Lopez. "Does your case rest completely on the testimony of this missing witness?"

"She's essential, Your Honor."

"Then it looks like you're between a rock and a hard place. Mr. Dupre has a right to have his case tried. This is the time we've set for the trial. You're going to have to choose between proceeding or dismissing."

Lopez moved for dismissal and Baron moved for a dismissal with prejudice. While they argued, Kerrigan turned to the detective.

"What do you think happened, Stan?"

He shook his head. "No idea. Andrews seemed standup. But Dupre can be a scary guy. Maybe she got cold feet."

Kerrigan shifted his attention to the front of the courtroom when Judge Robard began to speak.

"I've heard enough. The case will be dismissed on the motion of the district attorney. Bail will be exonerated."

"Is that dismissal with prejudice, Your Honor?"

"No it is not, Mr. Baron. Court is adjourned."

Everyone in the courtroom stood when the judge rose, and Kerrigan moved his head slightly so he could see Ally Bennett again. She turned toward him for a moment, and his gut tightened. Bennett was dressed in a black tailored jacket over a cream-colored silk blouse. A string of pearls graced her slender neck. A short black skirt showed off lightly muscled and tanned legs.

A dispirited Maria Lopez stuffed her paper-work in a file and marched, head down, up the aisle. Kerrigan and Gregaros fell in step beside her.

"It's not your fault, Maria," Kerrigan assured his disconsolate deputy. "I've been through this. So have most of the DAs in the office."

"We'll find Andrews," Gregaros assured her. "Then you'll put that arrogant prick away."

As they passed through the courtroom doors, Kerrigan cast one more glance at Ally Bennett, who was having an animated conversation with Dupre. She looked upset. Then the door closed behind Kerrigan, and the couple was lost from view.

That evening, Tim Kerrigan braved his wife's anger and daughter's disappointment and stayed late again, but he only pretended to work. There were cases to prepare and legal briefs to write, but he was too distracted to concentrate. By six, only a few stalwarts were still working. When all of the deputies and secretaries in the area had left, Kerrigan wandered over to Maria Lopez's desk. The cleaning people were starting to move through the office, but Kerrigan was not concerned about them, and he had a story prepared if another deputy spotted him.

The loose-leaf binders containing the Dupre case were neatly stacked on one corner of Maria's desk. Kerrigan's hand trembled when he opened the top binder. It contained the police reports in the case. He leafed through them until he found what he wanted. Then he wrote Ally Bennett's address and phone number on a slip of paper and walked back to his office.

His pulse was pounding when he closed his door. He sat down and stared at the white notepaper with his nervous scrawl. On his desk was a photograph of Cindy and Megan. Kerrigan squeezed his eyes shut. His blood roared in his ears.

Kerrigan reached for his phone and dialed Ally's number. The receiver felt hot in his hand. The phone rang twice. Kerrigan's grip tightened. He started to hang up.

"Hello?"

It was a woman. Her voice was husky.

"Hello?" she repeated.

Kerrigan replaced the receiver on the cradle, closed his eyes, and leaned his head back. What was he thinking? His heartbeat was rapid enough to alarm him, so he took long, deep breaths. After a moment, he picked up the phone and dialed again. Cindy answered.

"Hi, hon," he said. "I caught a break. Tell Megan I'll be home soon."

five

"Can you take a look at something for me?" Frank Jaffe asked from the doorway of Amanda's office. Amanda's father, a solidly built man in his late fifties, had a ruddy complexion and gray-streaked, curly black hair. A nose broken in his youth made him look more like a stevedore than a lawyer.

Amanda glanced at the clock. "I was wrapping up. I've got a date tonight."

"This won't take long." Frank walked over to her desk and handed her a thick file. "It's that new case I picked up in Coos Bay, the murder. There was a search at Eldrige's summer cabin and I want your opinion. I dictated a memo on the points I'm interested in. I'd do it myself, but I'm off to Roseburg for a hearing."

"Can't this wait until the morning?"

"I have to make some decisions in the case early tomorrow. Come on, help me here."

Amanda sighed. "You can be a real pain in the ass sometimes."

Frank grinned. "Love you, too. I have to be in court at nine in the morning, so call my motel room around seven. The number is clipped to the file."

As soon as the door closed, Amanda opened the file. When she pulled out a stack of police reports, some crime-scene photographs fell onto her blotter. One showed a woman's body sprawled on a beach where the tide had left her. Close-ups of her bloated and ravaged face documented the destruction the sea and its creatures had wreaked on her humanity.

A horrible memory overwhelmed Amanda. Without warning, she was naked, her hands bound, running in the dark, prodded by the point of a sharp knife. She fought for air, her breath coming in short gasps, just as it had on that terrible night in the tunnel. For a moment she even thought that she smelled damp earth. Amanda jammed her fist into her mouth to keep from screaming. She flung herself out of her chair and huddled on the floor in a corner of her office, bringing her knees to her chest and squeezing her eyes shut. The blood had drained from her face. Her heart was racing.

Amanda had a very clear memory of the first time she saw an autopsy photograph. She had graduated from New York University School of Law near the top of her class and had been offered a clerkship at the United States Court of Appeals for the Ninth Circuit. One morning, Judge Buchwald had asked her to review the file in a death penalty case. From the briefs, Amanda learned that the defendant's wife had died from shock after he shot her in the shoulder with a shotgun. Shortly before lunch, Amanda noticed an innocuous-looking brown envelope buried under some papers. She became curious and opened the flap. The envelope contained a stack of photographs. When she turned the first one over, she almost passed out. In retrospect, this black-and-white photograph of a dead woman on an autopsy table had been rather tame. The only wound was in the victim's shoulder. Without color, it was hard for Amanda to tell that she was seeing torn and mutilated flesh. Still, she had been dizzy and disoriented for the rest of the day.

In the intervening years, Amanda had viewed photographs portraying every manner of cruelty that can be inflicted on a human being. Soon the most gruesome sights had no effect on her. Then the surgeon—a sadistic murderer—had entered her life. Policemen or medical examiners are sometimes viewed as callous by civilians who hear them cracking jokes while standing over a victim, but people who deal with violent death on a daily basis have to shield themselves from the horrors that they encounter, so they can continue to function. Amanda's trauma had ripped away her shield.

When Amanda opened her eyes, she saw where she was. She didn't remember hiding in the corner. She had no idea how she'd gotten from her desk to the floor.

Amanda parked in the basement garage of a converted red-brick warehouse in Portland's Pearl District and took the elevator to her loft. It was twelve hundred feet of open space with hardwood floors, high ceilings, and tall windows that gave her a view of the metal arches of the Freemont Bridge, tankers churning the waters of the Willamette River, and the snow-covered slopes of Mount St. Helens.

Amanda double-locked her door and checked the apartment. It was irrational to think that someone was lurking inside, but she knew that she wouldn't be able to relax until she made sure that she was alone. Amanda thought back to her equally irrational reaction to Toby Brooks. She had to stop being afraid of everything. Every person she met was not a monster.

Amanda changed into sweats and went to her liquor cabinet. She was still upset by her reaction to the autopsy photographs and she needed a drink. The doorbell made her jump. Who . . . ? Then she remembered. She looked at her watch. How had it gotten so late? She peered through the peephole. Mike Greene was in the hall. He had a bouquet of flowers. Shit! What was she going to do?

Mike had been the prosecuting attorney in the Cardoni case, and Amanda had gone out with the deputy district attorney a few times since its violent conclusion. Mike was a bear of a man, with curly black hair and a shaggy mustache. Despite having a body that made people think football or wrestling, he had never competed in any sport. Greene was a gentle soul who played tenor sax with a local jazz quartet and had a passion for chess. She knew that he also cared about her, but she found it impossible to make any kind of emotional commitment since her encounter with the surgeon.

"Hi," Mike said when Amanda opened the door. Then he saw the way she was dressed.

"I'm sorry. I forgot we were going out."

Greene could not hide his disappointment. She felt terrible.

"I'm not feeling well," she said, only half lying. She felt drained and knew that she'd never have the energy to make it through their date. Greene's shoulders sagged. The hand holding the bouquet dropped to his side.

"What's going on, Amanda?"

She lowered her gaze, unable to look Mike in the eye.

"I know I should have called."

"I thought you forgot about our date."

"Don't cross-examine me," Amanda snapped, angry at being caught in a lie. "We're not in court."

"No, we're not," Mike said evenly. "There are rules in court. People have to follow them. You seem to be playing by your own rules when it comes to the two of us, and I have no idea what they are."

Amanda looked down at the rug. "I'm going through some . . . things. I just . . ."

She broke off and walked half way to the window. A river of headlights was flowing across the Freemont Bridge. She fixed on the lights.

"Look, Amanda, I know what you've been through, so I've tried to be understanding. I . . . I like you. I want to help."

"I know, Mike. I just can't. . . ."

She shook her head, her back still to him. She waited for him to say something, but he didn't speak and she did not hear him move. When she turned, she saw that Mike had laid the flowers on the coffee table.

"If I can help, call me. I'll be there for you."

Mike left, taking care to close the door quietly. Amanda sat on the couch. She felt terrible. Mike was so nice, and Amanda felt safe with him. She wondered if that wasn't what attracted her to him.

An image of Toby Brooks flashed into her head. If Mike made Amanda think of a teddy bear, Toby made her think of a cat. He made her think of someone else, too. She started to feel the way she had at the office. Fear began to overwhelm her again, and she struggled to hang on. All of a sudden, she was sorry that she had sent Mike away. She needed someone with her. She did not want to be alone.

six

A little after three on Thursday afternoon, Tim Kerrigan met with the detectives who were working a case involving a child pornography ring. Then he brainstormed with another DA about the best way to handle a tricky suppression motion. When the deputy left, Kerrigan checked his watch. It was after five, and Jack Stamm, the Multnomah County district attorney, would be by in forty-five minutes to take him over to the dinner that would kick off the National Association of Trial Lawyers convention.

There were so many other things Tim would rather be doing than attending that dinner. He put his feet up on his desk and closed his eyes. He rubbed his lids and drifted for a moment. His thoughts turned to the crumpled scrap of paper in his wallet, on which he had scrawled Ally

Bennett's phone number. Stan Gregaros said Bennett's working name was Jasmine. He said the name to himself, drawing it out. He felt a nervous buzz in his belly and heat below his waist.

Jasmine would not be the first prostitute he'd been with but, somehow, Kerrigan knew that Ally Bennett would be different from the others—different from any woman he'd ever been with. Her breasts would be perfect, her buttocks would be exquisite, and her mouth would perform miracles. "Tell me what you want," she would say, and he would tell her what he needed, he would tell her the things that he could never tell Cindy.

Someone knocked on his doorjamb. Tim's eyes opened. Maria Lopez was standing in the doorway, looking like she'd lost her best friend. Kerrigan dropped his feet to the floor. He was suddenly aware of the ringing of a phone and the murmur of conversations outside his office.

"Do you have a moment?"

Tim managed a nod. Maria crossed the room and sat down.

"What's up?" Kerrigan asked the young DA.

"A hiker found Lori Andrews in Washington Park."

"Ah shit."

"It's Dupre. He killed her."

"You know that for a fact?"

Lopez shook her head. "But I know he did it." She rubbed her forehead. "I saw the pictures, Tim. She was naked. She'd been beaten so badly. Then that bastard dumped her like a sack of garbage." Maria paused. She looked devastated. "Her little girl will probably go into foster care."

"Don't beat yourself up like this. We all make mistakes," Kerrigan said unconvincingly, thinking of his own.

Silvio Barbera, a senior partner in a major Wall Street law firm and the current president of the National Association of Trial Lawyers, looked out over the crowd in the Hilton ballroom from behind the podium that had been set up for the keynote speaker.

"I have been a football fan my whole life," he confessed. "I remember Doug Flutie throwing the Hail Mary pass that beat Miami and Franco Harris's Immaculate Reception, but my greatest football moment came eight years ago when Michigan played Oregon in the Rose Bowl. Remember the game? Both teams were unbeaten, and the national championship was on the line. When the fourth quarter started, Michigan led by twenty points and the announcers had written off the Ducks. That's when one of the greatest comebacks in college football history started.

"On the first play from scrimmage, Oregon's star running back ran sixty-five yards and Oregon was only down by thirteen. Michigan missed a field goal with seven minutes left on the clock. Two plays later, the same running back sliced through Michigan's line again for forty-eight yards and cut Michigan's lead to six. The teams traded field goals. When Oregon took over for its final series on its own ten, there were only forty-three seconds left on the clock.

"Oregon's quarterback had a good arm. Everyone expected him to fling a pass toward the end zone and pray for a miracle. Instead, he handed off to his back one more time. Ninety yards later, Oregon was the national champion. That year no one questioned who deserved the Heisman Trophy as the nation's best college football player.

"Now most young men who win the Heisman make millions by turning pro, but this young man was cut from a different cloth. He went to law school. As we all know, many young law-school graduates sign on with firms like mine, but this young man showed his character." Barbera paused while the audience laughed. "He turned his back on riches once again and opted instead for a job with the district attorney's office here in Portland, where he has dedicated his life to public service ever since.

"When I learned that this year's convention was going to be in Oregon I knew immediately who I wanted as our keynote speaker. He is one of the greatest college football players who ever lived, he is a great prosecutor, but most important, he is a man of great integrity and an example to us all.

"So, it is with great pleasure that I introduce our keynote speaker, Tim Kerrigan!"

Tim had lost track of the times he'd delivered "The Speech." He'd made it before youth groups and Rotary Clubs, at sports camps and churches. Appearance fees for "The Speech" had paid his law-school tuition and the down payment on his first house. Every time he gave "The Speech" it was greeted with enthusiastic applause. Afterward people wanted to shake his hand just so they could say they had touched him. Sometimes people told him that he had changed their lives. And Tim stood there and smiled and nodded, as a knife turned in the pit of his stomach.

Kerrigan had tried to beg off when Jack Stamm told him about Silvio Barbera's call. Stamm had misinterpreted his reluctance as modesty. He'd emphasized the honor of having a Multnomah County prosecutor as the convention's keynote speaker. Kerrigan gave in. If it wasn't for the scotch he'd consumed before going to the banquet and the other drinks he'd put down during dinner, he wasn't certain he would have been able to go through with it again.

As usual, when the speech was over, a crowd formed around Kerrigan. He put on his best smile and listened with feigned enthusiasm to everyone who spoke to him. When most of the well-wishers had cleared the ballroom, Tim spotted Hugh Curtin lounging alone at a table near the dais. Their eyes met and Hugh raised a glass in a mock toast.

It didn't take a genius to figure out why the former All-American lineman had been nicknamed "Huge." After four years of opening gaping holes for Kerrigan, Curtin had gone on to play pro ball for the Giants. A knee injury had ended his career after three seasons but "Huge," who had always seen pro ball as a quick path to financial security, had started law school while playing in the NFL.

He had just made partner at Reed, Briggs, Stephens, Stottlemeyer and Compton, Portland's biggest law firm.

As soon as the last well-wisher left, the smile drained from Tim's face and he slumped onto a chair next to Curtin, who had a tall glass of scotch waiting for him. Hugh raised his glass.

"To The Flash!" he said, using the nickname a publicist had dreamed up during Kerrigan's Heisman campaign. Kerrigan gave him the finger and downed most of his drink.

"I hate that name and I hate giving that fucking speech."

"People eat it up. It makes them feel good."

"A one-legged man could have run ninety yards with the holes you guys made for me. That was probably the best offensive line in college history. How many of you made it big in the pros?"

"You were good, Tim. You'd have found out how good if you'd turned pro."

"Bullshit. I'd never have made it. I was too slow and I didn't have the moves. I'd just have embarrassed myself."

It was the excuse he always gave for not turning pro. He'd given it so many times that he'd actually come to believe it.

Curtin rolled his eyes. "We have this same discussion every time you get maudlin. Let's talk about something else."

"You're right. I shouldn't cry on your shoulder."

"Damn straight. You're not pretty enough."

"I'd be the best-looking piece you ever had," Kerrigan retorted. Hugh threw his head back and laughed, and Kerrigan couldn't help smiling. Hugh was his best friend. He was a safe haven. Whenever he got down on himself, Hugh would trick him back through time to college and the parties and the beers with the team. Hugh could make him forget about the guilt that weighed him down like a two-ton anchor.

"You want to head over to the Hardball and tip a few brewskis?" Curtin asked.

"I can't do it. I promised Cindy I'd come home as soon as this fiasco was over," Kerrigan lied.

"Suit yourself. I have to be in court in the morning anyway."

"But we'll do it soon, Huge," Kerrigan said, slurring his words slightly. "We'll do it soon."

Curtin studied his friend carefully. "You okay to drive?"

"No problem. The old Flash isn't gonna get tagged for DUII."

"You're sure?"

Kerrigan got teary-eyed. He leaned over drunk-enly and hugged his friend.

"You always look out for me, Huge."

Curtin was embarrassed. He disengaged him-self and stood up.

"Time to get you home, buddy, before you start crying on the good linen."

The friends walked outside to the parking lot. It had rained during dinner and the cold air sobered Kerrigan a little. Curtin asked again if he was sure he could drive and offered Tim a lift home, but Kerrigan waved him off. Then he sat in his car and watched his friend drive away. The truth was that he wasn't okay and he did not want to go home. He wanted something else.

Megan was probably asleep by now and think-ing of her almost stopped him, but not quite. Kerrigan walked back inside the hotel and found a pay phone. Then he took the slip of paper with Ally Bennett's number out of his wallet and smoothed it out so he could read it. He felt sick as he dialed, but he could not stop himself. The phone rang twice.

"Hello?"

It was a woman and she sounded sleepy.

"Is . . . is this Jasmine?" Kerrigan asked, his heart beating in his throat.

"Yes?"

The voice was suddenly husky and seductive now that he'd used her working name.

"I heard about you from a friend," Kerrigan said. "I'd like to meet you."

Kerrigan's chest was tight. He closed his eyes while Bennett spoke.

"It's late. I hadn't planned on seeing anyone tonight."

Her answer let him know that he could change her mind.

"I'm sorry. I . . . I wasn't sure . . . I should have called earlier."

He was rambling and he forced himself to stop.

"That's okay, honey. You sound . . . nice. You might be able to charm me out of bed, but it will be expensive." There was a pause. Kerrigan heard her breathing on the other end of the phone. "Expensive, but worth every penny."

Kerrigan grew hard, and a pulse pounded in his temple.

"What . . . how much would it cost?"

"What's your name?"

"Why do you need to know that?"

"I like to know who I'm talking to. You have a name, don't you?"

"I'm Frank. Frank Kramer," Kerrigan said, giving her the name on a set of false identification he'd had made for this type of occasion.

"Who's your friend, Frank?"

She was being cautious. Kerrigan guessed it was because she knew that Dupre was under investigation. Kerrigan had read Bennett's file. It contained a list of johns with their phone numbers and addresses. There had been a guy from Pennsylvania in town for a convention six months ago.

"Randy Chung. He's from Pittsburgh. He spoke very highly of you."

"Did he? He had fun? He enjoyed himself?"

"Very much."

There was dead air.

"It wouldn't be all night or anything like that," Kerrigan said. "Just an hour or so. I know it's late."

"Okay, but I'll want five hundred dollars."

"Five. I . . ."

"It's your decision."

Kerrigan knew a motel where the night clerks asked no questions and were used to clients who paid for the night but stayed for an hour. Ally knew the motel too. They hung up. Kerrigan was light-headed. He thought that he might throw up. He tried to slow his breathing as he went back to his car. What was he doing? He should call back and call it off. He should just go home. But the car was already rolling.

Traffic was light. His mind wandered. He was going to use a false name, but what if Ally discovered his identity? Was that part of the thrill? Did he want to be ruined?

It was that run—that ninety-yard run. How he wished that a Michigan player had stopped him anywhere on that field short of the goal line. What he'd said to Hugh was true. No Michigan player had been close to him during those three Rose Bowl runs. His blockers wouldn't let them. But he got the credit. And then everything had snowballed out of control.

A car signaled into his lane, and Kerrigan dragged his thoughts back to the road. He tried to keep them there, but images of Ally Bennett intruded. Ally in court, what he imagined she'd look like naked. She was incredible, heart-stopping, and he would be with her in less than an hour. A driver honked, and Kerrigan's grip tightened on the wheel. That had been close. He forced himself to concentrate on his driving.

Even so, he didn't notice the black car that had been following him since he left the hotel.

Kerrigan parked in the shadows of the motel lot. The rain started to fall again, pinging on the car roof. The sound startled him into flashing on the night a week and a half before the Rose Bowl, when he'd sat in another car in the rain. Tim shook his head to clear the vision. His heart was beating too fast. He needed to calm down. Once he'd pulled himself together, he dashed across the lot to the motel office.

A few minutes later, Tim hung his rain-streaked trench coat in the closet of the room he'd rented for the night. There was a lamp on the end table next to the bed. He turned it on but left off the overhead light. He phoned Ally with his room number, then sat in the room's only armchair. He felt sick with fear and self-loathing as he waited for Bennett to arrive. Twice he started to leave, but turned back at the door. Several times he wondered if Ally would come to the motel and each time part of him hoped that she wouldn't show.

A knock startled Kerrigan. His stomach felt like it held a hot coal. When he opened the door, she was standing there, as beautiful and sensual as he remembered her.

In the lot, the man in the black car watched Kerrigan open the door for his visitor.

"Aren't you going to let me in, Frank?" Ally asked with a seductive smile.

"Yes, of course," Kerrigan answered, stepping back. She glided by him, taking in the room before turning to study her client. Kerrigan locked the door. His throat was dry and his lust made him dizzy.

"Here's the deal, Frank. You give me my fee and I give you your dreams. Does that sound like a fair trade?"

Ally was wearing a short wraparound skirt that showed her legs to the thigh, and a tank top that revealed the curve of her breasts. Her voice was huskier in person. Just hearing her speak made Kerrigan hard. Without taking his eyes from Ally, he removed the money from his pocket and held it toward her.

"Bring the money here, Frank," Ally said, establishing her dominance. It was what he'd hoped for and he obeyed, gladly surrendering his will to her.

Ally counted the money and put it in her purse. Then she peeled off her tank top and unwrapped her skirt until all she was wearing was a pair of black-lace bikini panties. Kerrigan's breath caught in his throat, and his knees almost gave way. If he could have invented a woman he would have invented the woman who stood before him.

"Tell me what you want, Frank. Tell me what you dream about."

Kerrigan lowered his eyes until he was looking at the floor. He whispered his wish.

Ally smiled. "Are you a shy boy, Frank? You spoke so softly that I didn't hear you. Say it again."

"I . . . I want to be punished."

Cindy Kerrigan turned on her light when Tim crept into the bedroom.

"It's almost two."

"I'm sorry. Hugh Curtin was at the dinner. He's having personal problems and needed to talk."

"Oh, really," she said coldly. "And how is Hugh?"

"Okay. You know. Hugh is Hugh."

Cindy sat up and leaned against the headboard of their king-size bed. One strap of her silk nightgown slipped down, revealing the curve of her left breast. She had ash-blond hair and lovely tanned skin. Most men thought that she was beautiful and desirable.

"Megan missed you," she said, knowing Tim would feel guilty. He could not avoid her without avoiding his daughter, whom he loved.

"I'm sorry. You know I wanted to come home," he said as he stripped off his clothes.

"What exactly was the problem?" Cindy asked in a tone that let him know that she saw through his lie.

"Office politics. Making partner wasn't all he thought it would be," Tim answered vaguely as he grabbed his pajamas. "It's complicated."

Cindy stared at him with contempt but dropped the subject. Tim walked into the bathroom. She clicked off her light. He thought about Cindy lying there in the dark, hurt and angry. For a moment, he almost went to her, but he couldn't. She'd see through him. And if the holding and the touching led to sex, he wouldn't be able to perform. He was spent. Of course, the likelihood of kindling any passion between them was remote. Sex had almost completely disappeared from their marriage.

Shortly after their wedding, it dawned on Tim that he had not married Cindy because he loved her. He had married her for the same reason he'd gone to law school. Marriage and law school were places to hide—islands of normalcy after the media frenzy that followed the Heisman award and his decision to forgo pro football. The moment Kerrigan had his epiphany, he felt like a gray cloth had been draped over his heart.

Cindy was the daughter of Winston Callaway and Sandra Driscoll. The Driscolls, the Callaways, and the Kerrigans were old Portland money, which meant that Tim had known Cindy his whole life. They had not become a couple until their last year in high school. When Cindy followed Tim to the University of Oregon, they continued to date, and they had married the weekend Tim received the Heisman Trophy.

Tim had hoped that having a child would make him love his wife, but that experiment failed miserably, as did every other attempt he made to force himself to feel something for her. Playing a role twenty-four hours a day was exhausting and had worn him down. Cindy was no fool. He wondered why she stayed with him when all he did was hurt her. Tim had considered divorce, but he could never bring himself to leave Cindy, and now there was Megan. He dreaded losing her or hurting her.

Kerrigan slipped onto his side of the bed and thought about his evening with Jasmine. Sex was not the magnet that had drawn him to her.

Freedom was the attraction. When he was naked in that seedy motel room, he had been truly free of the expectations of others. When he knelt before Jasmine, Kerrigan felt the mantle of the hero fall from his shoulders. When he used his mouth on her, he was perverted and not perfect, a deviate and a criminal, not an idol. Kerrigan wished that every person who had praised him and held him up as an example to others had seen him lying on those stained sheets, eyes closed, begging a whore to degrade him. They would turn away in disgust, and he would be free of the fame he knew was built on a lie.

seven

Harvey Grant, the presiding judge in Multnomah County, was a slender man of average size with salt-and-pepper hair, a life-long bachelor and friend of William Kerrigan, Tim's father—a hard-driving businessman and a perfectionist whom Tim had never been able to please. "Uncle" Harvey had been Tim's confidant since he was little, and he'd become Tim's mentor as soon as Kerrigan had made the decision to go to law school.

Normally, the judge attracted little notice when he was not wearing his robes. At the moment, however, he was preparing to make a key putt, and the other golfers in his foursome were focusing every ounce of their mental energy on him. Grant stroked his ball, and it rolled slowly toward the hole on the eighteenth green of the Westmont

Country Club course. The putt looked good until the moment the ball stopped on the rim of the cup. Grant's shoulders sagged; Tim Kerrigan, Grant's partner, let out a pent up breath; and Harold Travis pumped a clenched fist. He'd played terribly all day and he needed the missed putt to bail him out.

"I believe you gentlemen owe Harold and me five bucks apiece," Frank Jaffe told Grant and Kerrigan.

"I'll pay you, Frank," Grant grumbled as he and Kerrigan handed portraits of Abraham Lincoln to their opponents, "but I shouldn't have to pay a penny to Harold. You carried him all day. How you made that bunker shot on seventeen I'll never know."

Travis laughed and clapped Grant on the back.

"To show that I'm a compassionate guy I'll buy the first round," the senator said.

"Now that's the only good thing that's happened to me since the first tee," answered Kerrigan.

"He's just trying to buy your vote, Tim," Grant grumbled good-naturedly.

"What vote?" Travis asked with a sly grin.

The Westmont was the most exclusive country club in Portland. Its clubhouse was a sprawling fieldstone structure that had started in 1925 with a small central building and had grown larger and more imposing as membership in the club grew in prestige. The men were stopped several times by other members as they crossed the wide flagstone patio on their way to a table shaded by a forest green umbrella where Carl Rittenhouse, the senator's administrative assistant, waited.

"How'd it go?" Rittenhouse asked the senator.

"Frank did all the work and I rode his coat-tails," Travis answered.

"Same way you rode the president's in your last election," Grant joked. The men laughed.

A waitress took their order and Grant, Kerrigan, and Jaffe reminisced about the round while Senator Travis stared contentedly into space.

"You're awfully quiet," Jaffe told Travis.

"Sorry. I've got a problem with my farm bill. Two senators are threatening to keep it in committee if I don't vote against an army-base closure."

"Being a judge has its upside," Grant said. "If someone gives me a hard time I can hold him in contempt and toss his butt in jail."

"I'm definitely in the wrong business," Travis said. "I don't know about jail, though. Civil commitment would probably be more appropriate for some of my colleagues."

"Being a senator is a bit like being an inmate in a fancy asylum," Rittenhouse chimed in.

"I don't think I could win an insanity defense for a politician, Carl," Jaffe said. "They're crafty, not crazy."

"Yes," the judge said. "Look at the way Harold tricked us into letting him partner with you."

"I did read somewhere that not all sociopaths are serial killers," Jaffe said. "A lot of them become successful businessmen and politicians."

"Imagine what an asset it would be in business and politics to be free of your conscience," Kerrigan mused.

"Do you think guilt is innate or is it taught?" Travis asked.

"Nature versus nurture," Jaffe answered with a shrug of his shoulders. "The eternal question."

"I believe the potential to experience guilt is part of God's design," Grant said. "It's what makes us human."

Harvey Grant was a devout Catholic. He and the Kerrigans attended the same church, and Tim knew that the judge never missed a Sunday.

"But serial killers, professional criminals and,

as Frank pointed out, some politicians and busi-nessmen, don't seem to have a conscience. If we're born with one, where does it go?" Kerrigan asked.

"And what if there is no God?" Travis asked.

"Hey," Rittenhouse interjected with mock alarm, "let's not say that too loudly. All we need is a headline in the **Oregonian**: SENATOR TRAVIS QUESTIONS THE EXISTENCE OF GOD."

But Travis wasn't finished. "If there is no God then morality becomes relative. Whoever runs the show sets the rules."

"The point is moot, Harold," Frank said. "The fact that the judge missed that putt on eighteen proves beyond question that there is a God."

Everyone laughed and Travis stood up.

"On that note, I'll leave you gentlemen. Thanks for the game. It was a welcome break from work and campaigning."

"Our pleasure," Grant told him. "Let me know when you can sneak away again so I can win back my money."

Frank Jaffe stood, too. "Thanks for inviting me, Harvey. I love the course."

"You should think of joining the Westmont. I'll sponsor you."

"Hey, Harvey, I'm just a simple country lawyer.

I'd be in over my head in the company of you so-phisticates."

"Get out of here, Frank, before we have to start shoveling the patio clean," the judge answered.

Travis, Jaffe, and Rittenhouse headed for the locker room. "Harold was in a good mood," Kerrigan observed when they were out of sight.

"Why wouldn't he be? He's going to be the next president of the United States." Grant signaled the waitress for another round. "So, Tim, how have you been?"

"Overworked."

Grant smiled. "And Megan? How is she? I haven't seen her in a while."

"You don't need an invitation to drop over." Kerrigan smiled. "She asks about you."

"Maybe I'll come over next weekend."

"She's so sharp. I read to her every night. Lately it's been **Alice's Adventures in Wonderland**. A few days ago I caught her sitting on the floor in her room with the book in her lap sounding out the words."

"It's her good genes."

Talking about Megan made Kerrigan want to go home. For a moment, he wondered if he should desert the judge, who lived alone and who, Kerrigan imagined, must be lonely at times, despite the parties he threw and his constant round of social engagements. Then he thought about his own situation. He was married to a good woman, he had a wonderful daughter, but he still felt lonely. Maybe the judge was okay on his own. He had his work and the respect of the legal community. He also had integrity. Kerrigan stared out across the green expanse of the eighteenth fairway and wondered what that would feel like.

"Don't forget, we've got that fund-raiser at seven-thirty, tonight," Carl Rittenhouse told his boss as they left the clubhouse.

"The Schumans?"

"Right. I'll pick you up at seven."

"See you then."

Rittenhouse walked to the country club entrance to wait for the valet to get his car moments before another valet parked the senator's Range Rover near the bag drop. The valet put Travis's clubs in the back of the Rover then jogged away after the senator tipped him generously. Travis smiled as he walked to the driver's door. Everything was going so well. A recent CNN poll showed him fourteen percentage points up on the favorite to win the Democratic nomination in a head-to-head race, and the money for his campaign kept on pouring in.

The screech of tires tore Travis from his reverie as Jon Dupre's Porsche squealed to a stop next to him. Dupre threw open the door and hopped out, leaving the motor running.

"Lori's dead," Dupre shouted.

"Lower your voice," Travis answered, alarmed that someone might hear them.

"I'll keep my mouth shut just like I did when I was indicted. I could have caused a lot of trouble by telling the DA what I know about you."

"I appreciate that, Jon," Travis said, desperate to calm down Dupre. He could not afford to be seen having an argument with a pimp.

"I bet you do. And I'm certain the DA would be very interested in knowing about your relationship with a woman who's just turned up beaten to death."

"Lori was fine when she left me. I don't know what happened to her later."

"You know goddamn well what happened to her," Dupre said, jabbing a finger at the senator. "Look, I'll make this simple, Harold. I need money."

"Are you trying to blackmail **me**?" Travis asked incredulously.

"Blackmail?" Dupre answered with a smirk. "That's illegal. I'd never do something like that. No, Harold, I'm asking you to help me out, just like I helped you. The cops are all over me. I can't run Exotic right now. I took a huge risk bringing Lori to you and supplying those other girls."

"This is not the place to discuss this," Travis answered, his voice tight with anger.

"It's the only place I can talk to you, since you're not answering my calls."

"Phone me tomorrow," Travis said as he looked around anxiously. "I promise we'll settle this."

"You'd better, and don't even think about siccing Manuel or another of Pedro's boys on me."

Dupre handed him a copy of the cassette Ally had given him when he'd delivered Lori Andrews into Travis's hands.

"What is this?"

"A tape of your buddies talking about the biotech slush fund you used to crush the anti-cloning bill. They really loosen up with a pair of lips on their dick."

Travis paled.

"Keep it," Dupre said. "I've got copies. I want to settle this fast. If you're not interested in this tape I'm sure **60 Minutes** will be."

Suddenly, Travis saw Carl Rittenhouse walking toward him.

"Get out of here. That's my AA."

"I'm not messing around here," Dupre said as he jumped into his car. Rittenhouse arrived as Dupre drove away.

"You okay, Senator?" he asked, watching the car as it sped down the driveway.

"I'm fine," Travis answered, but his voice was shaky.

"Who was that?" Rittenhouse asked.

"Forget about it, Carl. It's not important."

"You're sure?"

"I'll be fine."

The incident bothered Carl, and after saying good-bye to the senator he jotted down the license number of the Porsche on the back of one of his business cards. In the meantime, Senator Travis left the Westmont. As soon as he could, he parked on a side street and punched in a number on his cell phone. He was sweating badly and his fingers trembled. When the person on the other end answered, Travis said, "We've got a problem."

eight

Two years ago, Amanda had represented Alan Ellis, a banker who'd been falsely accused of sexual molestation by a foster child. Eventually, the charges had been dismissed, but not before the banker had lost his job, his wife, his house, and most of his savings. Amanda was certain that her client was contemplating suicide, so she had asked around for the name of a psychiatrist who was competent and compassionate.

Ben Dodson's office was across from the library on the fourth floor of an eight-story medical building. Dodson was slender, with a dark complexion, and looked younger than forty-two. Granny glasses magnified the psychiatrist's blue eyes, and he wore his black hair almost to his shoulders. He stood up and flashed a ready smile when Amanda walked into his cozy office.

"It's good to see you again. How is Alan doing?"

"Last I heard, he was working for a bank in Rhode Island," Amanda said as she took a seat. "You really helped him."

Dodson shook his head. "I hope I never go through a tenth of what that poor bastard suffered. So, what brings you here? Have you got someone else for me to work with?"

Amanda had practiced what she was going to say in her apartment, in her office, and during the walk to Dodson's office, but now that she was here the words stuck in her throat. Dodson saw her distress and stopped smiling.

"Are you okay?"

Amanda didn't know how to answer the psychiatrist. She wasn't crazy, she felt fine most of the time. Maybe she'd made a mistake coming here.

"Pretty dumb question, huh?" Dodson said. "If you were okay you wouldn't be here. You want to tell me what's bothering you?"

Amanda still could not look at Dodson. "It's . . . it's stupid, really."

"But powerful enough for you to walk across town in the rain during your lunch hour. So, why don't you tell me about it."

Amanda thought about Toby Brooks and her nightmares and the flashbacks to the tunnel. It all seemed so silly in Dodson's office. Everyone gets scared, and she certainly had a good reason for her bad dreams.

"I'm probably wasting your time."

"I'm not doing much right now, so that's okay."

Amanda felt the heat rise in her cheeks. She hadn't felt this embarrassed since she'd made a fool of herself in her first trial.

"A week or so ago, I was at the Y, the YMCA. I work out there. Anyway, I was swimming and this man came over. He . . . he was very handsome, about my age. He seemed nice."

Amanda's voice caught. Dodson waited patiently while she gathered herself.

"I panicked. I was terrified. I couldn't breathe." She stopped, feeling utterly ridiculous.

"Has that ever happened to you before?" Dodson asked. His tone was calm and nonjudgmental, but Amanda didn't know what to tell him.

"Do you have any idea why you became so frightened?" Dodson asked when Amanda did not answer his question. She felt panicky now. She wanted to bolt. "Amanda?"

"I might."

"Can you tell me?" Dodson asked softly.

"How much do you know about what happened to me last year?"

"I read the stories in the papers and it was on TV. The surgeon who tortured those women attacked you."

It felt very hot, very close in Dodson's office, and that made her remember the tunnel. She stood up.

"I have to go."

Dodson stood with her. "Amanda, I want to help you and I think I may have some idea about how to do it."

Amanda froze. "How could you know anything? I haven't told you a thing."

"Can you sit down? Can I talk to you?"

Amanda lowered herself onto the seat. She felt dizzy.

"I'm going to get you a glass of water. Is that okay?"

Amanda nodded. Dodson stepped out for a moment and returned with a glass of water. He sat down and waited while Amanda drank half of the glass.

"Can I make a few guesses?" Dodson asked.

Amanda nodded warily.

"You approved of my work with Alan Ellis. Am I right?"

"Yes."

"And you came here to talk to me because you know from Alan's case that I can help people who are troubled."

Amanda's throat constricted and her eyes grew damp. She felt weak and ridiculous as she fought for composure, and she hated feeling weak and not in control of a situation.

"But most of all, you came to me because you trust me, because you know that what you tell me and what I tell you will stay between us, and because you know that I want to help you and that I will do everything I can to help you deal with this thing that's driven you to me."

The dam broke and Amanda started to sob. She made no sound but her head bobbed up and down. She jammed her fists in her eyes to stop the tears but she couldn't. Dodson let her cry. When her shoulders stopped shaking, he handed Amanda a box of tissues that had been sitting on his desk.

"I want you to tell me what happened last year with the surgeon," Dodson said when Amanda was calmer.

Amanda spoke with her head down and her eyes averted. She spoke without emotion, as if she was relating the plot of a movie she had seen a while ago. In the movie she was stripped naked, tape was placed over her mouth, her hands were secured behind her back with plastic restraints, and a hood was placed over her head. Then she was forced to run through a tunnel, her breath coming in short gasps, a sharp knife jabbing her buttocks to force her to move faster. And all that time the surgeon told her his plans for her and revealed his interest in testing how much pain a well-conditioned athlete could endure before she died or went insane.

"Before your escape, how did you feel?" the psychiatrist asked.

"Scared," Amanda answered. The short time in Dodson's office had exhausted her, and she wanted to curl up on his carpet and go to sleep. "I . . . I was certain that I was going to die."

"What about physiologically?"

"I don't understand."

"How was your breathing?"

"I had a lot of trouble. My mouth was taped, and a hood was pulled down over my head. There were moments when I thought that I might black out."

"What about your heartbeat?"

"It was elevated, really beating hard, and I was sweating."

"Have there been times since the incident, after you knew that you were safe, when you've reexperienced these physiological responses?"

"Yes."

"Okay. What about after you escaped? How did that feel?"

"At first I didn't know that I was free. I just ran, expecting him to catch me any second. Then the SWAT team found me. I was elated, really excited for a short time."

"It looked like the surgeon had escaped, too, at first, didn't it?"

Amanda nodded.

"How did you feel during that period?"

"Very frightened. I had a police guard, but I jumped at every sound and I always had the feeling that someone was watching me."

"How did you feel when you learned that your tormentor was dead?"

"I was with Dad. Sean McCarthy, the lead detective, drove out to the house. He told us in person. I remember not hearing what he said, at first. It was like what happens in a dream sometimes, when a person is right in front of you talking but the sound doesn't travel. I don't think I showed any emotion. I don't think I believed it. When I finally accepted what Sean had said, I almost collapsed from relief."

"Did you feel safe again?"

"For a time."

"When did that feeling of being safe fade away?"

Amanda felt anxious as she recalled the first time she'd had a flashback.

"Drink some water," Dodson urged. "When you're ready to talk about it, tell me what happened."

"This is really stupid."

"Try me," Dodson said, encouraging her with an understanding smile.

"I was home alone watching television, some cop show. I just turned it on without knowing the plot, and it was about a serial killer."

Amanda licked her lips nervously and took another drink of water.

"He grabbed a woman in a parking lot and locked her in the back of his van. She was screaming and pounding on the door. They were driving through the center of a big city and no one knew she was in that van. I broke out in a sweat, I panicked. It was as if I was back in the tunnel fighting for my life."

"What did you do?"

"I think I blacked out for a minute, because suddenly I was on the floor and I wasn't sure how I got there. I ran into the bathroom. I splashed water on my face. I took deep breaths. I was on edge all evening. I didn't sleep for hours."

"Have you had these feelings on other occasions?"

"Yes." She told Dodson about her recent panic attack in the office when she had seen the autopsy photographs by accident. "I've had nightmares, too."

"When you have a flashback, what is it like?"

"It's like I'm really there. Sometimes I can even smell the damp and feel the dirt. I . . . I feel like I'm going . . . like I'm losing it."

"Let's go back to the incident at the pool. Tell me about that again."

Amanda told Dodson about Toby Brooks's attempt to recruit her for the Master's swim team.

"My reaction was so stupid. Asking me to join the team was so normal. It was nice. Toby seemed kind. He was kind. But I was terrified."

"How did you feel when you were talking to Toby?"

"Feel? I didn't know him well enough to feel anything."

"But you just told me that you panicked when he spoke to you, that you were too spent emotionally to swim anymore."

"Yes."

"Why do you think you felt that way?"

"I don't know."

"Did you trust him?"

"I . . ." Amanda stopped. "I don't know." Her eyes dropped to her lap. "I guess not," she whispered.

"Are you finding it difficult to trust other people?"

"I don't know."

"Think about it. You have friends, don't you?"

She nodded.

"Have you seen a lot of them since the incident?"

"I guess I haven't. I don't feel comfortable around them anymore."

Amanda suddenly remembered the way she'd treated Mike Greene. She felt very bad.

"There's a man I've been dating a little. He's

very nice. I was supposed to go out with him the evening I saw the autopsy photographs and panicked. I was so rattled that I forgot all about the date. Then, when he showed up, I . . . I sent him away. I didn't explain why. I'm sure I hurt his feelings, and he's only been nice to me."

Amanda hung her head. She dabbed at her eyes with a tissue.

"You've been through a lot today and I think this is a good time to stop. But I'm going to talk a little before you go, and I want you to listen carefully and think about what I tell you—especially if you have another one of these incidents.

"First, you're not crazy. In fact, your reactions are so common that there's a name for them. What you are experiencing is called post-traumatic stress disorder. They used to call it shell shock in the First World War because soldiers who had been in combat manifested the problem most dramatically. We saw a lot of it in soldiers coming back from Vietnam. But it's not just war. Individuals who live through a psychologically distressing event that is outside the range of usual human experience can have the same symptoms. They can be triggered by a plane crash, torture, an earthquake, or a kidnapping—anything that involves intense fear, terror, and helplessness.

The problem seems to be more severe and last longer when the stressor is of human design, like the one you encountered.

"One of the most common symptoms of PTSD is the reexperiencing of the traumatic event through nightmares and flashbacks. The anniversary of the event can trigger feelings of panic or anxiety, and the same feelings can be triggered by something that reminds you of the event, like a movie with a serial killer or just meeting someone who reminds you of the person who caused your terror."

"Like Toby."

Dodson nodded. "I don't want to get into this too much right now, but I do want you to understand that your responses are reasonable."

"Why didn't I have them right after I was attacked? Why did it take a while before I started having these flashbacks and the nightmares?"

"Good question. At first, when you thought the surgeon was still at large and could hurt you, you went into a survival mode with a heightened state of alert and you suppressed all of your emotions so you could deal with the danger. But once you felt safe, you relaxed and gave your doubts and fears time to surface. Your guard was down. When you came in contact with a stimulus like the autopsy photo or Toby Brooks, you were forced to recall the incident without time to prepare yourself, and you started to wonder if it could happen again."

"What can I do to make this stop?" Amanda asked, her voice almost a whisper. "That's why I came here. I want it to stop. I was happy before. I was a happy person." Tears welled up in Amanda's eyes again. She dabbed at them with a tissue. "I want to be happy again."

Dodson leaned toward Amanda. When he spoke, he sounded confident and comforting.

"You are a very strong person, Amanda. It took strength for you to come here. I can't guarantee that you'll ever feel the way you did before the attack, but I can tell you that other people have fought through what you are experiencing. Right now I think it would help if you keep doing things you enjoy and are around people you like and trust. I'd also suggest that you try to avoid situations or books or movies that might trigger a reaction."

"What about my work, Ben? I'm a criminal defense attorney. I deal with murder and rape every day. What do I do about that?"

"That's a question I can't answer right now, but it's something that both of us need to think about."

Part Two

GETTING BACK ON THE HORSE

nine

Tim Kerrigan had just finished another chapter of **Alice's Adventures in Wonderland** and was tucking Megan in when he heard the phone ring.

"One more chapter, please," Megan begged.

"Not tonight."

"Why not?"

"If I read you another chapter we'll finish the book sooner and then it will be all done and you'll be sad because Alice and the White Rabbit will disappear."

"But you'll finish someday anyway and I'll be sad."

"But you'll be sadder later."

"And they won't disappear, because you can read it to me again."

Kerrigan kissed Megan's nose. "You are too smart, young lady."

Megan smiled and followed up her advantage. "One more chapter. Please."

Kerrigan was about to give in when Cindy walked into Megan's bedroom.

"It's Richard Curtis," she said. Richard Curtis was Tim's direct supervisor. Cindy looked put out, which was the way she always looked whenever his office called him at home.

"I'll take it in the study."

He turned back to Megan. "Sorry, Buttercup."

Kerrigan kissed Megan, gave her a hug, and said good night. Then he went into his den.

"What's up, Dick?"

"I hate to do this to you but I just received a call from Sean McCarthy. He's at a crime scene and I want you to cover it."

"Can't you find someone else?"

"Not for this one. It's Harold Travis."

"You're kidding! What happened?"

"He was beaten to death."

Tim closed his eyes. He remembered saying good-bye to Travis at the Westmont.

"I can't, Dick, I knew him."

"Everyone knew him."

"I played golf with him this weekend. Can't you send Hammond or Penzler? They'd give their right arms to see their name in the paper."

"Look, Tim, the death of a United States senator is going to be covered by the national media. You know how to deal with them. I need someone out there who won't grandstand if someone from **20/20** shoves a microphone in his face."

Kerrigan was quiet for a moment. Harold Travis. How could he be dead? He didn't want to see someone he knew dead.

"Tim?"

"Give me a minute."

"I need you on this."

Kerrigan sucked in some air. He felt light-headed. Then he closed his eyes and let out a breath.

"I'll do it."

Portland turns from city to country in the blink of an eye. Fifteen minutes from Kerrigan's house, the streetlights began to disappear; the only light was from a quarter moon. The prosecutor was afraid that he would miss the crime scene, but a police car had been stationed near the turnoff to keep out everyone without official business. He flashed his ID and turned onto a narrow, un-paved driveway.

Tim's car bumped along for an eighth of a mile. He had played blaring rock music as he drove out of town so he wouldn't have to think about where he was going and what he was going to see, but he turned off the radio when he spotted flashes of electric light through the trees. Then the dirt track turned and the prosecutor saw an assortment of official vehicles parked in front of a tiny A-frame house. It looked like every light in the cabin was on, and the light leaked across the lawn, bleeding out just beyond Kerrigan's car.

The A-frame was so small that only an unmarried person or a childless couple would tolerate it. Tim stood in the dark for a few minutes, fully aware that he was putting off the inevitable, before walking across the lawn. As he approached the house, he felt a little sick and disoriented, like a family member entering a funeral parlor.

The front door opened onto a stone entryway. In front of Kerrigan was an island with two high stools that separated the entryway from a narrow kitchen. To the left was a living room crowded with police officers and forensic experts, one of whom was talking to Sean McCarthy. The homicide detective had the alabaster skin of someone who never saw the sun; his red hair was streaked with gray. Tim had worked with McCarthy on several homicides and could not remember a time when the rail-thin detective did not look tired. McCarthy spotted Kerrigan and motioned him to wait while he finished up.

Tim stood beside a half-wall that separated the living room from the kitchen and stopped where the stone entryway met the living-room carpet. A flash from a camera attracted his attention to a loft that overhung the living room. Kerrigan had noticed the underside of the polished wood stairs that led up to the loft when he looked through the kitchen. He guessed that the bedroom must be up there where the roof narrowed. When he looked down, he saw a trail of smeared blood leading from the stairs through the kitchen and across the living-room carpet. Someone had run tape on either side so no one would step on the tracks. The end of the blood trail was hidden behind a cluster of people at the far side of the living room.

"I know you're not big on gore, so be prepared," McCarthy told Kerrigan when he ambled over. "This one is not pleasant."

Tim's stomach rolled.

"You up for this?" McCarthy asked, worried by the prosecutor's ashen pallor.

"Yeah. I'll be okay."

A photographer stood between Kerrigan and the body. He finished snapping stills of Travis and the surrounding area and stepped aside. Kerrigan squeezed his eyes shut, then opened them slowly to control the view. The senator was sprawled across the floor like a rag doll. His legs and arms were flung about at weird angles, and his head lolled on the carpet in an unnatural position. He was wearing jeans and a T-shirt, but no shoes or socks. His feet were a bloody mess. Someone had smashed every toe as well as the feet themselves. Travis's shins and kneecaps had also been smashed. Kerrigan guessed that Travis's killer had worked his way up the senator's body, ending at his head, where the senator's forehead, nose, mouth, and chin had been battered to pulp.

Kerrigan really wanted to be out of this room. McCarthy saw him sway and led him outside. The prosecutor walked behind the house to a bluff that dropped off into darkness. A chill wind blew up the ravine. Kerrigan concentrated on a solitary object lit by a string of lights moving slowly along a black ribbon that divided the valley, a tanker heading inland on the Columbia River to the Port of Portland.

"Has anyone notified Harold's wife?" Tim asked as soon as he was breathing normally.

"She's flying back from a medical convention in Seattle."

"This is fucking terrible," said Kerrigan.

McCarthy knew the DA did not expect a response.

"Have we found the murder weapon?"

"No, but I'm thinking a baseball bat or something like it."

"He looked like . . ." Kerrigan shook his head and didn't finish the thought.

"Dick called while you were driving over. He said you knew him."

"Yeah. I played golf with him this weekend."

"Can you think of anyone who'd hate him enough to do this?"

"I didn't know him that well. You should call Carl Rittenhouse. He's his AA. He might be able to help."

"Do you have a number?"

"No, but Judge Grant knows Rittenhouse. Hell, he knew Harold real well, too. Travis was his clerk during the summer before his last year of law school."

A man in a dark blue windbreaker walked up to McCarthy and Kerrigan and threw a thumb over his shoulder in the direction of the front of the house.

"We've got a visitor from an organization head-quartered in Washington, D.C.," said Alex DeVore, McCarthy's partner.

"I was wondering how long it would take for the G-men to put in an appearance. Is it anyone we know?"

"His name is J. D. Hunter and I've never seen him before."

"Tim?" McCarthy asked.

The prosecutor shook his head.

"Let's go meet our guest."

McCarthy led the way back to the entry hall where an athletically built man was studying the activity in the living room.

"Agent Hunter?"

The man turned. Horn-rimmed glasses perched on Hunter's small, broad nose, and his skin was deep black. McCarthy introduced himself and the senior deputy DA.

"You're not local, are you?" Tim asked.

"With the victim being a senator, Washington wanted an agent from headquarters on the case." He shrugged. "Politics. Anyway, I'd appreciate it if you'd fill me in."

"Sure," McCarthy said, "but we don't know very much yet. There's a service that cleans the house. They were told to come out late afternoon. One of the women found the body around five and called 911."

"Is this where the senator lived?" Hunter asked.

"No," Tim answered. "He's got a home in Dunthorpe."

"Then who owns this place?"

"We're not certain. A realty company deals with the cleaning service. They're closed, so we won't be able to find the name of the owner until the morning."

"Isn't there anything in the house that would let you know?" Hunter persisted.

McCarthy shook his head. "Forensics might give us a clue when they finish analyzing the prints, blood, etc. But the drawers in the bedroom are empty and there were no bills or notes on the kitchen bulletin board. We did find liquor and cocaine in a cabinet in the living room. . . ."

"Cocaine!" Kerrigan said.

"We dusted the baggie, so we'll know who handled it pretty soon."

"I hope to God it wasn't Harold," Kerrigan murmured to himself.

"Was there anything else?" Hunter asked.

"Yeah. Travis's body was found in the living room, but there's a blood trail leading downstairs from the sleeping loft. We think the killer started on him up there and chased him downstairs. One of the techs found an earring under the bed. It's a gold cross. Travis doesn't wear an earring. We're hoping that the killer does."

"That would be a break," Hunter said.

"The easier the better, I always say," DeVore answered with a smile.

"I'd like to take a look at the body, if that's okay," Hunter told McCarthy.

"Sure thing."

As he watched the FBI agent cross the living room, Kerrigan realized that something beyond the obvious was bothering him, but he couldn't put his finger on what it was.

Cindy was waiting for Tim when he returned home.

"I heard the car," she said and held out a glass of scotch. The ice clinked against the side of the glass, sounding like little bells. "I thought you could use this."

Tim took the glass, grateful for the kindness.

"Was it bad?"

"I've never known a victim before. The whole scene was surreal. We just played golf," he said, a sentence he'd been repeating all evening as if it was impossible for someone to die if you'd seen him only a few days before.

Tim downed his drink and set down his glass.

"Does Deborah know?" Cindy asked.

"She was in Seattle. She's flying back."

"It has to be awful for her. I can't imagine."

"I'll have to talk to her tomorrow," he said. "I'm not looking forward to that."

Cindy hesitated, then wrapped her arms around him. He resisted for a moment, then held her. Cindy rested her head against his chest. She'd showered while he was gone, and her hair smelled like fresh flowers. Cindy looked up. Her eyes and the soft pressure when she took his hand asked him if he wanted to go to bed. It had been so long. Cindy tensed, preparing for rejection. Tim knew how devastating it would be if he refused. Then he realized that he did not want to refuse, that he needed to be comforted and held. He kissed Cindy's forehead. He felt her relax, kissed her again, and felt something stirring. Cindy squeezed his hand and led him toward the bedroom.

ten

Dunthorpe was an exclusive residential neighborhood where substantial homes sat back from the road on large, tree-shaded lots, and the peace was rarely disturbed. But the morning after Harold Travis's murder, Sean McCarthy had to drive at a crawl to get past the television vans, the reporters, and the gawkers who crowded the narrow street that ran in front of the senator's house, a Tudor mansion shielded from view by a high hedge.

McCarthy flashed his ID at the policeman who was manning the barricade at the end of the driveway. The cop pulled back the sawhorse and waved McCarthy and Tim Kerrigan through. A maid answered the doorbell, and Kerrigan and the detective walked into a wood-paneled entry hall in which a crystal chandelier hung over a polished hardwood floor and the Persian carpet that covered most of it.

Carl Rittenhouse rushed over and grasped Tim's hand as soon as the prosecutor stepped through the front door. Rittenhouse had a doughy build and thinning gray hair that looked as if it had been combed in haste. His eyes were wide behind tortoiseshell glasses.

"This is fucking awful, Tim. Fucking awful."

"How is Deborah?"

"Holding up a hell of a lot better than I am. She's in there." Rittenhouse gestured toward the living room. "She's tough, keeping it in. I'm afraid she'll crash as soon as everyone leaves and she doesn't have to put up a brave front."

Kerrigan introduced McCarthy to the harried AA. "Look, Carl, before we talk to Deborah there are a few things we've got to ask you. Stuff we don't want to discuss in front of her. Is there somewhere we can talk?"

Rittenhouse led the way down a narrow hall decorated with delicate pen-and-ink sketches of Parisian boulevards, and into a den. Two walls were lined with bookshelves. A window took up most of the wall across from the door. Outside, the sky was gray and threatening.

"Do you have any idea who killed him?" Tim asked.

"No."

"He was going to be the nominee for president. You don't climb that high without making some enemies."

"Well sure, but I can't think of anyone who hated him enough to beat him to death."

"What about the house where Harold was killed?" McCarthy asked. "Who owned it?"

Rittenhouse colored.

"If you know anything you've got to tell me."

"It was the senator's place. I'm not certain Deborah knows."

"Why wouldn't she?" Tim asked.

Rittenhouse looked like he was in pain. "Come on, Tim. Do I have to spell it out for you? Harold fooled around."

"Do you know why he was there last night?" McCarthy asked.

"I might. Harold had an argument with a man in the parking lot at the Westmont after he played golf."

Rittenhouse told them about the incident.

"Did you recognize the man who was arguing with Harold?" McCarthy asked when he finished.

"No, but I saw him clearly. I'd know him if I saw him again."

"Great," Tim said.

"And I wrote down the license number of his car."

Rittenhouse took out his wallet and showed them what he'd written on the back of one of his business cards.

"What does the argument at the Westmont have to do with Harold being at the cabin?" Kerrigan asked while McCarthy used the phone on Travis's desk to call in the plate.

"A few of us met Harold here last night to plan campaign strategy. We've been doing that a lot since Whipple dropped out. We were all excited because the senator had a real shot at . . ."

Rittenhouse stopped. "Damn." He bit his lip in an effort to fight back tears.

"You want some water?"

Rittenhouse shook his head. "I'll be okay."

Rittenhouse paused until he had his emotions under control. "The meeting broke up around eight-thirty because Harold said he had a headache. He told me to cancel his plans for the morning. He said he felt run-down and wanted some time to himself. After Harold kicked everyone out, I asked him about the guy at the club again, because I'd been worrying about him. Harold had an odd reaction. He acted excited, like he wasn't worried at all, and told me to forget about it. He said 'Jon' was going to make it up to him that night. He looked like he'd forgotten that he was supposed to have a headache."

"Do you think the headache was a sham to get rid of everybody?"

"The thought crossed my mind."

"And you think he might have met the guy he argued with later on?"

"All I know is what I told you."

Kerrigan was about to ask another question when McCarthy interrupted. "The plate came back to Jon Dupre, 10346 Hawthorne Terrace, Portland."

Kerrigan could not conceal his surprise. "Describe the man who argued with the senator again."

"He was young, mid- to late twenties, good-looking."

"How tall was he?"

"Taller than Harold, maybe six feet."

"And his hair?"

"Uh, brown, I think."

"Any jewelry?"

Rittenhouse frowned. Then he brightened. "I think he had an earring."

"Can you describe it?" Kerrigan asked, fighting hard to mask his excitement.

"Uh, I think, yeah, it was a cross. A gold cross."

Kerrigan had a sudden flashback to the hearing in Dupre's case. He remembered the defendant strolling down the aisle, radiating arrogance the way his gold jewelry radiated light. One of those pieces of jewelry had been an earring in the shape of a cross.

"Sean, call Stan Gregaros. Tell him to put together a photo throw-down with a picture of Jon Dupre in it and get over here, pronto. Tell him to make it a great throw-down, one that will win a prize."

"Who is this guy, Tim?" Rittenhouse asked.

"Jon Dupre runs a high-class escort service that's a front for a call-girl operation. We got an indictment based on the testimony of one of his escorts, but we had to dismiss the case when she was beaten to death."

Rittenhouse turned pale. "Just like the senator," he said.

"Just like the senator," Tim echoed.

When Kerrigan and McCarthy entered the living room, Dr. Deborah Cable was seated on the sofa surrounded by friends. All conversation stopped, and Deborah's protectors stared at the detective and the prosecutor. Deborah stood up, and Tim walked over and hugged her. She was a substantial woman with graying brown hair, who normally exuded confidence and energy. Today she looked exhausted and bewildered.

"I wish this wasn't my case," Tim said after introducing Sean McCarthy.

"I wish this hadn't happened at all," she answered.

"Can we talk to you alone?" Tim asked, after casting a quick glance at the people who had come to comfort her. Deborah spoke quietly to her companions. Some hugged her and others squeezed her hand before drifting out of the living room.

"When did you get back?" Tim asked when they were gone.

"I caught a midnight flight. Carl picked me up at the airport. Thank God the press didn't know I was coming in. It's been a zoo out there."

Deborah sat on the sofa. Tim and the homicide detective took chairs across from her.

"Tell me how Harold died," Deborah asked as soon as they were seated.

Kerrigan hesitated.

"I'm a medical doctor, Tim, a neurosurgeon. I can handle the details."

Deborah sat up straight, her hands clasped in her lap, like a schoolgirl. Her body did not move when Kerrigan explained what he'd seen at the A-frame, but her hands tightened on each other.

"There are some questions that I have to ask if we're going to catch the person who did this."

"You don't have to walk on eggshells with me."

"Okay. Can you think of anyone who hated Harold enough to kill him so brutally?"

"No, but there was a lot about Harold's life that I didn't know." Dr. Cable fixed her large brown eyes on Kerrigan. "My work is here and Harold's was in Washington, D.C. That meant that we didn't see each other very much. For the past few years that's been intentional."

"I'm sorry."

Deborah flashed a tired smile. "Don't be. I wasn't. Our marriage was a mistake from the beginning, but we were both so busy with medical school and law school and our careers that we weren't together enough to notice. When I finally took a look at our marriage, it dawned on me that I didn't really know Harold at all." For a second her eyes darted down. When she looked up, Tim saw defiance. "I also learned that he was cheating on me every chance he got. Probably had been since we met."

"Why did you stay with him?"

"I don't know. Inertia, I guess. And I was too busy to take time out for a divorce, which would have hurt Harold's career. I didn't want to do that. I didn't hate him. We didn't know each other well enough to have intense emotions in either direction."

"Can you think of anything that will help us find Harold's killer?"

"I'm sorry, Tim. I can't give you a name. I didn't know any of his girlfriends. I do know that he was agitated for the past week. I asked him if something was wrong but he was evasive. I chalked it up to the excitement of sewing up the nomination."

"Do you think someone had threatened him?"

"He never said anything like that to me, but we didn't confide in one another. Besides, Harold was a United States senator. They have tremendous resources. If someone was threatening him he would have gone to the FBI."

"So you have no idea why Harold was upset?" McCarthy asked.

"No."

"Did you know that Harold owned the cabin where he was killed?" the detective continued.

Deborah flushed but her voice was steady when she told them that she knew nothing about the A-frame.

"Have you ever heard Harold mention a man named Jon Dupre?" Tim asked.

"Is he mixed up in this?"

"You know him?"

"Not personally, but his parents are members of the Westmont; Clara and Paul Dupre."

Tim's brow furrowed. "I don't think I know them."

"I'm not surprised. I don't either, except to say hello. They're much older than Harold and me. They had Jon late in life."

"Did Harold know Jon?"

"I'm sure he knew who he was, but I've never seen them together."

"Sean?" Tim asked.

"I don't have anything else."

"Then we'll leave you alone. If you think of anything else, or if you just want to talk, call me."

Sean McCarthy followed Tim out of the living room and Deborah's friends returned to her side. Carl Rittenhouse walked over and was about to ask a question.

"Let's go outside," Tim said. "I need some air."

The seasons were starting to change, and the wind was stirring the gold and red leaves that blanketed the lawn. Tim had worn a suit with no overcoat and he felt chilled, but the cold was refreshing after the stifling atmosphere in Travis's house.

"Did Deborah help?" Carl asked.

Kerrigan was about to reply when a car pulled past the barricade. Stan Gregaros got out and trudged up the driveway on the thick legs of a Greco-Roman wrestler. He spotted Kerrigan and McCarthy and waved a meaty hand that held a manila envelope.

"I got the pictures," he told Kerrigan.

"Carl, let's go some place quiet," Kerrigan said.

eleven

Jon Dupre's starkly modern house perched on the edge of a steep hill, separated from his neighbors by woods and facing an expanse of rolling hills and the low mountains of the coast range. The front of the house was curved tan stucco but the back was mostly glass, to take advantage of the spectacular view.

Two patrol cars pulled in behind Sean McCarthy's unmarked car. When McCarthy and Stan Gregaros walked toward the house, several officers grouped behind them. Gregaros grinned and loosened his jacket so his gun showed.

"Jon's not going to be happy to see me," he told McCarthy. Then he rang the doorbell hard and fast, three times. When the door opened, Gregaros flashed his badge at a bikini-clad

blonde. She glared at the detective as soon as she
recognized him.

"Is the gentleman of the house in?" Gregaros
asked.

"Go fuck yourself, Stanley."

She started to shut the door but Gregaros
stopped it with his foot.

"Don't be that way, Muriel."

The blonde turned her back on the detective
and walked away without a word.

"Lovely young lady," Gregaros told McCarthy
in a voice loud enough for the blonde to hear.
"Her real name is Muriel Nussbaum, but she's
Sapphire when she's working. The blond hair is a
dye job but her blow jobs are the real McCoy."

Muriel didn't give Gregaros the satisfaction of
a word or a glance as she waded through the deep
carpeting that covered the floor of a high-
ceilinged living room. She stepped aside when
she arrived at a sliding glass door that opened
onto a massive wood deck. Gregaros brushed
past her. Dupre and a glassy-eyed brunette were
chest-deep in a bubbling hot tub. A look of intense hatred suffused the pimp's handsome features as soon as he spotted Gregaros. A cell
phone was lying on a low glass table. Dupre mus-

cled his way out of the tub, grabbed it, and angrily speed-dialed a number. His eyes never left Gregaros as the detective crossed the deck.

McCarthy studied Dupre. He had the type of sleek, muscled body that is developed in a gym. His hair was short and styled. McCarthy was certain that Dupre's nails had been manicured. Then he shifted his gaze to Dupre's earlobe. There was a diamond stud in it.

"The motherfucker is here. He's in my house," McCarthy heard Dupre say into the phone, his anger under tight control. As soon as Gregaros got within arm's length, Dupre thrust the phone at him.

"My lawyer wants to talk to you."

"Certainly," Gregaros answered with an accommodating smile.

Dupre handed Gregaros the phone and the detective let it slip through his fingers.

"Oh, gee," he said, as he watched the phone sink to the bottom of the hot tub. "How clumsy of me. And I did so want to chat with Mr. Baron."

"Fuck you, Gregaros," Dupre answered with a low growl as every muscle in his body tensed.

"You're under arrest, Johnny boy," Gregaros informed Dupre, suddenly all business.

"For what?" Dupre asked belligerently.

"The murder of United States Senator Harold Travis, scumbag."

McCarthy thought that Dupre's shock was genuine, but he'd seen savvy crooks fake every emotion known to man.

"I didn't kill Travis," Dupre protested.

"I suppose you didn't argue with him at the Westmont, either."

Dupre started to answer, then clamped his jaws shut. Gregaros grabbed him roughly by the shoulder and turned him around so a uniformed officer could slap on a pair of cuffs. Dupre was wearing a low-cut swimsuit and nothing else.

"I'm not going downtown like this. Let me dress."

"Afraid someone will buttfuck you in the lockup? Funny, it doesn't bother you when someone does it to one of your girls. It'll do you good to learn how the other half lives."

Gregaros was trying to goad Dupre into attacking him, but McCarthy stepped in when Dupre tensed.

"I think we can let Mr. Dupre dress, Stan," he said, calmly moving between the detective and Dupre. Gregaros turned red with rage but held his tongue.

"Take Mr. Dupre inside and let him get dressed," McCarthy instructed a patrolman. "Watch him carefully, then cuff him."

As soon as Dupre had been hustled inside, Gregaros whirled toward Sean. "Don't ever do that again," he said.

"I know you'd like to kick the shit out of Dupre," McCarthy answered calmly, "but I don't want to hand Oscar Baron any more ammunition than you did by dropping that phone in the hot tub."

"Listen . . ."

"No, you listen to me, Stan," McCarthy cut in, his voice suddenly and uncharacteristically hard. "This is my case. You're along for the ride because you know a lot about our suspect. But I won't tolerate you letting this get personal. If Dupre killed Senator Travis I want him on death row, not back in his hot tub because you need to blow off steam."

When the guard let Jon Dupre into the noncontact visiting room at the jail, he looked as vicious as a raccoon that had once been trapped in Oscar Baron's garage. The lawyer was grateful that a wall of concrete and bulletproof glass separated them.

"Hey, Jon, how are they treating you?" Baron said, speaking into the receiver of the phone that hung from the wall on his right.

"Get me the fuck out of here."

"It's not that simple, Jon. You're charged with murdering a United States . . ."

"I didn't kill anyone. The charge is total bull-shit. That asshole Gregaros is behind this. I want you to sue him for false arrest and assault."

"Slow down. We're not suing anyone until we clear this up."

"Well, do it then. Find out what the bail is and get me out of here."

"I told you, it's not that easy. They don't have to set bail in a murder case like they do with other charges. We have to ask for a hearing. It will take time."

"I want out of here, Oscar. I don't want to be caged up with a bunch of degenerate morons."

"Hey, I don't want you locked up either, but there are procedures that have to be followed. I can't just break you out. And there's something else, too—my fee. We need to get that settled."

A vein started throbbing in Dupre's temple. "What kind of shit is this, Oscar? Haven't I always taken care of you?"

"Definitely, Jon," Baron said, keeping his tone businesslike, "but defending a murder case is different from handling that thing with the escort service. It's complicated and expensive. And they're probably going to go for the death penalty, which means twice the work you put in for a noncapital case. So we have to talk about money before I agree to hop in here."

"How much money are we going to talk about?"

Baron fought to keep his voice level. He was going to ask for more money than he'd ever received before and he was hoping that Dupre could come up with it.

"We're going to need an investigator—maybe more than one—and expert witnesses. . . ."

"Cut to the chase, Oscar."

"Okay." Baron's head bobbed up and down. "Let's say two hundred and a half for starters."

"Two hundred and fifty thousand dollars?"

"That's the retainer. It could go higher depending on the length of the trial and . . ."

Dupre laughed. "I can't come up with two hundred and fifty thousand dollars."

"Hey, Jon, don't go cheap on me. We're talking about your life."

"I don't have that kind of money."

"I thought you were doing okay with the girls and the other stuff."

"I was until the cops busted me. I haven't been able to run Exotic for months and I've had to lay low with the other stuff. Besides, you know I don't keep everything that comes in. There are other people who . . . you know."

Dupre grew intentionally vague, nervous about phone taps.

"Well, what can you come up with?" Baron asked.

"Right now? Maybe fifty."

"That's not even enough to get started in a case like this, Jon."

"I'm good for it, Oscar. I've always paid you."

"This is a death-penalty case. They're expensive. What about your parents? They have dough."

"My parents will probably cheer when they hear about my arrest. They cut me off when I was kicked out of college."

"Well, why don't you think it over, Jon, and give me a call," Baron suggested, anxious to get away now that it looked like Dupre couldn't come up with his retainer.

"This is bullshit," Dupre said, glaring at Baron

through the glass. "You can't bail on me, you greedy fuck."

Baron shot to his feet and glared back, very brave with a concrete wall and bulletproof glass keeping Dupre at bay.

"This greedy fuck just beat a case for you, you ungrateful shit."

Dupre didn't want Baron to leave him. He had to get out of jail.

"Hey, man, I'm sorry. Calm down, okay? I'm locked up and I'm a little tense."

The lawyer sat down, feigning reluctance. Dupre might be bluffing to get Baron to lower his retainer. Dupre's next words dashed his hopes.

"What if I can't get the money?"

"Tell the judge. He'll appoint you a lawyer."

"A public defender!" Dupre was livid. "I'm not risking my life with a free lawyer."

"Hey, they're okay, Jon. They screen them for murder cases. You'll probably get someone good." Baron looked at his watch. "Gee, I didn't realize the time. I've got someone waiting at the office. Meanwhile, see if you can get the dough for my retainer. You need a pro and I'm the best."

Dupre's hand tightened on the receiver.

"We'll be in touch," Baron said, backing out of

the room. As soon as he was in the corridor, the attorney breathed a sigh of relief. He hated dealing with angry clients, especially loose cannons like Dupre. Of course it was different if they could pay, but that didn't look likely. Too bad, a quarter of a million dollars would have been nice.

twelve

Once a month, Tim, Cindy, and Megan Kerrigan ate dinner with Tim's father and fourth wife in the oak-paneled dining room at the Westmont Country Club. These dinners were an ordeal for Tim, but Cindy, who found William Kerrigan charming, insisted on the ritual. Cindy also got along with Francine Kerrigan, who was twenty years younger than Tim's father and had the tight, sun-baked skin of a woman who sat poolside at expensive resorts all year, and a figure kept trim by starvation.

When they arrived at the club the night after Jon Dupre's arrest, Tim saw that his father had invited some other guests. Harvey Grant was seated at the table, along with Burton Rommel, a wealthy businessman who was prominent in the Republican Party, and Rommel's wife, Lucy.

William Kerrigan sported a year-round tan, had a full head of snow-white hair, and kept himself trim by working out in his home gym. Tim didn't see much of his father while he was growing up. Most of his energy had gone into his company, Sun Investments, but he did surface just often enough to make Tim aware of his disappointment in his only child. For instance, William let Tim know of his extreme displeasure when Tim chose "a state school" over the University of Pennsylvania, William's alma mater. He was appalled when Tim refused to pursue a multimillion-dollar career in pro football, and he had been dumbfounded when his son opted for a low-paying job in the district attorney's office. While she was alive, Tim's mother had been a buffer between father and son. When she died, Tim was saddled with a string of ever younger stepmothers who showed no interest in him at all, and a father who was around even less than before.

During the dinners at the Westmont, it was quite common for William to mention business opportunities with high earning potential, which Tim could pursue if he left the public sector. Tim always smiled politely and promised to consider them, while praying that someone would change the subject. Tonight, William was quieter than normal, but Harvey Grant picked up the slack, charming the women with titillating pieces of gossip, prodding the men to embellish their golfing accomplishments, and engaging Megan in conversation so she didn't feel out of place among the grownups.

"We had a tea party this morning," Megan told the judge. "Like Alice and the Mad Hatter."

"Were you the Mad Hatter?" Grant asked.

"Of course not."

"Were you the Dormouse?"

"No," Megan laughed.

Grant scratched his head and pretended to be confused. "Who were you then?"

"Alice!"

"Alice, but she was a pretty little girl and you're so huge. How could you be Alice?"

"I am not huge," Megan protested with a grin. "Uncle" Harvey was a big tease and she knew he was fooling.

When Megan's dessert arrived, Tim's father suggested that the men retire to the patio for a breath of fresh air.

"This business with Harold Travis is awful," said William, who never brought up unpleasant subjects at the dinner table.

"Jon Dupre has always been off. You have no

idea what he put his parents through," said
Burton Rommel, who was trim and athletic, with
hair that, at fifty-two, was still jet-black.

"You know them well?" Tim asked.

"Well enough to know how much they've
suffered."

"Everyone is shocked," Harvey Grant said.

"I hear that the governor is appointing Peter
Coulter to Harold's seat." William said.

"Isn't he a little old?" Tim asked.

"That's the point, Tim," William answered.
"He's going to warm that seat, not fill it. It's pay-
back for faithful service to the party. Pete will be
a U.S. senator for a year, then he'll step down.
He's safe, he won't do anything crazy, and it'll
look great in his obituary."

Burton Rommel looked directly at Tim.
"Listen, I asked your father to invite me tonight.
What happened to Harold is a tragedy, but we
can't dwell on that. We've lost a presidential candidate, we don't want to lose a senate seat, too.
The party needs someone with impeccable credentials to run next year."

It took a moment for Tim to catch on.

"You want me to run for the Senate?" Kerrigan
asked incredulously.

"You'd be surprised at the support you have."

"I'm flattered, Burt. I don't know what to say."

"No one expects you to commit tonight. The election is a year away. Think about it. Talk it over with Cindy. Then give me a call."

To Tim's relief, Harvey Grant changed the subject to U. of O. football, and Rommel and Tim's father lit cigars. When they decided that they had deserted the ladies long enough, Rommel and Grant went back inside. Tim started to follow them.

"Tim, wait a minute," William said. Tim turned toward his father. "You don't want to turn down an opportunity like this. You've chosen a career in public service. What greater way to serve than Congress?"

"I don't know a thing about politics, Dad. I'd be in over my head."

"You'd learn."

"I'd be in Washington most of the year, away from Megan."

"Don't be silly. They'd move with you. Cindy and Megan will love Washington. This is a golden opportunity, Tim. Don't squander it."

Left unsaid was "like all of your other opportunities."

"I'll give it serious thought," Tim answered to placate his father. "It's just a big step, that's all."

"Of course. And something that won't come again if you reject it."

Father and son were quiet for a moment. Then William placed his hand lightly on his son's shoulder. The uncharacteristic show of affection surprised Tim.

"We haven't always gotten along," William said, "but I've always wanted the best for you. If you decide to run, I'll use every contact I have to get you elected, and I'll make certain that you have the money you need."

Tim was overwhelmed. It had been a long time since his father had shown this much warmth.

"I appreciate that."

"You're my son." Tim's throat tightened. "Seize this opportunity. It's a once-in-a-lifetime chance to do something great for your country. You'll make a mark, Tim. I know what you're made of. You'll make your mark."

Tim was hanging up his clothes when Cindy returned to the bedroom after tucking Megan in.

"Do you have anything to tell me?" she asked with a mischievous smile.

"About what?"

"When you boys were on the patio, Lucy

Rommel told me that Burt was going to talk to you about something important."

"Burt asked me to run for Harold Travis's seat."

Cindy's face lit up.

"Oh, Tim! That's fantastic!"

"Yeah, well, I don't know . . ."

"Don't know what?"

"The whole thing is pretty overwhelming. I'm not certain that I want to do it."

"Are you serious? How could you even think about not running?"

Tim heard the excitement in Cindy's voice and felt the beginning of a pain in his stomach.

"I don't know if I can do it, Cindy."

"Of course you can do it. You're as smart as Harold Travis, smarter. It's the chance of a lifetime. Think what it will mean to Megan. She'll be so proud of you. Think of the people we'll meet."

"I know it's a great opportunity. I just need some time to get used to it."

Cindy hugged him and pressed her cheek against Tim's chest.

"I'm so **proud** of you." She held his face in her hands and kissed him. "I always knew you'd do something great."

Suddenly Cindy stepped back and took Tim's

hands. She looked up into his eyes. He thought she looked frightened.

"Tim, I love you, but I know . . . There have been times during our marriage when I felt that you didn't love me."

"Cindy . . ."

"No, let me say this." She took a deep breath. "I've always loved you, even when I seemed angry or cold. I acted that way because I was afraid that I was losing you. I know you love Megan. I know we've had hard times. I don't know what I've done wrong, but I'll change if you tell me." Her grip tightened. She looked fierce. "I want our marriage to work. I want you to be the person you were meant to be, and I want to be there to help you." Her grip slackened. "I also know that there are times when you don't believe in yourself, that you think you don't deserve the rewards life has given to you." Tim's eyes widened with surprise. He had no idea that Cindy suspected the doubts and fears that bedeviled him. "But you're wrong, Tim. You are good and kind and you do deserve to be a star. Accept the offer, run for the Senate. Don't doubt yourself and never doubt me."

After they made love, Cindy fell into an exhausted sleep but Tim lay awake. He imagined himself striding through Washington's corridors of power: Tim Kerrigan, United States senator. It sounded unbelievable, and the thought of running scared him to death. Still, it was an important position he could use to help people, and it was a way to pay back Cindy for the pain he'd caused her. She would be part of the Washington social whirl. A senator's wife threw parties and dined with ambassadors and generals. A senator's wife would be on television and would be interviewed in magazines. It was a role that she was born to play.

But a senator can't hide. What if someone found out what had happened in the park just before the Rose Bowl? He was almost certain that his secret was buried so deep that no one would ever uncover it, but he'd never been up against the resources of a national political party.

Tim turned on his side. He didn't know what to do. He was afraid. But then he was always afraid.

thirteen

The Justice Center was a sixteen-story, concrete-and-glass edifice located a block from the courthouse. The Multnomah County jail occupied the fourth through tenth floors of the building, which also housed the central precinct of the Portland Police, a branch of the district attorney's office, and several courtrooms. A pack of reporters was waiting for Wendell Hayes in the Justice Center's glass-vaulted lobby. The defense attorney was easy to spot because he was as wide as he was tall.

"Can you tell us why Judge Grant appointed you to represent Jon Dupre?" one reporter asked.

"Isn't it unusual for you to accept a court appointment?" another shouted.

Hayes greeted several reporters as he huffed past the curving stairs that led up to the courtrooms on the third floor and walked into the jail reception area. He was a large man gone soft, and the short walk from the courthouse to the jail had winded him. Even expert hand-tailoring could not disguise his girth. Hayes pulled out a handkerchief and mopped the sweat from his flushed face. His broad back was to the two sheriff's deputies who watched the show from the protection of the reception desk. The television cameramen turned on their lights and the deputies blinked as Hayes was washed in a white glow. The reporters crowded around him and repeated their questions.

Hayes flashed the brethren of the Fourth Estate a warm smile. He loved them. It was their reports of his colorful courtroom exploits that had made the attorney a household name. In return, Hayes was always good for a quote and had no compunction about leaking information when it was to his advantage.

Hayes held up a hand and the questions stopped. "As you know, I rarely accept a court appointment, but I did in this case because Judge Grant asked me. He's an old friend and a hard man to turn down."

"Why didn't Judge Grant use one of the lawyers on the court-appointment list?" shouted a reporter from one of the network affiliates.

"Jack Stamm is going to seek the death penalty, which limits the list to death-qualified lawyers. Judge Grant wanted to avoid any suggestion that Mr. Dupre was not going to be treated fairly because of Senator Travis's prominence."

"What's your defense going to be?" a reporter from the **Oregonian** asked.

Hayes smiled. "Grace, I haven't talked to Mr. Dupre yet, so I can't possibly answer that question. But I'm going to do that now. So, if you'll excuse me . . ."

Hayes turned to one of the deputies manning the reception desk, a huge man with red hair who was almost as tall as the lawyer.

"Hey, Mac, help me make my escape from this rabble, will you?" he said loudly enough so the reporters could hear him. A few laughed.

"Sure thing, Mr. Hayes."

The lawyer started to hand the deputy his bar card, but he waved him off.

"I'll need to check your briefcase, though."

A metal detector stood between Hayes and the jail elevator. He handed over his briefcase and took his keys, coins, and a small Swiss Army knife out of his pocket. Then he stripped off his coat and handed it and the metal objects to the guard.

"How'd you think the Blazers made out in that

trade?" Hayes asked as the guard laid down the jacket and gave the papers in his briefcase a cursory going-over.

"I don't know about that forward from Croatia. I'd have gone for Drake."

"The guy from Dallas?" Hayes said as he walked through the metal detector. "He's big but he can't shoot."

"Yeah, but he can block shots, and the Blazers are definitely hurting on defense." Mac handed back everything but the knife. "Sorry, Mr. Hayes. I gotta hold on to this."

"I'll pick it up when I'm through," Hayes said as he put on his jacket. "Beam me up, Mac."

It was Hayes's standard line, and Mac flashed his usual smile as he walked over to the jail elevator and keyed Hayes up to the floor where Jon Dupre was being held.

One of Adam Buckley's jobs as a jail guard was escorting attorneys to the three soundproofed visiting rooms designated for face-to-face meetings with their clients. Buckley could see into these rooms when he walked along the narrow corridor that ran in front of them, because each had a large window. The corridor ended at a thick metal door. A small glass window in the top half of the door looked out on another hallway into which the elevators from reception emptied.

"I'm here to visit Jon Dupre," Wendell Hayes said as soon as Buckley opened the door.

"I know, Mr. Hayes. I got him in room number two."

"Thanks," Hayes answered as he glanced through the glass at a woman in a business suit and a young black man who were huddled over a stack of police reports in the room nearest the elevators.

Buckley led Hayes to the second visiting room and let him in through a solid-steel door. A second door at the back of the room led to the unit where the prisoners on the floor were housed. Jon Dupre, dressed in an orange jail-issue jumpsuit, was sprawled in one of the two molded plastic chairs that stood on either side of a round table secured to the floor by metal bolts. Hayes walked past Buckley, and the guard pointed to a black button that stuck out from the bottom of an intercom that was recessed into the yellow concrete wall.

"Press that if you need assistance," he told Hayes, even though he knew that the lawyer was familiar with the routine.

Buckley relocked the door just as his radio came to life and the dispatcher notified him that another attorney was on the way up. He ambled down to the door and watched a harried public defender walk out of the elevator, reading a police report. Buckley recognized him and let him into the corridor.

"Hey, Mr. Buckley, I'm here for Kevin Hoch."

"They're bringing him down."

Buckley was passing the second contact room when Wendell Hayes crashed into the glass window.

"What the . . ." Buckley started to say, but he froze with his mouth half open when Hayes turned his head and blood poured out of his left eye socket, smearing the glass. The public defender made a strangled cry and tried to burrow through the far wall as Hayes pushed off the glass and turned toward Dupre. Buckley watched the prisoner stab the lawyer, then snapped out of his trance when more blood sprayed across the window and Hayes sank to the floor. He wanted to break into the room but his training took over. If he opened the door, he would be facing an armed man without a weapon and endangering everyone else on the floor.

"Major assault, major assault in contact visiting room two," Buckley shouted into his radio as he rushed to the window. "A man is down."

Buckley pressed against the window so he could judge Hayes's condition. Dupre thrust a jagged metal object at the guard. Buckley jumped back, even though the glass was between them.

"I need backup," Buckley shouted. "Weapons are involved."

Dupre kicked the window. The glass shuddered but didn't break.

"What is the man's condition?" the dispatcher asked.

"I don't know, but he's bleeding bad."

Dupre ran to the door at the back of the room and slammed his hands into it, but the steel door didn't move. He began pacing frantically and muttering to himself.

"Who else is on the floor?" the dispatcher asked.

"I've got a lawyer and prisoner in room one and an attorney in the corridor," Buckley answered as Dupre turned his attention to the other door.

"Evacuate. I'll get the sergeant."

"Get out, now," he told the public defender, as he opened the hall door. When it was relocked, Buckley opened the door to visiting room one and told the woman to leave. Her client looked confused.

"There's an emergency," Buckley told the inmate, keeping his voice calm. "The guard will be here for you in a moment."

The woman started to protest just as Buckley heard Dupre slam a chair against the glass window. The window was thick but Buckley wasn't certain that it would hold.

"Out!" he yelled, grabbing the attorney by the arm and hustling her into the hall. The prisoner got to his feet.

"My papers," she started to say. Then the chair hit the window again and she clamped a hand to her mouth when she noticed the blood-smeared glass for the first time. Buckley locked her client in and pushed the woman into the hall with the elevators. This time she didn't protest. Buckley followed her and locked the door. If Dupre broke through the glass he would still be trapped in the narrow hall outside the visiting rooms.

"This is Sergeant Rice. What's the situation?" a voice asked over Buckley's radio.

"There's a prisoner in one. I just locked him in. I don't know if there's an inmate in three yet, but someone was supposed to bring Kevin Hoch down. I'm in the hall outside the elevators with two attorneys. I think Wendell Hayes is dead." Buckley heard an intake of air. "He's inside room two with Jon Dupre. Dupre stabbed him several times. He's got some kind of knife."

"Okay. Hold your position, Buckley. The jail is locked down and I'll have help to you in another minute. Then I'll go in through the back door with the CERT boys."

As they spoke, the elevator doors opened and ten members of the Corrections Emergency Response Team rushed out of the elevator in flack jackets and face shields. They were all carrying nonlethal weapons, like Mace, and three of them had man-sized Plexiglas shields.

"Buckley?" one of the men asked. Adam nodded. "I'm Sergeant Miller. What's our situation?"

Buckley repeated what he'd told Sergeant Rice.

"Let's go in," Miller said. Buckley opened the door to the hallway. Over the radio, Buckley could hear Sergeant Rice talking to Dupre.

"Mr. Dupre, this is Sergeant Rice. I'm on the other side of this door with fifteen armed men. If you look into the corridor, you'll see many more armed men."

Dupre spun toward the window. He looked desperate. Both of his hands were bleeding and he was holding something shiny. Wendell Hayes was sprawled on his back. His throat and face were drenched in blood.

"We don't want to hurt you," Sergeant Rice told Dupre. "If you put down your weapon and surrender we'll just cuff you and return you to your cell. If you don't surrender I can't guarantee your safety."

Dupre's eyes darted to the men in the corridor. They looked intimidating in black, with their weapons and shields.

"What will it be, Mr. Dupre?" Sergeant Rice asked calmly.

"Don't come in here," Dupre shouted.

It was quiet for a moment. Then the rear door crashed into the room and four men swarmed in, their body shields leading the way. The room was narrow and there was nowhere for Dupre to run. He jabbed at the shields as he was driven into the wall. A CERT team member sprayed Mace in his eyes. Dupre screamed, and two of the men grabbed his legs and brought him down while the other two wrestled the knife from his hand. In less than a minute, Dupre was cuffed and in custody. Buckley saw another deputy rush over to Hayes. She searched for a pulse, then shook her head.

fourteen

Court adjourned early, so Amanda decided to head to the Y for a workout. It crossed her mind that she might see Toby Brooks, a possibility that made her uneasy. She tried to stop thinking about him but that was impossible. "This is stupid," she said out loud. "He's a normal guy. He won't hurt you." Then she felt sad. Before the Cardoni case, meeting someone like Toby Brooks would have excited her. The greatest casualty of her degradation at the hands of the surgeon had been her ability to trust people.

In the locker room, Amanda changed quickly, grabbed her goggles, stuffed her long black hair under her swim cap and headed for the pool. As she neared the revolving door, she grew short of breath and felt foolish. Brooks probably wasn't even working out. And if he was, he'd be swimming and there was no way she'd be able to talk to him.

But Toby was at poolside. As soon as he saw Amanda, he grinned and waved.

"Change your mind about swimming on the team?" he asked.

"Nope," she managed. "I'm just here for a workout."

"Too bad. Senior Nationals are in a few months. Then there are the Senior Worlds. They're in Paris, this year."

"Chlorine in Paris. How romantic," she said, forcing a smile.

Toby laughed. The Masters swimmers finished a set and started to group by the pool wall.

"I've got to get these guys moving. Have a good workout."

Toby turned to his swimmers and yelled out their next set as Amanda grabbed fins and a kickboard from a pile on the pool deck. She was putting them on the edge of the pool in front of her lane when she saw Kate Ross walking up the ramp from the locker room, dressed in tight jeans, a blue Oxford work shirt, and a bomber jacket and carrying her shoes and socks. A twenty-eight-year-old ex-cop whose specialty was computer crime, Kate was a muscular five seven, with a dark complexion, large brown eyes, and curly black hair. Several months before, while working as an investigator at Portland's largest law firm, she had asked Amanda to represent Daniel Ames, a first-year associate who was charged with murder. Amanda had helped clear Daniel's name, then hired him as an associate at Jaffe, Katz, Lehane and Brindisi. Shortly after, Amanda lured Kate to the firm.

"Come for a swim?" Amanda asked, her good mood fading because she realized that Kate's appearance meant her workout plans were kaput.

"I don't do water."

"What's up?"

"Judge Robard tried to reach you in Judge Davis's courtroom, but you'd skedaddled. He's waiting for you in his chambers. Your dad sent me to find you."

Amanda's shoulders sagged. Judge Robard had made her life miserable in the few trials that she'd been unfortunate enough to have before him. The only solace in being in his court was that he made life equally miserable for the prosecution. Now he'd ruined her workout. Unfortunately, there was no way that she could turn down an urgent summons from a circuit court judge without ruining her legal career.

"I'll change and go straight downtown," she sighed. "You can go back to my dad and tell him you've accomplished your mission."

"He's cooking dinner for you at his house and wants you to drop by after you see Robard."

Judge Ivan Robard was a fitness fanatic who spent his vacations running marathons. A vegetarian diet and all that exercise had left him with zero body fat on his five-foot-six frame. Robard's sunken cheeks and deep eye sockets reminded Amanda of a shrunken head she'd seen in a New York City museum. It was Amanda's theory that the judge would be much more pleasant if he ate more and worked out less.

Robard was seated behind his desk writing an opinion when Amanda was shown into his chambers. The walls were covered with pictures of the judge racing along city streets in Boston, New York, and other marathon locales, standing on top of mountains, hang gliding, bungee jumping, and white-water rafting. Just looking at them was exhausting.

"At last," Robard said without looking up from his work.

"My investigator dragged me out of the pool," Amanda answered. If she was looking for sympathy from a fellow athlete, she didn't get it.

"Sorry about that," Robard answered without conviction as he stacked the papers on which he was working in a neat pile and finally looked at Amanda, "but we've got a situation."

A punch line from an old joke—"What you mean **we**, white man?"—raced through Amanda's head, but she held her tongue.

"You heard about Wendell Hayes?"

"It's all anyone's been talking about."

"You know anything about the guy who killed him, Jon Dupre?"

"Only what I read in the paper."

"He's a pimp, a drug dealer. I just heard a prostitution case where he was the defendant."

Amanda suddenly knew the reason for Robard's hasty summons and she didn't like it one bit.

"What happened?" she asked, to stall for time.

"I had to dismiss. The state's key witness no-showed. After I dismissed, she turned up dead. Anyway, Harvey Grant got the bright idea of assigning me the homicide because I handled the other case. So, as I said, we've got a situation. The

Constitution says that I have to appoint counsel for Dupre, but that wonderful document doesn't tell me what I'm supposed to do when every attorney I call says that they would rather not represent someone who stabbed his previous lawyer to death."

Amanda knew what Robard wanted her to say but she wasn't going to make it easy for him, so she sat silently and waited for the judge to continue. Robard looked annoyed.

"What about it?" he asked.

"What about what?"

"Miss Jaffe, the one thing you are not is stupid, so don't fence with me. I asked you here because you've got more guts than any lawyer in town, and I need a lawyer with guts on this case."

Amanda knew that he was thinking about Cardoni, and she wanted to tell him that her lifetime allotment of courage had been used up last year.

"You should hear the excuses I've been getting from your fellow advocates," Robard went on. "What a bunch of babies."

"I thought Dupre had the money to hire a lawyer. The papers said his parents are rich."

"They disowned Dupre when he was kicked

out of college and decided to deal drugs and sell women."

"What about the lawyer who handled the promoting case?"

"Oscar Baron? Don't make me laugh. He's as scared as the rest. Says Dupre can't afford his fee. And he's got a point. Only millionaires can scrape up the money to pay a lawyer in a capital case. Besides, he's not qualified to handle a death-penalty case. So, what do you say?"

"This is a bit overwhelming, Judge. I'd like some time to think, and I'll want to talk it over with my father."

"I spoke with Frank earlier," Robard answered with a weaselly smile. "I can tell you that he's all for it."

"Oh he is, is he? Well, I'd like to know why. So it's either give me some time or I'll politely decline your kind offer to spend the next few months with a homicidal maniac."

"Time is of the essence, Miss Jaffe."

Amanda sighed. "I'm having dinner with my dad tonight. I'll get back to you tomorrow."

Robard's head dipped a few times. "That's fair, that's eminently fair. I'm usually here at seven." Robard scribbled something on his business card. "Here's my back line. My secretary doesn't get in until eight."

Amanda Jaffe's mother had died the day Amanda was born, and Frank Jaffe was the only parent she'd ever known. In his youth, Frank had been a man's man, a brawler and carouser who believed that a woman's place was in the home. He had never imagined himself raising a little girl by himself. Then Amanda's mother died, and Frank put every ounce of his energy into the job. Because he had no idea what he was supposed to do, Frank did everything. There had been dolls and ballet lessons, but Amanda had also learned to raft white water, pump iron, and shoot a gun. When she showed an aptitude for swimming fast, Frank became her biggest supporter, praising her when she won—which was often—and never getting down on her when she didn't.

Six years ago, Amanda had hesitated when Frank offered her a job as an associate in his firm. She wondered at the time if her father wanted her for her legal skills or because she was his daughter. In the end, she'd accepted the offer over several others because criminal law was the only type of law Amanda wanted to practice and

Frank Jaffe was one of the best criminal lawyers in the country. Now her reputation was approaching that of her father's and there were only rare occasions in her professional life when Frank acted like a parent and not a law partner. When that happened, Amanda set him straight, which was what she was determined to do when she pulled her car into the driveway of the steep-roofed East Lake Victorian where she had grown up.

Frank was only an adequate cook, but he excelled at matzo-ball soup and potato pancakes, his mother's specialties. When Amanda was a little girl, Frank had prepared these dishes for her as a special treat. When Amanda saw the fixings on the kitchen counter she knew her father was feeling guilty.

"I always thought we got along, and I haven't heard that the firm needs to downsize," she said as she chucked her coat onto a chair. "Is there some other reason you want me to die?"

"Now, Amanda . . ."

"Did you tell the Honorable Ivan Robard that I would accept his offer to represent a lawyer killer?"

"No, I did not. I simply said that you were up to the job."

"So are you. How come you didn't volunteer to help this poor unfortunate boy?"

"I can't take the case. I knew Travis. I was in a foursome with him at the Westmont, last week."

"Oh, I see. You can't be a human sacrifice because Travis is an old golfing buddy, but I don't play golf, so I'm fair game. What on earth were you thinking?"

"I had a few reasons for suggesting that Ivan ask you to take the case. There's the general one about every defendant deserving the best representation possible, and it bothers me that lawyers are refusing to take on this case because they're scared. But neither of those is the reason I'd like to see you represent Dupre."

Frank paused. When he spoke, he looked concerned.

"That business last year was awful. You know how proud I am of the way you handled it, but I also know that since the Cardoni case ended you've stayed away from cases involving violence. I can see why you'd do that. I wish I could wipe out the bad memories. And I was thinking that maybe one way you can get past what happened is by getting back on the horse."

Amanda had to admit that since **Cardoni** she had been involved in only a few murder or assault cases, and even there, with the exception of Daniel Ames's case, she had limited herself to helping other attorneys in the firm with legal research or pretrial motions. She just did not want to see any more violence. And that presented a problem when you were practicing criminal law.

"You're right, Dad. I have been running scared. But that case . . ." She flashed on the Mary Sandowski video, and a shudder ran through her. "It's been very hard for me."

Frank's heart ached at the memory of what his daughter had gone through.

"I know, kid," he said, "and I wouldn't blame you if you tried something else, another area of law. But you've got to face up to your fears if you're going to stick with criminal law. It's your choice and I'll support any decision you make, but this is as good a way as any to test yourself if you want to stay with the practice."

"I'll think about it."

"Good, but you can't do that on an empty stomach. So, enough law. Let's eat."

Part Three

THE PRESUMPTION OF INNOCENCE

fifteen

Shortly before quitting time, Jack Stamm summoned Tim Kerrigan to his office. When his senior deputy arrived, the Multnomah County district attorney waved him into a chair and signaled his secretary to close his door. Stamm, who was usually upbeat, was not smiling.

"Can you believe this mess with Wendell Hayes? In the jail of all places. It makes everyone in law enforcement look like a boob."

Stamm ran his fingers through his thinning brown hair. His eyes were bloodshot and there were dark circles under them. Kerrigan guessed that the DA had slept very little since the Hayes killing.

"I want you on this, Tim. I want Dupre on death row for the murders of Wendell Hayes and Harold Travis."

This was not what Kerrigan wanted to hear. The case would be huge, but there was Ally Bennett to consider. She hadn't shown any sign that she knew who he was when they'd had sex at the motel, but his face would be on television and in the newspapers every day if he prosecuted Jon Dupre. What would she do if she discovered who he was? He'd be wide-open to blackmail.

"Can't someone else handle it?" Tim asked.

Stamm failed to hide his surprise at Kerrigan's reluctance to prosecute these headline-grabbing cases.

"Your unit had Dupre's pimping case," the DA answered, "and you're already on the senator's case."

Kerrigan needed time to think, so he asked a question to divert Stamm.

"Are we even going after Dupre for Travis's murder? The evidence is skimpy. We don't have him anywhere near the scene. . . ."

"You've got that earring, you've got him arguing with Travis the day before the senator was murdered. Besides, it doesn't matter how much evidence we have in Travis's case. We'll piggyback the trials. Go after Dupre for Hayes first. That case is a walk in the park. Dupre was locked in with Wendell. We've got an eyewitness. The little prick brought the murder weapon with him to the conference. Proving intent and deliberation will be a snap."

"If it's that easy you don't need me for Hayes. A rookie DA could get a death sentence for a violent pimp under these circumstances."

"It's not that simple, Tim." Stamm leaned forward. "I've received a few calls from some very influential people. They told me that you've been offered a shot at Harold Travis's seat."

Kerrigan stifled a curse. He should have seen this coming.

"These cases will put you in the spotlight for months and, as you just told me, Wendell's case is open and shut—so simple that a rookie DA could get a death sentence. You couldn't ask for a better way to get exposure. You'll have national coverage."

Kerrigan wanted to turn down the case but what excuse would he give Jack? He couldn't tell him about Ally Bennett.

"Can we resolve the case with a plea?" Kerrigan asked. "There's no defense in Wendell's case. His lawyer is going to offer a plea in exchange for a life sentence."

Stamm shook his head. "We don't plead this one. That little punk killed a United States senator. Then he had the audacity to murder one of the state's most prominent attorneys in our own fucking jail. I'm sorry, Tim, but my mind's made up. This son of a bitch invaded our home. He's going to death row and you're going to take him there."

Maria Lopez walked into Tim's office as soon as he returned from his meeting with Jack Stamm. Many of the other deputies had left, and the sky outside Tim's window was edging toward gray.

"Do you have a minute?" Maria asked.

"Sure."

"There's a rumor that you've been tapped to prosecute Jon Dupre."

"It's not a rumor," Kerrigan sighed. "I'm it."

Maria focused all of her energy on Kerrigan.

"I want to second-chair. I want a chance to help put him away."

"I don't know . . ."

"Who knows more about Dupre than me? I'll be able to tell you who'll make a good witness in the penalty phase, where to find everything you need to show future dangerousness." She tapped her temple. "It's all up here, ready to go. Anyone else will need to spend hours finding out what I can tell you right now."

What Maria said was true, but she had no experience in trying a death-penalty case. On the other hand, her passion would help her put in the sixteen-hour days, seven days a week, that were standard operating procedure when you were asking the state to execute a human being.

"Alright," he said. "You've got it. You're second chair."

Lopez grinned. "You won't regret this, boss. We'll get Dupre, I promise you. We'll put him down."

Tim Kerrigan called Hugh Curtin a little after seven. Hugh was an unmarried workaholic and Tim knew that he'd meet him for a drink anytime, anywhere, if he didn't have a date with one of his many girlfriends. They agreed to meet at the Hardball, a workingman's bar near the baseball stadium, because the patrons minded their own business and the odds of running into someone they knew were mighty low.

Tim waited for his eyes to adjust to the dark before scanning the bar for his friend. It only took a few seconds to spot Hugh in a booth toward the rear. Hugh poured Kerrigan a tall one from a large pitcher as soon as he saw him. Tim slid into the booth and downed half of it. As soon as he put down the mug, Curtin topped it off.

"So," Curtin said, "are you going to explain why you're interfering with my twenty-eighth viewing of **Predator,** starring my all-time favorite action hero, Jesse 'The Body' Ventura?"

"I need your advice."

"Of course you do."

Curtin emptied the pitcher and signaled for another. In college, Tim had seen "Huge" chug a pitcher with no ill effects.

"I had my monthly dinner with my father at the Westmont."

"And survived."

Tim nodded. "We didn't dine alone. He invited Burton Rommel and Harvey Grant." He paused. "The party wants me to run for Harold Travis's seat in the next election."

Curtin paused with his mug halfway to his lips. "You're kidding!"

"Don't you think I could do it?" Kerrigan asked anxiously.

"Of course you could do it. Look at the morons who've served in Congress. It's just a shock. Fuck, if you became a senator I'd have to be civil to you. You could have the IRS audit my god-damn taxes."

Kerrigan smiled.

"The real question is, **should** you do it? There's a ton of prestige that goes with the position, and the chance to do a lot of good for a lot of people. But being a senator is a twenty-four-hour-a-day job. You'd never be home. Megan would miss you. You'd miss a lot of her growing up. Still, the chance to be a United States senator . . . It's a tough call. What does Cindy want you to do?"

"She wants me to run."

"I don't suppose there's any question about what your old man wants?"

"He wants me to go for the gold. I thought the top of his head was going to pop off when I didn't jump at the offer."

"But you told him you're thinking about it?"

"Oh, yeah. I didn't want him to have a coronary."

"It would mean a lot to him, Tim."

"Yeah, he could brag about having a senator in the family."

"He wants what's best for you."

"He wants what's best for William Kerrigan."

"You're being hard on him."

"He's a hard man. He always has been. No matter what I did it was never enough. Not even winning that goddamn trophy. It became so much tin to him when I didn't go pro and cash in.

"And he was never around when Mom was dying." Tim took a drink, then continued. He looked down at the tabletop. "I always suspected that he was spending time with one of his women. I still can't imagine it. My mother is wasting away from cancer and he's balling some bimbo."

"You don't know that."

"No, not for certain. But he sure married number two fast enough."

Kerrigan could never bring himself to say the name of the woman who had succeeded his mother as mistress of the house.

"Maybe I'm wrong, maybe I'm being unfair to him, but what business deal could be so important that he couldn't put it off? Mom was dying, for Christ's sake. He knew she only had a little time left. Didn't he want to spend it with her?"

"So Cindy wants you to run," Hugh said to distract his friend. "Your father wants you to run and the party wants you to run. What do you want to do?"

"I don't know if I can handle being a senator." Hugh could see the pain in his friend's eyes. "Why me, Huge?"

"I'm going to tell you the answer, but you won't like it."

"That's why I'm asking you. You're always straight with me."

"They're asking you because they think you can win and that's all that counts in politics. And they think you can win because you're 'The Flash.' And it's time you got comfortable with the fact that 'The Flash' is always going to be part of who you are, whether you like it or not. It's almost ten years since you got the Heisman. I know you think you didn't earn it, but there are a lot of people—including me—who think you did. And it's about time you came to grips with that and moved on.

"Look at it this way. This is a chance to start from scratch, to do some good, to see if you really are 'The Flash.' And I think that's what scares you. You're worried that you'll win and won't be able to handle the job.

"You've heard me quote Oliver Wendell Holmes more than once. 'Life is passion and action and each man must take part in the passion and action of his times at peril of being judged not to have lived.' I believe that. You've been hiding in the DA's office trying to avoid being noticed, but you've got to come out sometime. It'll be scary, pal. You'll be risking failure. But who knows, maybe you'll surprise yourself."

sixteen

Nightmares wrecked Amanda's sleep and she was drenched in sweat when she awoke in the dark, exhausted and slightly nauseous, an hour before her alarm was set to go off. Amanda usually started the day with calisthenics, occasionally followed by a decadent pancake breakfast at a café that had been a neighborhood fixture since the fifties. This morning, she settled for an ice-cold shower, a toasted bagel, and tea.

Amanda's loft in the Pearl, a former warehouse district, was a brisk fifteen-minute walk from her office. She left her car in the garage in hopes that the cool weather and mild exercise would calm her anxiety. She would be sitting opposite a violent killer later this morning but, she reminded herself, it would not be the same person who had inspired the horrors that had invaded last night's sleep. That person was dead. Jon Dupre would be manacled, and Kate Ross would be with her in the interview room. Logically, there was no reason to worry, but she still felt light-headed when she arrived at the law offices of Jaffe, Katz, Lehane and Brindisi. The fear stayed with her while she worked—a tiny insect she could feel skittering across the pit of her stomach no matter how hard she tried to distract herself.

Kate Ross had picked up the discovery in the Travis and Hayes cases from the district attorney's office, and it was waiting on Amanda's desk when she arrived. Amanda read the police reports first and avoided looking at the crime scene and autopsy photographs until she could no longer put off the task.

Amanda spread the photos of Harold Travis's and Wendell Hayes's bodies on her desk, praying that they would not trigger a flashback. She told herself that viewing the pictures was part of her job—an unpleasant part, but an important part. Amanda took slow breaths as she studied the crime-scene photos. She had read the autopsy reports and went through the autopsy photos quickly. When she was done, she shoved the photos into the case file and noticed that her hands were trembling. She closed her eyes, leaned back in her chair, and tried to relax. The worst was over—she'd seen the pictures and had not had a flashback—but still Amanda wondered if she had made a mistake when she agreed to accept the Dupre case.

Amanda and Kate arrived at the Justice Center at ten-thirty. They showed their IDs to the guard at the jail reception desk, and Amanda asked for a contact visit with Jon Dupre. The guard made a phone call. As soon as he hung up, he told Amanda that Jail Commander Matthew Guthrie wanted to speak to her. A few minutes later, Guthrie lumbered into the reception area. He was in his early fifties, a bright-eyed Irishman with salt-and-pepper hair, broad shoulders, and the beginning of a beer gut.

"Morning, Amanda."

"Good morning, Matt. Is this a social call?"

"Afraid not. I'm not allowing contact visits with Dupre. I wanted to tell you in person because I know you're gonna scream and holler."

"You got that right. I don't want to talk to my client through a sheet of bulletproof glass like he's some sort of animal."

"Well there's your problem," Guthrie answered calmly. "Dupre **is** an animal. The last time we let him have a contact visit with one of your brethren he stabbed him in the eye and cut his throat. I'm not giving him the opportunity to do it again. And before you say it, it's not because you're of the female persuasion. I didn't know who was gonna get stuck with this dreamboat when I made the prohibition."

"Look, Matt, I appreciate your concern for my safety, but I need to meet face-to-face with Dupre if I'm going to establish trust between us. The first meeting is very important. If he thinks I'm afraid of him he won't open up to me."

"I'm not changing my mind on this. One dead attorney on my watch is enough."

"You can manacle him. And Kate's with me. She's an ex-cop and she's very good at self-defense."

Guthrie shook his head. "Sorry, Amanda, but I'm sticking to my guns. It's a noncontact visit or nothing."

"I can get a court order."

"You'll have to."

Amanda saw that it was useless to argue and she knew that Guthrie meant well.

"I'll take what I can get, for now, but I'm going right to Judge Robard as soon as I'm through."

Guthrie nodded. "I expected you would. No hard feelings I hope?"

"This just reinforces my opinion that you're a narrow-minded redneck," Amanda said with a smile.

"And proud of it," Guthrie laughed. Then he sobered. "You watch yourself with this son of a bitch. Don't let him con you and don't you let your guard down for an instant. Jon Dupre is very, very dangerous."

"Don't worry, Matt. He's one client I am definitely not going to underestimate."

"Okay, then." He stuck out a massive paw, which Amanda shook. "Say hi to your dad for me."

Guthrie left and Amanda showed the contents of her briefcase to the guard, then went through the metal detector. As she waited for Kate to follow, Amanda had to admit that she was relieved that there would be a concrete wall and bullet-proof glass between her and Jon Dupre.

The noncontact visiting room was so narrow that Kate Ross had to stand behind Amanda with her back pressed against the door. Amanda sat in a gray metal bridge chair and rested her notepad and file on a ledge that projected out from a wall that was directly in front of her. The bottom of the wall was concrete and the top was bulletproof glass. It was impossible to hear through the glass, so attorney and client communicated through phones attached to the wall on both sides.

A door opened on the other side of the glass, and a guard pushed Jon Dupre into an identical space. Amanda's first impression of her new client was that he was handsome and hyperalert. Dupre's ankles were shackled, which forced him to shuffle forward unsteadily. The prisoner riveted his eyes to Amanda's, and they stayed on her. It was unnerving, but Amanda sensed fear as well as aggression. When he drew closer, she saw that Dupre's eyes were red and swollen, and there were bruises on his face.

The guard pressed Dupre down onto his chair and left. The jumpsuit her client was wearing was short-sleeved. He placed his manacled hands on the metal ledge, revealing a row of stitches on his right forearm and cuts on the sides of his fingers on both hands.

Amanda forced a smile as she picked up the receiver of her phone and gestured for Dupre to do the same.

"Who the fuck are you?" he asked.

"I'm Amanda Jaffe and I've been asked by the court to be your attorney."

"Jesus, they sent me a cunt for a lawyer. Why don't they just give me my lethal injection now."

Amanda stopped smiling. "You've been appointed a cunt for a lawyer, Mr. Dupre, because all the swinging dicks were too scared to take your case."

"And you're not?" Dupre said, tapping the receiver against the bulletproof glass.

"The jail commander wouldn't let us meet face-to-face. As soon as I'm through here, I'm going across the street to the courthouse to get an order forcing him to let us meet in a contact room."

Dupre pointed the receiver at Kate. "Is she your bodyguard?"

"No, Mr. Dupre. She's **your** investigator. Now, are you going to keep testing me or can we get down to work? I've got a number of questions I'd like to ask you. You're in a lot of trouble. You murdered a prominent attorney and you're looking at a very real possibility of a death sentence."

Dupre sprang to his feet, leaning against the ledge to maintain his balance. Even though there was a wall between them, Amanda pushed her chair back, stunned by Dupre's sudden rage.

"I didn't murder anyone and I don't need a DA's flunky for an attorney. Get the fuck out."

"Mr. Dupre," Amanda shouted into the phone. Dupre smashed the receiver against the glass, struggled to the rear wall, and slammed his man-acled hands against the steel door. The door opened and the guard stepped back to let Dupre into the hall that led to his cell. Amanda sagged onto her chair.

"What an asshole," Kate said.

Amanda gathered her papers, her eyes still on the door through which her client had disappeared.

"What are you going to do now?" Kate asked as she opened the door into the hall.

"I'm going to give Dupre time to cool off while I get a court order from Robard. Then I'll set up a contact meeting and hope it goes a little better."

"Good luck."

"Meanwhile, you and I will draw up a game plan for the trial and the penalty phase."

Kate pressed the button for the elevator.

"We should spend most of our time on figuring

out how to keep the jury from sentencing Dupre to death. I've read the police reports. I don't think that the guilt phase is going to take too long."

"That's negative thinking," Amanda answered with a tired smile. "We don't do that at Jaffe, Katz, Lehane and Brindisi."

"Hey, I'm positive. I've even got a few theories of defense. Martians may have beamed powerful thought rays through the concrete walls, which forced Dupre to chop up Mr. Hayes, and the Sci Fi channel had this movie about demonic possession. I'll write for their research file."

The elevator took them down to the reception area of the jail. When the doors opened they could see a group of reporters milling around.

"Oh, shit," Amanda said. "Someone tipped them off."

The reporters shouted questions at Amanda as she walked through reception. She stopped in the lobby. The lights from one of the TV cameras blinded her for a moment, and she squinted.

"Are you representing Jon Dupre?" one reporter asked.

"Did you meet with him face-to-face?"

Amanda held up her hand and the questions stopped.

"Judge Robard asked me to represent Mr. Dupre and I've just come from a meeting with him. . . ."

"Were you frightened?" someone shouted.

"Did Dupre admit that he murdered Senator Travis?"

Amanda waited patiently until the reporters quieted down.

"Those of you who know me know that I believe that the proper place to resolve a matter of this seriousness is in a courtroom and not in the press. So, I won't be discussing the case with you and I certainly will not reveal any attorney-client communications."

Several reporters continued to ask questions. Amanda waited patiently for the shouting to subside.

"I'm not going to comment on this case in the press," Amanda repeated. "I'm sorry, but that's my position. Let's go, Kate."

Amanda and her investigator walked away from the reporters and through the main doors of the Justice Center just as Tim Kerrigan jogged up the stairs from the street. The prosecutor stared for a second as if trying to place her, then smiled when he did.

"Hey, Amanda, it's been a while."

"Two years, the Harrison case."

"In which you were a graceful winner, if I remember correctly."

"You know my investigator, Kate Ross? She used to be PPB."

"Sure. You were involved in the Daniel Ames case."

"That was me," Kate answered.

The reporters and cameramen had been walking away when they spotted Kerrigan talking to Amanda. They surged toward them like a pack of ravenous wolves.

"What's with the reporters?"

Amanda looked over her shoulder and grimaced. "I'm handling Jon Dupre's case."

"Then we've got something in common. I'm prosecuting. Maybe I'll get to even our record."

"We'll see," Amanda answered without much confidence.

"Mr. Kerrigan," someone shouted.

"I'll leave you to your public," Amanda said.

"Gee, thanks," Kerrigan answered.

As the reporters closed in on her adversary, Amanda and Kate raced down the stairs and started to put some distance between themselves and the press.

"He's the jock, right?" Kate asked.

"Not just any jock. He won a Heisman about ten years ago."

Kate whistled. "How is he in court?" she asked.

"Good. He's smart and he works very hard." Then she sighed. "But the way this case is shaping up, he won't have to break a sweat."

seventeen

Oscar Baron's office was on the eighteenth floor of a modern glass-and-steel office tower. The waiting area was tastefully furnished and gave the impression that Baron was doing well, but Amanda knew that he was renting space from a firm and had nothing to do with selecting, or paying for, the reception-area furnishings.

The receptionist buzzed Baron and told him that Amanda was waiting for him. After five minutes, she started thumbing through a copy of **TIME**. Fifteen minutes later, Baron hurried into the waiting room.

"Sorry," he said as he extended a hand. "I was talking with a lawyer in New York about a case we're cocounseling."

Amanda pretended to be impressed that Baron was working with a New York lawyer as he led her down a long hall and into a moderate-sized office with a view of the river.

"So, Robard stuck you with Dupre," Baron said when they were seated.

"I took the case as a favor because no one else would touch it. I'm surprised you aren't representing Dupre. You'd have gotten a lot of media exposure."

"Yeah. I can see it now." Baron held up his hands as if he was a director framing a shot. "OSCAR BARON'S CLIENT GETS THE CHAIR." He laughed. "Or maybe, MAD PIMP CLAIMS SECOND LAWYER VICTIM. Just the kind of publicity I need. Besides, he couldn't afford my fee." Baron leaned forward and dropped his voice a notch. "And between us, I'm glad. Poor Wendell." He looked at Amanda wide-eyed. "There but for the grace of God, huh? I'm telling you, I've had nightmares about that little bastard. It could have been me in that room at the jail."

"You think Dupre might have tried to kill you?"

"Who knows what that lunatic is capable of."

"Did he threaten you while you were representing him?"

"Well, no, not directly. But the guy is scary. I always felt he was ready to explode. I guess I just got lucky. So, how are you two getting along?"

"We're at the feeling-out stage. You know how that is."

"Oh, sure. That's when they don't trust you and lie to you. Then you pass that stage and they trust you **and** lie to you."

Baron barked out a laugh and Amanda forced a smile.

"How long have you been representing Jon?" she asked.

"It was just this one case, but I represented a few of his girls when they got in trouble."

"The women who worked in his escort service?"

Baron nodded.

"Tell me about the escort-service case."

"I can't reveal any confidences without Jon's okay."

"Of course, but I'm interested in public knowledge. Information that's in the police reports. I'll need copies from you, anyway. I thought you could give me an abridged version now."

"Why do you need the police reports from the escort case?"

"The penalty phase. I understand that Dupre was rough with some of the women. The DA will try to introduce those incidents as evidence of his propensity to be dangerous in the future."

"Right, of course." Baron paused. "You know, that's a big file. It's going to cost a lot to make the copies."

"We'll pay for the costs, Oscar."

Baron looked relieved.

"Now about the escort service, how does that work?"

"Exotic Escorts is a pretty simple operation. Jon recruits the girls. . . ."

"How does he do that?"

"You've met him. He's a stud, and he's smooth. He'll go to the clubs where young girls hang out. He likes college girls. He'll pick up a freshman who's away from home for the first time. He'll fuck her silly, give her a little coke, and let her hang out in his hot tub. She falls hard for him. That's when he tells her about his business problem. How he runs this escort service and has this very good client who's in town for the evening, but the girl who was supposed to go out with this guy is sick. He tells her it's just like going out on a blind date, then he'll show his pigeon the jewelry and designer clothes she'll wear—all knock-offs, of course."

"Do they realize that they'll have to have sex with the customer?"

"Jon will be all embarrassed when he tells them

about that part. He'll admit that the guy will probably ask for sex, but he says that it's up to her. That's when he mentions how much extra money she can make by doing this little extra favor for him."

"And this always works?"

"Of course not. But it worked often enough for Jon to build quite a stable. He hooks the girls on the easy money or the coke. He's clever about not using a girl too often, unless they're really into it."

"Don't the women catch on? Don't they see he's using them?"

"Some do."

"What happens then?"

"He lets them walk away, unless they're going to cause trouble. Jon can be pretty rough on girls who get out of line."

"Is the DA going to put on a parade of women who'll testify that Dupre beat them?"

Baron shrugged.

"How bad does it get?"

"It's in the reports. Besides, they're all whores. I would have clobbered them on cross."

"How does Dupre get clients?"

"The usual way. Some of the concierges at the better hotels are in his pocket. He doesn't pay them up front, except maybe with a free sample of the goodies." Baron flashed Amanda a knowing smile, and she wondered how often he'd sampled the goodies. "The real money is in the cut they make on every customer they refer. He has the same deal with the bartenders at the strip clubs.

"Of course, the best advertising is word of mouth, but Jon also runs ads in the singles magazines. You know, 'Spend a night with your fantasy girl.' He runs this disclaimer, 'Legal inquiries only,' but there's a nude or two in the ads in a sexy pose that's worth a thousand words. Most of the time, the customers want to date the girls in the ad. Of course, they're models, a come-on. Dupre has a girl named Ally Bennett working the phones. She diverts them. She's really special. Just listening to her is like getting laid."

"Is she a business partner?"

"Jon doesn't have a partner. And, if he did, it wouldn't be a woman. He has no use for women. He despises them. I'm surprised that he's willing to have a woman represent him."

Amanda smiled but said nothing.

"So what's his relationship with Ally Bennett?"

"She's his go-between. She fields the calls, sends out the girls, and collects the money."

"He must trust her."

Baron shrugged. "As much as he trusts anyone. Ally also handles some of Jon's heavy hitters."

"Like?"

"Now there we're getting into attorney-client confidences. Jon will tell you if he wants to. You'd be surprised at some of the names."

"What's this costing the customer?"

"There's a three-hundred dollar call-out fee just to get the girl to the room. Jon made it high to cut out the penny-ante trade. Once the girl arrives, there's a fee schedule for lap dances or artistic posing. When that's done, the girl will ask about a tip. That's a cue for the customer to spell out what he really wants. That brings another fee schedule into play."

"It sounds like it can get pretty steep."

"It is. I told you, Jon's operation is strictly high-end. There's more money that way and less trouble. The cops are going to think twice before hassling a state senator or a circuit court judge, which means that there's less chance of feeling heat. And, if some crusader does make a bust, what have the cops got? Jon has Ally record all of the incoming calls, and there she is, telling Mr. Judge that Exotic Escort girls don't do the nasty for money."

"What about the girls? They can testify."

"Sure, but they don't. If they're busted, Jon pays the girl's legal fees, and the penalties for prostitution aren't stiff enough so the girls will turn."

"So how did the DA make a case against Dupre?"

"Lori Andrews. She was a single mother and the cops threatened to take her kid away."

"She was murdered, right?"

"Yeah, that was tragic," Baron said without real emotion. "When she didn't show for Jon's trial, the state had to dismiss. Of course, after what happened with Wendell, Kerrigan probably won't need much testimony to get a death sentence in this case. Then again, you might get a jury composed of people who hate lawyers. My suggestion: Tell a lot of lawyer jokes during jury selection and choose the folks who laugh the loudest."

eighteen

Tim Kerrigan heard shoes tapping rapidly on the marble floor of the Multnomah County Courthouse, and someone called his name. He turned and saw J. D. Hunter, the FBI agent he'd met at Senator Travis's cabin, walking toward him.

"Your office said you'd be here," Hunter said. "I'm glad I caught you."

"I just finished arguing a motion."

"Did you win?"

"It was a push."

"You have time for coffee? It's almost three. Coffee-break time where I come from."

"Thanks for the invite, but I'm up to my neck in work and I've got to get back to my office."

"Can I walk with you?"

"Sure. What's up?"

"Jon Dupre. The Wendell Hayes killing."

"Why are you interested in that? There's no federal crime."

"No, not directly, but Dupre may be connected to an international drug dealer who is financing terrorism. So it's peripheral, this interest in Dupre. Just loose ends."

"Who's the drug dealer, in case I run across something?"

"Mahmoud Hafnawi. He's a Palestinian living in Beirut. Let me know if Dupre mentions him."

"I will."

Hunter shook his head. "Dupre is one weird dude."

"Why do you say that?"

"The guy murdered his lawyer. Why do you think he did it?"

"That's a question we're all asking."

"Did Hayes and Dupre know each other? Was there bad blood between them?"

"Hayes knew Jon through his parents, but we haven't found any other connection. Dupre didn't even hire Hayes. The presiding judge asked him to take Dupre's case as a favor."

"I'd have thought he'd already have his own lawyer."

"He did. A guy named Oscar Baron, but Baron

wouldn't represent Dupre because Dupre couldn't pay his fee."

"Any question about Dupre's guilt?"

"Of the Hayes murder? None. Wendell was killed in a contact visiting room up in the jail. They were locked in together. It's as clean a case as I've ever seen."

Hunter was quiet for a moment. Then he shook his head. "Considering the trouble he's in, it sure is odd he'd off his lawyer."

"Have you ever figured out why these people do the things they do?"

"You've got a point. Still, Hayes was one of the best, no?"

Tim nodded.

"You'd think Dupre would want a guy like Hayes running his defense, creating reasonable doubt, saving him from death row. If I was in Dupre's shoes, Wendell Hayes would be the last guy I'd kill."

"But he did. We have an eyewitness, a jail guard. He saw the whole thing. Poor guy was shaken up so badly that he's on administrative leave."

"I'm not surprised. Watching someone get sliced up like that and not being able to help. What did Dupre use?"

"A piece of jagged metal," Tim answered. "It looks like the lever they use to open and close the air vents in the jail. It had been sharpened to a point."

"Where did he get it?"

Kerrigan shrugged. "It's your typical jailhouse shiv, homemade. We're checking Dupre's cell and the rest of the housing unit to see if he made it himself, but Dupre could have bought it from someone."

They arrived at the elevators. Kerrigan pushed UP and Hunter pressed DOWN. The UP arrow turned green.

"You heading back to D.C.?" Kerrigan asked as the doors opened.

"In a bit."

"Safe journey."

"Hey, I forgot," Hunter said. He handed Kerrigan one of his business cards. "In case anything comes up."

Hunter was smiling when the doors closed, like he knew some secret. Something about the agent bugged Kerrigan. He remembered feeling the same way when they'd first met at the Travis crime scene. There had been something about Hunter that had bothered him then. Suddenly he realized what it was. The cleaning people had discovered the senator's body only a few hours before Richard Curtis had called Tim and told him to go to the cabin. J. D. Hunter had told Kerrigan that he was picked to investigate Travis's case because the FBI wanted an agent from Washington involved in the murder of a senator. How had Hunter gotten to Portland so quickly? It would have taken time for Washington to learn about the senator's death. Even if Hunter flew to Portland on an FBI jet, there was no way he could have gotten to Travis's house as fast as he had.

Kerrigan was still mulling over this thought when he walked into the reception area of the district attorney's office and found Carl Rittenhouse waiting for him, unshaven, his eyes bloodshot, looking worse than the last time they saw each other. Tim's first thought was that he was taking his boss's death extremely hard.

Rittenhouse stood as soon as he spotted Kerrigan. "Tim, do you have a minute?" he asked anxiously.

"Sure, Carl."

Kerrigan motioned Rittenhouse to follow him to his office.

"Yesterday, at the house, you were talking about Dupre," Rittenhouse said as soon as Tim shut his office door. "You said he ran an escort service and some woman was killed."

"That's right." Kerrigan dropped his files on his desk and sat behind it.

"I wanted to tell you then, but I wasn't certain, so I found the article about her murder in the paper. There was a picture." Rittenhouse hung his head. "It was the same woman."

"I'm not following you, Carl."

"I'd seen the woman before, Lori Andrews. I took her to the cabin."

"The Senator's cabin?" Kerrigan leaned forward. "When was this? The night she was killed?"

"No, a few months before. We were back in town for a round of fund-raisers. Harold asked me to meet her and drive her out. That's all. I never saw her again."

"Why are you telling me this?"

"What if the argument Dupre had with the senator at the Westmont was about Lori Andrews? What if the senator was involved in her death?"

Rittenhouse was sweating.

"Have you helped the senator with women before, Carl?"

"Once or twice. I'm not proud of it."

"Did he ever do anything to any of them that would make you think he hurt Lori Andrews?"

The AA looked down. He wrung his hands.

"There was one time, this one girl. It was in D.C. There had been a party at an embassy. He called me at home, late, about three in the morning. I brought her home, to her apartment. She had a black eye and some bruises."

"The senator beat her?"

"He said that she'd had an accident."

"What did the woman say?"

"Nothing. She was really scared and I didn't ask. Harold told me to bring money, five hundred dollars. I gave it to her. The senator never mentioned it again."

Kerrigan asked Rittenhouse a few more questions, told him that he would have Sean McCarthy take his statement at a convenient time, then thanked him for coming. As soon as Rittenhouse was gone, Kerrigan grabbed the police reports in Travis's case. On page seven of a report written by one of the investigators from the crime lab, there was mention of traces of blood found on the baseboard of a wall in the living room. This blood appeared to be old.

Kerrigan called the lab and spoke to the person who had written the report. Before he hung up, the prosecutor asked the investigator to run a DNA test to see if the blood on the baseboard was Lori Andrews's.

nineteen

As soon as Amanda returned to her office after talking to Oscar Baron, she looked up Ally Bennett's address in the police reports. Forty minutes later, she and Kate Ross were at the door of a garden apartment in Beaverton.

Amanda was curious to see what a high-class call girl looked like, and she was a little disappointed. Ally's black hair was cut short, framing a face that was pretty, but not striking. With the proper makeup and clothing, she would probably look sexy, but today, without makeup, wearing sweat socks, jeans, and a T-shirt, she had the tired look of a co-ed who was cramming for exams.

"I'm Amanda Jaffe," she said, holding out a business card, which Ally looked at but did not take.

"So?"

"I'm an attorney. This is my investigator, Kate Ross. I've been appointed by the court to represent Jon Dupre. We'd like to talk to you about him."

Amanda hesitated for a moment, hoping for a response. When she didn't get one, she forged on.

"He's facing a possible death sentence, Miss Bennett. Kate and I want to save his life, but we need information to do that. Right now I don't know very much about him. That's why we're here."

Ally opened the door and ushered Amanda and Kate into a small, spotless front room. The floor was partially covered by a throw rug. Framed Monet and Van Gogh prints decorated the walls. The furniture was inexpensive but in good taste. Ally dropped into a chair and folded her arms across her breasts; her body language told Amanda that Bennett didn't trust her.

"What do you want to talk about?" Ally asked.

"The DA has charged Jon with killing Wendell Hayes, a lawyer who was appointed to represent Jon before I was, and U.S. Senator Harold Travis. We're interested in anything you can tell us about Jon or these two men that will help us defend him."

"I don't know anything about Hayes, but I can tell you about Travis," Ally said angrily. "The papers are making him sound like a choirboy but he was scum."

"Why do you say that?"

Ally's eyes misted. "He murdered Lori."

All good trial lawyers develop an ability to keep their emotions hidden when the unexpected happens, so Amanda managed to conceal her surprise.

"Are you talking about Lori Andrews?" Kate asked. "The woman who was found in Washington Park?"

Ally nodded.

"The police think Jon killed Lori Andrews to keep her from testifying at his trial," Kate said, keeping her voice level.

"The day Lori disappeared, Travis asked for her specifically. He had one of Pedro Aragon's men take her someplace so he could meet her later."

"How do you know that?" Kate asked.

"I was there. Travis had a fund-raiser for a bunch of high rollers at this big house in the country. He arranged for Jon to bring me, Lori, and some other girls to entertain these special guests after the regular guests had left."

"You're talking about sex?" Amanda said.

"What do you think?" Ally asked with a roll of her eyes.

"What happened with Travis and Lori?"

"Me and the other three girls were at the party most of the evening. We were told who our dates would be, but we circulated most of the night so no one would catch on about the real party that would take place after the straight guests left. As soon as we were the only ones left, Jon drove up with Lori, and Travis told one of Aragon's men to take her away." Ally paused. When she spoke again there was a catch in her voice. "Lori was scared to death. I tried to get Jon to stop it but . . ."

Ally shook her head.

"Why would Pedro Aragon be getting women for Senator Travis?"

Ally shrugged. "All I know is that Travis dated Lori before. The first time he beat her bad. One of Aragon's men drove her to emergency. He told her if she called the cops he would kill her and her daughter, Stacey."

"If Travis beat her, why did Lori see him again?" Amanda asked.

Ally looked sick.

"She didn't know what Jon had done until she got to the fund-raiser. Then it was too late."

"Why did Jon put Lori in that position?"

"He needed the money. Ever since he got busted, he's had trouble running his business. I'm guessing that Travis paid Jon a lot for the evening."

"Wasn't it dangerous for the senator to deal with a pimp who was under indictment?" Kate asked. "What if it got in the newspapers?"

"Lori worked for Jon, and Travis had this thing for her. She was small and she looked young. Travis made her pretend she was a bad little girl. Then he would punish her." Bennett's eyes welled up with tears. "And I'm sure it never entered his mind that he could get in trouble. He was going to be president. He probably thought he could get away with anything."

Bennett paused and her features hardened. "A little rough stuff was something we've all put up with, but what he did . . . I picked up Lori at the hospital after he got through with her that first time. You should have seen her."

Bennett shivered.

"I don't suppose she considered going to the police," Kate said.

"She wouldn't tell anyone but me what happened. She was afraid of Aragon but she was just as afraid that Children's Services would take Stacey away from her if she admitted what she did, which is what happened anyway. Besides, who would have believed her? Lori was a whore and Travis was a big shot."

"Do you like Jon?" Kate asked.

The question surprised Bennett. "What's that got to do with anything?"

"If you testify for Jon, the prosecutor can ask you about anything that would give you a motive to lie for him," Kate explained.

Ally thought about the question. Then she straightened up and clasped her hands in her lap, her shoulders folding in from tension.

"It doesn't matter whether I like Jon. I owe him."

"Why?"

"My mother died a few years ago and my father . . . He needed a woman," she said bitterly. "I was the closest one. I got out of there as fast as I could and I ran as far as I could and ended up living in an apartment in the same building as Lori. I was barely making it when she introduced me to Jon." She shrugged. "It was easy money and I'm good," she added forcefully. "But Jon saw that I was smart, too. No one ever saw that in me before. He showed me how to run the phones, then he showed me how to handle the accounting."

Ally looked down at her lap. When she looked up, Amanda saw strength in her that had not come through before.

"Jon trusts me and he made me believe in myself. I've even started taking some courses at Portland Community College to get my GED. Jon encouraged that."

"Are you and Jon lovers?"

"Lovers?" Ally laughed. "We've screwed, but our thing is different. Jon fucks the other girls and he parties with them, but I'm the only one he trusts. I'm the woman he sends when someone important wants one of his girls. And no one else knows anything about the business. When the cops tried to frighten me into turning on Jon I told them to get fucked. So, no, we're not lovers, but Jon means something to me."

"Ally, I've got a problem and you can help me solve it. Jon may trust you, but he doesn't trust me. When I met him at the jail he walked out on me. You need to know that I am the only lawyer in Oregon who will take his case, which means that I'm the only lawyer in Oregon who can keep Jon off of death row. I need you to talk to him, to tell him to cooperate with me. Will you do that?"

"I'll talk to Jon. He'll see you."

twenty

Jon Dupre had been confined to a narrow single cell since killing Wendell Hayes. It had a metal cot that was bolted to the wall, a toilet, a metal sink, and nothing else. It didn't matter that his cell locked shut at night: Dupre was afraid to go to sleep, because he was certain that was when they'd come for him. One way or another, he was a dead man.

Tonight he struggled to stay awake until exhaustion overcame his will. But even while he slept, part of his animal brain searched for danger, listened for the telltale squeak of an approaching footstep. So, when he heard a click at his cell door, he sprang up, fists clenched, ready for combat.

A solidly built black man stepped into his cell, and the door slammed shut behind him. Dupre looked terrified. He was taking short, shallow breaths.

"Relax, Jon," the man said. J. D. Hunter recognized flight-or-fight behavior when he saw it, and there was no place for Dupre to run. The agent held his hands up, palms out, knowing that if he had to, he could curl them into fists faster than Dupre could cross the cell.

"Easy. I'm here to help you." Hunter kept his voice calm and low. "I'm the agent who was working with Lori Andrews, and, believe it or not, you weren't the prize we were after. Help me and I can help you, and you need all the help you can get."

Dupre had not relaxed one bit. His upper body was swaying, his eyes were riveted on Hunter.

"Who sent you?" Dupre asked. His voice was hoarse and choked by fear.

"I'm with the FBI."

"Bullshit!"

Hunter slowly reached into his jacket pocket to take out his identification.

"I want you out of here," Dupre said.

"This could be your only chance, Jon."

"Don't come a step closer," Dupre warned.

"Okay, Jon, if that's the way you want it, I'll leave."

Hunter rapped on the door and it swung open. Before he left, the agent flipped his card onto the bunk.

"Do yourself a favor and call me."

"Get out!"

The cell door slammed shut and the light went out. Dupre dropped to the cot and put his head in his hands. He was shaking. After a while, he calmed down and lay on his back. His hand dropped to his side and his fingers brushed Hunter's card. It had the seal of the FBI and J.D. HUNTER embossed on it. Dupre's first instinct was to rip it to shreds, but what if Hunter really was with the FBI and could help him? He pulled the card in front of his eyes so he could study it in the dark. The card looked real, but that didn't mean a thing. He started to crumple it up but stopped and slipped it in the pocket of his jumpsuit. He was too stressed out to think. In the morning, if he could sleep and clear his mind a bit, he would try to come up with a plan.

twenty-one

Amanda's hands were clammy and she felt a little dizzy as she waited for the guard to let her into the contact room where Jon Dupre had murdered Wendell Hayes. Judge Robard would only agree to sign the court order compelling the jail to permit a contact visit if she agreed to go along with the safety measures that Matt Guthrie proposed, so she knew that guards would be posted outside both doors to the contact room and that Dupre would be in chains. Still, she could not calm down. The jail commander had also wanted Kate Ross present for the interview, but Amanda had drawn the line there. She knew that she had to meet one-on-one with Dupre if she was going to repair the damage caused by the noncontact visit.

Amanda fought the urge to run when the guard

locked her in. "I can do this," she told herself. "I can do this."

There were no visible signs of the killing, but Amanda had seen the crime-scene photographs and she kept her back to the spot where Hayes had died. To distract herself, Amanda took out her pad and her file. She was arranging them on a small, circular table, when the lock on the back door snapped open and the guard motioned Jon Dupre into the room. He stared at her for a moment before shuffling to the table and sitting down.

"We'll be right outside," Dupre's escort told her, gesturing toward the guard who was watching through the window in the corridor. Amanda studied her client. He looked just as angry and defiant as he had during their first meeting, but she thought she sensed something else—desperation.

"Good afternoon, Jon," Amanda said when the guard had locked them in.

Dupre slouched in his chair and didn't answer her. Amanda decided to go over some basics, to try and get Dupre involved and because it would help her calm down.

"Before we discuss your case I want to make sure you understand the attorney-client relationship."

"Oscar Baron told me all this shit."

"You may find that Oscar and I practice law a little differently, so humor me, okay?"

Dupre shrugged.

"First, anything you tell me is confidential, which means I won't tell anyone about our conversations without your permission, except the attorneys in my firm who are working on your case and Kate Ross, our investigator.

"Second, you are perfectly free to lie to me but I'm going to use the information you give me to make decisions in your case. If you do a great job fooling me and it causes me to do something that loses your case, please remember that you'll go to jail and I'll go home and watch cable TV.

"Third, I will not let you lie under oath. If you tell me that you murdered Senator Travis, I'm not going to let you testify that you were in Idaho when he was killed. I won't tell on you because we have the attorney-client relationship, but I will remove myself from the case. What I'm getting at here is that I am very honest and very ethical and you need to know that about me up front so that we don't have any misunderstandings down the line. Any questions?"

"Yeah. What's in this for you? Court-appointed lawyers aren't paid shit. You must be pretty hard up if you'll work for peanuts."

"Trying a death case is a specialty. Very few attorneys have the training to handle a capital case. Judge Robard asked me to represent you as a favor to him."

"Why is that?"

"I'll be straight with you, Jon. He asked me for two reasons: First, I'm a very good lawyer, and second, the other lawyers who could handle death cases were afraid of you."

"And you're not?" Dupre said with a smirk, holding up his manacled hands, giving Amanda another look at the cuts on his hands and forearm.

"You have no idea what I had to go through to get Judge Robard and the jail commander to agree to a contact visit of any kind."

"Yeah," Jon answered sarcastically, "I bet you'd be dying to be locked in with me if these chains were off. You're scared to death."

"Do you think that my fear is unreasonable? Please focus on the fact that I'm willing to fight very hard for you knowing that you murdered your first lawyer."

Dupre leaped to his feet. He looked furious.

"Fuck you, bitch. I told you the last time I didn't murder anyone, and I don't want a lawyer who thinks I did."

The front and rear doors flew open seconds after Dupre leapt to his feet and started screaming at Amanda.

"Please . . ." Amanda started as the guards grabbed Dupre, but her client cut her off.

"Get me out of here," he screamed. The guards obliged.

The doors slammed, temporarily locking Amanda in with her thoughts. This was never going to work. Dupre was a lunatic. He'd murdered two men and he deserved anything he got. It suddenly occurred to Amanda that Dupre's rage had been sparked by her assertion that he had murdered Wendell Hayes. Now that she thought about it, Dupre had also gone ballistic the first time she'd implied that he was guilty. Dupre had insisted that he hadn't killed anyone both times, which was ridiculous in light of the evidence. Then she remembered something that she had forgotten in the excitement, something that had bothered her the first time she met with Dupre and continued to bother her now—something that made her wonder whether it was possible that Dupre was telling the truth.

Oscar Baron's receptionist buzzed to tell him that he had a collect call from Jon Dupre. Baron debated taking the call, but Dupre could still refer clients to him.

"Hey, Jon. How are they treating you?" Baron asked in a hale-and-hearty tone as though he didn't know that Dupre had gutted a fellow attorney.

"They're treating me like shit, Oscar. They've got me in fucking solitary and they stuck me with a cunt for a lawyer. Some bitch who's scared to be in the same room with me."

"Amanda Jaffe, right?"

"How did you know?"

"She visited me."

"What was she doing at your office?"

Dupre sounded outraged. Baron smiled.

"Calm down. She just wanted the police reports from the case I got dismissed."

"Don't give her shit, Oscar. I'm getting rid of her as fast as I can."

"Did you come up with the dough for my fee?"

"No, I can't make that."

"Then you might want to stick with Jaffe. She's okay."

"I don't want 'okay,' Oscar. This is my goddamn life we're talking about."

"She did that serial case and the case for the associate at Reed, Briggs. She knows her way around."

"Look, I didn't call so you could give me a pep talk about Amanda Jaffe. I need you to do something for me."

"What?"

"I don't want to talk about it over the phone. Come over to the jail. And don't worry about getting paid. Ally is on the way over with enough money to cover the fee for what I want you to do."

twenty-two

The offices of Oregon Forensic Investigations were located in an industrial park a few blocks from the Columbia River. Late in the afternoon of the day after her unsuccessful meeting with Jon Dupre, Amanda drove along narrow streets flanked by warehouses until she found the complex where Paul Baylor worked. A concrete ramp led up to a walkway that ran in front of the offices of an import-export business and a construction firm. The last door opened into a small ante-room. It was furnished with two chairs that stood on either side of an end table on which were stacked several scientific journals. She rang a button on the wall next to a door, for assistance. Moments later, Paul Baylor walked into the ante-room. Baylor was a slender, bookish African

American with a degree from Michigan State in forensic science and criminal justice, who had worked at the Oregon State Crime Lab for ten years before leaving to set up his own shop. Amanda used him when she needed a forensic expert.

Baylor ushered Amanda into a small office outfitted with inexpensive furniture. A small desk was covered with stacks of paperwork, and a bookcase was crammed with books on forensic science.

"I've got a few questions I wanted to ask you about a new case I've got," Amanda said as she opened her briefcase and took out a manila envelope.

"The Travis and Hayes murders?"

Amanda smiled. "You got it on the first try."

"It wasn't hard. I can't read a paper or turn on my TV without seeing you. I should probably get your autograph."

"If I gave you my autograph you'd be able to sell it and retire. Who'd do my forensic work?"

Baylor laughed as Amanda took a stack of photographs out of the envelope and handed them to him.

"Jail personnel took these right after Wendell

Hayes was stabbed to death. What do you make of these cuts?"

Baylor shuffled through the pictures, stopping to study some of them longer than others.

"They're defense wounds," Baylor said when he was ready. "When you have a homicidal attack with a knife, the victim's wounds will normally be deep or long and haphazardly spaced. You're going to find cuts like the ones in the photos on the victim's hands, fingers, palms, and forearms, because he's going to throw up his hands and forearms automatically to ward off the attack, or he'll try to grab the weapon. That's what we have here. A long deep cut on the forearm, a slice on the webbing of the hand, and cuts on the palms and fingers."

"Is there any way that the person wielding the knife could have received those wounds?"

"Sure, if this was a knife fight where both people were armed or one person lost the knife and the other person got it for a while. But those wounds were received by someone who was being attacked."

"Very interesting."

"Not to me. They're exactly what I'd expect to find on Wendell's arms and hands."

"Oh, I agree there. Only these arms and hands belong to Jon Dupre."

Frank Jaffe worked in a spacious corner office decorated with antiques, which was basically unchanged since the firm was founded shortly after his graduation from law school over thirty years ago. When Amanda rapped on Frank's doorjamb, he looked up from a brief.

"Do you have a minute, Dad?"

Frank put down his pen and leaned back. "For you, always."

Amanda threw herself onto a chair that stood before Frank's immense desk and told her father about Dupre's violent reaction when she suggested that he might be guilty of the Hayes and Travis murders and about Ally Bennett's assertion that Senator Travis had attacked Lori Andrews. Finally she told her father about her meeting with Paul Baylor.

"What's your take?" Frank asked when Amanda was through.

"Those defense wounds bother me. Dupre was treated for them immediately after his arrest in the visiting room."

"Any chance they're self-inflicted?" Frank asked.

"Why would he cut himself?"

"To fashion a self-defense argument in a case that's impossible to win any other way."

"Who would believe Dupre, Dad?"

"No one. Which is the problem you're going to have trying to sell this theory to a jury. The logical explanation for those cuts is that Dupre brought the shiv into the visiting room and Hayes somehow got the knife away from him and stabbed Dupre in self-defense. Before you can argue that Dupre acted in self-defense, you're going to have to prove that Hayes smuggled the shiv in, which presents another problem. What motive could Hayes possibly have to attack Dupre?"

"What motive did Jon have to kill Hayes?" Amanda countered. "Don't forget the fix Dupre was in when Hayes came to the jail. If he's convicted of killing Senator Travis, he'll get life in prison or a lethal injection. Wendell Hayes was a terrific trial lawyer. Why kill someone who could have saved his life?"

"Good point. Unfortunately the prosecutor doesn't have to prove motive."

"Yeah, I know." Amanda looked dejected. "There is something else that's bothering me, though. If Dupre brought the shiv to the interview room because he wanted to kill Hayes, he'd have to know that Hayes was the lawyer who was coming to visit him. Grant didn't appoint Hayes until shortly before Hayes went to the jail."

"So, we need to know when Dupre learned that Hayes was going to be his lawyer."

"Right. If Jon didn't know that Hayes was going to be his lawyer until he met him in the visiting room, why would he bring a shiv with him?"

"He may have had it for protection from other inmates."

"Jon wouldn't have had it on him when he went to see Hayes. He'd never risk having it found during a frisk."

"Maybe Dupre planned to kill any lawyer who showed up so he could plead insanity."

"Then why isn't Jon acting crazy or suggesting that he is?"

"And he's got those cuts," Frank muttered to himself.

"What do you know about Wendell Hayes?"

"Not a lot. We socialized at Oregon Criminal Defense Lawyers Association meetings, Bar Association meetings, stuff like that. I've been on panels with him and we've had drinks together."

"Did you ever hear anything that would suggest he was dirty?"

"There are always rumors when a lawyer handles a lot of drug cases."

"Such as?"

"Money-laundering, that type of thing. But how would that explain Hayes attacking your client?"

"I don't know, but it makes it more likely that he'd try to kill someone if he was bent."

"Wendell's career did start with a bang. There was the Blanton case and that one with the hit man—I can't remember the case name. Things really broke his way in those cases."

"What do you mean?"

"The DA had a slam dunk in **Blanton** until his eyewitness recanted, and the key evidence disappeared from the police property room in the other case. Most people thought he was lucky, but there were a few DAs I know who suggested that the breaks weren't just luck."

"Hayes didn't do much criminal stuff anymore, did he?"

"Wendell still took on a few high-profile criminal cases but, mostly, he was handling business problems for people with money."

"What type of problems?"

"He secured a very lucrative federal construc-

tion contract for Burton Rommel's firm and he's
maneuvered a few land-use planning rulings for
developers that were worth millions. That type of
thing."

"Deals that require political clout."

Frank nodded. "Wendell had plenty of that. He
was part of the Westmont crowd, old Portland
money. He grew up on intimate terms with the
people who make this state run."

Amanda talked to her father a little longer. Since
they were both working late, they decided to have
a quick dinner downtown in an hour. Amanda
went to her office and spent the time reviewing
everything she knew about Dupre's case. One
thing that she thought about was the picture Ally
Bennett had painted of Harold Travis. It was far
different from the picture the press was present-
ing. Unfortunately, the only evidence that Ally
could offer about Travis's character was Lori
Andrews's hearsay statements, which were inad-
missible in court. And proving that Travis was a
degenerate didn't disprove the state's allegation
that Dupre had murdered the senator. Ally's information actually hurt Jon's case. If Travis beat
up one of Dupre's escorts after Jon warned the

senator about hurting her, it would provide Jon with a motive to kill Travis.

On the other hand, if Tim Kerrigan tried to introduce evidence about Lori Andrews's murder at Jon's trial, evidence that the senator had beaten Andrews would be useful. Amanda was thinking about ways to get Ally's hearsay into evidence when she remembered that cocaine had been found in the senator's house. She wondered if the lab had recovered Travis's prints from the baggie, so she checked the police reports and found that the prints on the baggie were too smudged for comparison. Amanda was disappointed, but she thought of another way to prove that the senator had used cocaine. She found the autopsy report. The tox screen had not found cocaine, but it had picked up something else. According to the report, there were traces of alprazolam in the senator's blood. Amanda wondered what that was. She was about to do some research when her father buzzed her on the intercom to tell her that he was ready to go. Amanda was exhausted and starving. She made a note to find out about alprazolam, grabbed her coat, and left her office.

twenty-three

Oscar Baron was ready to pack it in. Sitting in an abandoned gas station at two in the morning in the fucking cold was definitely not his idea of a good time. He was a lawyer, for God's sake. People waited for him, not the other way around. If Jon Dupre hadn't agreed to the outrageous fee Baron was charging him, he'd have been long gone. Even at the rates that he had gouged out of Dupre, Baron was starting to wonder if it was worth it.

First he'd had to deal with that stuck-up bitch, Bennett. She'd brought his money and Jon's bargaining chip to Baron's office about an hour after Baron had taken Dupre's call. Baron had suggested a friendly blow job to celebrate his being back on the case, and she'd had the temerity to turn him down, like she was too good for him.

Then, Oscar had had to put up with Dupre's ravings at the jail. Jesus, could he go on and on. But Baron was pretty good at tuning out clients, and he could put up with the most unmitigated bullshit for what Dupre was paying him.

Finally, there was this ridiculous meeting in the middle of nowhere. Dupre had insisted that Baron deal with an FBI agent named Hunter. Baron had called the local office and left his number. Hunter had called him at home and told him they had to meet immediately behind this abandoned gas station on a deserted stretch of the highway to the coast. When Oscar pointed out that it was one in the morning and he was in bed, the agent had insisted that the clandestine rendezvous was necessary for security reasons. Oscar would have told the agent to go fuck himself if Dupre hadn't promised a sizeable bonus for a good deal.

A car turned into the lot and Oscar stubbed out his cigarette. It was about time. The lawyer got out of his car and turned up the collar of his camel's-hair overcoat to protect his cheeks from the wind. Overnight, the weather had turned and it was close to freezing. The car pulled alongside Oscar, and the driver reached over and opened the door. He was Hispanic, with a flat, pockmarked face and a wisp of a mustache. That didn't seem right. Oscar was certain that Dupre had told him that Hunter was black. Well, this guy was dark. Baron didn't really care; as long as he was being paid, he'd deal with anyone.

"Agent Hunter was called away on another case, Mr. Baron." He held out his credentials. "I'm Agent Castillo."

"Hunter just called me."

"He was as upset as you are, but something came up. I really can't discuss his other case. You understand."

"All I know is that he got me out of bed in the middle of the night," Oscar complained as he slid onto the passenger seat.

"If we weren't concerned for your safety I would be snug under the covers myself."

"Yeah, well, let's get this over with. I'm freezing my nuts off."

"What does Mr. Dupre want?"

"To get out of jail."

"That may be difficult. He killed a United States senator. . . ."

"He denies that."

"Yes, well, then there's the little matter of murdering Mr. Hayes, which is a state matter over which the Bureau has no jurisdiction. Besides, I'm not certain I should be talking to you. I've been told that Amanda Jaffe represents Mr. Dupre."

"Do you see Jaffe sitting here? She's a court-appointed lawyer. Jon doesn't trust her. He doesn't trust anyone except me."

"So, she doesn't know anything about these negotiations?"

"Not a thing. Now, let's get down to business, so I can go home. You figure out a way to help Jon and Jon will help you fry some very big fish."

"Such as?"

"Pedro Aragon, for one."

"Go on." Castillo said it as if he wasn't impressed, but his body language suggested otherwise.

"My client has knowledge of Aragon's operation. He can show you how his people bring the stuff in, he can draw you an organizational chart. . . ."

"We know a lot of this already, Mr. Baron."

"But can you prove it? Jon's been secretly taping and filming conversations with Aragon's men; it's an insurance policy for situations like this. With Jon's evidence you can bag some of Ara-

gon's lieutenants. Maybe they'll turn. And Jon says he's got other stuff that will make busting Aragon seem like small potatoes."

"Oh. What would that be?"

"He didn't tell me. He just said to tell you that what he has is dynamite."

Baron pulled a tape recorder out of his coat pocket and laid it on the seat between them.

"Let me play you a sample of the stuff he's got against Aragon."

Baron hit the PLAY button and a tape started to roll. Halfway through, Oscar zoned out. The stuff was good evidence, but pretty boring. A lot of drug jabber about quality and prices. It could have been two guys at a used-car lot. Oscar didn't snap out of his trance until Castillo flashed the car's headlights.

"What's that for?" the lawyer asked just as his door was yanked open. A hand grabbed his coat collar, and a huge man started to pull him out of the car. Oscar hung on to the dashboard. A gun butt smashed his fingers, and he screamed. He was on the ground before it registered that it was Castillo who had crushed his fingers. Oscar opened his mouth to protest, but the muzzle of another gun ripped past his lips and smashed his teeth. Oscar tried to scream again, but he choked on the muzzle. The man who had pulled him from the car pushed the gun barrel deeper into his mouth. Castillo walked into Oscar's line of sight.

"If you make a sound, the gun will be pushed down your throat and you will choke to death. Nod if you understand."

Oscar jerked his head up and down. The metal barrel was tickling his throat and he had to fight his gag response. Castillo nodded. The gun slid out of Oscar's mouth and he gasped for air.

Castillo squatted beside Baron, grabbed his ear, and twisted. Baron grimaced, too frightened to cry out.

"You said that this tape is a sample. Do you have others?"

"Aah. Please. There's more in my safe."

Castillo released the pressure on Oscar's ear.

"You're at our mercy, Oscar. No one is going to come to your rescue. Whether you live or die depends solely on how much you cooperate. Do you understand me?"

Oscar nodded.

"Good. We've had taps on your phone and we've had your home and office wired since you were at the jail yesterday. That's how we knew that you called the FBI. So don't bullshit me."

"I won't."

"I want the combination to your safe and the keys to your home and your office. We'll take you to a safe place. If you've been honest you'll be released unharmed. If you've lied, you will be tortured. Do you understand?"

Baron nodded. He understood perfectly. He could identify his captors, so he would have to die. His only hope was that if he cooperated completely, his death would be quick.

twenty-four

Jon Dupre had called Ally Bennett from the jail and given her the combination to a safe hidden in the basement of an isolated house on the Willamette, several miles south of Portland, which Jon had purchased under another name. Sometimes Jon's "special" customers wanted a place to party where they wouldn't be seen, even by chance. There was money in the safe, and envelopes containing video- and audiotapes. She had taken some of the money and a few audio- and videotapes to Oscar Baron. Jon had not told her what was on the tapes, but he had been confident that they would get him out of jail.

In addition to Baron's retainer, Ally had taken some of Jon's money for herself. She'd been having trouble making ends meet since the cops closed down Exotic Escorts and had been forced

to tend bar evenings at a tavern near her apartment. She hated it, but she had to earn a living.
She'd finished her shift at the bar and was pulling
into her apartment complex when she heard
Oscar's name on the car radio.

". . . was found brutally murdered in his home.
Police told reporters that Baron had been tortured and robbery appeared to be the motive."

Ally slowed down. She didn't believe in coincidences; the murder had to be connected to the
tapes she'd given to Baron. With a chill, she realized that Oscar knew her name. What if he told it
to his killers? What if they discovered where she
lived?

All of a sudden, it didn't seem smart to go up
to her apartment. Ally switched off her headlights
and made a slow U-turn. She was almost at the
entrance to the apartment complex when headlights came on at the far end of the lot. Ally
jammed the accelerator to the floor and peeled
out across traffic. She turned right at the first
street and began weaving in and out of side
streets. Ally slowed down but kept a constant
watch in her rearview mirror. After a few minutes, she started to feel silly. Was her high-speed
flight caused by paranoia? Maybe, but Ally decided not to take any chances. She took out the

loaded .38 she carried ever since one of her customers had smacked her around, and placed it next to her on the passenger seat. When the car from the lot did not materialize, Ally headed toward the freeway.

Jon Dupre's safe house had a deck that overlooked the river. It was cold outside but Ally pulled her coat tight against her throat. She needed fresh air and a place to think. Ally lit a cigarette and wondered about the tapes she had given to Oscar Baron. If Jon was convinced that the tapes would help him beat the rap for killing a United States senator, there had to be something earthshaking on them. There were other tapes hidden in the safe. She crushed out her cigarette and went inside.

The safe was under a cover of loose linoleum in the basement laundry room. As soon as she opened it, she counted the money. There was twenty thousand dollars left. If someone was after her, she could take it and run. But she couldn't run. Not without Stacey, Lori Andrews's kid. The thought of Stacey languishing in one foster home after another was eating her up. If she had enough money . . .

Ally rummaged through the contents of the

safe. She found some business ledgers and glanced through them. They contained the names, phone numbers, and addresses of Exotic Escort customers, and were cross-referenced to the tapes. Ally selected a few videotapes at random. There was a big-screen TV in the basement. She turned it on, put a cassette in the VCR, and pressed PLAY. What she saw was what she'd expected to see. A fat, older man, whom Ally recognized as an influential politician, was groping a naked Asian girl named Joyce Hamada. She watched for a while before taking the tape out and popping in another. It was more of the same, only the partners were different. Ally was puzzled. These tapes would be interesting to the cops, but no one was going to let Jon off in exchange for them. Whatever Jon was counting on had to be a hell of a lot different from what she'd seen. Then she remembered the cassette she'd slipped into Jon's pocket at the Travis fundraiser.

At Jon's instructions, Ally had secreted mini tape-recorders in the den and several bedrooms as soon as she'd arrived at the country house. She had collected the recorders and all of the tapes before the night was over. The girls were always under orders to get their dates to talk about themselves, and this wasn't the first time she'd brought tapes to Dupre. Though Jon had given her a bonus every time she helped him tape a client, he'd never told her what he did with the tapes, but she wasn't stupid. Ally was certain that he used them for blackmail if the information was juicy enough. There had been a lot of very important people at Travis's party.

Ally went back to the safe. The tapes from the fund-raiser were small, and it took her a while to find them. They were much more interesting than the sexcapades she'd viewed earlier.

twenty-five

Jon Dupre was still in manacles when Amanda walked into the contact visiting room, but he exhibited none of the aggression and tension she had noticed during her previous visits. Instead he sat slumped forward, resting his arms on the table, with his head in his hands, looking subdued and exhausted.

Amanda sat opposite her client. She was on edge but not as frightened as she had been when they'd met before. Dupre looked up. His eyes were bloodshot and he was unshaven.

"Thank you for seeing me, Jon."

"I need your help," he answered.

Amanda knew that sociopaths were very skilled at faking sincerity—she had been conned before—but no alarms were going off.

"I've always wanted to help you."

"Yeah, I know. I'm sorry."

"Then let's forget the last two visits. Why don't you tell me how you got the cuts on your hands and forearm?"

The question startled Dupre. "Why do you want to know that?"

"I thought you were going to trust me."

Dupre twisted in his seat.

"Jon?"

"You won't believe me."

"Try me."

Dupre looked away from Amanda.

"You know why I'm here, Jon," she said in a steady voice. "I'm the only lawyer who would take your case, the only person who wants to help you. But I can't work in a vacuum."

Dupre met Amanda's eyes. He spoke slowly, weighing each word.

"Wendell Hayes cut me."

"With the shiv?"

"That's right."

"How did he get the shiv?" Amanda asked. "Did he wrestle it away from you?"

"Hayes brought the knife into the jail. It was his. He attacked me, not the other way around. I know it sounds insane, but that's what happened." Dupre brought his cuffed hands to his

face and rubbed his forehead. "This whole thing
is a nightmare."

"How could Hayes smuggle a knife through the
metal detector?"

"I don't know. All I know is the moment the
guard was out of sight Hayes was on me." Dupre
pointed to the stitches along his forearm and the
cuts on his hands. "I got these blocking the knife.
I'm not dead because I caught Hayes in the
throat with a lucky punch. He dropped the shiv
and I grabbed it and stuck him in the eye."

"Why didn't you stop then?"

Dupre looked incredulous. "He was trying to
murder me. I was locked in with him. Hayes is
huge and I didn't know if he had other weapons.
I had to finish him."

"I've got to level with you, Jon. This sounds . . .
far-fetched. Why would Wendell Hayes want to
kill you?"

Dupre looked down at the table and shook his
head.

"Did he even know you before Judge Grant appointed him?" Amanda asked.

"Not really. My parents knew him, but they
weren't friends. Before I was banned from the
club I saw him at the Westmont a few times."

Amanda shook her head. "This isn't going to fly."

"You think I'm lying?" Dupre asked angrily.

"I didn't say that. In fact, I have a witness who supports your story."

Amanda told him what Paul Baylor had concluded after viewing the photographs from the jail infirmary.

"Unfortunately, Paul's testimony alone won't be enough to acquit you," Amanda concluded. "Can you think of any other way to prove that Hayes attacked you?"

"No."

"Then you see our problem. Your word is not going to be enough to convince a jury that a prominent attorney would try to kill a client he hardly knew. What's Hayes's motive? How are we going to counter the argument that Hayes couldn't have smuggled the shiv through the metal detector? You didn't go through a metal detector, and the weapon is the type of homemade job that jail inmates make."

"I could take a lie detector test."

"The results aren't admissible in court."

Dupre threw his head back and slammed his hands on the table. The guard on the other side of the window started to raise his radio to his mouth as he moved toward the door. Amanda waved him off.

"Forget Hayes for a moment. Tell me about Senator Travis," Amanda said.

"I didn't kill him."

"Why did you argue with him the day before he was killed?"

"He dated one of my girls and she turned up dead."

"Lori Andrews?"

Dupre nodded. "The last time he dated her he beat her up."

"Did Travis admit that he had anything to do with Lori Andrews's murder?"

"No. He said he didn't touch her. But I didn't believe him."

"I'm surprised that you cared about Andrews. Her disappearance helped you, didn't it? It got your case dismissed."

"I'm glad Lori didn't show up, but I didn't want her dead."

"The police found an earring at the Travis crime scene that's supposed to be identical to one you were wearing when you argued with Hayes at the Westmont."

"They did?"

"You didn't know?"

"No. What did it look like?"

"It's gold, a gold cross."

"I have one like it, but I have no idea why it would be at Travis's place. I've never been there."

"Did you talk to Travis again after you saw him at the country club?" Amanda asked.

"No."

Amanda made a note on a legal pad. "What about the evening that Travis was killed? Was anyone with you?"

"A few of the girls were over earlier in the evening. I got high and passed out. When I woke up in the morning they were gone."

"I'll need a list of the women who were at your house so Kate Ross can check them out."

"Joyce Hamada was there. She's a student at Portland State. And Cheryl . . . uh, Cheryl Riggio. Talk to them."

"Okay. We have a bail hearing set for tomorrow. Don't get your hopes up about getting out. There's no automatic bail in a death-penalty case."

"Yeah, I know." Dupre was suddenly very quiet. "Oscar told me."

"I take it you've heard?"

Dupre nodded. "Do you know what happened to him?"

"Only what I read in the paper and heard on the radio, which wasn't much."

"Was he tortured?"

"That's what the paper said."

"Burglars, right?"

Amanda nodded. "It seems unreal. I was talking to him a few days ago about your case."

"Yeah," Dupre agreed, "unreal."

twenty-six

When the Multnomah County Courthouse was completed in 1914, it occupied the entire block of downtown Portland between Main and Salmon and Fourth and Fifth, and was the largest courthouse on the West Coast. The exterior of the concrete building was brutish and foreboding, but the lobby had a majestic elegance until it became cluttered with metal detectors and guard stations.

Amanda and Kate had to fight their way past the TV cameras and through the throng of reporters who started to shout questions at Amanda as soon as they entered the lobby. They hurried up the wide marble stairway toward Judge Robard's courtroom on the fourth floor, hoping that the uphill run would discourage the heavily loaded cameramen and the sedentary reporters, but a few hearty souls jogged after them, panting questions, which Amanda ignored.

The corridor outside the courtroom was packed with people who were trying to get a seat. They had to wait in line and go through another metal detector to get inside. Amanda flashed her ID, and she and Kate were waved through. Judge Robard had seniority and one of the older courtrooms. Amanda couldn't help thinking how the high ceiling, marble Corinthian columns, and ornate molding made the setting ideal for a judge with such an exaggerated sense of his own importance.

The spectator benches were almost full, and Tim Kerrigan was already at the prosecution counsel table; his second chair was a young Hispanic woman whom Amanda had never met. Kerrigan heard the stir in the courtroom when Amanda came in, and turned his head toward the doorway. The prosecutor whispered something to his colleague and they both stood.

"Hi, Amanda, Kate," Kerrigan said. "This is my second chair, Maria Lopez."

The women nodded at Maria then Kate took the end seat at the defense table.

"You're not really asking for a full-blown bail hearing, are you?" Kerrigan asked Amanda.

"Yup."

"Robard will never grant bail."

"Then I'll be wasting my time."

The prosecutor laughed. "I knew you'd be a pain in the neck."

"Hey, it's my job."

Kerrigan was about to say something else, when Jon Dupre was led into court in manacles and leg chains. With a look of deep satisfaction, Maria Lopez watched Dupre struggle forward. Amanda remembered that Lopez had prosecuted the prostitution case, which had been dismissed.

"Sit down with your attorney," ordered Larry McKenzie, one of Dupre's guards.

"Aren't you going to take his chains off?" Amanda asked when McKenzie made no move to unshackle her client.

"Orders. He's supposed to have them on during the hearing."

"We'll see about that."

"Don't get mad at me. I'm just following orders."

"Sorry, Mac," Amanda told the guard.

"No problem, Ms. Jaffe, but I wouldn't argue too hard to have them taken off, if I was you. I was on the admitting desk when Wendell Hayes came to the jail the day he was killed. I wish I'd told him to be more careful."

Amanda pulled out Dupre's chair and helped him sit down before sitting next to him. The bailiff rapped his gavel and Ivan Robard walked briskly through a door behind his dais.

"Be seated," he ordered. "Call the case."

"This is the time set for a bail hearing in the case of State of Oregon versus Jonathan Edward Dupre."

As soon as the bailiff finished reading the case number into the record, Tim Kerrigan stood and told the judge that he was ready to proceed.

"Amanda Jaffe for Mr. Dupre, Your Honor. Before we start the bail hearing, I would like to have my client unshackled. He . . ."

Robard held up his hand. "I'm not going to do it, Ms. Jaffe. Feel free to file a motion with authorities so you can make your record for the appellate courts, but I've talked to the jail commander and he believes that Mr. Dupre is too dangerous to leave unshackled."

"Your Honor, this is a bail hearing. You are going to have to decide whether Mr. Dupre should be released from custody. Your ruling to have him kept in chains shows that you have prejudged his case, and I'd ask you to recuse yourself."

Robard cracked a humorless smile. "Nice try,

but it won't work. I'm keeping the shackles on for security reasons, and so would any other judge in this courthouse. I haven't heard any evidence yet. If Mr. Kerrigan doesn't make a case for holding your client, we'll talk about bail. So let's get to it."

Judge Robard shifted his attention to the prosecutor.

"Mr. Kerrigan, Mr. Dupre is charged with, among other things, two counts of aggravated murder. ORS 135.240(2)(a) says that I have to grant release unless you can convince me that the proof is evident or the presumption strong that Mr. Dupre is guilty. What's your proof?"

"Your Honor, I'm planning on calling one witness in the case against Mr. Dupre for murdering Wendell Hayes. That should be sufficient to convince the court that there is a strong presumption that Mr. Dupre is guilty in that murder case. The state calls Adam Buckley, Your Honor."

Like most of the jail guards, Adam Buckley was a big man, but he had lost weight since witnessing the death of Wendell Hayes. He was dressed in an ill-fitting sports coat that hung loosely on his slumped shoulders; he kept his eyes low to the ground as he walked to the witness stand. Amanda had read the report of his interview and she knew that he was on administrative leave as a result of his trauma. She felt sorry for Buckley because she knew what he was going through.

"Officer Buckley," Kerrigan asked after the guard had been sworn and testified to his occupation, "did you know Wendell Hayes?"

"Yes, sir."

"How did you know him?"

"He came up to the jail to talk to prisoners from time to time. I let him in and out."

"On the day of his death, did you let Mr. Hayes into a contact visiting room at the Justice Center?"

"Yes, sir."

"What prisoner was he meeting?"

"Jon Dupre."

"Do you see Mr. Dupre in this room?"

Buckley cast a quick look at Dupre, then looked away. "Yes, sir."

"Can you identify him for the judge."

"He's the man sitting with the two women," Buckley said without looking at the defense table.

"Was Mr. Dupre in the visiting room when you let Mr. Hayes into it?"

"Yes, sir."

"You saw him?"

"I went into the room with Mr. Hayes. Dupre was sitting in a chair in the room. I told Mr. Hayes to press the call button if he needed help, then I locked them in."

"Was anyone else in the contact room?"

"No. Just Mr. Hayes and the defendant."

"Was Mr. Dupre shackled as he is today?"

"No, his hands and feet were free."

"Thank you. Now, Officer Buckley, shortly after you locked the two men in together, did you see them again?"

Buckley paled. "Yes, sir," he answered in a shaky voice.

"Tell the judge what you saw."

"Mr . . . Mr. Hayes . . . He was pressed up against the glass window." He paused. "It was awful," he said, shaking his head as if to clear it of his memory of the event. "There was blood all over the window. It was coming from his eye."

"What did you see next?"

Buckley pointed at Dupre. "He was stabbing him."

"Could you see what Mr. Dupre was using?"

"No. He was moving it back and forth too fast."

"Your Honor," Kerrigan said as he picked up an evidence bag containing the shiv, "Ms. Jaffe has agreed to stipulate, for purposes of this hearing, that Exhibit One is the weapon that was used to stab Mr. Hayes."

"Is that right?" Robard asked.

"Yes, Your Honor," Amanda answered.

"Officer Buckley, did you see what happened to Mr. Hayes as a result of Mr. Dupre's attack?"

"Yes, sir. He was bleeding badly from several places."

"Did Mr. Dupre try to attack you?"

"I was pressed up against the glass trying to see how bad Mr. Hayes was hurt, and he made stabbing motions at me."

"Where was Mr. Hayes at that time?"

"On the floor."

"Your Honor, for purposes of this hearing, Ms. Jaffe has agreed to stipulate that Mr. Hayes died as a result of wounds inflicted by Mr. Dupre with Exhibit One."

"So noted. Any further questions, Mr. Kerrigan?"

"No."

"Ms. Jaffe?" Judge Robard asked.

"A few, Your Honor," she said, standing and walking toward the guard. "Officer Buckley, where did you first encounter Mr. Hayes?"

"When he came off the elevator he rang me to get into the hall with the interview rooms."

"And you took him to the interview room where Mr. Dupre was waiting?"

"Yes."

"Did you search Mr. Hayes before you let him into the interview room?"

Buckley looked surprised by the question. "I don't ever do that. They search the lawyers downstairs before they send them up."

"So your answer is that you did not search Mr. Hayes?"

"Right. Yes."

"Did you have Mr. Hayes and Mr. Dupre in your sight continuously after you locked Mr. Hayes in?"

"No."

"Why not?"

"Another lawyer came up on the elevator and I let him in to see a prisoner."

"How long were Mr. Dupre and Mr. Hayes out of your sight from the time you locked in Mr. Hayes until you saw the two of them fighting?"

"I don't know. Probably a minute, maybe two."

"So you have no idea what happened in the interview room between the time you locked Mr.

Hayes in and the time you saw the men in the middle of their fight?"

"No, ma'am."

"No further questions."

"No further questions," Kerrigan said, "and no other witnesses, Your Honor."

"Ms. Jaffe?" Robard asked.

"One witness, Your Honor. Mr. Dupre calls Larry McKenzie."

"What?" the startled jail guard said.

Kerrigan and the judge also looked surprised but Robard recovered quickly and beckoned the redheaded bodybuilder to the stand. McKenzie glowered at Amanda as he walked past her, but Amanda was concentrating on her notes and didn't notice.

"Officer McKenzie," Amanda asked when the guard was sworn, "you were manning the reception desk at the jail on the day that Wendell Hayes was killed, were you not?"

"Yeah."

"Please describe the reception area and the process you go through when an attorney comes to the jail for a contact visit with a client."

"Reception is on Third Avenue off the Justice Center lobby. When you come in, we're behind a desk. To the side of the desk, between the reception area where you can sit down and the elevators that go up to the jail, is a metal detector."

"Okay, so say I come into the jail to visit a prisoner and I come up to your desk, what happens then?"

"I ask for your Bar card and I check your ID."

"Then what?"

"You empty your pockets of any metal objects and you give me your briefcase to search, if you've got one. Then you go through the metal detector."

"What time did Mr. Hayes come into the reception area?"

"Around one, I think."

"Was he alone?"

McKenzie snorted. "He had a circus with him—TV cameras, reporters shouting questions."

"Did Mr. Hayes hold a press conference?"

"He answered a few questions. The reporters had him backed up against the reception desk. When it got too bad, he asked me to rescue him."

"By letting him into the jail?"

"Right."

"What did you do?"

"What I always do. I checked his ID and passed him through the metal detector."

"Did Mr. Hayes have a briefcase?"

"Yeah, but I checked that, too."

"Did you send the briefcase through the metal detector?"

McKenzie started to answer, then stopped.

"No, I don't think so. I think I just went through it."

"What was Mr. Hayes doing while you were going through this procedure?"

"He was . . . Let me think. Yeah, we were talking."

"About what?"

"The Blazers."

"While you searched the briefcase?"

"Yeah."

"So your full attention wasn't on the search?"

"Are you saying I didn't do my job?"

"No, Officer McKenzie. I know you **tried** to do your job correctly, but you had no reason to think that Wendell Hayes would try and smuggle anything into the jail, did you?"

"Hayes didn't smuggle anything in."

"Did he go through the detector with all of his clothes?"

McKenzie gazed upward, trying to recall everything that had happened. When he looked back at Amanda, he was worried.

"He took off his jacket and . . . and he folded it up and handed it to me with his briefcase and the metal stuff in his pockets, like his keys and a Swiss Army knife. I kept the knife."

"Did you search the jacket thoroughly?"

"I patted it down before I handed it back," McKenzie said, but he did not look as sure of himself now.

"Were the reporters still milling around your desk?"

"Yeah."

"Were they talking?"

"Yeah."

"I was watching a TV news story about Mr. Hayes's death. The station had pictures of him going through the metal detector. Were they filming Mr. Hayes during the search?"

"I guess so."

"So those bright lights were still on and there were a lot of other distractions?"

"Yeah, but I was thorough."

"Think hard about this, Officer McKenzie, please. Did you hand back Mr. Hayes's jacket and briefcase before or after he was through the metal detector?"

McKenzie hesitated for a moment. "After."

"Is it possible, then, that Mr. Hayes could have slipped something by you in his jacket or brief-case while he was talking to you about the Blazers and the reporters were distracting you with their bright lights and chatter?"

"Something like what?"

"Something like Exhibit One."

McKenzie's mouth gaped open, Kerrigan shot Amanda an incredulous look, and a low rumble erupted in the spectator section. Judge Robard rapped his gavel.

"It didn't happen like that," McKenzie insisted.

"But it could have?"

"Anything is possible. But Hayes didn't smuggle in a knife, and even if he did, your boy committed murder."

"Move to strike that last response, Your Honor," Amanda said. "And I'm through with the witness."

"I'll strike it, Miss Jaffe," Judge Robard said, "but I'm having trouble seeing where you're going with this. I assume you'll clear up my confusion when you make your argument."

"I don't have any questions for Officer McKenzie," said Tim Kerrigan, who looked amused.

"Any other evidence for either side?"

"No," Amanda and Kerrigan said.

"Argument, Mr. Kerrigan, since you've got the burden."

"The question before the court is whether the state has met the burden imposed by ORS 135.240(2)(a) of proving that Mr. Dupre's guilt in the murder of Wendell Hayes is evident and that the presumption of that guilt is strong. If we do, the court must deny release. Officer Buckley testified that there were only two people in the contact visiting room—the victim, Wendell Hayes, and the defendant—and they were locked in. He also testified that he saw Mr. Dupre stab Mr. Hayes, and it is stipulated that Exhibit One is the weapon that was used to kill Mr. Hayes. I don't think I've ever heard more convincing evidence of guilt, Your Honor."

Kerrigan sat down and Amanda stood.

"Let's cut to the chase here, Ms. Jaffe," Robard said. "Are you going to argue that Wendell Hayes smuggled Exhibit One into the jail?"

"There's no evidence that contradicts that position."

Robard smiled and shook his head. "I have always considered you to be one of the brightest and most creative attorneys in the Oregon Bar, and you have not disappointed me, today. Why don't you tell me the next logical step in your argument."

"If Wendell Hayes smuggled the knife into the

jail, my client acted in self-defense, negating Mr. Kerrigan's proof of guilt."

"Well, that's right, if there was any evidence that Mr. Hayes attacked your client, but the only thing I heard was that Mr. Dupre was wielding the knife. He even threatened Officer Buckley."

"Officer Buckley didn't see everything that happened in the interview room during the crucial time between locking Mr. Hayes and Mr. Dupre in together and seeing my client stab Mr. Hayes."

Robard chuckled and wagged his head. "You get an A—no, an A-plus—for effort, but no cigar. I'm denying release in the case involving Wendell Hayes, and setting bail of one million dollars in the case involving the murder of Senator Travis. Unless there's something else, this hearing is adjourned."

"He didn't listen to a thing you said," Dupre said bitterly.

"I didn't expect him to, Jon."

"So you're saying I'm dead?"

"Not at all. I told you that our forensic expert will testify that your cuts are defense wounds that you could only have gotten if you were being attacked by a knife."

"Why didn't you tell that to the judge?"

"I don't think it would have swayed a hardnose like Robard, and I want to save some surprises for trial. We're working on other leads, too, so don't give up."

Amanda and Dupre spoke for a few more minutes before she signaled Larry McKenzie that her client was ready to go back to the jail.

"I hate to see this cockroach jerking you around," McKenzie said as he tugged on Dupre's chains to get him to stand.

"I'm sorry if I surprised you, but I didn't think of calling you until Officer Buckley testified."

"No hard feelings," McKenzie told her, but Amanda wasn't certain that he meant it.

"I appreciate the preview of coming attractions, Amanda," Tim Kerrigan said when Dupre was out of earshot.

"We aim to please."

"You're not really going to argue that Dupre killed Wendell Hayes in self-defense, are you?"

"We'll see."

"Good luck."

Amanda was stuffing her file into her attaché case when Grace Reynolds, a reporter from the **Oregonian**, walked up to the low fence that separated the front row of the spectator section from the counsel tables. Grace was a slender brunette in her late twenties. She'd interviewed Amanda on two occasions for feature stories and had once double-dated with Amanda when they were both going out with attorneys from the same firm.

"Hi," Grace said. "You certainly wowed the judge. I haven't seen Ivan the Terrible smile that much since he imposed his last death sentence."

"Are we off the record, Grace?"

"You're not going to be Amanda 'No Comment' Jaffe with your old drinking buddy, are you?"

"Afraid so."

"I was hoping you'd give me an exclusive on the homicidal pimp."

Amanda winced. "You're not going to call him that, are you?"

"We're taking it up at the editorial meeting. Of course I might argue against it if you gave me some reason to believe that I'd be committing libel. And don't try to sell me on the cockamamie story you gave the judge."

"I must be losing my debating skills."

"Or your mind. That was the most outrageous argument I've heard since the Twinkie Defense."

"Didn't that win?"

"I don't remember. So, do I get my exclusive?"

"No can do, right now. But I'll promise to think

of you when the time is right, if you'll answer a question for me."

"Ask."

"You were at the jail when Hayes was killed, right?"

"Down in Reception." She shook her head. "What a bummer."

"I checked with Harvey Grant's clerk. Grant appointed Wendell Hayes to represent Jon Dupre a little before one on the day that Hayes was killed. He made the appointment in his chambers, not in open court, and the press wasn't invited. Hayes walked over to the Justice Center half an hour after he was appointed. How did you and the other reporters know that Hayes was going to be at the jail?"

"We got a tip."

"From who?"

"Mr. Anonymous."

"Do you know if the tip was anonymous for everyone?"

"I didn't ask."

"Okay, thanks."

"What's going on, Amanda?"

"I promise you'll be the first to know when I figure it out."

"Lets get together for a beer or a movie sometime," Grace said. "No business."

"Sounds good."

Kate had watched the exchange. "Why the question?" she asked once Grace left the courtroom.

"Only Judge Grant, Wendell Hayes, and Grant's clerk knew that the judge was going to appoint Hayes. If Hayes wanted to distract the guard at the desk so he could smuggle in the shiv, it would help to have a pack of howling journalists flashing lights in Larry McKenzie's eyes and causing their usual havoc."

twenty-seven

The reporters were waiting when Tim Kerrigan and Maria Lopez left the courtroom. Most of the spectators were gone, but Kerrigan noticed a young blond woman with sunglasses, dressed in jeans, a T-shirt, and a leather jacket, leaning against a marble pillar and studying him with intense concentration. A cameraman moved and blocked his view. When the cameraman moved again, she was gone.

As soon as the press conference was over, Stan Gregaros and Sean McCarthy joined the prosecutors.

"What did you think about the hearing?" Kerrigan asked the detectives.

"Slam dunk," Gregaros answered. "You're gonna have a ball at the trial if Jaffe sticks with her bullshit theory that Dupre acted in self-defense."

"We've got some more evidence to use against Dupre," McCarthy said. "Remember Rittenhouse telling us that Travis said that 'Jon' was going to make everything okay on the night of the murder?"

Kerrigan nodded.

"I had Dupre's phone records sent over. A call was made from his house to Travis's place in Dunthorpe on the evening Travis was killed."

"Another nail in Johnny boy's coffin," Gregaros said.

The detectives and the prosecutors conferred for a few more minutes before Tim and Maria took the elevator to the district attorney's office.

"I've actually got some work to do in another case, Maria," Kerrigan said. "Why don't you do some research on the evidentiary issues we talked about and we'll touch base tomorrow."

"I'll get right on it."

Maria walked away and Kerrigan entered his office. He dumped his files onto his desk and hung his jacket on a hook, closing the door behind him. As he was loosening his tie, he found himself remembering the blonde he'd seen briefly in the courthouse. Something about her seemed familiar.

Kerrigan's intercom buzzed.

"There's a Miss Jasmine on line two," his secretary said.

Kerrigan froze, and in that second he pictured the blonde again and knew for a fact that she was Ally Bennett.

Kerrigan lifted the receiver.

"Hello, Frank," a husky and familiar voice said.

"I think you've got the wrong person," he said carefully.

"Do I, **Frank**? Should I go to the press and let them sort it out?"

"I don't think you'd get very far."

"You don't think they'd be interested in a story about a DA who is prosecuting a pimp while having **very** raunchy sex with one of his whores?"

Tim closed his eyes and forced himself to stay calm. "What do you want?"

"Let's meet where we did the last time and I'll tell you in person. Eight o'clock. Don't be late, **Frank,** or Jasmine will be very angry."

Kerrigan felt himself begin to grow hard as an image from their last meeting was triggered by her words. An insane desire to have sex with

Jasmine again welled up in Kerrigan, despite the knowledge that meeting with her could only lead to his destruction.

Then he thought about Cindy. Something was going on between them that he hadn't anticipated. They had grown closer since she'd comforted him after his return from Senator Travis's crime scene. When he made love to his wife, there was none of the energy he'd felt with Bennett, when lust and shame had combined to produce a cocktail of illicit pleasure, but he'd felt dirty when he left the motel and he'd felt at peace when he was in Cindy's arms.

For a moment, Kerrigan thought about defying Ally, but he didn't have the courage. There were so many things she could do to hurt him; she could go to the press, to Jack Stamm, or, worst of all, she could go to Cindy. Tim felt defeated. Ally Bennett had ordered him to return to the motel and he was too weak and afraid to disobey.

Part Four

THE VAUGHN STREET GLEE CLUB

twenty-eight

Joyce Hamada wasn't hard to spot in the crowd of students that surged out of Smith Hall shortly after three. Kate Ross had found her picture in the case file Oscar Baron had given to Amanda, but the picture did not do her justice. Baggy jeans and a loose-fitting Portland State sweatshirt could not conceal her voluptuous figure. Jet-black hair hung to Hamada's waist and gleamed in the afternoon sun as if it had been polished. Her almond-shaped eyes were wide and alive, the highlight of a face that would have looked great on the cover of a fashion magazine.

Kate followed the nineteen-year-old sophomore across the street to the parking garage. She lagged behind when Hamada walked up a flight of stairs to the third floor, and closed the gap while she was tossing her books into the back of a beat-up Mazda.

"Miss Hamada?"

The woman spun in panic, her eyes wide. Kate held out her credentials.

"Sorry, I didn't mean to frighten you. My name is Kate Ross. I'm an investigator working for the lawyer who's defending Jon Dupre. Do you have a minute?"

"You've got the wrong person. I don't know this man."

"I'm talking to you here, Miss Hamada, because I don't want to embarrass you in a more public setting."

"I'm late. I have to go," Hamada said as she opened the driver's door.

"You were arrested for prostitution three months ago but the charges were dropped. Jon Dupre posted your bail and paid Oscar Baron's legal fees. That's a strange thing for someone you don't know to do."

Hamada swore and her shoulders slumped.

"I don't want to hurt you. I'm not interested in things you may have done. I just want to talk about some things that might be relevant to Jon's case."

Hamada sighed. She got into the car and motioned Kate around to the passenger side.

"Ask your questions," Hamada said when Kate shut the door.

"Why don't you start by telling me how you met Jon?"

Hamada laughed, but her eyes didn't. "I was fresh off the bus from Medford, my first time in the big city, if you can believe that. About two weeks after school started, I went to one of the clubs with some girls from school. Jon made a move on me and I didn't know what hit me. He's this great-looking, older guy, he dresses well, and he's ultrasmooth, not geeky like most of the freshman boys. The next thing I know I'm in this house I'd only seen in the movies, high on cocaine, and he's fucking my brains out. I thought I'd died and gone to Hollywood."

"How did he convince you to work for him?"

"I don't want to get into that stuff. I'm out of the life now that he's locked up." Hamada paused and shook her head. "The way he killed that lawyer, that could have been me."

"Did Jon ever hit you?"

"Yeah," Hamada said, hanging her head.

"Why didn't you leave him?"

She laughed harshly. "You think it's easy to walk away from someone like Jon?"

"Jon says that you were at his house with another girl on the evening that Senator Travis was killed."

"So?" Hamada asked defensively.

"Were you there?"

"Yeah."

"Do you remember Jon calling anyone that night?"

"He was always on the phone. I didn't pay any attention."

"Did you hear him mention Senator Travis?"

"No, but we weren't always in the same room. Besides, we left early."

"Why is that?"

"Jon got pretty fucked up on some drug he was doing, and Ally chased us out."

"Ally Bennett?"

"Yeah. She was like a mother hen when she was around Jon. Always trying to act important."

"You and Bennett didn't get along?"

"It wasn't like that. She's just territorial where Jon is concerned. She could be nice, too."

"The DA may subpoena some of the women who worked for Jon to convince the jury that he has a violent nature. If you're a witness, what can we expect from you?"

"He roughed me up once when I didn't want to

go out on a job. He scared me more than hurt me. Once I did what he wanted he was nice again."

"Can you think of anything that would help Jon?"

"Not really. I'm sort of relieved that he's in jail. I wanted to quit, but he made it hard. I hated it, really. Having some fat pig slobbering over me. I always took a long shower afterwards. Sometimes it didn't help. There'd be this smell that would stay with me."

"Was being afraid of Jon the only thing that made you stay?"

"Look, the money was great. My folks don't have much and it really helped. But, all in all, I'm glad I have an excuse to get out."

Kate headed for Ally Bennett's apartment as soon as she finished talking to Joyce Hamada. She had to find out how long Ally Bennett had stayed with Jon Dupre on the night Travis was murdered. Kate tried to remember if the medical examiner had estimated a time of death. If Bennett had stayed most of the night, she could be Jon's alibi.

Kate pulled into the lot at Ally's apartment complex and walked to Ally's door, which was ajar. She knocked. No one answered.

"Ally?" Kate called as she pushed the door all the way open. It looked like a freight train had driven through the apartment at full throttle. The Van Gogh and Monet prints had been thrown to the floor, cracking the glass, the cushions on the sofa had been ripped to shreds, books littered the floor, and the bookshelf had been overturned.

Kate crossed the living room and walked down the hall to the bedroom, hoping that she would not run across Bennett's body. The bedroom had suffered the same fate as the living room. Sheets and blankets were strewn across the floor and the mattress had been ripped open. Every drawer in the dresser had been pulled out and Bennett's clothes had been tossed about.

After a brief look at the kitchen and bathroom, which had also been trashed, Kate left, pulling the door shut and wiping her prints from the knob. Then she drove to the parking lot of a nearby supermarket and phoned Amanda.

"What do you think happened?" Amanda asked after Kate told her about her interview with Joyce Hamada and her visit to Bennett's apartment.

"I can't begin to guess, but finding Bennett should be our chief priority."

"If she can alibi Jon for the evening of Senator

Travis's murder I might be able to convince Tim Kerrigan to back off on those charges."

"I'll get right on it."

"And I'll call Sally Grace and see if she has an estimate of Travis's time of death."

"Okay. Phone me with it if you get one."

"Will do. Where are you going to start looking?"

"I'll hit the computer to see if Bennett has used a credit card recently and I'll talk to people at her apartment complex. Maybe see if Hamada or that other woman knows if she's working somewhere now that Exotic Escorts is on hiatus."

"Sounds good."

They rang off and Amanda thought about this new twist. Why had Bennett's apartment been trashed? Bennett could be dead, or so scared that she'd run. And what if she was dead? Amanda hoped that they could find her, and that she was safe.

Amanda's mother had died in childbirth, but she'd had one great parent and a carefree childhood. She always felt incredibly lucky about the breaks life had dealt her. Amanda shivered. Growing up with a sexual predator for a father, having to sell your body because it was the only way to get by. She thought about the psychological scars she carried from her one brief brush with depravity. What if every day of your life was like the moments she'd spent as a prisoner of the surgeon?

Amanda hoped that Ally had escaped the people who'd invaded her apartment and she hoped, for Jon's sake, that Kate could find her. A call girl was not the greatest alibi her pimp could have, but it would be a lot better than what they had now.

twenty-nine

Tim parked in the motel lot. He'd told Cindy that he would be out late meeting with a reluctant witness, and he didn't know if she believed him. He'd lied to her before and merely felt uncomfortable, but this time he felt as if he was losing a part of himself. The other times he'd gone to prostitutes, there was almost no risk. Ally Bennett was not merely a threat to his career. He had finally admitted to himself that she was a threat to his family. What had he been thinking? If Bennett went to the media, Megan would grow up with the shame of his disgrace, and Cindy . . . It would be terrible for her.

Ally was already inside, dressed in a black turtleneck and jeans, smoking a cigarette and watching television. Ally snapped off the set when

Tim walked in and closed the door. She was sitting in the shadows, in the room's only armchair.

"Take a seat, Mr. DA," she said motioning toward a chair at the desk. Tim pulled it out and sat down. The desk was on the other side of the small room. He was glad to have the bed between them.

"What do you want?" Kerrigan asked.

"Getting right to the point, are we? Don't you want to engage in a little foreplay first?"

Kerrigan did not answer.

"Does Cindy like foreplay?"

"Keep her out of it," Kerrigan said angrily, rising to his feet. Ally showed him her .38.

"Sit," she commanded. Tim hesitated, then sat back down.

"That's right, Timmy. Be a good boy and do what you're told and you won't get hurt."

Kerrigan's fists knotted but he did not dare move. Ally placed the gun on the table beside her chair.

"I've been finding out all sorts of interesting things about you. I didn't know that you were a big strong football hero," she taunted. "You didn't seem very strong the last time we were together."

"There's got to be a point to this, Ally. So why

don't you get to it. Is it money? Is that what you want?"

"Yeah, money. But I have other demands."

"Such as?"

"I want you to dismiss the case against Jon Dupre."

"That's impossible."

"But you'll do it anyway if you want to hold on to your job, your family, and your reputation."

"I couldn't dismiss the charges even if I wanted to. Jack Stamm is the district attorney for the county. I just work for him. He'd dismiss the charges if I could give him a reason, but he'd overrule me if I tried to do it on my own."

"Then give him a reason."

"Like what?"

"Jon didn't kill Senator Travis."

"I don't believe that for a second, but even if it was true there's no question that he killed Wendell Hayes."

"Tell Stamm that Jon killed Hayes in self-defense, like Amanda Jaffe said."

"There's absolutely no proof that Dupre was acting in self-defense. Were you in the courtroom when the jail guard testified?"

Ally nodded.

"Then you heard what he said."

"He didn't see everything."

"Ally, there is nothing I can do for Jon Dupre."

"Then I'll destroy you."

Kerrigan felt the fight go out of him. He hung his head.

"You want to know the truth? There's not much to destroy. I'm a civil servant and an unfaithful husband."

"If you're looking for pity, forget it." Ally stood up. "Just figure out how to get Jon out of jail. And figure out a way to get me fifty thousand dollars." Kerrigan looked shocked. "And don't waste your breath telling me you're a poor civil servant. Your wife and your father are rich. Get them to give you the money or get it someplace else, but get it."

Ally pulled a minicassette from her pocket. "Cheer up, Timmy. I give value for my money. You should know that." She held up the cassette. "When I get the money, you get this. It'll make your career."

"What is that?"

"A recording of a conversation I taped at Senator Travis's fund-raiser. It's got some interesting information on it about the way the anti-cloning bill was killed in the Senate. You'll be able to make headlines with this tape that will make everyone forget about Jon Dupre. See you soon."

Ally held the gun on Kerrigan while she moved toward the door.

"How will I get in touch?" Tim asked.

"Don't worry. I'll call you."

The door closed behind Ally. Tim didn't move. The desk chair was uncomfortable but he didn't notice. An image of a toppling house of cards flashed in his head.

The last time they had met in this motel room, Jasmine had asked him what he wanted her to do to him and he had told her that he wanted to be punished. It would have been more accurate to tell her that he **needed** to be punished, that he **deserved** to be punished.

Kerrigan closed his eyes and let his head fall back. He was a prosecutor. His job was to make certain that criminals suffered the consequences of their acts, but he had escaped the consequences for his worst act for so long that he'd deluded himself into believing that he would escape punishment forever.

The weeks before the Rose Bowl had been a blur. The press was everywhere and the

practices had been intense; and compounding the confusion were the discussions of his wedding to Cindy. It was almost impossible to find a place where he could be alone and think. Too many people wanted a piece of him, and Cindy wanted to be with him every second of the day. Tim was sharing a house with Hugh Curtin and two other players that was a nonstop party.

On a wet and cold Thursday, a week and a half before the big game, Tim had escaped to a dark booth in a workingman's bar off the interstate. The tavern was only three miles from campus but it catered to hard drinkers and had none of the ambience that attracted a college crowd. It was a place where the Pac-10s star running back could drink without being noticed.

By two in the morning, empty shot glasses were lined up in front of Tim on the scarred wood table. He'd made a solid dent in his sobriety, but he was no closer to solving his personal problems. Cindy was expecting him to marry her, but did he want to get married? He was young and he had his life ahead of him. How did he know that Cindy was The One? One thing he knew for certain—Cindy would be crushed if he broke off their engagement. But wouldn't a momentary tragedy be better than a lifelong one?

It was well past the curfew set by the Oregon coach. If he was caught here, drunk or sober, Coach could suspend him. Tim looked around. The bar was emptying out and he still had not decided what he was going to do. Fresh air might help.

Tim pushed himself to his feet and headed for the door. A gust of wind blew cold darts of rain into his face. Tim's car was in the lot but he knew better than to drive. He'd have Huge drive him over tomorrow morning. The walk back would give him time to think and sober up.

Tim had no idea how long he'd been walking when a car slowed down and paced alongside him. It was new and expensive, a rich kid's car—the kind the sons and daughters of the Westmont Country Club crowd drove. The passenger window rolled down.

"Tim. Hey."

It was a girl's voice. He stumbled over and ducked down so he could see the driver. She was alone.

"It's me. Melissa Stebbins."

Tim placed her immediately. She was one of Cindy's sorority sisters. Melissa had a reputation for doing drugs, drinking, and sleeping around.

"Get in," Melissa said.

Tim thought about refusing, but the rain had sobered him up enough to make him feel miserable walking in it. The dome light switched on when Tim opened the door. It had given Melissa a chance to see his pale face and bloodshot eyes. It had also allowed Tim to notice Melissa's breasts outlined beneath a tight sweater. He had the beginnings of a hard-on by the time he sat down.

"What are you doing out?" Melissa asked. "Don't you jocks have a curfew?"

"I had something to do. Coach said it was okay."

Melissa could smell the booze from across the car, and Tim looked like shit.

"Right," she laughed. She saw the concern on Tim's face. "Don't worry. I won't turn you in."

The car swerved and almost went off the road.

"Whoops," Melissa laughed as she brought the car back to the pavement. Tim realized that he wasn't the only drunk in the car and that they were heading away from his house.

"I'm over on Kirby," Tim said.

"Fuck Kirby," Melissa laughed.

"Are you okay? You want me to drive?"

Melissa didn't answer. She turned into the park and headed for the heavily forested section known since the advent of the car as Lovers' Lane. Melissa smiled at Tim. There was no doubt what had prompted her look. If he'd been sober he would have been scared, but the booze had mashed down his inhibitions.

Sometime between parking and their first kiss, Melissa slipped her hand into Tim's lap and began stroking his penis through his jeans. When she broke the kiss, Tim noticed that her eyes were glassy, but he didn't notice much else.

"Want one?"

Melissa was holding out a handful of pills. Even as wasted as he was, Tim knew better than to mess with pharmaceuticals. He shook his head. Melissa shrugged. She shoved the pills into her mouth and washed them down with something from a bottle Tim hadn't seen before. The hand returned to Tim's lap.

Melissa pulled down his zipper and unbuck-
led his pants. He was conscious of the rain
pelting against the roof of the car. For a
second, Tim thought about Cindy. Then
Melissa's mouth was on him and he wasn't
thinking about anything. His eyes closed and
his buttocks tightened. He was about to come
when Melissa pulled away roughly.

Tim's eyes snapped open. Melissa's eyes
rolled back in her head. A moment later, she
was thrashing against the driver's-side door.
Tim pressed backward, stunned and too terrified to think. Melissa was flailing. He knew
that he had to do something, but he had no
idea what. Suddenly, she collapsed, con-
vulsed again, and stopped moving.

"Oh, my God. Melissa! Melissa!"

Tim forced himself to lean toward Melissa
and touch her neck, checking for a pulse.
Her flesh felt clammy and he pulled back.
Had there been a pulse? He wasn't certain.
He just wanted to get out of the car.

The rain was still falling. He zipped up his
pants. What should he do? Call someone, he
guessed, an ambulance, the cops. But what
would happen to him if he did? He was
drunk, breaking curfew, an engaged man

getting a blow job from a girl high on God knew what. Would the cops think he'd given her the drugs?

Better get out of here, he told himself. Tim ran. Then he stopped. He had to make a call. If he left her and she died . . . He didn't want to think about that.

Another thought occurred to Tim—fingerprints. He'd seen cop shows. They'd dust the car, wouldn't they? Where had he touched it? After that night, every time he was tempted to rationalize what he'd done, Tim would remember wiping the door handles and the dashboard.

The rain was starting to let up when he sprinted out of the park. He was two miles from home. There were houses across the street but they were all dark. He should pound on a door and tell them about Melissa. He could make up a story, say he was . . . what? Walking through the woods in the rain at three in the morning, drunk. And they'd know him. He was famous. If the cops told Coach what he'd been doing—that he was intoxicated—Coach would kick him off the team. He'd have no choice.

Tim kept running. There was a twenty-four-hour convenience store a few blocks from his house. He detoured past it and checked the lot for cars. A guy was inside, getting cigarettes. Tim waited until he left, then jogged to the pay phone and called the police anonymously, hanging up as soon as he was certain that the cops knew where to look for Melissa.

Tim's house was dark and quiet. He let himself in and stripped off his clothes in his room. Melissa was probably okay, he told himself. Yeah, she'd probably just passed out. She'd been wasted. That was it. She was okay.

Tim went to bed, but he didn't sleep. Whenever he closed his eyes, he saw Melissa pressed against the car door, her eyes rolled back, drool clinging to her lower lip. When he sobered up, he cried, but he wasn't sure if he was crying for Melissa or himself.

The next day at practice Tim learned that Melissa was dead. The paper said something about a preexisting heart condition and drugs and booze. There was no mention of a passenger. Tim wondered if Melissa would have survived if he had called for help as soon as he left the park. Was she dying while

he was running for his life? Would a doctor have saved her?

Worst of all, he had spent time wiping away his prints to protect himself. Had those few moments meant the difference between Melissa living or dying? If he'd stayed with her until the ambulance arrived, would Melissa Stebbins have survived?

Tim waited for the police to come for him all week long. Some of the time, he longed for the knock on the door and the chance to confess and unburden himself of his guilt, but it never came. So much for justice. Instead of going to jail, Tim won the big game and was awarded a trophy declaring him to be the greatest college player in the United States of America. He was hailed as a hero. Tim knew better.

thirty

Billie Brewster waved to Kate Ross across the dining room of Junior's Café, where you could get coffee, strong and black, but no lattes; and apple pie a la mode, but never ever a tiramisu. Brewster was a slender black woman with close-cropped hair who worked Homicide. She and Kate had been friends when Kate was with the Portland Police Bureau and they had reestablished their friendship during the Daniel Ames case. Kate paused at the counter to give Junior her order before joining Billie.

"How have you been?" Kate asked as she slid into the booth.

"I've been better. The Parole Board passed on my brother this morning."

"Did you go down there for the hearing?"

"No. I get too bummed out."

"I'm so sorry."

Billie had been forced to raise her younger brother from the time she was sixteen, the year her father deserted the family and her mother started to work two jobs just to get by. Billie blamed herself for her brother's failings. He was locked up at the Oregon State penitentiary for committing an armed robbery.

"When does he come up again?" Kate asked.

"It doesn't matter. This is his third fall and he's not getting out soon." Billie took a sip of her coffee. "Maybe it's for the best. Every time he's on the outside he messes up."

Billie shook her head. "Enough of this negative shit. What's behind the mysterious phone call?"

"Sorry I couldn't be more specific. I'm really just fishing around."

"Fish all you want, girl, as long as you're paying for my pie and coffee."

"You know Amanda is representing Jon Dupre?"

"Who doesn't?"

"Do you know what happened at the bail hearing?"

Billie threw her head back and laughed. "I sure do. That girl's got balls. Self-defense!"

"I'm glad we're able to bring some joy to your life."

Billie laughed again. "You aren't serious about this, are you Kate? You're the brain who went to CalTech. Don't tell me you went on a football scholarship?"

Kate said nothing. Billie stared for a moment. "You are serious."

"I know it's far-fetched but we have some evidence to back up Dupre's claim."

"That I'd like to see."

"When we're ready. But enough of your questions." Kate pointed at Billie's pie and coffee. "I'm paying this exorbitant bribe to pump you for information."

"Go for it."

"Have you ever heard that Wendell Hayes was dirty?"

Billie savored a piece of pie while she thought.

"If you're asking whether we have an investigation going, as far as I know, we don't. Of course, there are always suspicions when a lawyer represents drug dealers, and Wendell represented Pedro Aragon's people. You must have heard rumbles while you were working Narcotics."

"I wasn't in long enough," Kate answered, trying to keep the bitterness out of her voice. The Portland Police Bureau had recruited her out of CalTech, where she'd majored in computer science, to investigate computer crime, but Kate had gotten bored and asked for a transfer to Vice and Narcotics. While working undercover, she had been involved in a shootout at a mall that had left civilians and a key informant dead. Kate had been the department's scapegoat and had been driven off the force.

"The only other thing I can think of falls under the heading of an urban legend."

"Spill."

"Have you ever heard of The Vaughn Street Glee Club?"

"No."

"About seven years ago, while I was still in uniform, I was the first officer on the scene when Michael Israel, a prominent banker, committed suicide. It was classic. He shot himself in the head in his study and he left a note confessing to the murder of Pamela Hutchinson, a young woman he said he'd gotten pregnant."

"Was there a murder that matched up?"

"Yeah. Eight years earlier. Hutchinson worked as a teller at Israel's bank and she was pregnant. After Israel's suicide we ran a ballistics check on the gun that Israel used on himself. It was the same weapon that was used to kill Hutchinson.

"Was Israel ever a suspect in Hutchinson's death?"

"Never. He was questioned at the time, but it was routine. We talked to everyone at the bank. Besides, there was no reason to suspect Israel. He was married, a member of a prominent Portland family. Hutchinson was found in a parking lot miles from the bank. She'd been beaten and shot. Her purse was missing. Everyone thought that she was killed during a robbery."

"How was Hayes involved?"

"Don't be impatient," Billie said as she took another mouthful of pie. "The year I made detective, the DEA arrested Sammy Cortez, a Mexican national who worked for Pedro Aragon. The feds had Cortez cold for a major drug conspiracy rap that carried a life sentence without parole. Cortez was talking a blue streak in hopes of cutting a deal, and one of the things he claimed he could clear up was the murder of a banker in Portland a few years before."

"Israel?"

Billie nodded. "He said that there was a conspiracy of well-connected, wealthy men who had ordered Israel's death and wanted it to look like a suicide. Cortez said that these men and Aragon went way back."

"Did he say that Hayes was involved?"

"He never mentioned any names, wouldn't say anything else without a deal, except for one thing. He said these men had been together so long that they even had a nickname for the group—The Vaughn Street Glee Club."

Kate looked skeptical. "What did Aragon ever have to do with a glee club?"

"Beats me, and Cortez couldn't explain the name either. He said it was an inside joke. Anyway, DEA thought Cortez was full of shit about the glee club thing but they notified us anyway. I went over to the federal lockup to talk to him because I knew about the Israel case. When I got there I learned that a lawyer had just spent half an hour with Cortez. When they brought Cortez into the visiting room he looked scared to death and he wouldn't say another word about anything. Want to guess who the lawyer was?"

"Wendell Hayes?"

Brewster nodded. "Now, I knew a little about Cortez from another case. He was a genuine tough guy, but he was also a strong family man. On a hunch I checked on his wife and their eight-year-old daughter. The daughter hadn't gone to school the day before Hayes visited or the day of his visit, but she went back the day after Cortez stopped cooperating. I tried to talk to the daughter, but the mother wouldn't let me near her."

"You think she was snatched to shut him up about this club?"

"Maybe, or maybe the talk about the club was bullshit. Cortez could have told the feds a lot about Aragon's organization. They had plenty of motivation to shut him up."

"Is Cortez still in prison?"

"Cortez is in hell. He was knifed in the yard soon after he started serving his term."

thirty-one

Tim Kerrigan needed help from someone with power and connections. Hugh Curtin was Tim's best friend, but what could "Huge" do about Ally Bennett? William Kerrigan had power and connections, but telling his father about his sordid relationship with a prostitute would only confirm every belief his father held about his son's failure to measure up. When Kerrigan thought about it, there was only one person he could go to for help.

Harvey Grant lived alone high above city center, behind stone walls, in a secluded area of the West Hills. Tim stopped at the iron gate that blocked access to the judge's estate and spoke into a black metal call box. Victor Reis, an ex-cop in his fifties, who acted as a combination butler, bodyguard, and secretary for the judge, answered. Moments later, the gate swung open and Tim drove up a long driveway before stopping in front of a three-story brick house of Federalist design.

Most of the windows in Grant's mansion were dark, but the house was often alive with light and sound. The judge was famous for his large parties and intimate get-togethers. An invitation to one of Judge Grant's soirees was eagerly sought and cherished because it signified that you were one of Portland's elite.

Tim parked in front of a recessed portico where Harvey Grant was waiting.

"Come into the study," the judge said solicitously. "You look like you can use a strong drink."

"I've done something incredibly stupid," Kerrigan said as they walked down a side hall to a wood-paneled den.

"Wait until you've calmed down," Grant said as he sat Tim in an armchair near a fireplace with a carved cherrywood mantel, in which a fire had been laid. Tim leaned his head back and soaked up the warmth. As soon as he closed his eyes he felt bone-weary.

"Here," Grant said. Kerrigan jerked awake. He had not realized how much the meeting with Ally Bennett had taken out of him. The judge pressed a cold glass into Kerrigan's hand and took a sip from a glass he'd filled for himself.

"Thanks," Kerrigan said as he gulped down half the glass.

Grant smiled warmly. Kerrigan had always been amazed by his mentor's steadiness. Even in the most contentious courtroom situation, Harvey Grant floated above the fray, counseling the combatants with the calm, reassuring voice of reason.

"Feeling a little better?" Grant asked.

"No, Judge. It's going to take a lot more than a glass of scotch to fix my problem."

"Tell me what happened."

Kerrigan could not look Harvey Grant in the eye as he told him about his sordid evening with Ally after his speech at the trial lawyers' convention, and its aftermath. The judge took an occasional sip but his expression did not change as he listened. Kerrigan felt lighter after unburdening himself. He knew he was taking a risk going to an officer of the court, but he was certain that Grant would protect his confidence and he hoped that the judge would find a solution to his dilemma.

"Is this the only time that you've done this sort of thing?" Grant asked.

"No." Kerrigan hung his head. "But I've always

been so careful. With Ally . . . I don't know what I was thinking. I was drunk, I was depressed. . . ."

Kerrigan stopped. His excuses sounded weak and unconvincing.

"Cindy is a good person, Tim."

When Kerrigan looked up, there were tears in his eyes.

"I know that. I hate myself for lying to her. It makes me sick."

"And there's Megan to think about," Grant reminded him.

Kerrigan fought back a sob. Everything was tumbling down around him. Grant sat silently and let Kerrigan grieve.

"Have you talked to your father about Miss Bennett?" Grant asked when Tim stopped crying.

"God, no. I couldn't. You know how it is between us."

"So, you came straight here?"

Tim nodded.

"Is it your impression that Miss Bennett has kept what she knows to herself?"

"I don't know, but she'd lose her advantage over me if our relationship became public knowledge."

"What do you think would happen if she went to the press and you denied her allegations?"

"Do you mean can she prove we spent the night together?"

Grant nodded. Kerrigan rubbed his forehead. He tried to remember what had happened that evening.

"I registered with false ID, but the clerk at the front desk might remember me. And I went there again tonight. I may have left prints in the room. Fingerprints last a long time. They don't clean very thoroughly at that place."

"Most likely, though, it would be her word against yours, no?"

Kerrigan thought of something. "Phone records. I phoned Ally from my office the night I first saw her and I used a pay phone in the hotel where I gave my speech. No one could prove I made either call, but the phone records would be powerful circumstantial evidence that she's telling the truth.

"And what does it matter if she can prove what happened? Once that type of allegation is made it sticks with you forever, no matter what the truth is."

"You're right, Tim. If this got out it would be

disastrous, and it would ruin your chance to be a senator."

Grant paused and took a sip of his drink. His brow furrowed. "What do you make of this business with the cassette?"

"Dupre ran a pretty high-scale operation. We know that politicians and wealthy businessmen used it. Bennett could have been in a position to tape incriminating evidence that Dupre could use for blackmail."

Grant nodded, then became pensive again. Kerrigan waited, exhausted, grateful for the pause. When the judge spoke, his tone was measured and thoughtful.

"You've acted very foolishly, Tim, and placed yourself and your family in a precarious position, but I may be able to help you. I want you to go home and let me work on this problem. If Miss Bennett contacts you, stall her. Promise her that you are going to do as she asks but you need time to figure out how best to accomplish her purpose. I'll call you when I know more."

Grant got up and Tim rose with him. Standing was like climbing a mountain. His body seemed to be as heavy as stone and he felt a weakness of spirit that was close to a wish for death.

"Thank you, Judge. You don't know how much just talking to you means to me."

Grant placed his hand on Kerrigan's shoulder. "You can't see it, Tim, but you have everything that most men wish for. I'm going to help you hold on to it."

thirty-two

Amanda went to bed early and spent another night tossing and turning until exhaustion forced her into a deep, troubled sleep. In her dream, she was on a cruise ship. Amanda had no idea where the ship was sailing, but the sea seemed smooth and the sky was clear. Still, she felt a vague unease. It was as if she sensed that the weather could change at any minute.

The corridors of the ship seemed to lead nowhere and Amanda was alone and lost, searching for someone whose identity remained a mystery to her. She came to a cabin that looked familiar. When she touched the door, it moved inward in slow motion to reveal a man who was standing with his back to her. He started to turn as slowly as the door had moved. Just before she could see his face, Amanda jerked awake.

For a moment, Amanda was unsure of whether she was in bed or on the ship. Then she saw the glowing red numerals on her clock and knew that she was home. It was five o'clock. Amanda made a short, half-hearted attempt to get back to sleep but soon gave up. The dream had been very unsettling. The idea of taking something to help her sleep was getting more and more appealing, and she decided to talk to Ben Dodson about it at their session in the afternoon.

The Y was open for early risers. Amanda drove over for a workout that she hoped would clear her head. As she swam, she thought about her relationship with Mike Greene. She liked him, and she felt comfortable with him, but there was no spark.

Amanda had been away from Oregon, except for short visits, since she started college at Berkeley. When she returned to work in Frank's firm, she'd found that most of her high school friends had moved away. Many of those who remained were either married or in serious relationships and she was often the odd wheel when they got together. A few of her women friends had chosen career over marriage, but when they met for dinner or drinks, men were a frequent topic of conversation. Amanda loved her work, but her happily married friends had a closeness that she envied, and she was often depressed when she left them.

Mike had gone through a bad divorce in L.A. before moving to Portland; even so, she had a sense that he might want more out of their relationship. Amanda cared for Mike, but deep down she knew that something was missing. He was a safe haven. When she married, she didn't want to settle for safety. She wanted to be in love.

After her workout, Amanda drove downtown. There was a brief that was due in the court of appeals by next Friday, and she could get a lot of work done because the phones didn't ring in the office until the receptionist came in at eight. Amanda grabbed a scone and a latte at the coffee bar at Nordstrom, then entered the Stockman Building. She passed Daniel Ames's office on the way to her own.

Daniel's early life had been terrible. In his late teens, he had run away from an alcoholic mother and a series of abusive "fathers," living on the street until he'd joined the army out of desperation. After the army, Daniel had worked his way through college and law school, finishing high enough in his law-school class to get a job offer from Portland's largest firm.

Daniel was consulting a medical text as he waded through a stack of doctor's reports in a medical malpractice case. He looked up and grinned. Daniel was handsome, with solid shoulders and a great smile. It was almost impossible now for Amanda to remember how frantic and hopeless her friend had seemed when they'd first met in the Multnomah County jail. Daniel had been framed for the murder of one of his firm's senior partners and Kate and Amanda had saved him. Daniel had been living with Kate Ross since Kate's investigation, and Amanda's courtroom skills had cleared his name.

"I didn't think the bosses got to work this early," Daniel joked.

"I'm just here to keep an eye on the help."

"Kate's in, too. She wanted to talk to you about something."

Amanda carried the latte and the bag with the scone down the hall to the investigator's narrow, messy office.

"What have you got for me?" Amanda asked as she pushed papers away from the edge of Kate's desk and put her food on the cleared space. As Kate told her about her meeting with Billie Brewster, Amanda munched on her scone and sipped her latte.

"So, what's your conclusion?" Amanda asked when Kate was through.

"If this 'Vaughn Street Glee Club' exists, and Wendell Hayes was part of it, he could have been sent to the jail to kill Dupre."

"Why?"

Kate shrugged. "Beats me. Did Dupre have any idea why Hayes was after him?"

"No."

Amanda finished her scone and washed the last piece down with a sip of her latte.

"What are you doing next?" she asked Kate.

"I set up a meeting with Sally Grace to go over the autopsy report on Michael Israel to see if there's any evidence that he was murdered."

Amanda stood up. "Let me know what you find."

"First thing."

Amanda shook her head. "This case isn't getting any easier."

Amanda was still awkward about her visits to Ben Dodson and she'd told no one—including her father—that she was seeing a psychiatrist.

"I've been reading about you in the papers," Dodson said when Amanda was seated in his office.

"The reporters won't leave me alone," Amanda answered self-consciously.

"Have you had any trouble handling the pressure?"

Amanda nodded. "The first two times I met with Jon Dupre I was terrified."

"I don't think that's an abnormal reaction given the fact that he'd killed his previous lawyer." Dodson smiled. "I guarantee you, I'd have been pretty nervous if you asked me to evaluate him."

Amanda laughed and felt her anxiety ease a bit. "I guess you're right."

"See, not every fear reaction is irrational."

"I didn't let my fear paralyze me," Amanda said proudly. "I was scared to death, but I forced myself to sit in the same room with Jon."

"That's good. What I want to know is whether you've had any more flashbacks—the kind of feelings that are unexpected."

"Seeing the autopsy photographs of Senator Travis and Wendell Hayes upset me, and that was unusual. I mean, you see those kinds of things all the time in my line of work."

Dodson flashed Amanda a reassuring smile.

"Anyway, the photos did get to me, and my fear of meeting with Dupre was much more intense than the normal tension I always experience when I'm in close quarters with my more dangerous clients."

"But you dealt with it."

Amanda nodded.

"When we talked during your first visit, you expressed some anxiety about continuing to work as a criminal defense attorney. How are you feeling about that?"

"Pretty good, actually." Amanda paused. "There's something funny about Dupre's case. I can't get into the facts . . ."

"Of course."

". . . but Jon may be innocent, and that made me remember why I got into this business in the first place—to protect people who couldn't protect themselves. So, the case is making me feel better about what I do."

"That's good. What about the nightmares? How are you sleeping?"

"Not too well. I don't have nightmares every night but it happens a few times a week. And it's hard for me to fall asleep. I think I'm afraid to go to sleep because of the nightmares. I've been exhausted a lot since I took on Jon's case."

"Maybe we should consider medication."

"I don't know," she said, even though she'd

planned on bringing up taking a sleeping pill. For some reason, this idea embarrassed her.

"Why don't you think about it and tell me what you want to do the next time we meet."

As Amanda rode the elevator to the lobby of Dr. Dodson's building, she thought about The Vaughn Street Glee Club. The idea of a high-level conspiracy going back decades was fascinating but far-fetched. It was a stretch to think that there was a connection between Israel's death and Dupre's case.

The elevator doors opened. Amanda paused in the lobby. Connections—conspiracies were, by definition, acts of people working in concert. Sammy Cortez had told the police that the conspiracy between Pedro Aragon and the others went way back. Was there some connection between Aragon and Hayes that started before Hayes became a lawyer? Amanda walked outside and found herself in the shadow of the Multnomah County Public Library. An idea occurred to her. She crossed the street.

The library, which took up a city block, was Georgian in style, with a ground floor fronted by cool gray limestone, and upper stories of red brick. Amanda climbed the broad granite steps that led to the public entrance and went directly to the History Department on the third floor where she found the library index; row after row of low-tech, wooden drawers stuffed with musty index cards arranged by name, which gave citations to newspaper articles in which the individual on the card was mentioned. Amanda pulled out the drawer marked ANIMALS TREATMENT and flipped through the cards until she found several for Pedro Aragon. She listed every newspaper-story reference on her yellow, lined legal pad, then did the same for Wendell Hayes. When she was finished, Amanda made a separate list of all of the stories that mentioned both men.

Periodicals were on the second floor. Amanda decided to work from the oldest stories forward, and the oldest reference was an **Oregonian** article from 1971. The newspaper stories from that far back were only on microfilm. Amanda found the appropriate roll. She fitted it on a spindle attached to a gray metal scanner and turned the dial. The microfilm raced across the screen fast enough to give her a headache, so she slowed it down. Eventually she reached the Metro section for January 17, 1971. At the bottom of a column was an update of a story about the investigation into a massacre that took place in December of 1970 in North Portland, in which Pedro Aragon was a suspect. The January story concerned the discovery of three handguns in a landfill on the outskirts of Portland. They had been positively identified as weapons used in the December shootout. The handguns had been traced to the home of Milton Hayes, a wealthy Portland lawyer and gun collector, who had reported the weapons stolen in a burglary that had been committed on the evening of the shootings. Buried in the story was an explanation of how the burglars had gained entry to Hayes's house. His son, Wendell, who was home from Georgetown University for the holidays, had forgotten to set the alarm when he left the house with several of his friends to attend a Christmas party.

Amanda found the microfilm spool for December 1970 and located the story about the drug-house massacre. Dead bodies had been found scattered around the first floor of an abandoned house. Most of the victims had been shot to death, but a man in the front hall had had his throat slashed. Traces of heroin had been discovered in several rooms. The police had been able to identify several of the victims as members of a black gang with Los Angeles connections, and the others as Latinos associated with Jesus Delgado, who was suspected of working for a Mexican drug cartel. One of the dead men, Clyde Hopkins, had ties to an organized crime family in Las Vegas. Pedro Aragon, a known associate of Delgado, had been arrested the day after the murders but had been released when the police could not break his alibi.

Could Hayes and Aragon have been involved in the drug-house massacre? Amanda had a hard time picturing a West Hills preppie wiping out armed druggies in a shootout in one of Portland's worst neighborhoods, but Hayes might have been at the house buying drugs, or he could have stolen his father's guns to trade for dope.

Amanda wondered who Hayes's buddies were in December of 1970. They were probably the friends he was with on the night his father's guns were stolen. It would be interesting to get the police reports and find out the names of the boys who were with Hayes when the B-and-E occurred.

Amanda took a break from viewing microfilm and found Wendell Hayes's obituary. Hayes had graduated from Portland Catholic in June of 1970, the same year as the drug-house massacre. He had attended college and law school at

Georgetown University. Amanda asked the reference librarian where she could find the yearbook for Portland Catholic. She took it to a table and started leafing through the book.

Hayes had been the senior class vice president, and the president had been Harvey Grant. As she thumbed through the yearbook, Amanda found more familiar names. Burton Rommel and William Kerrigan, Tim's father, were teammates of Hayes on the football and wrestling teams. Amanda remembered that Grant was also a graduate of the law school at Georgetown, and she was pretty certain that he'd received his undergraduate degree from the school.

Amanda checked out the backgrounds of Burton Rommel and William Kerrigan. Neither had gone to Georgetown. Rommel had a BA from Notre Dame and Kerrigan had received degrees from the Wharton School at the University of Pennsylvania.

Amanda returned to the microfilm projector and threaded in another spool, which contained an early reference to Pedro Aragon. She was curious to learn how someone who started out running a drug house in Portland got to be the head of a cartel in Mexico. An hour later, Amanda had learned that Aragon's rapid rise had been made possible by a series of murders, which had started in 1972 with the assassination of Jesus Delgado, Pedro's immediate superior, in the parking lot of a Portland 7-Eleven.

Amanda spent more time going through stories that mentioned Pedro Aragon and Wendell Hayes, but the majority were accounts of cases in which Hayes had represented a client with connections to Aragon. She returned the microfilm and headed back to her office. Amanda had not really believed Sammy Cortez's story about The Vaughn Street Glee Club when she walked into the library, but one piece of information in the newspaper stories had really gotten her thinking: The drug house where the massacre took place was on Vaughn Street.

thirty-three

Tim Kerrigan and Maria Lopez had been discussing trial strategy for an hour, and it was getting close to five o'clock. Kerrigan had his jacket off and his tie at half-mast. Lopez had slung her jacket over the back of a chair, and her hair was a mess because she kept running her hands through it.

"Jaffe filed a motion to keep evidence of the Travis murder out of the Hayes case," Tim said. "What do you think? Can we get evidence about Travis's murder in when we try Dupre for killing Hayes?"

"I'd concede the point," Maria answered. "Why risk a reversal? Hayes is an easy win. The trial should take less than a week, if you don't count jury selection. Our case will take a day, two at the most. If Jaffe defends with this self-defense bullshit, she could turn the trial into a circus, call all the reporters, do a demonstration with the metal detector at the desk in reception. But I still see it as a slam dunk. Once we have a conviction we can introduce it for impeachment if Dupre takes the stand when we try him for killing the senator."

"Good thinking. But . . ."

The phone rang. Tim looked annoyed as he picked up the receiver. "I'm in conference, Lucy. I don't want to be interrupted."

"I know, but there's a Miss Bennett at the front desk. She's very insistent."

Kerrigan felt the blood drain from his face. Ally Bennett had called several times but he'd had the receptionist tell her that he was out. Kerrigan glanced at Maria to see if she'd noticed his discomfort. She was looking at her notes.

"Okay, patch me through to reception," Kerrigan said. A moment later, Ally was on the line.

"Thank you for coming by," Kerrigan said quickly. "I'm in a meeting, but I do want to get together with you."

"Yeah," Bennett said, "I think you'd better do that."

"Let me call you when I'm through here, say in an hour?"

"I'll be waiting, and I'll be very, very disappointed if I don't hear from you."

The line went dead. Kerrigan could feel sweat beading his forehead. He never expected Ally to show up here. Maria knew who Ally was. What if she'd seen her in reception?

"Are you okay?"

Maria was staring at him. He forced a smile.

"I think I'm coming down with something. Why don't we stop now?"

"Sure." Maria stood and gathered up her files. "I hope you feel better."

"Thanks. You're doing a great job, Maria."

Lopez blushed. She backed out of his office, pulling the door shut behind her. Kerrigan dialed the extension for Harvey Grant's chambers.

"Bennett was here, Judge, in reception," Kerrigan said as soon as Grant was on the line.

"Did anyone see her?"

"I don't know who was out there."

"What did you do?"

"I talked to her over the phone on the reception desk."

"So no one saw you together?"

"No. I got rid of her by promising I'd call her in an hour. That's fifty minutes from now."

"Okay, calm down."

"What am I going to tell her?"

There was silence on the line. Kerrigan waited, his hand clammy against the plastic, his stomach in a knot.

"Tell Miss Bennett that you think you'll have everything worked out by next week."

"How am I going to do that?"

"Say that you've almost put the money together, then intimate that you're working with a detective who owes you a favor. Be vague. Tell her that this detective can make evidence disappear, but won't tell you how he's going to work it."

"What happens next week, when Dupre is still in jail?"

"We'll discuss that tonight."

Kerrigan fortified himself with scotch before meeting with Harvey Grant. He looked like he'd slept in his clothes. Victor Reis opened the door before Tim could ring the bell. The bodyguard's craggy face broke into a smile. Kerrigan was certain that Victor noticed his disheveled state, because he noticed everything, but Reis made no mention of Tim's condition.

"Come on in. The judge is in the den. Have you eaten?"

"I'm fine. I'll find him. Thanks."

Kerrigan walked down the hall to the room where he and Grant had last met. The judge was dressed in khaki slacks, a plaid shirt, and a baggy sweater. A book on English military history was lying at his elbow. He smiled warmly and waved Tim onto a seat.

"How are you holding up?" Grant asked.

"Not real well," Tim answered as he slumped into an armchair.

"Can I get you a drink?"

Tim shook his head. "I've had a couple already."

Grant's smile became wistful. "How long have I known you, Tim?"

"My whole life."

Grant nodded. "I was at your baptism, your first birthday, and your first communion. I've always been very proud of you."

Kerrigan cast his eyes toward the floor. They misted and his voice caught in his throat.

"I'm sorry I let you down."

"You haven't, son. You're just human. We all make mistakes."

"This is more than a mistake."

"No, no. What's happening to you is a bump in the road. No more. It seems colossal now, but we'll take care of it. A year from now you won't remember how upset you were."

Kerrigan looked up hopefully.

"Tim, do you trust me?"

"Yes."

"And you know that I have only your best interests at heart?"

Tim wanted to tell the judge that he felt closer to him than he did to his own father, but he could not say the words.

"I have a solution to your problem," the judge said. "This woman is a whore, gutter trash. We're not going to let someone like that destroy your life."

Kerrigan leaned forward, eager to hear Grant's plan.

"Do you remember Harold Travis's musings about the existence of God when we were on the terrace of the Westmont, after we played golf?"

"It was the last time I saw him alive."

"Let me ask you something, Tim. Do you think that there is a God, a supreme being who sees everything that we do and punishes our bad acts?"

Tim didn't know how to answer. He'd been

raised to believe in God, and there were times when life itself seemed like a miracle. He remembered having the most certainty when Megan was born; and now and then he'd have days when the world around him was so filled with beauty that he had to believe in a divine plan. But most of the time he found it hard to accept the idea of such a plan. It was difficult to believe in a merciful God when you were interviewing an abused child whose face was devoid of all emotion and whose body was covered by evidence of a life that had known only pain and despair. The everyday routine in the district attorney's office tended to erode faith.

"It's natural to hesitate when asked a question like this," Grant said, "and it's difficult for a person trained to use logic to accept the existence of anything—let alone a supernatural, all-knowing being—without evidence. That's one of the downsides of a legal education, I guess."

"But you believe in God?"

"Harold believed that the concept of God was invented to keep the riffraff in line," Grant answered, sidestepping Tim's question. "He was very cynical, but was he right? If the poor didn't believe in a reward in the afterlife, would they suffer in this one or would they rise up against their betters? Harold believed that God and Law were invented by superior men to control the masses, and he believed that morality was relative."

"There are rules, Judge. Morality isn't relative. We know in our heart when we do something wrong." Kerrigan hung his head. "I know."

"That's guilt, which we experience when we believe—on faith—that there are divine rules of conduct. But what if you knew for a fact that there was no God and no rules other than those that **you** made? If that were true, you would be a free man, because the restraints that kept your desires in check would be released."

"What does this have to do with Ally Bennett?"

"If God does not exist, if superior men play by their own rules, if there is no divine punishment, then Ally Bennett would cease to be a problem."

"You mean that she could be killed?"

"Removed, Tim, the way you erase a disquieting sentence in a brief that you're writing or slap away an insect that has interfered with your peace of mind."

"But there are rules, there are laws."

"Not for everyone. Harold knew that for a fact."

"What are you getting at, Judge? I'm not following you."

"You're afraid to follow me. There's a difference. Answer me this: What would you do if I could assure you that there would never be any consequences if you removed Ally Bennett from your life?"

"You can't give me that assurance. No one can."

"Pretend that I could."

"I . . . I couldn't kill someone even if I knew that I could get away with it."

"What if a burglar broke into your house and was going to kill Megan? Are you telling me that you wouldn't kill him?"

"That's different. That's self-defense."

"Aren't we talking about self-defense? Isn't this woman threatening your life and the lives of those you love? Imagine yourself as a United States senator. That's within your grasp, Tim. Now think forward a few years. Can you see yourself as president of the United States, the most powerful person in the world?"

Kerrigan's mouth dropped. Then he laughed. "Look at me, Judge. I'm not presidential material. I'm a hard drinker, a man who goes with whores to motels where you pay by the hour."

"That is your image of yourself, but ask anyone in Oregon what they think of Tim Kerrigan and they'll tell you that he's a man of great character who has sacrificed personal wealth and fame for public service. Only one person can prove otherwise. Only one person can destroy your marriage and the way Megan perceives you. Only one person stands between you and your dreams and the happiness of your family."

"I can't believe you're saying this. You believe in God. You're a devout Catholic."

Grant didn't answer. He took another sip of his drink.

"You're not seriously thinking of having Ally Bennett murdered?" Tim said. "Tell me that this is a put-on."

Grant continued to sit quietly. For a brief moment, Kerrigan imagined Ally Bennett dead. All of his problems would disappear. He could keep trying to heal the wounds in his marriage and create a life for Megan in which she would be proud of him. But thinking about Megan brought him back to reality.

"I've known you my whole life, Harvey," Tim said, using the judge's first name for the first time in recent memory. "I can't believe that you could kill someone in cold blood, and I can't either. How could I face Megan if I killed someone? It would eat me alive."

Tim stood and began to pace. "And all this talk about morality and God doesn't mean a thing anyway, because if there's one thing I've learned as a district attorney it's that everyone gets caught eventually."

"You're afraid, Tim. That's natural. But you would see things differently if you knew that there were no consequences." The judge paused for dramatic effect. "And that is something that I can guarantee."

"How can you possibly guarantee that we wouldn't be caught?"

"You have more friends than you know, Tim. People who believe in you and want to help you."

"Who are these people?"

"Friends, good friends. That's all you need to know for now. They are policemen who will control the investigation, district attorney's . . ."

Tim's head snapped up.

"Yes, Tim, in your own office. You'll be covered. When Ally Bennett is dead you'll be free. Think about that. Think about what that would mean to Megan."

Grant lifted up the book of military history and took hold of a file that had been under it.

"This shouldn't be that hard for you. You've played by your own rules for years. I have to believe you did it because you believed that there would be no consequences for your actions."

Grant handed the file to Kerrigan, and he opened it. On top was a photograph of Ally Bennett entering his motel room on the night they had sex. There were other shots of them, inside the room, in various sexual positions. Beneath these photographs were pictures of Tim in other places, with other women. The photos covered sexual encounters that had occurred years before. In several pictures, Kerrigan was snorting cocaine or smoking marijuana. The invasion of his privacy that the photographs represented should have made Tim furious, but all he experienced was numbing shock.

"How . . . ?"

"We've known for some time. It's what persuaded us of your potential."

Kerrigan slumped back onto his chair and put his head in his hands.

"I think of you as my son, Tim. I only want to help you out of this terrible predicament. Everything I've said is new, a shock. I can appreciate that it will take some getting used to. But you'll see that everything I've said makes perfect sense and is in your best interest."

"I won't kill her. I can't. I'll resign my job. I'll

go to the press and confess to . . . to what I've done. I just can't murder anyone."

"I expected this reaction, Tim. I know it's hard to take the first step. Go home and sleep. You'll think much more clearly in the morning. You'll see that killing Ally Bennett is the only rational way to solve your problems. Your choice is between eliminating someone who wants to ruin you and your family, and protecting your family. Do you want to trade the future of everyone you hold dear for the life of a whore?"

Halfway home, Kerrigan pulled to the side of the road, opened the door, and vomited. He sat with his feet on the ground and his head between his knees. After a while, Tim wiped his mouth with his handkerchief, then threw it away. It was close to freezing, and the cold stung his cheeks. He looked up. The night was clear and the stars were sharp, but the world seemed to waver.

Harvey Grant, a man he would trust with his life, a man he revered more than his own father, had known his most intimate and sordid secrets for years, had been recording his degradation and sharing his knowledge with people Tim probably saw every day. Who were they? How many of them had treated him as if he were normal, while picturing him naked in the most demeaning positions, begging for punishment and reveling in his own debasement?

If Harvey Grant was telling him the truth, the world he thought he knew was being manipulated by a cadre of people who believed themselves to be above the law, people who would kill without compunction to achieve their ends and who were commanding him to kill.

Going to the police or another DA was out of the question. If Harvey Grant, the presiding judge and one of the most powerful people in the state, was involved with this group, then anyone could be in it.

What about the FBI? He could contact someone in Washington, D.C., but what would he say? The story sounded insane. And the judge had those photographs, which would completely discredit him.

There was suicide, of course. Kerrigan wiped his eyes. We all die. Why not go now and save himself this pain? He'd made a mess of his life, so why not end it? The idea of escaping to the peace of death was tempting.

Then Kerrigan thought about some of the things that Grant had told him. The judge was certain that he could kill Bennett with impunity.

If he did do this one terrible thing, his immediate problems would be solved and his future could be something he had never even dreamed about. At first, the suggestion that he could become a president of the United States seemed preposterous, but it did not seem so ridiculous when he examined the idea objectively.

Winning an election to the Senate was easy to imagine. He looked like a senator, he was famous and popular throughout the state. And once he was a United States senator, it was easy to imagine himself as president. Any senator was in a position to try for the highest office.

Kerrigan remembered how excited Cindy was about the prospect of his running for Travis's seat. Megan would know that her father was someone very important. So many doors would open for her. He might even win the respect of his father.

Kerrigan no longer felt the cold. He was no longer aware of where he was. It was as if he was on the border of a world far different from the one he had known his whole life. One step and he would be over that border and in a new world without limits, where he could do anything he wanted to do without fear.

The judge was right about so much he'd said.

Ally Bennett was a whore—a whore with the power to ruin his life. And how was she using her power? She wanted Tim to set free an unrepentant killer. There was no way that Tim could do what she wanted anyway. That meant that Ally Bennett was going to destroy his life and make his lovely, innocent daughter go through her life carrying the burden of her father's shame.

Kerrigan looked up. The stars no longer wavered, his sight was sharper, and his mind was clearer. No longer was he asking himself if he **should** kill Ally Bennett. He was contemplating a new question: **Could** he kill Ally Bennett?

thirty-four

Ben Dodson was in a good mood when he arrived at his office on Monday morning. He had a full schedule of patients, but his secretary told him that his four o'clock had canceled, which meant he'd be able to go home early. As Ben went to his filing cabinet to find the file for his first patient of the day, he noticed a slip of paper that was half hidden under his desk. He picked it up and discovered that it was a note that he had scribbled to himself about Amanda Jaffe during one of their sessions. Dodson frowned. The note should have been in Amanda's file. What was it doing on the floor?

Dodson found Amanda's file and opened it. Everything looked in order. He put the paper back in the file and replaced the folder in its proper place. He took out the file for his nine o'clock and sat down to review it. After a few minutes, he paused, distracted by thoughts of the slip of paper from Amanda's file. In his mind's eye, Dodson could see himself placing the slip in the file and replacing the file after Amanda's session. He buzzed his secretary and asked her if she had taken the file from the cabinet. She had not.

Dodson was certain that he had not reviewed Amanda's file since their last appointment, which was when he'd written the note. Amanda had come to see him on Friday. Was it possible that the paper had lain unseen under his desk all day? That had to be what happened because the only other explanation would involve someone breaking into his office.

As soon as she was at her desk on Monday, Amanda phoned the Portland Police Bureau's police report requests number. A recording told her that all requests for police reports had to be in writing, but it gave her a phone number for Records. A woman answered the phone.

"I'm Amanda Jaffe, an attorney, and I'm trying to get my hands on some old police reports from the early nineteen seventies."

"Gee, we only keep records for twenty-five years. I'm pretty sure we wouldn't have them."

"Even in a homicide case?"

"Oh, that's different. Those we don't destroy, because there's no statute of limitations."

"So, I can get them?"

"You might be able to, but I couldn't give them to you. Those reports are in a locked cabinet in a locked room. The only people who can get them are Records techs."

"Can I talk to one of them?" Amanda asked.

"You could, but they won't give you the reports. They have to be authorized to get them."

"Who can do that?"

"The detectives who handled the case."

"They're probably retired, don't you think?"

"Yeah."

"So?"

"Any homicide detective can authorize the request if the original detective isn't available."

"Thanks."

Amanda dialed Homicide and asked for Sean McCarthy.

"How's my favorite mouthpiece?" McCarthy asked.

"Hanging in there."

"Is this call about Mr. Dupre?"

"Sherlock Holmes has nothing on you, Sean."

McCarthy laughed. "What can I do for you?"

"I'm trying to get my hands on some police reports from the early nineteen seventies. Records won't give them to me without the authorization of the detective who worked the case or, if he's not available, another homicide detective."

"Are the reports connected to Dupre's case?"

"They might be. I have to read them to be certain."

"What do you think you'll find?"

"I'd rather not say until I'm certain I'm going to use them."

"Then I can't help you."

"I'll just file a discovery motion. Why make me go through that?"

"Kerrigan is running this case. He's the one you should talk to. If he tells me it's okay to authorize the release, I'll make sure you get the reports, but I'm going to let him make the decision."

Amanda had hoped that Sean would give her the reports without asking for her reason for wanting them, but she had expected him to refuse. Nothing was ever easy.

thirty-five

The weekend had been hell for Tim Kerrigan. Every moment that he was home he worried about getting a call from Ally Bennett. When he wasn't worrying about Ally's call he was tortured by the choice he would soon have to make.

On Sunday, Tim and Cindy took Megan to the zoo. Tim was grateful for the outing. His absorption in Megan's antics helped him to forget his problems. As soon as Megan was in bed, Tim went into his study on the pretext of doing work. By the time he went to bed, he had decided what he would do. That night, he made love to Cindy with incredible passion.

When Kerrigan arrived at his office on Monday, he was exhausted from lack of sleep. One of the few tasks he could handle was reviewing his mail. There was a report from the crime lab on the old blood that had been discovered in Harold Travis's A-frame. The blood was the same type as Lori Andrews's blood. DNA testing would show conclusively whether or not the dead call girl had bled in the senator's cabin. If it turned out that Senator Travis had murdered the escort during rough sex, it would be unethical for Tim to use evidence of Andrews's murder to convince a jury that Dupre had killed her. It also made no sense from the standpoint of strategy to argue that Dupre had killed Travis to avenge Andrews. That would only create sympathy for Dupre and make the jurors hate Travis. Kerrigan was still trying to decide what to do with the evidence of the senator's perversion, when his intercom buzzed.

"Amanda Jaffe is here to see you," the receptionist said. Tim was in no mood to talk to Jon Dupre's attorney but it would look odd if he refused to see her, and it was essential that he act naturally now that he had made his decision.

"Amanda," Kerrigan said as soon as she was shown in, "to what do I owe this pleasure?"

Tim was usually neat and well dressed. Today, his eyes were glassy and there were dark circles under them. His hair looked like he'd run a comb through it without concern for the results, and the top of his white shirt showed because the knot in his tie had not been pulled tight. Amanda also noticed an uncharacteristic quaver in his voice.

"I heard that you weren't busy enough," she joked to conceal her surprise, "and I don't want you to get laid off, so I brought you something to do."

Kerrigan forced a laugh. "Gee, thanks."

Amanda handed him a motion for discovery that she'd worked on as soon as she'd finished talking to Sean McCarthy. Kerrigan thumbed through it. There was a general request for discovery of all evidence uncovered in the investigation that would tend to prove that Jon Dupre was innocent. Kerrigan wondered if he had a statutory or constitutional duty to disclose the lab report to Amanda. Did it exculpate? Finding Lori Andrews's blood in Travis's cabin would be evidence Amanda Jaffe could use to argue that Dupre did not murder Lori Andrews, but did it have any tendency to disprove the cases against Dupre for the Travis and Hayes murders?

Under the general request was a series of specific requests, which he skimmed because he was anxious to be by himself. His eye passed down the list and was almost to the bottom when something in the middle of the demands made him go back. Amanda was requesting production of a set of police reports from the 1970s. Kerrigan was tempted to ask Amanda how they could possibly be relevant to Dupre's case, but he held his tongue.

"I'll review your motions and get back to you if there's a problem."

"Great." Amanda looked closely at Kerrigan. "Are you feeling okay?"

"I think I might be coming down with something," he answered, faking a smile.

As soon as Amanda left, Kerrigan buzzed Maria Lopez and asked her to come to his office. When she walked in, he handed her Amanda's motions.

"Amanda Jaffe filed these. I have two assignments for you. One is going to upset you a little."

Maria looked puzzled.

"Jon Dupre may not be responsible for the murder of Lori Andrews," Kerrigan said.

"Then who . . . ?"

"Senator Travis had a penchant for rough sex and he'd been with Lori Andrews. We also found Lori Andrews's blood in Travis's cabin."

Kerrigan briefed Maria on the lab report. "And there's more," he continued. "Carl Rittenhouse was Senator Travis's administrative assistant. He told me that he brought Lori Andrews to the cabin where Travis was murdered, a few months ago. Then he told me about an incident in D.C. where it appeared that Travis had beaten up a woman."

"Travis might have beaten up Lori, but that doesn't clear Dupre," Maria insisted. "Dupre could have murdered her to keep her from testifying after Travis beat her at the cabin."

"That's a theory," Kerrigan agreed. "What I need to know is whether we have a legal obligation to disclose to Jaffe the information we have about Andrews's death."

"I'll look into it."

"There's something else. Amanda wants all the police reports of a 1970 shootout at a drug house in North Portland and a drug killing from 1972."

"Why does she want that?"

"That's what I need you to tell me. Get the reports and tell me why they bear on this case. If Amanda wants them, there's got to be something in them that will cause us trouble."

thirty-six

The state medical examiner's office, a tree-shaded, two-story red-brick building on Knott Street, looked more like a real estate office than a morgue. Kate Ross parked in the lot at the side of the building, crossed the well-tended lawn, and climbed the steps to the front porch. She asked for assistant ME Sally Grace at the front desk, and moments later she was sitting in Grace's office.

Dr. Grace, a slender woman with frizzy black hair, had a dry sense of humor and a sharp intelligence that made her an excellent witness. Kate had seen her testify on several occasions, and had spoken to her in the course of a few investigations.

"I pulled the file on Michael Israel," Grace said after they got the small talk out of the way.

"Norman Katz did the autopsy, but he's not with the office anymore."

"Did Dr. Katz conclude that Israel committed suicide?"

"That's the official finding."

Kate heard the hesitation in the ME's voice. "You don't concur?"

"It would probably be my finding, too, but there are a couple of anomalies. Not enough to challenge Norm's conclusion," Dr. Grace said quickly, "but, on the phone, you did ask me to see if there was any way that Israel's death could have been a homicide, so I looked at everything from that angle."

"What did you find?"

"Two things. First, Israel had six hundred nanograms per milliliter of temazepam in his blood. Restoril is the trade name. It's like Valium, and the usual therapeutic level would be somewhere between one-hundred-ninety and five-hundred-seven nanograms per milliliter, so the level is high."

"Could someone have drugged Israel and faked the suicide?" Kate asked.

"It's possible, but taking a sedative makes sense if Israel was going to commit suicide. He might

have needed to calm himself to get up the
courage to do the deed. Now six hundred nanograms per milliliter is high, but it's not so high
that it suggests that someone drugged him. He
could have just taken too much."

"Okay. You said two things bothered you. Give
me the rest of it."

Dr. Grace showed Kate a color photograph of
the crime scene. Israel's upper body lay on a
green desk blotter stained red by the blood that
had pooled under his head. Grace pointed to a
raw red spot on Israel's temple.

"That's the entry wound. Do you see the black
halo of gunshot residue that surrounds it?"

Kate nodded. The residue looked like a perfect
circle that had been drawn with a compass.

"When a person commits suicide by gunshot,
they usually eat the gun or shoot themselves in
the temple. With a temple shot, the victim is going to screw the barrel into his skin, so I would
expect to find a tight contact wound, not this circle of gunpowder. Israel's wound was a near contact, which means that the gun barrel was not
touching his temple when it went off. Six hundred nanograms per milliliter of temazepam
might not have been enough to put out Israel
completely. If it did put him under, the dose is

light enough so he could have awakened. If Israel was drugged first and someone put the gun in Israel's hand and held it next to his temple, he could have flinched and that could account for the near-contact wound.

"Of course, this is pure theory. Israel might have flinched anyway before he pulled the trigger."

"You're sure he shot himself?"

"I'm sure he was holding the gun when it went off."

Grace pointed to Israel's right hand in the crime scene picture. A layer of soot peppered Israel's thumb and index finger and the webbing between them.

"That's gunshot residue on his hand, which you'd expect to find if he was holding the gun when it was fired."

Kate took a moment to digest what she'd been told.

"If you had to bet—suicide or homicide—where would you put your money?"

Dr. Grace tossed Kate a copy of the suicide note that she'd found in the file.

The note said:

Pamela Hutchinson was carrying my baby. When I refused to marry her she

threatened to expose me. I shot her with the gun I am using to take my life. I made the murder look like a mugging gone wrong. No one suspected me, but I have never been able to forget what I did and I can no longer live with my guilt. Maybe God will forgive me.

"What do you think?" Grace asked when Kate had read it.

"The note is pretty formal. I'd expect something a little more emotional. But . . ." Kate hesitated then answered: "Suicide."

"Me too. And it would take very clear evidence to make me change my mind. What made you look into this after all these years?"

"A fairy tale, Sally. A fairy tale."

thirty-seven

Tim Kerrigan parked in Harvey Grant's driveway at eight o'clock at night. A heavy rain was falling, and the prosecutor dashed from the car to the shelter of the portico where he jabbed repeatedly at the bell.

"She called my house," Kerrigan said as soon as Grant opened the door. The judge could smell alcohol on his breath. "**My house!** Cindy answered the phone."

"Come in, Tim."

Kerrigan ran a hand through his hair as he pushed past the judge and headed for the den. He looked wild and on the brink of doing something desperate.

"I take it that you've made a decision," Grant said when Kerrigan was seated with a glass of scotch in his trembling hand. The prosecutor stared at the floor.

"She hasn't left me a choice. She says that she's going to the police next week if Dupre's case hasn't been dismissed. I kept trying to explain the problems with a dismissal but she wouldn't listen. She's . . . she's irrational. So . . ."

Kerrigan could not finish. He took another stiff drink.

"You've made the right decision, Tim."

Kerrigan put his head in his hands. "What have I gotten myself into?"

Grant laid a hand on Tim's shoulder. "Nothing you won't survive as a much stronger person. Right now your emotions are dominated by fear and doubt. Once Bennett is dead you'll realize how grand your future is going to be."

"I'll go to Hell."

"There is no Hell, Tim, and there is no eternal punishment. For you there will only be freedom when Ally Bennett is dead. Your family will be safe. You will become a United States senator and be in a position to do good for a great number of people."

"What do I do now?"

"Nothing rash. You have to detach yourself from what you're going to do. It's the only way you'll be able to handle the pressure. You must be calm. You must always remember that you're doing this for your family."

Tim took a deep breath. He closed his eyes.

"Have you thought about how you're going to accomplish your task?" Grant asked.

"I've thought about some of my cases, what went wrong. I don't want to make a stupid mistake."

"Good."

"My big problem is that I don't know where Bennett lives. I had her address from the police reports in Dupre's case. I called the manager. She's gone. She moved out in the middle of the night and stiffed him for the rent."

"She'll contact you, Tim. She wants her money. You'll have to kill her when you meet."

"Yes. I'll . . . I'll do it then."

"There's one thing we haven't talked about," Grant said. Tim focused on the judge. "Bennett mentioned some tapes."

"She wants to sell them for fifty thousand dollars."

Grant smiled. "Remember I told you that there are people who care about you, friends who want to protect you and see you succeed?"

Tim nodded.

"The money will be no problem. It will be provided in any form that Miss Bennett demands."

"Judge, I . . ."

Grant held up a hand. "The money means
nothing compared to the welfare of you and your
family. But you can't give it to her unless she
gives you these tapes. Do you understand?"

"Of course."

"They're very important."

"I'll get them."

"I know you will. I have great confidence in
you. When you hear from Miss Bennett, call me
immediately."

"I will."

"And relax, Tim. You're not alone. You're with
your friends. No one can touch you now."

"I wish I could believe that."

Grant touched him on the shoulder. "You can,
Tim. Alone, you're just a man, but with us to pro-
tect you, you will be invincible. Now go home to
Megan and Cindy."

The judge walked Kerrigan to the front door and
watched him drive away. As soon as Tim's car was
out of sight, Grant returned to his den and made
a phone call.

"It's done," he said as soon as the phone was answered.

"Do you think he'll follow through?"

"He really has no other choice. But there's backup if he falters."

"Good."

"We have another problem that I wanted to run by you," Grant said. "Amanda Jaffe made a motion for discovery in the Dupre case."

"So?"

"She wants the police reports for the nineteen-seventy shootings at Pedro's drug house and the reports about Jesus Delgado's murder."

"Do you think she's onto the club?" Grant's friend sounded concerned.

"I don't know but I don't think we should take any chances."

"You want to kill her?"

"No. The next lawyer who was appointed would see the motion and want to know what was in the reports, and we don't know who in her firm knows about the request." Grant laughed ruefully. "We can't kill everyone."

"So what do you suggest?"

"We need to control Jaffe," Grant said. "I've had a tail on her since she started representing

Dupre. She's seeing a psychiatrist because of what happened while she was representing Vincent Cardoni. I've got a copy of her psychiatrist's file. I think she can be frightened into backing off on the reports and laying down on Dupre's cases."

thirty-eight

Amanda worked until seven-fifteen on a motion to suppress. She could have worked a little longer, but she was tired, and Agatha Christie's **Witness for the Prosecution** was on TV at eight. After locking the office, she headed for the eight-story garage where her car was parked. A cold rain was falling, and there were few people on the street. Amanda hunched under her umbrella. When she reached the garage, a slender man followed her into the elevator. He wasn't carrying an umbrella, and his long dark hair was beaded with water. The man smiled. Amanda nodded and pressed the button for six. The man punched the button for seven.

The garage was open to the elements, and Amanda felt a blast of wind as soon as she stepped out of the elevator. There was no one else around, and only a few cars were left at this hour. Amanda's heartbeat sped up and she became hyperalert, something that happened often in isolated situations since the attack by the surgeon.

Amanda heard footsteps. The man from the elevator was walking a few paces behind her. Amanda fought to keep her panic at bay. She told herself that he was just looking for his car, but she still slid her keys between her fingers, points out, after using the remote on her key chain to unlock her car.

Amanda quickened her pace. To her relief, the footsteps behind her stayed steady. The distance between them widened and she started to relax. Then two men stepped out of the shadows, cutting her off from her car. One of the men stared past Amanda to the man who was following her, and the other man smiled. Amanda spun, sick with fear, and drove her keys into the face of the man behind her. He screamed as Amanda raced by him toward the exit stairs. If she made the street, she could shout for help, but her attackers were coming fast. She'd never have time to open the steel exit door. Amanda veered right and raced down the ramp seconds before a shoulder crashed into her, knocking her off her feet. She threw out her hands to break her fall. The keys went flying as her knees smashed into the concrete. She ignored the pain and struck out, but the man who had tackled her buried his head in her back and she had no place to land a punch. Then the other two men were looming over her. The man she'd punched with the keys was bleeding. He knelt down, said "Bitch," and slammed a fist into Amanda's face. Her head bounced off the concrete, stunning her.

The wounded man drew back his arm again. Before he could strike, the third man grabbed his coat and yanked him back. Amanda stared at the third man's flat, pockmarked face. Their eyes met. Amanda screamed. A hand clamped over her mouth. The man with the pockmarked face took a rag and a bottle of liquid out of his pocket. Amanda felt a surge of adrenaline and almost broke free. The hand over her mouth released, and the rag took its place. She tried to hold her breath but the fumes worked their way into her nostrils. A moment later, she passed out.

It took a second for Amanda to feel damp and cold as the water from the puddle in which she'd been dumped worked its way through her clothes.

"Sleeping Beauty is getting up," someone said.

Amanda turned toward the voice. A sharp pain in her head made her grimace. Raindrops bounced off her face.

"Do we get to fuck her now?" the wounded man asked.

"Patience," answered the man with the pock-marked face, who was obviously the leader.

"I want to make this bitch scream. Look at my face."

The leader nudged Amanda with the toe of his boot.

"What do you say, **señorita?** You want us to make sweet love to you? It would be something you'd never forget. We are very good lovers."

A wave of nausea swept through Amanda. She rolled to her side and fought the urge to throw up, afraid to show any weakness.

The leader turned to the man who'd tackled Amanda. "I don't think she likes us." He looked down at her. "But that doesn't make any difference, does it, Amanda."

It took a second to register that they knew her name. She looked up at the leader.

"What you want to do, what you don't want to do, doesn't matter one bit. We own you. We can fuck you, beat you, cut up your face and make you look real ugly so no one would ever want to fuck you again. It's all up to us."

Fear heightened Amanda's senses. She looked around. They'd driven her into the woods. The black silhouettes of trees towered over her. She pushed herself into a sitting position. It hurt to move.

"If you're thinking of running, don't. Running will only earn you a beating. Do you want a beating?"

Amanda stared at her tormentor but did not answer. He reached down, grabbed a handful of hair, and jerked her head up. Amanda gritted her teeth.

"Let's get one thing straight. You don't have free will anymore. Understand? If we tell you to do something, you do it. If we ask you a question, you answer. Now, do you want a beating?"

"No," Amanda gasped. He released her hair and she fell back on the ground. As she lay on the wet dirt, terror overwhelmed her. She had escaped the surgeon only to find herself trapped and helpless again, and this time she was alone, without hope of rescue.

"What are these?"

Amanda tried to focus on the object that dangled from the leader's hand.

"My keys," she answered.

"That's right. We have the keys to your condo, the keys to your father's house, the keys to your office. You can't keep us out. We could go to your condo right now and destroy everything you own. We could go to your father's house and slit his throat. We can do whatever we want. You understand?"

Amanda nodded.

"Stand up."

Amanda struggled to her feet. She was still woozy from being drugged, and her limbs felt like spaghetti.

"Take off your clothes."

Amanda's eyes began to tear, and she bit her lip but could not move any other part of her body. The leader hit her hard in the solar plexus. She doubled over and sank to her knees. This time she did throw up. The men watched her without speaking. She fell on all fours and vomited some more. When she stopped, a hand reached down. It was holding a handkerchief. She recognized it as one she had in her purse.

"Here. Clean up," the leader said.

She wiped her mouth.

"We'll try again." His voice was calm and patient. "Stand up and take off your clothes."

Amanda struggled to her feet and removed her raincoat. She was wearing a skirt and blouse and her fingers tripped on the buttons. The leader showed no emotion as Amanda stripped, but the other two looked excited. As soon as she stepped out of her skirt and took off her blouse, goose bumps rose on her skin. The rain and the wind chilled her to the bone and she began to shiver. Her hair hung limp and heavy with water.

"Lose the bra and the panties."

Amanda did as she was told. Her tears mixed with the rain that coursed down her cheeks. She stared past the men into the dark forest.

"That was good. You did what you were told. Now I have a question for you. You ready to answer?"

Amanda nodded, too afraid to speak.

"What can we do to you?"

"What?"

The leader nodded, and the man she'd punched with her keys grabbed her right nipple and twisted. Amanda screamed. The man twisted again. When she reached for his hand, he hit her in the ribs. Amanda fell to the ground, gasping for air. The men waited. She started to struggle to her knees, but the leader put a toe in her side, and Amanda toppled back into the mud.

"Stay there," he commanded. "It'll make it easier for us to fuck you if you miss this question again. Now, listen up. What can we do to you?"

"What . . . whatever you want."

"Good answer, but be more specific."

"Ra . . . rape me."

"Correct. What else?"

"Beat me."

"Anything else?"

Amanda's body was shaking from cold and fright.

"Kill me."

"Good. But you forgot one thing that's worse than anything you mentioned."

Something else occurred to Amanda, but she couldn't say the word.

"No," she gasped between sobs.

"I think you figured it out, haven't you? We can take you to someplace cold and dark, where no one will ever find you, and conduct experiments in pain."

Suddenly, Amanda was back in the tunnel. She was naked then, too, and the surgeon was priming her fear by telling her how he would subject her to experiments in pain. Amanda curled in a ball.

"You get it now, bitch? You understand?"

Amanda was too terrified to answer. She braced for punishment, but no one hit her.

"Now listen to me. I'm going to tell you how you can save yourself." Amanda stared into space.

"I'm going to tell you to do something. If you do it, you'll be safe. If you don't, those you love will die and you will be taken away to spend the rest of your life in agony. And it will be a long life, very long. Now ask me how you can save yourself."

"How . . . how can I save myself?"

Amanda's teeth chattered and she barely got the words out.

"You will stop investigating Jon Dupre's case and you will make certain that Dupre is convicted of murder and sentenced to death. Do that and you will survive. Keep poking your nose into the case and you know the consequences. Now get dressed."

Amanda wasn't sure she'd heard the man correctly until her panties fell across her face. They were sopping wet and covered with mud, but she scrambled into them. She rolled over and found the rest of her clothes. As she dressed, her keys landed next to her feet.

"Walk straight ahead for a quarter mile and you'll find a logging road and your car."

The men turned their backs to her and faded

into the darkness. Amanda struggled into her shoes and stood up. Her body was trembling uncontrollably. She wanted to get to her car and the heater, but she was afraid that the men were waiting for her in the woods, that they had built up her hopes so that they could capture her again and crush them. When the shaking began to rattle her teeth, she forced her feet forward. Then she ran. Normally, Amanda could run a quarter mile in a little over a minute, but tonight her feet tripped over themselves. When she broke out of the woods onto the logging road, she sobbed with relief. The men were gone and her car was at the side of the road. Amanda got in and locked the doors. Her hand shook so badly that it took forever to fit the car key in the ignition. Then the car started and the heater, cranked to maximum, began pumping out hot air. She started driving, sobbing quietly. What was she going to do? She couldn't bear being alone. She wanted to run to her father, but what if she was followed? They could kill Frank to demonstrate their power. They were right. They could do anything they wanted to do.

Amanda parked her car in the condo garage but she didn't get out immediately. She imagined her kidnappers lurking in the dark waiting to take her again—the punch line to a cruel joke. When she mustered the courage to leave her car, she took the stairs instead of the elevator and peered down the hall before racing to her condo. Once inside, she double-bolted her door. Then she checked every inch of her loft. When she was certain that she was alone, she went into the bathroom and ripped off her clothes. In the shower, tears of shame and frustration flowed as the hot water washed away the grime.

Amanda lost track of how long she stood under the cascading water and how many times she soaped herself. At some point, she left the shower stall and dressed in sweats and heavy socks. Her body felt clean, but she felt soiled and empty. She curled up on her couch and stared through her high windows at the lights of nighttime Portland. What was she going to do? If she was responsible for Jon Dupre's execution, she would be a murderer. If she didn't follow her captors' instructions, innocent people, including her father, could die. She didn't want to think about what might happen to her.

Amanda wrapped her arms across her breasts. She felt so helpless and she hated that feeling. But she was helpless. These people knew exactly how to control her. They'd made her relive her terror at the hands of the surgeon and they had threatened her father—the person she loved most in the world. But who were they?

This was the first time since she'd been attacked in the parking garage that Amanda had been composed enough to ask that question. Once she did, the answer was obvious. The Vaughn Street Glee Club did exist.

Part Five

AN EYE FOR AN EYE

thirty-nine

Amanda dragged herself into the bedroom at eleven-thirty and tried to sleep, but every time she closed her eyes she was back in the woods. She curled into a fetal ball, shivering despite the blankets. Exhaustion finally knocked her out a little after two-thirty, but she jerked awake several times with night sweats from bad dreams. When she woke up for good, it was still dark. A machine-gun rain rattled her windowpanes. She had no energy for calisthenics. Amanda went to the kitchen, but all she could tolerate was toast and tea. She cried while the water boiled.

Amanda would not even think of leaving her apartment. What if the men were waiting for her in her garage or outside her door? At nine, she called the office to say that she was sick. She asked Daniel Ames to cover an afternoon court appearance, then got back into bed but she could not sleep. She tried to read but she couldn't concentrate. She kept on reliving the terror of the kidnapping.

Amanda went into the living room and turned on the television. An old movie distracted her for a while, but she started crying in the middle of it. At noon, she forced herself to fix lunch because it gave her something to do. She was making a sandwich when the phone rang, startling her so much that her knife clattered to the floor. She let the answering machine take the call but picked up when she heard Kate's voice.

"How are you feeling?" Kate asked.

"Not so good."

"A cold?"

"Yeah, a bad one."

"Well, I may be able to cheer you up."

Kate told Amanda about her visit to the medical examiner and what she'd learned about Michael Israel's death. A day ago, Kate's news would have excited Amanda, but today she just felt numb.

"When I left the ME I started looking for similar suicides in Oregon," Kate said. "I only found one, but it was very interesting. Twelve years ago, Albert Hammond was on the Multnomah County circuit court. Do you remember him?"

"Dad tried a big murder case in his court when I was in junior high. Didn't he get in trouble with the Bar?"

"Big trouble. Hammond was arrested for DUII and assault on Dennis Pixler, the arresting officer. He was facing possible disbarment. Hammond told the papers that Pixler was crooked and had set him up. About a month later Pixler killed himself. He left a suicide note exonerating Hammond. It said that drug dealers who wanted revenge for a sentence that the judge had handed down had paid him to frame Hammond. The police questioned the dealers but they denied hiring Pixler, which you would expect.

"Anyway, Pixler had life insurance but the insurance company wouldn't pay off when the medical examiner ruled the death a suicide. Pixler's widow refused to accept the finding and sued the insurance company. The autopsy report was entered in evidence during the trial. Pixler had six hundred milliliters of temazepam in his blood. That's the same drug that was found in Michael Israel's blood, and the same quantity."

"That's interesting, Kate, but Robard would never let us introduce this stuff at trial."

"I agree, but it does make you think. And there's something else. Do you remember what happened to Albert Hammond?"

"Didn't he disappear?"

"Without a trace, about a year and a half later," Kate said. "But not before he got in more trouble with the law. Another drunk-driving arrest, but this time they also found cocaine in the glove compartment and a young woman in the car who wasn't his wife. Hammond swore that the woman put the drugs in his glove compartment when the cops pulled him over. He said she was a hitch-hiker he'd picked up because he was worried about a young woman hitchhiking alone. But the woman had a record for prostitution. She said that Hammond was full of shit about the cocaine and that he'd begged her to say it was hers as soon as they were pulled over."

"So, what happened?" Amanda asked, feeling that she had to say something to keep up her side of the conversation.

"Hammond posted bail and he was never seen again. The week that he disappeared, his wife was killed by a hit-and-run driver and his son and daughter-in-law were murdered in a home-invasion robbery."

"You're kidding."

"The week after Michael Israel died, his wife and child died when their house burned down. Interesting coincidence, huh?"

"I'd like to believe that we've found evidence of some big conspiracy here," Amanda said finally, "but this could just be wishful thinking. These incidents are years apart."

"If we could find a way to hook them up—find a connection between Israel, Hammond, and Travis. . . ."

Amanda had become so intellectually involved in Kate's report that she'd forgotten for the moment what would happen to her if her kidnappers learned that she was actively investigating Dupre's case. When she did remember, fear gripped her again.

"Thanks for calling," Amanda said, "but I'm really feeling lousy. I want to get some sleep."

"Sure," Kate said, her tone showing that she was upset by her boss's lack of enthusiasm for what she thought was some pretty classy detection. "Sorry I bothered you at home but I thought you'd want to know."

"I do. We'll talk more when I get back to the office."

Amanda hung up and looked at her sandwich. She couldn't eat it. She shuffled to the couch.

The remote was on the coffee table. Amanda channel-surfed but nothing interested her. She was so tired. She wished she could sleep. Ben Dodson could give her something to make her sleep but she would have to leave her apartment to get it. What were the chances that someone was waiting for her? It was the middle of the day. There were people all around. But even while she told herself she was safe, her body shook and tears welled up in her eyes.

Amanda dressed in a hooded sweatshirt, jeans, and sneakers. She pulled up the hood and donned dark glasses to hide her bruises. No one was waiting outside her door and there was no one in the elevator. She was afraid to go into the garage, so she rode the trolley across town, comforted by the people who surrounded her but constantly scanning the crowd for danger.

Ben Dodson was shocked when his receptionist showed Amanda into his office. She looked like a homeless person, and she hadn't been able to conceal all of the purple-and-yellow bruises.

"What happened to you?" he asked, staring at her battered face.

Amanda looked down. "I'm okay," she mumbled.

"Are you sure?"

"Please, Ben, I don't want to discuss it."

Dodson opened his mouth then shut it. Amanda was his patient and he wouldn't press her.

"Why are you here?" he asked. "This isn't a scheduled appointment."

"You said you could give me something to help me sleep. I . . . I really need it."

Amanda choked back a sob and Dodson guided her into a chair.

"Has something happened to make your situation worse?" Dodson probed.

"Please, Ben. Just give me something to help me sleep. Can you do that without asking questions?"

"Yes. I can prescribe some alprazolam."

The name of the drug startled Amanda. "What is that?"

"It's an antianxiety drug. You've probably heard the trade name, Xanax. Why?"

"When they did the autopsy on Senator Travis, alprazolam showed up in his tox screen. I didn't know what it was and I was going to ask someone, but I forgot. Do you think there's anything odd about his taking the drug?"

"What was the dosage?"

"I don't remember, but I can call my office and find out."

"Use my phone."

Amanda called her secretary and told her to get the information from the Dupre file. Amanda relayed the results of the tox screen to Dodson. He seemed surprised.

"Are you sure your secretary read the report correctly?" Dodson asked.

"Yeah. I remembered the result once she told it to me. Why?"

"The readings are not what I'd expect to find if a person was taking a prescription amount."

"What's the problem?"

"That strong a dose would leave him dopey as hell."

"What do you mean by dopey?"

"He'd be ambulatory but his legs wouldn't work all that well and he'd have trouble thinking clearly."

"Why would Travis take so much that he'd get dopey?"

"I have no idea. Maybe he was double-dosing or maybe he just made a mistake."

While Amanda remembered what Kate had said about the tranquilizers found in the Israel and Pixler autopsies, Dodson studied her battered face again.

"Are you involved in something dangerous, Amanda?"

She looked up. Dodson saw fear in his patient's eyes.

"Why would you ask that?" Amanda said.

"Your face for one thing and . . . well, something happened. . . ."

"Something involving me?"

She was terrified. Had Ben been threatened? Were the men who attacked her coming after him?

"I may be wrong but I think someone broke into my office and went through your file."

Dodson explained about finding the paper from Amanda's file under his desk.

"My secretary didn't look at your file and I'm certain that the paper was not under my desk the evening before I found it because I remember dropping a pen on the floor. The paper was sticking out. I'd have seen it when I picked up the pen."

Amanda stopped listening to Dodson. The men who had kidnapped her had read her file and Dodson's diagnosis of post-traumatic stress disorder. The pockmarked man had used the phrase "experiments in pain." When she'd been taken hostage by the surgeon, he terrified her with his plans to subject her to experiments that would measure her pain threshold. The surgeon had stripped her, and that is why her captors had forced her to strip. Amanda's fear was replaced by anger. The bastards had intentionally manipulated her emotions to force her to relive the horror of her capture by the surgeon.

"Amanda?"

Dodson's voice brought her out of her reverie.

"I don't want to frighten you, but I felt that I had a duty to let you know."

"I'm glad you told me," Amanda said. Dodson was struck by the steel in her voice. "You've helped a lot."

forty

Amanda shut the door to her father's office. He came to his feet when he saw her face.

"Jesus, Amanda—what happened?"

"I was attacked last night. Three men kidnapped me in the parking garage."

Frank rounded his desk. "Are you okay? Did they . . ."

"They hit me a few times, but they didn't do anything else. Physically, I'm fine. I'm just scared, and that's what they wanted. But I'm mad, too."

"Did you call the police?"

"No. I can't. You'll understand when I explain what happened. Sit down, Dad, this could take a while."

Amanda started by telling Frank Billie Brewster's story about the Michael Israel suicide and the assertion of Pedro Aragon's man, Sammy Cortez, that Israel had really been murdered on the orders of powerful men who worked with Aragon and called themselves The Vaughn Street Glee Club.

"Cortez was willing to talk about Pedro Aragon and the club until Wendell Hayes visited him at the jail. Billie thinks that Aragon's men kidnapped Cortez's daughter to shut him up and used Hayes as the messenger."

"Any lawyer would tell a client not to talk to the cops."

"I don't think that Hayes was just any lawyer. Remember Paul Baylor told me that he thought the wounds on Dupre's hands and forearm were defense wounds?" Frank nodded. "Dupre says that Hayes smuggled the knife in and attacked him."

"I don't know, Amanda. This sounds very farfetched."

"Jon Dupre supplied Senator Travis with women, including Lori Andrews, the woman whose body was found in Forest Park. Travis was connected to Aragon. And I discovered a connection between Aragon and Hayes that goes back to the seventies."

Amanda told Frank about the drug-house massacre and the guns stolen from Wendell Hayes's home that were linked to it.

"Here's the kicker, Dad. The house where the massacre took place was on Vaughn Street. I think that The Glee Club exists. I think it started at that drug house when Aragon and Hayes were still in their teens."

"This is pretty hard to believe, Amanda. I know these men."

"How well, Dad? You said that you didn't really socialize with Hayes. You played golf with Senator Travis shortly before he was killed, but how well did you really know him?"

"Not that well," Frank admitted. He was quiet for a moment. When he spoke, he sounded distraught.

"You've got to resign from Dupre's case."

"I can't. If I drop off, it could put us in danger and they would just go after the next lawyer who was appointed to represent Dupre. Besides, the more I learn about Dupre's case, the more convinced I am that he's innocent of both murders."

Frank pounded a fist on the arm of his chair. "There's got to be something we can do."

"I haven't come up with a thing. I feel like I'm sealed in a box."

Frank started pacing. It was comforting to see

her father working with her on a case and to know that he was there for her.

"Okay, help me on this," Frank said. "The case against Dupre for killing Wendell Hayes is almost impossible to win, isn't it, even with this theory about this conspiracy?"

"Judge Robard won't even let me argue its existence without hard evidence and I don't have any."

"Then why did they come after you? Why let you know that you're onto them?" he paused. "You did something that scared them enough to force them into the open."

"I know about the suicide victims with the same drugs in their systems, but they were so far apart, and there's no evidence connecting the deaths. Besides, how would they know about Kate's investigation? She only told me about it this morning."

"There's got to be something else."

"Paul Baylor's opinion that Jon's wounds are defense wounds will give me a chance to argue that Hayes tried to murder Jon, but I can't see them trying to kill me over that."

"What did you say?"

"I can't think of anything I've done that would make them want to kill me."

Frank snapped his fingers. "They didn't kill you."

"I don't understand."

"If they wanted you dead they would have killed you last night. For some reason you're more valuable to them alive than dead."

"They want me to throw Dupre's case."

"The case is open and shut. They don't need you to throw it. No, you did something that can't be corrected by killing you. You must have left a trail of breadcrumbs that a new lawyer would follow even if you were dead. They think a lawyer who was assigned to replace you would see what they don't want seen."

"Which is what? I can't think of a single thing that would represent a huge threat to these people. Hell, Dad, we can't even prove they exist."

"It's not something you know, it's something . . . What have you filed with the court?"

"Motions, jury questionnaires, a lot of stuff."

"Whatever it is that's scaring them could be in the circuit court files. Otherwise they would have forced you to bring them your paperwork. But the court has your motions; the judge has them, the DA's office. They can't get rid of all the copies of everything you filed. And any lawyer appointed to represent Dupre would read what you filed. Go over your pleadings. You've stumbled onto something very dangerous to these people. You have to figure out what's keeping you alive."

"What will you do?"

"I don't know yet," Frank answered, but he had an idea he didn't want to discuss with Amanda until he'd worked it all out.

forty-one

Frank insisted that Amanda move in with him until they could figure out what to do. She had protested half-heartedly that she was probably being watched and the move would signal that she'd told her father what had happened to her. When Frank refused to change his mind, Amanda gave in without much of a fight.

Frank went with Amanda to her apartment and waited while she packed her bags. The first thing Frank did when they arrived at his house was to give her a .38 snubnose to carry with her. Frank had taken Amanda shooting since she was a little girl and she was comfortable with guns. The idea that she might have to shoot a person made her queasy, but after what she'd been through she knew she could do it. She wished that she'd had a gun in the parking garage.

Frank cooked dinner while Amanda put away her clothes in her old room. Frank still kept her trophies on a shelf and framed clippings about her swimming triumphs on the walls. There was something reassuring about her old room but she doubted that she'd feel safe tonight.

Amanda still did not have much of an appetite, but she forced herself to eat the salmon and rice that Frank cooked for her. During the meal, neither Jaffe spoke much. Afterward, Frank went into his den and made a phone call.

"I've got to meet a client," Frank said when he came out. "Don't worry, I shouldn't be too long. Keep the doors locked and keep a gun with you while I'm gone."

"Okay," Amanda answered, certain that her father was keeping something from her. She didn't want to stay alone but she knew Frank wouldn't desert her if he didn't have a good reason.

The music pouring out of The Rebel Tavern was so loud that Frank Jaffe could hear it in the gravel parking lot of the biker bar. An obese, bearded man in a motorcycle jacket staggered out just as Frank reached the door. He was anchored to a heavily tattooed woman dressed in black leather and wearing a dog collar.

Frank watched the couple stumble toward a big Harley, then stepped inside, where he was greeted by smoke and noise. He squinted through the haze and found Martin Breach sitting alone in a back booth. Scattered around the bar near the booth were three of the gangster's bodyguards.

Breach was dressed in lime-green polyester pants, a loud plaid jacket, and a Hawaiian shirt. His sense of style hadn't improved since the last time Frank and Amanda had met him at one of his strip joints during the Cardoni case. Breach was squat and heavyset with thinning, sand-colored hair. His skin was pale as plaster, because he rarely went outside. He waved to the attorney who had represented several of his associates over the years.

"Hey, Frank!" Breach said, flashing a wide grin as Frank slid into the booth.

"Thanks for meeting me, Martin."

"Beer, some hard stuff? It's on the house," said Breach, who owned The Rebel.

"Beer's fine," Frank answered as he filled a glass from the pitcher that stood in the middle of the table.

Breach had a silly grin and often looked sleepy or stupid. The gaudy, ill-matched clothes helped create an image of incompetence that disguised a sharp intelligence and a truly psychotic personality. Many a rival had figured this out moments before suffering a violent death.

Frank had thought long and hard before setting up this meeting. He had been dealing with criminals for more than thirty years and had no illusions about Breach. Doing business with the man was as close as he would ever come to doing business with the devil. But Frank would trade his soul to Satan to protect Amanda.

"So, Frank, what can I do for you?"

"You remember my daughter, Amanda?"

"Sure. Great kid, gutsy, too."

"Amanda is representing Jon Dupre."

"So."

Frank leaned forward. "This has to stay between us, Martin, because Amanda . . . She could be hurt badly if . . ."

"Talk to me, Frank."

"Three men kidnapped Amanda last night. They . . . they made her strip. They threatened to kill me and torture her if she didn't throw Dupre's case."

Breach showed no emotion. "Why are you here, Frank?"

"Have you ever heard of The Vaughn Street Glee Club?"

Surprise flickered across Breach's features. "Keep talking," he answered.

"Amanda thinks they're behind her kidnapping. It has something to do with the Dupre case."

Breach leaned back against the booth. He did not look nervous or afraid, but he did look wary.

"She needs help, Martin."

"Kidnapping, that's something you usually report to the police."

"We think that these people have someone in the cops—maybe more than one person."

Breach waited for Frank to tell him what he wanted. Frank hesitated, knowing that this was his last chance to step back from the brink. He jumped.

"Can you get these people to lay off Amanda?"

"I can't help you directly, Frank. I want to. I like your daughter. But I can't get involved with these people. You're right about the cops, but it goes deeper than that. These people could make me very uncomfortable. I'm not even sure who's who. Wendell Hayes was one of them. Him I'm sure of. I heard rumors about Senator Travis, and I know for sure that Pedro Aragon's people are involved. We have a truce, Pedro and me. He does his thing and I do mine. If it was Aragon's people who snatched your daughter, I can't get involved."

Frank's shoulders sagged. Coming to Breach had been a long shot, anyway. He started to stand.

"Sit down. I said **I** couldn't help you. But I may be able to put you in touch with someone who can watch Amanda's back."

"A bodyguard?"

"Something like that. This guy is freelance, ex–Delta Force. He's not cheap, but he's the best."

"Give me the number."

Breach shook his head. "It doesn't work that way. You just go about your business. Wait for a guy named Anthony to make contact."

Frank held out his hand. Breach took it.

"I won't forget this," Frank said.

"What are friends for?" Breach answered. Frank wondered what he'd gotten himself into.

forty-two

It took a moment or so for the flashing light in his rearview mirror to register, and a few more seconds for Tim to figure out that the police car wanted him to stop. He pulled to the side of a winding stretch of road in the West Hills where the lots were large and there was little traffic. Once the other car had parked behind him, Kerrigan saw that it was unmarked. Stan Gregaros got out. Kerrigan gripped the wheel and fought his panic. Was it possible that the detective knew about the plot to murder Ally Bennett? Was he going to be arrested?

Gregaros came around the passenger side and rapped on the window.

"Stan!" Kerrigan said a little too loudly after lowering the window. "Don't tell me I was speeding."

"No, Tim," the detective answered. "It's something bigger than that. Let me in."

Kerrigan unlocked the passenger door and Gregaros slid into the seat, propping a briefcase on his lap.

"So, what's up?" Kerrigan asked, trying to keep calm.

Gregaros grinned. "Welcome to the club."

"The club? I don't . . ."

Gregaros laughed. "It's okay, Tim. Didn't Harvey tell you that you'd have friends who would help you get through this problem with Ally Bennett? Well, I'm one of them."

Kerrigan closed his eyes and leaned back in his seat, his relief palpable. Gregaros opened the briefcase and took out two sheets of paper, a clipboard, and a plastic bag containing a revolver. Kerrigan's eyes fell on the revolver. Something about it looked familiar. Then he realized that it had been evidence in one of his earlier cases.

"Is that the revolver from the Madigan case?"

"I took it from the property room. The case is closed, so no one will be looking for it, but the use of a gun that was an exhibit in one of your cases will add to the authenticity of your confession if we ever have to use it."

"What confession?"

Gregaros handed Tim one of the sheets of paper, which Tim read.

I'm sorry for any pain that my death causes, but I could not live with my guilt anymore. I had a relationship with Ally Bennett, one of Jon Dupre's escorts, while our office was prosecuting his case. She threatened to expose me if I didn't dismiss Dupre's murder charges. I killed her with this gun. God help me.

"What is this?" Tim asked.

"Our insurance policy. Not everyone knows you as well as Harvey and I do. And even the best person can become weak under stress, so every new member signs one of these."

"You . . . you'd kill me?"

"We've had an occasion or two where we misplaced our trust. Those people were dealt with, and so were their families and close friends, anyone they could have told about us."

"You're threatening Cindy and Megan?"

Gregaros stared directly into Kerrigan's eyes. "It would be out of my hands, Tim, and there are those of us who believe that there are no limits where self-preservation is concerned."

The detective fastened a blank sheet of paper to the clipboard.

"I want you to copy the note in your own hand and sign it."

"What if I refuse?"

"You'd be completely on your own, and so would your family. I'm sure Harvey would try to convince the others that you wouldn't tell anyone about us, but they all know how much pressure you're under. I wish I could promise you that nothing would happen to you or your wife and kid, but I can't."

Suddenly Kerrigan's car felt like a cage. He was having trouble breathing.

"Look at you," the detective said. "You're a wreck, and why? That bitch, Ally. Think how good it's gonna feel when she's gone. That's the way to be safe, pal. Putting that whore in the ground will help your disposition better than a bottle of tranqs."

Gregaros handed Kerrigan a pen. Tim's hand shook when he copied the note and it looked as if it had been written in a moving car. When he was done, Gregaros put the signed confession in a plastic evidence bag and took back the note that Kerrigan had copied. Then he handed Kerrigan the pistol.

"This is the gun you'll use. You won't wear gloves. I'll be there to help if you need me, but you won't see me. When she's dead, I'll take the gun. You got all that?"

Kerrigan nodded because his mouth was too dry for him to try to speak. Gregaros looked Tim in the eye and waited until he was certain that Tim was listening.

"You ever killed anyone?"

Melissa Stebbins's face flashed in Tim's head but he shook his head anyway.

"That's what I figured. You never know, though." Gregaros grinned. "I'm gonna tell you how. It's easy if you do what I say. So pay attention."

forty-three

Amanda hadn't had much of an appetite since her kidnapping, and the first sign that she was starting to get back on her feet was the rumble of her stomach shortly before one. She walked down the block to a Mexican restaurant and ordered a taco salad. As she ate, her mind drifted to Jon Dupre's case. Even with everything she knew, she had a hard time seeing herself convincing a jury to acquit Jon for the murder of Wendell Hayes. Tim Kerrigan could prove beyond any doubt, let alone a reasonable doubt, that Jon had killed his lawyer, so the only way to win was to convince the jury that Jon had acted in self-defense. To do that, she had to prove that one of the state's most prominent attorneys had risked his career by smuggling a shiv into the jail to murder someone he hardly knew. She might get some mileage out of Paul Baylor's testimony, but Hayes's motive was the sticking point. After all, Dupre was already facing the death penalty. Why risk everything to kill Dupre when there was a good chance that the state would do it for you?

Amanda paused with her fork halfway to her lips. That was a good question. She played around with it. What circumstances would force Hayes to act so quickly? There was only one answer that occurred to Amanda. Hayes had to believe that Jon knew something that could severely damage him or his fellow conspirators. What could Jon possibly know that was that explosive? Only one person could answer that question. Amanda ate quickly then headed for the jail.

Jon Dupre had adapted to the restrictions his chains placed on his movements and he slid onto his chair with a practiced motion.

"How come a high-priced lawyer like you is visiting the jail instead of taking a power lunch?" Dupre asked.

"Hey, Jon, the defense never rests."

Dupre smiled. Amanda realized that this was the first time she'd gotten him to lighten up. Maybe she was finally cracking Dupre's shell.

"So," he asked eagerly, "do you have some news?"

"Not really, just questions."

"About what?"

"Did Wendell Hayes try to kill you to keep you from talking to the cops about a conspiracy of powerful men that includes Pedro Aragon?"

"What the fuck is this? Who are you working for?"

"I'm working for you, Jon, but you don't make it easy. Talk to me."

Dupre cast a quick look at the guard who was watching them through the glass. He leaned forward and dropped his voice so low that Amanda could barely hear him.

"Stay away from this. You can't help me and you'll get yourself dead."

"Jon . . ."

"Listen to me." He moved so the guard could not see his face. "When we talk, cover your mouth."

"What?"

"You have no idea what you're dealing with. The guard could be one of them, he could be a lip-reader."

"You're serious?"

"Just do it."

Dupre's outburst convinced Amanda that he

believed they were in danger. She trusted the guards but did as Dupre asked, to humor him.

"They sent Hayes to shut me up," Dupre whispered. "These people are everywhere. They murdered Oscar Baron."

"Baron was killed by burglars."

"That's how they made it look. I sent Baron some evidence to show the FBI."

"After I started representing you?" Amanda asked angrily.

"Calm down. This was after our first contact visit. I didn't trust you, so I paid Oscar to negotiate a deal. I was going to fire you as soon as he had it in place. Only they must have found out and killed him."

"Whoa, slow down. What did you have to bargain with?"

"I've been taping my drug deals with Pedro Aragon's people. I figured I could use them if I was ever busted and my case went south." He hung his head. "I had Ally bring them to Oscar. The newspaper said he was tortured before he was killed. Knowing Oscar, I don't think he'd hold out for long, so they must have everything Ally gave him."

Now Amanda knew who had searched Ally

Bennett's apartment and what they were looking for.

"Have you heard from Ally since Baron was killed?" she asked.

"We haven't talked since I asked her to take the tapes to Oscar."

"Kate Ross was at her apartment. Someone trashed it."

Dupre looked alarmed. "You don't think . . . ?"

"I don't know what to think. If she ran, where would she go?"

"I don't know, Amanda. Honestly, I don't."

"If she contacts you, make certain that she calls me. So far, she's your best chance of beating the Travis charge."

"What do you mean?"

"Kate talked to Joyce Hamada. She said she and another woman were at your house on the night that Senator Travis was murdered but Ally chased them out when you had some trouble with a drug you took. If Ally was with you when Travis was murdered she can testify about that. If the jurors believe her they'll have to acquit you. We need to get in touch with her."

"They don't give me many calls," Dupre said. "The one time I tried to call after Oscar was killed there was no answer at her apartment and she didn't answer her cell phone."

Amanda got both phone numbers from Dupre.

"Do you think that Hayes tried to kill you to protect Aragon?" Amanda asked.

"No one knew about those tapes when Hayes came after me."

Something about the sound of Jon's voice made Amanda pause. She cocked her head and studied him. He couldn't meet her eye.

"Then why did Hayes do it?" she asked. "Why did he feel that he had to act so quickly?"

"Maybe he was worried that I'd try to make a deal with the cops."

"And tell them what?"

"About Senator Travis and these people who protected him. Travis liked rough sex. When he finally went too far with one of my girls he used one of Pedro's men to clean up his mess."

"This was Lori Andrews, right?"

Dupre nodded. "He really had a thing for Lori and he thought I'd keep him from seeing her, so he tried to get on my good side. He hinted that he could protect my operation so I'd never have to worry about the cops. I didn't believe him, so he told me about these people."

"Did he tell you who they were?"

"No. He didn't mention any names, but he hinted that there were judges and cops in it, even DAs. It sounded far-fetched until Hayes tried to fillet me."

Something was still troubling Amanda, something that didn't make sense. It took her a moment to figure out what it was.

"You didn't tell Travis about the tapes, did you?"

"No."

"And you couldn't prove that Travis was in this club?"

Dupre nodded.

"And you didn't know anyone else in the club, right?"

"Only Travis, and I wasn't sure that he wasn't bluffing to keep me from hurting him."

"It doesn't sound like these people would be worried about you hurting anyone. They didn't know about the tapes and they wouldn't know that you knew about the group unless Travis told them. Even if he did, he'd also tell them that you didn't know anyone's identity but his, and Travis was dead by the time Hayes tried to murder you. So why did he do it? It doesn't make any sense, something's missing. What aren't you telling me?"

Dupre averted his eyes and licked his lips nervously.

"This isn't twenty questions, Jon. If you want to have any chance of walking out of here you have to tell me everything. I told you I'll hold it in confidence, and it's not going to do you any good if you're dead."

Dupre took a deep breath. "Okay, I'll tell you. There are some other tapes. I only held out because they're all I've got left. I was counting on them to bargain with if things got really bad."

"I've got news for you, things are really bad right now, and they are going to get worse if we don't get some breaks. Now, what is on those tapes?"

Amanda had a hearing in another case at three. She called Kate on her cell phone as she walked across the street from the Justice Center to the courthouse. Kate was out, and Amanda left a message saying that it was urgent she call her. As Amanda went through the security checkpoint, her eyes darted around the main floor, lingering for a moment on a tall man in a leather trench coat before shifting to a slender man in a windbreaker and a Mariners' baseball cap, lounging on a bench, and finally passing over a muscular woman in a navy-blue pea coat who was staring at her. Everyone looked dangerous.

Amanda walked up to the fifth-floor court-room. Inside, she saw a few lawyers and court personnel she knew. There were also some court watchers; unemployed or retired men and women who preferred watching court cases to viewing the daytime soaps. None of the men who had kidnapped her were in the room.

Frank was waiting for Amanda outside the courthouse to take her home when she was finished with her hearing. He slipped her the .38. When they got to the parking garage, Frank pressed the button for their floor. Just as the elevator doors closed, Amanda thought she saw someone start up the stairs. Was he the slender man in the windbreaker and baseball cap she'd seen in the courthouse? Amanda tightened her hold on her gun.

They got to their car and drove home without incident. Frank parked in the garage. Amanda hefted her briefcase and waited for Frank to open the door and punch in the alarm code. They walked through the kitchen and into the living room. Amanda pulled her .38. A man was sitting in the dark. He was over six feet tall, rangy, and dressed in tan slacks and a dark turtleneck sweater. His shiny black hair was fastened in a ponytail, and he had the high cheekbones and bronze complexion of a Native American. The gun didn't seem to bother their visitor, because he smiled when Amanda sighted on him.

"I'm George. I work with Anthony," he said in a deep clear voice.

Frank relaxed. "Put the gun down, Amanda. He's here to help you."

"Who . . . ?"

"He's a bodyguard. I hired him."

George stood up and crossed the room with a confident stride.

"It's a pleasure to meet you, Ms. Jaffe." He smiled warmly. "I hope you'll forgive my dramatic entrance but I wanted to test Mr. Jaffe's security procedures. Obviously they're wanting, but we'll shore them up."

"Where is Anthony?" Frank asked him.

"You won't see him unless there's trouble, but he's around."

Amanda was still holding her gun.

"Do you know how to shoot your weapon?" George asked.

Amanda nodded.

"Good, but I don't want you shooting one of

the good guys. Our code word is 'red.' If there's a problem and someone shouts it out, you'll know they're friendly." George's smile widened. "Don't shoot them.

"I've had you under observation for a couple of days. There are some procedures I'd like to go over. I'll try not to make them cumbersome but they are necessary if we're going to keep you safe."

"How intrusive are you going to be?" Amanda asked.

"I'll be with you all the time but I'll try to blend in as much as possible."

Amanda looked skeptical. George would stand out in any crowd.

"I know," he smiled, as if he'd read her mind, "but part of the value in having a bodyguard is that it scares some people away. The people you're dealing with don't scare that easily, so it helps if they think I'm all you've got. Think of me as a diversion. The people you won't see until they're needed are very good at what they do."

forty-four

Kate waited until the sun went down before driving to Jon Dupre's riverfront house. In her pocket was the combination to his safe and a description of the envelope containing the tapes from the Travis fund-raiser, which Dupre had given Amanda at the jail; a .45 lay on the seat next to her. If she ran into any of Pedro Aragon's men, she wanted to be carrying a gun with stopping power.

Kate left the highway several miles south of Portland and drove along an unlit, two-lane country road for fifteen minutes before turning off onto a long dirt driveway. As she approached Jon's house from the side, she saw a deck projecting out over a swath of lawn that ended at the river. Kate parked her car around the side of the house where it wouldn't be seen from the road.

Then she went around the back, with her gun leading the way. All the doors were locked, but Kate had a set of lock picks she'd taken off of a perp when she was a cop. She'd practiced with them for fun but found that they occasionally came in handy. Now she jimmied the rear door and let herself into a finished basement. The alarm started to hum but she had the code.

Kate switched on her flashlight and played its beam over the finished basement. There was a wet bar at one end of the room and a pool table in the middle. A large-screen TV dominated one wall. Someone had been watching it recently. A beer can and a half-eaten pizza sat on a table next to a lounger.

According to Jon, the safe was under the floorboards in the laundry room at the bottom of the basement stairs. Kate decided to check out the rest of the house before opening the safe, to make sure that she was alone. The pizza and beer bothered her.

Kate crept up the stairs and opened the basement door slowly. The lights were off in the house. Kate stood still but heard no sounds on the main floor. She searched through the rooms quickly until she reached the bedroom. The rest of the house had an unlived-in feel, but someone had been using the bedroom recently. The blanket and top sheets had been thrown back as if someone had just gotten out of bed. A carrying bag with woman's clothes sat on the floor next to the dresser. There were men's clothes, probably Dupre's, in the dresser.

Kate checked the bathroom and found a toothbrush, a half-used tube of Crest, and a hairbrush on the sink. A small black kit with more bathroom items sat on a shelf. Kate hurried back to the basement determined to find the audiotapes and get out before the person staying in Dupre's house returned.

The safe was concealed under several linoleum tiles. Kate pried up the tiles and used Dupre's combination to open it, listening all the time for any sound from the top of the stairs. The safe was crammed full of videotapes, ledgers, and papers. Before she could sort through them, headlights swept across the back lawn. Kate drew her gun and listened. Moments later, car doors slammed and the front door opened.

Kate closed the safe and replaced the linoleum tiles. She was halfway across the basement when the door at the top of the stairs opened and the lights came on. Kate ducked behind the bar. A huge man wearing a parka and a smaller man in a windbreaker stopped at the bottom of the stairs. The big man was carrying a duffel bag.

"Look at that TV," the smaller man said. "It's almost as big as the one at the sports bar."

"We're not here to watch the tube. We're supposed to clean out the safe."

"There's a boxing match on ESPN, Chavez–Kramer. It'll be great on a big screen."

"I'm doin' what I'm supposed to. You do what you want."

The big man went into the laundry room. The small man grabbed the remote. Kate felt sick. On the big screen, two welterweights were circling each other. Halfway through the round, the large man hurried out of the laundry room and covered his ears. There was an explosion and the small man jumped out of his seat, a gun in his hand.

"Why didn't you tell me you were ready to blow the safe?" he screamed, waving the gun at the big man.

"I didn't want to interrupt your viewing pleasure."

"Fuck you. You scared the shit out of me."

The big man sighed. "Turn that off, will you. Let's get this over with."

"I'm watching the fight," the smaller man insisted stubbornly as he stuck his gun back in the pocket of his windbreaker.

A few minutes later, the big man emerged, carrying the duffel bag. Kate had a decision to make. There was no way she could get out the back door without attracting attention, but, if she waited for the men to leave, they would get away with the contents of the safe. Kate was an excellent shot and she was in a perfect position to take out both men, but she had no idea who they were. What if they were cops?

Kate stood up, gun drawn.

"Freeze, police!" she shouted. Both men jumped.

"You, watching the TV, take your gun out with your fingertips and drop it on the floor."

The small man hesitated and Kate blew out the TV screen.

"Geez," the man screamed, throwing an arm up to block the flying glass.

"Do it now!" Kate yelled, aiming between his eyes.

The small man did as he was told. Kate told him to kick the gun over to her. When the gun skittered over to her she bent down and put it in her belt.

"Okay, you," she said, pointing the gun at the big man. "I want the duffel and your gun. Be smart and I won't have to shoot you."

Without warning, the large man hurled the duffel bag at Kate and pulled out his own .45. Kate shot him in the knee a fraction of a second before the duffel hit her in the shoulder, knocking her off balance. The large man screamed as he collapsed. His gun went flying.

The other man charged. Kate shot him in the hip, knocking his legs out from under him. He grunted and crashed to the floor. The big man's teeth were clenched from pain but he was crawling toward his gun.

"You stupid fuck," Kate shouted at the big man. His fingers were inches from his gun. "Grab it so I can kill you."

The way Kate sounded made the big man freeze. She walked over and kicked him in the head, furious that he'd forced her to shoot both men. She grabbed the gun and the duffel. Then she backed out the door and pulled it shut. She didn't take a breath until she was on the freeway and she was certain that no one was following her.

Kate parked in Frank's driveway and Amanda walked out to meet her. Once she saw the grim look on her friend's face, she expected the worst.

"I just shot two guys," Kate said. "I hope it was worth it."

Amanda knew Kate's history with guns and was very concerned.

"Are you okay?" she asked.

"I'm shaking like a leaf."

Amanda led Kate into Frank's den. Kate dumped the duffel bag on the desk and sat down. Amanda went to the liquor cabinet and poured her friend a drink. Kate leaned forward, resting her forearms on her knees. She had been in two shootouts before this and it was always the same for her. During the action she was calm and focused, as if she was in a bubble that sealed off her emotions and slowed time to a crawl. When the action stopped, she was like a junkie going through withdrawal cold-turkey, and the raw emotions she'd sealed away while she was fighting for her life came flooding back. Her senses overloaded, filling her with fear because she had almost died, and self-loathing because she'd enjoyed the rush of combat.

"Tell me what happened," Amanda said as she handed Kate a glass of scotch. Kate's hand shook when she took her first drink but it was steadier by the time she finished telling Amanda about the gunfight at Dupre's house.

"Any idea who they were?" Amanda asked when Kate was finished.

"No, but they were after the contents of the safe."

"Did you call the cops?"

"Not yet. I wanted to check with you first."

"We should call. Jon gave you permission to go to his home and take the stuff in his safe. Those two men are burglars. They had no right to be there. They were stealing."

"Stealing what, though? If we send the cops to Dupre's house we'll have to tell them why I was there. They'll want to see what's in that duffel bag. I'm guessing that won't help our client."

"Let's find out," Amanda said, dumping tapes and papers onto the desktop. The audiotapes from Travis's fund-raiser were supposed to be in a plain white envelope. Amanda found several such envelopes containing audiotapes, but they had dates on them that did not match the evening of the Travis fund-raiser. Amanda played them on a tape recorder but she could tell within minutes that, although interesting, the tapes were not the right ones.

Kate had been going through a ledger while they listened. Every once in a while she would pick up a videotape and compare it to a notation in the ledger.

"If these tapes show what I think they do we could destroy a lot of careers."

"But not the careers I'm interested in," Amanda responded. "The tapes from the fund-raiser aren't here."

There was a television with a VCR in the den. Kate turned it on and slipped a tape into the VCR. She and Amanda watched quietly.

"Damn, I didn't know you could do that," Kate said as one of Dupre's escorts engaged in a series of sexual contortions.

"I certainly didn't think **he** could do that," Amanda answered. "I don't know how I'll ever be able to appear in court with him again with a straight face."

"If we give this stuff to the cops, they'll charge Jon with every prostitution crime in the criminal code, and the lives of every person on these tapes will be ruined," Kate said. "So, what do we do?"

"Good question," Amanda answered. She looked troubled. "I don't think we have any obligation to turn over these tapes. They're not evidence of any crime that's been charged. I'll call the state bar in the morning and talk to one of the lawyers who answers ethics questions, to see what they think.

"We've got to call the police about the shooting, though," Amanda said. "Those men could be seriously hurt. Now, go home and get some sleep."

"If I can."

Amanda placed her hands on her friend's shoulders and squeezed. "You didn't do anything wrong, Kate. You just protected yourself. I'll see you in the morning."

forty-five

On the evening of February 17, 1972, a clerk on a smoke break had seen three men gun down Jesus Delgado in the parking lot of a 7-Eleven in Northeast Portland. The clerk had written down the license number of the beat-up, dark blue Toyota in which the three killers had escaped. Moments after dispatch broadcast this information, the car passed Portland police officer Stanley Gregaros.

Stan was riding solo because his partner had developed a bad case of food poisoning early in their shift. The young cop followed the suspects as they zigzagged to a warehouse in a deserted industrial block. Gregaros crept around the side of the building expecting to find a gang of brutal thugs. Instead he saw three white kids in their early twenties, dressed in rugby shirts, crewneck sweaters, and chinos. They looked more like fraternity brothers than a trio of assassins. What gave the lie to the picture were the weapons, ski masks, and black clothing that the boys had piled on the hood of their car.

Gregaros knew that he should not approach three suspected murderers alone, no matter how uncharacteristic their looks and attire, but the only other car in the lot was a shiny black Ferrari—exactly the type of car these rich kids would drive. He feared that the frat boys would be gone by the time he radioed for backup, so he walked around the corner of the building and ordered the trio to freeze.

Gregaros expected the boys to quake with fear but, after their initial surprise, they had calmly followed his instructions to put their hands against the warehouse wall and spread their legs. While he was patting down his prisoners, Harvey Grant, the smallest boy, wondered aloud what the young policeman would do with fifty thousand dollars? Gregaros had laughed at the brazen and ridiculous bribe. Fifty thousand dollars was a lot of money for someone like Stan, who had been born poor, grown up hard, and joined the force after a tour in Vietnam with the Marines.

When Gregaros asked Grant where he would get that kind of money, Grant asked him if he knew that Jesus Delgado was the dead man in the 7-Eleven parking lot. Gregaros stood back and looked at the boys again. "No, it's not possible," he told himself. These guys couldn't be connected to Mexican gangsters. Then he took another quick look at the automatic weapons and ski masks stacked on the hood of the Toyota.

"Let us go and we'll take care of you," Grant had said. "Who knows, this might not be a one-shot deal. We can use a man inside the Portland police."

Gregaros hesitated.

"There's a downside to rejecting the offer," Grant continued.

"Oh?" Gregaros had said.

Grant had turned his head and smiled. Stan thought that he looked like one of those nerds on College Bowl.

"If you arrest us," Grant said, "we'll swear that we parked our car in this lot so we could smoke some weed, and found the Toyota just as it is, moments before you arrested us. It will be your word against ours. Do you know who we are?"

"Three punks who are starting to piss me off."

"Bzzz! Wrong answer," chimed in Wendell Hayes. "You're looking at the sons of three very influential and very rich men."

"Our daddies will never let us go to jail," Grant said. "We'll have the very best attorneys that money can buy, but we won't need them. Want to know why?"

"I'm listening."

"You're the only witness and you'll be dead."

Stan's response had been to pistol-whip Grant. The blow had brought the future judge to his knees. When he staggered to his feet, blood from a scalp wound trickling down the side of his face, there was a twisted smile on his lips.

"Police brutality," Grant had said cheerfully. "Now you're facing massive lawsuits and your credibility on the stand will be shot to hell. I'm just a little guy, sir, and you're a big brute. Boo-hoo. We'll have the journalists in a feeding frenzy and there won't be any pension for you. That's assuming, of course, that you're alive to collect it. Is that fifty thou sounding better?"

Gregaros had never regretted his decision to let the three boys go. He was rich beyond his dreams and more powerful than he ever thought possible, even if few people knew it.

While on the force, Gregaros had made evidence and people disappear in cases that affected the club's interests. Pedro Aragon's muscle was used for everyday intimidation, but Stan was used in special cases, like the one tonight.

The club had orchestrated Harold Travis's climb up the ladder of national politics. Then, just as he was on the brink of realizing the organization's greatest dream, the senator's ego had turned him into a liability. First, there was the cocaine and his brutal sexual encounters, culminating in the murder of Lori Andrews. Then, Travis had put himself into a position to be blackmailed by Jon Dupre.

McCarthy had arrested Jon Dupre for Travis's murder before the club could get to him. Then Wendell Hayes had failed to kill Dupre in the jail. It looked like their luck had changed when Oscar Baron brought Dupre's tapes to the meet with Manuel Castillo, but Baron didn't have the tape that could destroy all of the hard work that had gone into killing the anti-cloning bill. Some of the club members had invested heavily in the biotech companies that the bill was aimed at, and they stood to lose billions if anything went wrong.

Pedro's men had not found the tape when they ransacked Ally Bennett's apartment, and Bennett had disappeared the evening that Baron died. All of the club's efforts to find her had gone for naught—until Bennett surfaced to demand fifty thousand dollars for the very tape the club wanted.

Several hours earlier, Tim Kerrigan had visited Harvey Grant in his chambers to tell him that he was going to kill Ally Bennett this evening; a fact that the judge had known for half an hour. Gregaros had installed taps on Kerrigan's home and office phones hours after Kerrigan told Harvey Grant that Ally Bennett had the tape. When Bennett called Kerrigan to tell him where to make the exchange, a trace had located Dupre's safe house. It would have been easy for Gregaros to kill Bennett at the safe house, but the club needed to bind Kerrigan to it. They had lost one chance to win the presidency. Kerrigan presented them with another viable candidate.

Gregaros would take out Bennett if Kerrigan lost his nerve. If Kerrigan came through, the detective would take the murder weapon to the judge, who would put it with the weapons and confessions that the founding members of the club used to secure the loyalty of new members. To make certain that Dupre had nothing else that could hurt them, Gregaros had dispatched a team to the safe house moments after Bennett left for her meeting with Tim Kerrigan. After tonight, everything would be back where it should be.

Gregaros had been following Bennett in a nondescript black Chevy since she'd left Dupre's riverfront house. Stan let a few cars get between them, then settled in behind his quarry. Everything was proceeding smoothly until Bennett left the freeway. Less than a mile later, a police car pulled in behind Gregaros. He checked his speedometer to make sure that he was driving under the speed limit. Bennett passed a car, then pulled back into the right lane. The patrol car's bubble light started flashing. Stan slowed down until he was certain that the cop was pulling over Bennett. There was a strip-mall entrance on his right. He drove in and switched off his lights.

The patrolman approached Bennett's car and began talking to her. Bennett handed over her license and registration. The patrolman walked back to his car to run the information through his computer. When he was through, he walked back to Bennett and returned the paperwork. Then he pointed to her left taillight. Of course. The light was out. Stan hadn't noticed. The cop talked to

Bennett for a minute more before returning to his car. It looked like he'd only given her a warning.

Gregaros settled in behind Bennett as soon as she pulled away from the curb. He passed the cop car and saw that the officer was on his radio. A moment later, the patrol car made a U-turn and drove off in the opposite direction.

Traffic thinned as Bennett headed out of town. Gregaros lagged back. There was only a quarter moon and Bennett's car was dark blue, but her lone rear light was all he needed for his tail. When she turned onto a two-lane road that led into Forest Park, Stan turned off his lights and let the distance between them widen.

Bennett turned right, then left onto a narrow road. Stan knew that Bennett had insisted that the meeting be in a secluded meadow on the edge of a deep ravine near the boundary of the park. Gregaros knew the spot and didn't have to worry about staying close anymore. Bennett made a turn onto a dirt-and-grass road that led to the meadow. Suddenly the headlights of a park maintenance truck blinded Gregaros. It was hauling a small trailer loaded with gardening equipment, and had turned out of a side road. Stan figured that the driver had not spotted him because the Chevy's lights were off. The detective pulled to the side of the road to avoid the truck and hoped that the driver didn't honk his horn. The truck drove by silently. Gregaros looked up the road in time to see the red glow of the single rear light of Bennett's car moving like a firefly toward the meadow.

The dirt road was bounded by a row of neatly planted bushes, which Gregaros could barely see in the dark. When he drove past them, the road curved. He turned the car around so it was facing downhill, and parked. His gun was on the passenger seat, concealed under a magazine. He got it and walked up the road to the meadow, then moved into the cover of the trees. When he reached the edge of the copse, he stood behind a tree trunk and watched.

Bennett had stopped on the edge of the ravine. Kerrigan's car was beside her car, with the length of two parking spaces between them. Gregaros saw Kerrigan walk up to Bennett's open window. He was carrying a briefcase with the money that the judge had provided. Bennett said something. Stan could hear her but he couldn't make out her words. Kerrigan opened the briefcase, closed it, and placed it in the back seat of Bennett's car. When Kerrigan closed the rear door, he turned, so his back was blocking Gregaros's view of Bennett, but the detective heard Kerrigan demand the tape. Bennett spoke, and Kerrigan stuck out his left hand and then placed something in the left-side pocket of his coat. The DA's right hand went into his right-side pocket, and he shoved his arm in the driver's window. The muzzle flash from Kerrigan's gun illuminated the inside of Bennett's car for a second. Bennett screamed and blood sprayed across the window. Kerrigan pulled the trigger twice more. Bennett slumped sideways and disappeared from view.

Kerrigan grabbed the briefcase with the money, ran to his car, and returned with a gas can. After splashing the gasoline around the interior of Bennett's car, Kerrigan flipped in a match. He staggered back as the interior of the car lit up. Gregaros stepped out of the trees. Kerrigan was so intent on his task that he didn't hear him. Instead, he leaned forward, rested his hands on his knees, and dry-heaved several times.

"Good work."

Kerrigan leaped back, startled.

"It's me, Stan."

Kerrigan sagged from relief. Gregaros looked into the car. Blood had spattered across the inside of the windshield. Bennett's legs and lower body were still on the edge of the driver's seat, but her upper body was sprawled face-down across the passenger seat as if she'd been twisting away from Kerrigan when he shot her. Blood pooled under her head and torso, and flames raced through her hair and across her hands. Her clothes and the upholstery were on fire. Gregaros smelled flesh burning. He pulled back because of the heat.

"Give me the gun," Gregaros said.

"Let's get out of here before the car explodes," Kerrigan answered, eyeing the flames anxiously.

Gregaros held out a plastic Ziploc bag. "The gun."

Kerrigan pulled it out of his pocket and dropped it in the bag.

"And the tape."

Kerrigan took it out of his left-side pocket and handed it over.

"You did good," Gregaros said. "The judge will be proud of you."

Kerrigan didn't answer. Even in the dark, the detective could see that the prosecutor was ghost-white. He knew exactly how Kerrigan was feeling. He'd felt sick after his first face-to-face kill. The second hadn't bothered him at all.

Kerrigan ran to his car and Gregaros trotted back through the woods. Kerrigan drove by while Stan was getting into his car. Gregaros headed back toward town. Moments later, an explosion in his rearview mirror lit up the night sky.

forty-six

At five in the morning Stan Gregaros knocked loudly on the door to Harvey Grant's bedroom and entered without waiting for an invitation.

"What's going on?" Grant asked as he groped for his glasses.

"We have a problem."

"Is Bennett still alive?"

"No, she's dead. Kerrigan did just fine." Gregaros put the plastic bag with the murder weapon on Grant's end table. "He got the tape, too, but I didn't trust Bennett when she promised to turn over all of the tapes Dupre made at the fund-raiser, so I sent two men to Dupre's safe house after Bennett left. They were supposed to get everything out of his safe and bring it to me. They emptied the safe but someone shot them and took the bag with the tapes."

"What do you mean, someone shot them? Were they waiting for them? Do we have a leak?"

"I don't know, but I don't believe in coincidences. I think Jaffe knows about the tapes."

"Amanda Jaffe?"

Gregaros nodded. "Pedro's men made it to one of our doctors, and he called me. They told me that the shooter was a woman. Amanda Jaffe's investigator is very good with a gun. I showed them a snapshot. They identified her right away."

Grant paced back and forth across his bedroom. This was a very serious situation. No one knew what Dupre had recorded. Jaffe could be in possession of evidence that would destroy everything Grant had taken a lifetime to build.

If she was still investigating Dupre's case aggressively, she would go after the police reports in Delgado's murder and the murders at the drug house. Those reports contained the only clue to the identity of the original members of The Vaughn Street Glee Club—the names of the boys who were with Wendell Hayes on the evening that Wendell took three guns from his father's locked gun cabinet.

"Get Castillo on this right away," Grant said. "I want that bag and I want Jaffe dead."

"I'll call him on the road."

"Where are you going?"

"McCarthy paged me on the way over here. He wants me at Bennett's crime scene."

"Why?"

"No idea."

"You don't think he knows you were there, do you?"

"I don't see how he could. I'll tell you what's going on later."

The sun was just coming up when Stan Gregaros parked behind one of several police cars at the Bennett crime scene. Two men from the lab were making casts of a tire track, and two uniforms charged with keeping gawkers away were shooting the breeze, because no civilians had made the trek to the murder scene yet. Wisps of smoke hung in the air over the burned-out hulk of Ally Bennett's car, and an acrid smell similar to overcooked barbecue—typical of an arson murder—assailed Gregaros when he drew closer.

Sean McCarthy broke off a conversation with one of the forensic people when he spotted Gregaros.

"Hell of a way to start the day, huh Stan?"

"Hey, you know me. I love the smell of charred flesh first thing in the morning. To what do I owe this honor?"

McCarthy gestured toward the car. "We ran a trace on the plates. It belongs to Ally Bennett."

"She's one of Dupre's girls."

McCarthy nodded. "The body was badly burned, but it's female and fits Bennett's general description."

"Lori Andrews. Now Bennett."

"Don't forget Oscar Baron."

"You think the three murders are connected?"

"Two of Dupre's women and his attorney murdered so close together. What do you think?"

"Dupre is in jail. He couldn't have killed Baron or Bennett."

"That's why I called you out. You know all about Dupre's operation. Did he have a partner, someone who'd get rid of witnesses for him?"

"No. He was a loner. I . . ."

"Sean!"

The detectives turned. Alex DeVore was crossing the meadow followed by a heavyset man wearing a green uniform.

"This is Dmitry Rubin. He's with park maintenance. Dmitry made the 911 call last night."

"Glad to meet you, Mr. Rubin," McCarthy

said. "I'm Sean McCarthy. This is Stan Gregaros."

"I just finished taking Mr. Rubin's statement. Tell them what you told me."

"I was driving back to the garage last night when I passed a car. What made me remember it was it was driving without headlights. It came out of nowhere. There could have been an accident."

"Can you describe it?" Gregaros asked, trying to keep his voice even.

"Nah. I figured it was kids, you know, going up to the meadow to make out."

"Go ahead, Mr. Rubin," DeVore said.

"The explosion was a few minutes after. I pulled over when I heard it. Then I turned around and headed back. When I was halfway here, a car came barreling by."

"The same one you saw before?" Gregaros asked.

"No, a different one. But the car that was driving without headlights came by a few seconds later."

"Can you give us a make or model on either car?"

"Mr. Rubin did better than that," DeVore said. "He got most of the license number on the car he saw right after the explosion."

"I didn't get it all," Rubin said apologetically. "It went by too fast."

"What about the car that was driving without headlights?" Gregaros asked.

Rubin shook his head. "I was writing down the license number. My head was down. By the time I looked, it was too late."

"Don't worry about that," McCarthy said. "This is a great help to us."

"Yeah, nice work," Gregaros added, successfully hiding his relief that Rubin had missed his car. Still, if they traced the partial plate to Tim Kerrigan, there would be trouble.

An hour after Stan Gregaros left the meadow, Kate Ross walked into Amanda's office.

"Did you listen to the local news this morning?" Kate asked.

"Was there something about the shooting at Jon's house?"

"No, nothing. But Ally Bennett is dead."

"What!"

"She was murdered. They found her body in Forest Park."

Amanda looked stricken. "She recorded the tapes at the Travis fund-raiser and she brought the tapes of the drug deals to Oscar Baron. The people who killed Oscar probably got to her."

"I bet she was the woman who was staying at Dupre's safe house."

"The men you shot last night may have killed her. Are they in custody?"

"I don't know."

"Could they have left on their own steam?"

"Maybe. They were in a lot of pain but the big guy was tough. Have you made a decision on what to do with the evidence in the duffel bag?"

"Not yet. If the two men got away, maybe we don't have to do anything. Just hang tight and we'll talk later."

forty-seven

Manuel Castillo wished that he'd had some time to make up a plan for the best way to hit Amanda Jaffe, but he was under orders to do it fast. His first idea was to take her in the parking lot where he'd kidnapped her, but her father and a big Indian were with her. Castillo had the Indian, with his ripped muscles and ponytail, pegged as a rent-a-cop who'd wet his pants when the bullets started flying. But he couldn't risk Jaffe getting killed before she gave him the stuff from Dupre's safe.

Castillo had decided on a home invasion. People were all fogged up by sleep in the early morning hours. He'd storm in while the home alarm was scaring the shit out of the Jaffes and kill everyone except Amanda. Once he had the bag, he'd play with her a little before killing her.

She'd looked tasty without her clothes, and she definitely needed to be taught a lesson for disobeying him. When the driver parked the van in front of Frank Jaffe's house at three A.M., Manuel was deep in a fantasy in which Amanda was naked, tied to the posts of his king-size bed and screaming.

Castillo pulled down his ski mask and rapped with the butt of his gun on the wall that separated the cab of the van from the back. The driver would stay in the van and keep the motor running while Castillo and his crew took care of business. All of the men were dressed in black and carried automatic weapons. The van was painted black and had stolen plates.

The house was dark and there was no moon. Castillo crossed the lawn quickly and surveyed the door for a few seconds before blowing out the lock. One of his men kicked it in and rushed into the house.

George, Amanda's bodyguard, was waiting for them. He shot the first man as he came through the front door. Castillo hit the floor and fired a burst of automatic fire. It laced across George's side and shoulder. The next man through the door shot the bodyguard in the midsection. George went down firing. His round sliced through the gunman's kneecap. Castillo ignored the chaos and raced up the stairs to the second floor. The alarm shrieked so loudly that he did not hear the last man through the door drop from a bullet that drilled through the back of his head.

The house alarm shrieked and Amanda leaped out of bed, forgetting her gun. It was pitch-black in her room and she was disoriented. Her door flew open.

"It's me," Frank yelled. "Move."

Amanda heard shots and raced onto the landing. The sharp bark of automatic weapons fire sounded over the alarm. Frank dragged Amanda toward a narrow back stairs that led to the kitchen. They were almost there when shots stitched a line down the landing. Frank turned and fired his shotgun. In the flash, Amanda saw a man in a ski mask dive into her room.

"Go!" Frank yelled.

Amanda raced for the back stairs. Castillo stuck the muzzle of his automatic weapon into the hall and pulled the trigger. Amanda was halfway down the stairs when she heard Frank grunt. She turned and Frank tumbled by, almost bowling her over. He landed in the kitchen in a heap.

"Dad!"

Frank's shoulder and his pants leg were drenched with blood. Amanda bent over him.

"Get out," Frank gasped. "Go!"

Amanda looked for the shotgun, but it had fallen out of Frank's hand on the upper landing when he was hit. She dragged her father into the butler's pantry, hoping the darkness would hide him. Over the shrieking alarm, she heard footsteps pounding down the back stairs. The door to the basement was in front of her. Amanda wrenched it open and leaped down the stairs in the dark.

A little moonlight filtered through the dirty basement windows. It was barely enough to see, but Amanda had grown up in this house and knew every inch of the basement by heart. Frank had stacked a cord of wood against the unpainted concrete wall to the right of the stairs. Next to the logs was an axe. A light bulb hung from the ceiling in front of the stairs. Amanda grabbed the axe and shattered the bulb. There were three other bulbs hanging from the ceiling. Amanda raced through the room smashing them. She had just finished when she heard the basement door fly open.

Evenly spaced through the unfinished basement were massive wood beams that supported the ceiling. Amanda hid behind one and waited. The few times she had hunted with her father, he had shown her how to move through the woods quietly. She tried to remember her father's lessons now.

Someone started down the basement stairs. Amanda tightened her grip on the axe. In the dim light she saw a man holding an automatic weapon. He turned away from her and looked at the cord of wood. When he was satisfied that Amanda wasn't hiding behind him, the man turned in Amanda's direction. He was wearing a ski mask.

"Hey, sweetie, come out."

She recognized the voice of the pockmarked man who had kidnapped her, and she started to shake.

"If you surrender to me now I'll make it fast," he said as he moved across the concrete floor. "If you piss me off I'll take you with me. It will be just you and me hour after hour, day after day."

Amanda knew what she had to do if she and her father were going to survive this night.

"I read about some guy," Castillo went on. "He kept a woman chained up, with tape over her mouth, in a box under his bed. When he wanted her he would take her out and fuck her. Some days he'd even feed her. Then she'd go back in the box, like a deck of cards. I have a nice bed. There's plenty of space for a coffin under it."

Terror threatened to paralyze Amanda; she forced herself to block out the killer's voice and visualize what she had to do, just as she did before a swim meet. When her tormentor was within reach, Amanda would move and swing and swing again, the way she stroked in a race—powerful strokes, rhythmic strokes, one after the other.

Castillo was close to the beam now. She could hear his feet slide toward her along the concrete floor. The moment his back was to her, Amanda stepped out and swung with all her might. The axe bit into Castillo's right shoulder with a sickening thud. He grunted and his gun clattered to the floor. As Amanda yanked out the axe and raised it again, Castillo stared at her in disbelief. Amanda's light-colored flannel pajamas were spotted with his blood. More blood speckled her face. She looked insane.

The blade sliced into his knee. Castillo shrieked. The next blow took him in the side. Blood spurted from his shoulder, his knee, and this new wound. He crashed to the floor face-first, unable to move his hand to break his fall.

Amanda straddled him, screaming with each blow.

"Don't," Castillo croaked as the blade descended one last time. The axe sliced through the killer's throat and cut off his words. Amanda stepped on his shoulder and wrenched out the blade. She prepared to swing again, but footsteps brought her around. The slender man in the Mariners' baseball cap, whom Amanda had seen in the courthouse and thought she'd seen in her garage, leaped to the bottom of the stairs. He swung a gun toward Amanda's midsection and froze. She raised her axe.

"Red! Red!" he shouted. "It's okay, Amanda. You're safe."

The killing rage still had hold of her and she took a step forward. The man lowered his gun.

"They're all dead. You're safe," he said softly. "I'm Anthony."

Amanda gripped the handle. What if it was a trick?

"I've got to get an ambulance for your father. He's hurt. He has to go to a hospital."

Suddenly her arms were too heavy to hold the axe and it clanged to the floor.

"We've got to call for an ambulance," Anthony insisted as he turned and raced up the stairs with

Amanda on his heels. While Anthony called 911, she dropped beside Frank and rested his head in her lap. When the police and the medics found her, Amanda was still sitting on the floor with Frank, but Anthony and the Indian were gone. Amanda tried to remember what the man in the cap looked like but she could not recall a single feature.

forty-eight

Mike Greene's car skidded to a stop and he leaped out. Several lab techs were working in the back of a black van that was parked at the curb by Frank Jaffe's house. A photographer snapped a picture as Mike went by, and the flash illuminated the driver of the van. His head was tipped back. Before the light from the flash faded, Mike saw a jagged red line stretching across the driver's throat.

Lights had been set up on the front lawn where another corpse sprawled face-down. The man was dressed in black. A forensic specialist was peeling off his ski mask to reveal a blood-encrusted wound. In the entryway, two more dead men were being photographed.

"Mike."

Greene looked up and saw Sean McCarthy and

Stan Gregaros walking out of the hall that led to the kitchen.

"Where is she, Sean?"

"Upstairs, away from this mess."

"Is she okay?"

"She's in shock. The first cop who got here found her sitting on the floor in the kitchen. Frank's head was in her lap and she was rocking back and forth."

"Is Frank . . . ?"

"He was shot twice and bleeding badly, but the medics got to the house in time. He's at the hospital now. The doctors think he'll make it."

"Thank God."

"There's something else," McCarthy told Greene. "There's a dead man in the cellar. Amanda killed him with an axe."

"It's self-defense, all the way," Gregaros added. "The guy in the basement is Manuel Castillo, an enforcer for Pedro Aragon."

"What would Aragon want with Frank and Amanda?" Mike asked Gregaros.

"She was pretty shaken when we talked. I didn't press her," McCarthy answered. "We're hoping that Amanda can clear up everything when she's calmer."

"Shit. It's not fair after what she went through with Cardoni."

"She'll be okay, Mike," McCarthy said.

"I want to see her."

Greene started toward the stairs but McCarthy stopped him.

"Amanda needs a friend, right now. That's why I called you. This is not your case. You've got a conflict. Comfort her, but don't question her. Understood?"

Greene nodded then shook off McCarthy's hand and ran upstairs. Amanda was being photographed by a lab tech. She startled when Greene ran into the room. Greene stared at her blood-streaked face and pajamas.

"Are you okay?" he asked. She nodded but the fear he saw told him she wasn't.

"I'm through, Mike," the photographer said, "but we'll need the clothes."

A policewoman had been sitting with Amanda. "Let's go to your room," she said. "We'll get these things off of you and get you warm."

Mike followed the women down the hall and waited outside Amanda's door while she cleaned up and changed. At the far end of the hallway, another lab tech was examining blood that had splashed on the wall across from the back stairs.

Amanda looked terrible. He couldn't imagine what she'd gone through. She was tough—he'd been there when she'd set herself up as a sacrificial lamb so they could trap the surgeon—but she was basically a decent and gentle person. Mike knew policemen who had killed criminals in self-defense. No matter how justified the killing, most of them were scarred psychologically from the experience.

The door to Amanda's room opened, and she came out dressed in slacks and a sweater. She was pale, and her hair was damp from a quick shower. Mike hesitated, not certain that Amanda would want to be touched.

"Can I . . ." he started, but Amanda cut him short by falling against his chest. He held her while she sobbed.

"Sean heard from the hospital," Mike said as he led her down the hall and into the study, where they'd have some privacy. "Your dad is going to be okay."

"I killed him, Mike. I lost control."

Mike forgot what Sean had said about discussing the case with Amanda. He stepped back and put his hands on her shoulders and forced her to look in his eyes.

"You had to."

"You don't understand. I wanted to kill him. I couldn't stop. My arms just kept moving."

"Amanda, listen to me. You didn't do anything wrong. The man you killed was Manuel Castillo, an enforcer for Pedro Aragon. It was him or you."

Mike was about to say something else when a man knocked on the doorjamb. He was an African American with glasses and a sturdy build, and Greene had never seen him before.

"I'm sorry to interrupt, Mr. Greene, but I'd like a few words with Miss Jaffe."

"Who are you?" Greene asked.

"J. D. Hunter. I'm with the FBI."

"Can't this wait for later?"

"I've been informed that Ms. Jaffe had been kidnapped by one of her assailants." Mike stared at Amanda. "Kidnapping is a federal crime."

"What's he talking about?" Mike asked.

Amanda put a hand on Mike's arm. "It's okay, Mike. Let me talk to him."

"I'd like to question Miss Jaffe alone, if you don't mind."

Mike knew that he had no business being in the room, but he didn't want to leave Amanda. She flashed him a tired smile.

"I'm still a lawyer. I know how to protect myself."

Amanda squeezed his hand and watched as he left the room.

"Who called you?" Amanda asked as soon as the door closed behind Greene.

"Sean McCarthy," Hunter said.

"It seems like a funny thing to do, calling in the feds at this point."

Hunter laughed. "You don't miss a thing, do you? I heard you were sharp."

"So, what's this really about?"

"I'm afraid I can't tell you, not yet. But I'd appreciate it very much if you'd take it on faith that Jon Dupre may benefit from my investigation."

Amanda thought about that for a moment. "Ask your questions."

"Tell me about the kidnapping."

Amanda took a deep breath. Her kidnapper was dead but her emotions hadn't fully accepted that yet.

"I was captured in my parking garage a few days ago. The man in the basement and the two dead men in the living room took me out in the woods. They threatened to . . . to do things to me."

Amanda stopped, unable to repeat Castillo's threats.

"Do you know why you were kidnapped?"

Amanda nodded. "They wanted me to throw the cases against Jon Dupre."

"From what I've heard, they're easy cases to win. Why would Pedro Aragon have to fix them?"

Amanda hesitated. There were policemen, a senator, lawyers, and judges in The Vaughn Street Glee Club. Why not an FBI agent? Amanda closed her eyes. She didn't care anymore. After what had happened this evening, she decided that her best defense was to make what she knew about the club public. Keeping quiet had almost gotten her father killed.

"Despite the way things look, Jon Dupre may be innocent of both murders," Amanda said. "I'm certain that Wendell Hayes was sent to the jail to murder Jon and that he, not Jon, smuggled the shiv into the visiting room."

Amanda watched for Hunter's reaction and was surprised to see none.

"Who do you think sent Hayes to kill your client?"

"Have you ever heard of a group called The Vaughn Street Glee Club?"

"Yes, but I'm impressed that you have. Why don't you tell me what you know about them."

"I think Pedro Aragon met Wendell Hayes in nineteen seventy when they were in their teens or early twenties and formed a pact to help each other. I think some of Hayes's childhood friends were part of the group. Over the years, Wendell and his friends rose to power and they drafted new recruits into their club. If I'm right, there are bankers, judges, politicians, district attorneys, and police involved. How am I doing?"

"Keep going, Miss Jaffe," Hunter responded noncommittally.

Amanda told Hunter about the evidence that pointed to Senator Travis as the man who murdered Lori Andrews. Then she told the agent Jon Dupre's version of the Hayes killing and the evidence that supported it, including Paul Baylor's opinion that Dupre had been attacked.

"My investigator has discovered two suicides going back many years, which may have been murders committed by these people. But I think that the real reason they want to shut me up is that I filed a motion for discovery for the police reports in a multiple murder in a drug house that occurred in nineteen seventy. Here's the kicker: The drug house was on Vaughn Street."

Hunter's poker face was transformed by a wide smile.

"Weapons taken from Wendell Hayes's home were used in the shooting. The police concluded that a burglar stole the guns but I think Wendell took them. Hayes had an alibi for the night of the killings. Supposedly he was at a party with college friends who were home on Christmas break. I'm willing to bet that somewhere there is an interview with these boys. I think they were the original members of The Vaughn Street Glee Club and this is the only record that can point us to them."

"Miss Jaffe," Hunter said, "if you ever get tired of practicing law there's a spot for you in the Federal Bureau of Investigation."

"Then you believe me?"

"Oh, yes. I've been on this case for a while. Senator Travis had a penchant for rough sex and a thing for Lori Andrews. Dupre was buying his drugs from Pedro Aragon. When Portland Vice arrested Andrews, she agreed to work as an informant to help them get Dupre. The Bureau has been trying to break Pedro's cartel and we found out about Lori. During a debriefing, she told an agent about the senator, and I was brought in. We'd heard rumors that Pedro was connected to several prominent people in Oregon, and I'd heard Sammy Cortez's story about The Vaughn Street Glee Club. When Wendell Hayes tried to kill Dupre I started taking the story seriously.

You've given me the last piece of information that I needed."

"To do what?"

"Again, I'm afraid I can't tell you that, not until we close the loop. But I can tell you that you've performed an invaluable service by opening up to me."

"Since I've been so helpful to you, do something for me."

"If I can."

"Can you take me to the hospital? I've got to see my father."

Part Six

THE NINETY-
YARD RUN

forty-nine

Harvey Grant was taking off his robe when Tim Kerrigan burst into his chambers and collapsed onto a chair.

"You've got to help me," Kerrigan pleaded.

"What's wrong, Tim?" Grant asked, alarmed. Kerrigan looked like a drunk or a crack addict. If he came apart it would be a disaster.

"I . . . I have dreams. I see her burning, and I can still see the way her face looked when I pulled the trigger. It exploded. There was so much blood."

The judge sat next to Kerrigan. "I'm glad that you've come to me, Tim. I'm glad that you know that you can trust me to help you."

"You're the only one I can talk to." His head dropped into his hands. "I can't take it. I can't live like this. Maybe I should go to the police. I'd tell them it was all my idea. I wouldn't tell them about you or anyone else."

Grant kept his voice calm. He had to stop Kerrigan from coming unglued.

"You're not thinking straight," the judge said. "A confession would destroy Cindy. And think of Megan. She would always be known as the daughter of a murderer, and she'd lose her father. You know what happens to children who grow up with that curse. You would be destroying her chance of happiness."

Kerrigan nodded. "You're right. I have to think of Megan. But what can I do? I feel lost. I can't find any peace."

"Time will make the pain go. Two years from now you won't remember how sad you are today. You'll be in Washington, D.C., with Megan and Cindy by your side. You'll be one of the most powerful men in America and Ally Bennett will seem like someone who only existed in a dream."

Kerrigan looked at Grant hopefully. "Do you think that will really happen?"

Grant squeezed Kerrigan's shoulder. "Trust me, Tim. This empty feeling, your guilt, it will all fade away. You'll be fine and your life will be good."

Kerrigan embraced Grant. "Thank you, Harvey."

Grant patted Tim on the back. Then he got him a glass of water and waited while Tim pulled himself together. They talked for a while more and Kerrigan was calmer when he left. As soon as the door closed behind the prosecutor, Grant sagged.

"Detective Gregaros is here, Judge," Grant's secretary said over the intercom.

"Send him in," Grant said.

The judge had rarely seen Gregaros rattled, but he looked bad today.

"What happened last night?"

"Castillo fucked up. He's dead and so are his men."

"What about Amanda Jaffe?"

"She's the one who killed Manuel."

"She's a goddamn girl."

Gregaros shrugged. "Manuel is still dead."

"This just keeps getting worse," Grant said. "Tim Kerrigan was just here."

"I saw him leave," the detective said. "He looked like shit. What happened?"

"He's a mess. I calmed him down for the moment, but I'm concerned."

"You should be. We've got real problems.

Remember I told you that that maintenance guy wrote down most of Kerrigan's license plate? Fucking McCarthy. The son of a bitch is too smart. He ran the partial license number through the Department of Motor Vehicles computer and spotted Kerrigan's name on the printout. Then he checked Kerrigan and Bennett's phone records. Bennett phoned Kerrigan's house a few days before he killed her. And they both called a motel near the airport. McCarthy got a positive ID on both of them from a clerk at the motel."

"What is McCarthy planning to do?"

"I convinced him to move slow. I told him Kerrigan's career would be ruined if we went public without an airtight case. He's going to talk to Jack Stamm before he talks to Tim, and Stamm is out of town until tomorrow. We don't have much time to decide what to do."

Grant closed his eyes. Events were getting out of hand.

"I hate to admit it but bringing Tim in was a mistake," the judge said.

"What are we going to do about that?"

"I'll call the others. I'm going to suggest that we cut our losses."

fifty

"Tim!"

Kerrigan turned and saw Maria Lopez hurrying after him, her shoulders hunched against the teeming downpour. She was carrying a briefcase in one hand and a thermos in the other, leaving no hand free for an umbrella. Her hair was sopping wet and disheveled from the rain. She was wearing a raincoat but she'd forgotten to button it, so her blouse was streaked with raindrops.

"What's going on?" Tim asked, shielding her with his umbrella.

"A woman called," Maria said when she'd caught her breath. "She says that she can prove Dupre murdered Senator Travis. She wants to meet us at Travis's cabin."

"When?"

"Now. Travis taped his sex acts secretly, and the tape was running when Dupre killed him. The tape is at the cabin. We have to go now because she's leaving town tonight."

"Hold on. Who is this woman?"

"She wouldn't give me her name. From what she said I'd guess she was one of Dupre's escorts, one of the women he beat up."

"This doesn't sound right. We searched the cabin and didn't find any tapes."

"Maybe she brought it with her."

Tim thought for a moment. "I'm going to call Sean McCarthy. I want him with us."

"She said no cops. She'll run if she sees anyone else."

Tim hesitated.

"We've got to go," Lopez insisted. "Our case against Dupre for the senator's murder isn't that strong. If this tape is what the woman claims, we'll nail him."

"All right. Let's go. My car is in the lot."

"No. She wanted to know what car we'd be driving. I described mine. If she sees another car she may bolt."

"I hope this isn't a wild goose chase."

"She sounded scared, Tim. I don't think she was faking."

. . .

"What a miserable night," Kerrigan said as Maria drove toward the cabin. The rain was coming down so hard that the wipers could barely deal with it.

"Everything okay with you, Tim?" Maria asked. "You look like you've been through the wringer."

"It's nothing. I'm just worn out."

"Have some coffee," Maria said. "It'll warm you up."

"Good idea."

Tim unscrewed the top of Maria's thermos and filled it with steaming coffee.

"You want any?" he asked Maria.

"I'm fine."

Kerrigan finished his coffee just as Maria turned off the main road onto the unpaved driveway that led to the cabin. No lights showed through the trees and Kerrigan began to wonder if they weren't on a fool's errand.

"It doesn't look like there's anyone here," he said, looking for a car.

Maria parked in front of the cabin. Kerrigan opened the door and started to stand. The movement made him dizzy and he sat back down.

"What's wrong?" Maria asked.

He shook his head. "I'm fine. Let's go."

Kerrigan pulled himself up and followed
Maria. She was carrying the thermos and her
briefcase and seemed oblivious to the rain. It
took Tim a while to join her at the front door. He
was having trouble focusing.

"Here, let me help you," Maria said, taking his
elbow and supporting him as he stumbled inside.

"I don't feel well," Tim said. Maria flipped on
the living room light and helped him to the couch.

"Must be something you ate," she said. The
words sounded as if they came from far away.
Tim looked up. Maria was holding out the plastic cup that acted as a cover for the thermos.
"Drink some more coffee. It will wake you up."

Tim swallowed half a cup, dribbling some of it
on his raincoat. His mouth didn't work well.

"Let's get you out of that coat," Maria said as
she slipped off one sleeve of Kerrigan's raincoat.

Tim looked around. "There's no one here," he
managed. Saying the words took an effort.

"Guess we've been stood up," Maria answered.
She was opening her briefcase and extracting a
sheet of paper. It looked familiar. He was so focused on the paper that he didn't notice the gun
in the Ziploc bag until it made a noise when it hit
the coffee table in front of the couch.

"Wha's that?" Tim asked. He tried to sit up but he didn't have the energy. The paper looked like the confession he'd signed for Stan Gregaros, but he couldn't get his eyes to focus long enough to read it.

"I'm sorry this didn't work out," Maria said. "No one realized how weak you are."

It took a moment for her comment to register. By the time it did, Maria had slipped on gloves and had taken the gun out of the bag.

"What . . . What are you . . . ?"

"I'm getting ready to help you kill yourself. The drug should kick in completely in a moment or two."

Kerrigan shook his head. "I don' unerstand."

"Of course you don't. You still think that I'm a dumpy, enthusiastic deputy DA." She laughed. "I'll admit, the dumpy part has been a little tough to carry off, but the enthusiasm has been genuine. I enjoy my work."

Kerrigan stared at Maria.

"Let me introduce myself, Tim. I'm Pedro Aragon's daughter."

Tim shook his head again, trying to clear it. He was fading fast, but he was still fighting.

"You might as well give in to the drug, Tim. I dosed the coffee like you wouldn't believe."

Kerrigan tried to stand and toppled sideways. Maria shrugged.

"Suit yourself."

Tim was almost under. When he was out, Maria would press the gun into his hand, twist the muzzle into his temple, and pull the trigger. Kerrigan's eyes closed. Maria picked up the gun and walked around the table. She checked Kerrigan's pulse and sighed. She did like Tim. He was such a hunk. If everything had gone as planned, she might have even bedded him at some point. With her weight off, she was pretty sexy, and she knew that Timmy was having problems at home.

Ah well. Maria pressed the muzzle of the gun against Kerrigan's temple.

"Sweet dreams," she said.

fifty-one

Harvey Grant had met Maria Lopez in the park across the street from the courthouse during the noon recess, and given her Tim Kerrigan's confession and the weapon Kerrigan had used to murder Ally Bennett. Grant ate dinner while Kerrigan and Lopez were driving to the cabin. The judge went to bed at ten and slept soundly, expecting to wake up to news that Tim Kerrigan was dead. The bad news was waiting with his morning paper.

The judge usually enjoyed a hearty breakfast before going to work, but the story on the front page of the **Oregonian** killed his appetite and made Grant feel something he had not felt in a long time—fear.

DEPUTY DA ARRESTED IN MURDER PLOT

Maria Lopez, a deputy district attorney in Multnomah County, was arrested last

night by the FBI and charged with the attempted murder of former Heisman Trophy winner Tim Kerrigan, her direct superior at the district attorney's office. The murder attempt took place at the cabin where Jon Dupre, the owner of Exotic Escorts, allegedly murdered United States Senator Harold Travis. Kerrigan and Lopez are prosecuting Dupre for Travis's murder and the murder of prominent Oregon attorney Wendell Hayes.

In a prepared statement, FBI agent J. D. Hunter stated that he and several other agents were involved in an ongoing investigation—the details of which he could not disclose—when they followed Lopez and Kerrigan to the cabin and set up surveillance. The agents arrived as Deputy District Attorney Lopez fired a gun at Kerrigan. They arrested Lopez, who is now in custody. The agents would not comment on Kerrigan's medical condition or reveal his whereabouts.

There was more to the story—most of it recapping Kerrigan's football career and his achievements in the district attorney's office.

Grant took pride in the control he had over his emotions. He exercised it now and willed away his doubts and fears while reviewing his assets and liabilities. Maria Lopez was in custody and looking at some serious time. Attempted murder if Kerrigan wasn't dead; murder if he was. But Maria wouldn't cooperate. She was Pedro's daughter and completely loyal to her father and the club. What if she did crack? It wouldn't be for a while. Besides, her word alone wouldn't be enough to support charges against him, Grant reasoned. Then he realized that it wouldn't be just her word. The FBI had the gun Kerrigan used to murder Ally Bennett, and Kerrigan's suicide note. This gave them an ironclad case against Kerrigan and the leverage they needed to force him to cooperate, and Kerrigan would cooperate once he figured out that the judge gave Maria the order to kill him.

"Tim knows that we'll kill Cindy and Megan if he talks," Grant said out loud. "But the Bureau's had him since early yesterday evening. Cindy and Megan could be in protective custody by now."

Grant grabbed the phone and dialed Kerrigan's home.

"Yes?" Cindy answered hesitantly. She sounded scared.

"It's Harvey."

"Thank God. I thought you might be another reporter." Grant could hear the relief in her voice. "They haven't stopped since early morning. There's a camera crew camped outside our driveway."

"I just read about Tim in the morning paper. Is he okay?"

"He's alive, but no one will tell me anything else. Tim's father is going to meet with Katherine Hickox this morning," she said, naming the United States attorney for Oregon.

"If anyone can find out what's going on, Bill can."

"I'm so worried about Tim. The story in the paper said that woman tried to murder him. They work together. Why would she do that?"

"I don't know any more than you do but I'll talk to Jack Stamm and see what I can find out. Meanwhile, you take care of Megan. This could be tough on her."

"Please call me if you find out anything. I don't even know if Tim is hurt or . . ."

"Don't let your imagination get the best of you, Cindy. The paper said that Lopez was being charged with attempted murder, so Tim must be alive."

"Oh, God. I hope so."

"You have to be strong. Whenever you're tempted to panic think of your daughter."

"I will, Harvey. Thank you so much. You mean a lot to us."

Grant hung up. Cindy and Megan were home, which meant that Kerrigan wasn't cooperating yet. How much longer would that last?

Katherine Hickox, a member of the Westmont Country Club, had known William and Tim Kerrigan for years. She and another man were in her office when William and his attorney, Peter Schwab, arrived. She shook Schwab's hand quickly, but held Kerrigan's.

"I'm so sorry to hear about all this, Bill. Are you okay?"

"I'm holding up, but I'll feel a lot better when I know how Tim is doing."

Katherine released Kerrigan's hand and introduced the other man in the room.

"This is J. D. Hunter. He's the FBI agent in charge of the case."

Hunter shook hands with Kerrigan and Schwab while the U.S. attorney sat behind her desk.

"How is my son?"

"When we broke into the cabin, Maria Lopez had a gun to Tim's head. It went off as she was turning toward us. The gun moved, so Tim only suffered a minor head wound. It's nothing serious. We have him in the secure wing at OHSU. I thought it would be better to hold your son at a hospital instead of a jail."

"Why would you hold him at all?"

"Tim is the prime suspect in the murder of a prostitute who was shot to death in Forest Park a few days ago."

Kerrigan's mouth opened. He stared at Hunter for a moment, then turned toward Katherine. She nodded.

"You're serious?"

"I'm sorry, Bill," the U.S. attorney said.

"Are you planning on transferring Tim to jail when he's able to move?" Schwab asked.

"No. We're releasing him sometime today."

"If he's a suspect, why are you letting him out?"

"I can't get into that. I will tell you that we're handing over everything we have to the state. Katherine doesn't see a federal crime here. There's evidence that the lab is still checking. If they get the results we think they will, I'm certain the state will indict."

"From what I know, it doesn't look good for Tim," Hickox said.

"Everyone I talk to says nothing but the finest things about your son," Hunter said. "He must have been under tremendous pressure. I'd like to help him, and you can play an important part in making sure that he gets a lenient sentence."

"What can I do?"

"Before I go any further I'll need your word that you won't discuss what I tell you with any-one else."

"I don't understand."

"And I can't explain without your promise."

Kerrigan conferred with his attorney. When they were through he turned back to Hunter.

"I give my word that I'll keep your confidence. Now tell me how I can help Tim."

"Tim's assistance in a larger investigation could have an impact on his charges and his sentence, but he's refusing to cooperate. If you want to help him, go to the hospital and talk sense into him. Believe me, he needs all the help he can get."

fifty-two

An armed police officer manned a desk in front of the thick steel door that barred entry to the secure wing of the state hospital. William Kerrigan signed in. The officer checked his ID then pressed a button under the desk. Moments later, the steel door opened and an orderly escorted Kerrigan down a corridor surfaced with linoleum that smelled faintly of antiseptic. Halfway down the hall, another officer was sitting in front of Tim's hospital room. He checked Kerrigan's ID a second time before unlocking the door to the room.

Tim turned toward the door when his father entered. He was pale. A thick bandage covered a good part of the right side of his head and there was a dark bruise where the bandage did not cover his skin. There was no life in his eyes.

"Are you okay?" William asked.

"I messed up, Dad." A tear formed. "I really messed up."

William pulled a chair next to the bed. Tim looked away from him and wiped his eyes.

"It'll be okay, son. I talked to J. D. Hunter, the FBI agent in charge of this case. You're going to be released from the hospital, today. Once you're out of here, we'll get the best lawyers and we'll get you through this."

"No, I don't think so. You don't even know what's happened to me."

"Hunter said that you killed a woman. You didn't do it, did you, Tim?"

"I did kill her." Tim looked so lost. "God forgive me. I . . . I shot her then I set her on fire." Tim couldn't meet his father's eye. "I'm a terrible person. I've ruined Cindy's life and Megan's."

"Hunter said that he'll help you if you cooperate with him. He didn't tell me what he wanted you to do, but he assured me that something will be done if you assist the FBI in an investigation."

"I can't, Dad. If I . . ."

"What is it?"

"I can't tell you. I'd be putting you in danger."

"I don't care, Tim. You're my son. What is it that they want you to do?"

"You don't understand. They'll kill Cindy and Megan if I talk. They might even come after you."

"Who are you talking about?"

Tim shook his head.

"The people who threatened you aren't more powerful than the federal government. I'll make sure that Cindy and Megan are protected."

"You can't guarantee that. You don't understand who you're dealing with."

"Then you have to tell me."

Tim stared out the window. His father waited patiently. Then Tim seemed to make a decision.

"Maybe you can help me. Maybe we can work this out."

He thought some more. Then he took a deep breath.

"It's Harvey, Dad. Harvey Grant. He's the one who threatened me."

William's mouth dropped open. Then he laughed in disbelief.

"Harvey is my oldest friend. We go back to junior high. He loves you. He's your godfather."

"Please don't hate me, but I went to Harvey when I got in trouble. I didn't go to you. I felt that he . . . that you . . ."

"You don't have to say any more, Tim. I understand why you didn't come to me. I'm not the warmest person. It's hard for me to show affection. But I've always loved you. If I've been hard on you it's because I wanted you to be the best."

"I always thought you were disappointed in me, that you wished I . . . that I wasn't your son."

"Oh, no, Tim. You've always made me proud. Now tell me what this is all about."

Tim told his father about his evening with Ally Bennett and her attempt to blackmail him into dismissing Jon Dupre's case. Then he told him about his meetings with Harvey Grant and what had happened in Forest Park.

"I can't believe this," William said. "I've known Harvey my whole life. I never suspected . . ."

"It's true. And now you see why I can't cooperate. He'd have Cindy and Megan murdered. But I have something I can use against him. I know a way to find out the names of the members of his group."

"How will you do that?"

"When I signed the suicide note, Stan Gregaros told me that every new member does the same thing. The notes are confessions. The murder weapons have the member's fingerprints. If the police had them, they'd have a list of all the members and an airtight case against each one for murder. I want you to negotiate with Harvey. I'll go with you. We can meet in a public place so we'll be protected. The Westmont would be perfect."

William looked at Tim's bandaged head. "Are you sure you're up to this?"

"We have to act now. I told Hunter that Maria was insanely in love with me but I rejected her and she killed Ally Bennett to frame me. I said that she must have gotten my prints on the gun when I was unconscious and that she wrote the note. But the lab will analyze the note. Any minute, Hunter could learn that it's my writing. I'll be back in custody. That's why we have to meet with Harvey tonight."

"What do you want from Harvey?"

"A promise that he won't hurt my family. I won't help the authorities if he leaves everyone alone. I'll fight the murder charge but I'll take my medicine if I get convicted." Tim hung his head. "I'll deserve what I get, anyway."

Then Tim looked up. He seemed very determined.

"You tell Harvey that he has to promise not to hurt Cindy or Megan. If he won't agree I'll do everything I can to destroy him."

fifty-three

Harvey Grant was in his chambers when William Kerrigan called him on his cell phone from Tim's hospital room.

"How's Tim?" the judge asked.

"He's being released in half an hour."

"That's wonderful. I've been really worried."

"Have you, Harvey?"

"Of course. All it said in the paper was that Maria Lopez tried to kill him. No one's been able to tell me how he was doing, until now."

"Well, he's doing fine. In fact, he wants to have dinner with you and me at the Westmont tonight."

"Doesn't he want to be with Cindy and Megan?"

"Yes, but it's more important that he makes sure that they're safe."

"I don't understand."

"I think you do. Tim and I had a long talk. He told me about the visits he paid to you recently."

"I see."

"I don't want to discuss this over a cell phone. Do you?"

"No."

"Then let's get together at the Westmont at eight. And Harvey, I think you should wait to hear what we say before you do anything rash. Tim's figured out how to bring down your whole house of cards."

"What are you talking about?"

"He'll tell you tonight. He's already committed his thoughts to paper. Peter Schwab will have it as soon as I leave here."

"I'd never do anything to hurt Tim. I think of him as a son."

"I'm glad, Harvey. Keep thinking of him that way."

"How can Tim hurt us?" Gregaros asked, after the judge told him what Kerrigan had said.

"Did you tell Tim that the other members of the club sign suicide notes when they join?"

"Yeah."

"If the police get their hands on the notes and

the weapons they'll have an open-and-shut case for the murder each member confessed to. Someone will cut a deal. Then it won't just be Kerrigan's word or Maria's word against ours."

"Kerrigan doesn't know where they're hidden."

"They'll get a search warrant for my house. They'll tear it apart looking."

"Then we have to get rid of the evidence."

"No. If we destroy the confessions we'll lose our hold on the others. Fear keeps them in line. We just have to move the evidence off my property. Don't worry. I've worked everything out. We have to act quickly, so we'll do it tonight, before Kerrigan can tell anyone."

A few hours later, Harvey Grant put the suicide notes and the guns into a large carton, which Victor Reis, his assistant, carried into the kitchen. A door from the kitchen opened into Grant's garage, so no one watching the house could see what they were doing. As soon as Reis put the carton in the trunk of Grant's Cadillac, he drove Grant to his meeting with the Kerrigans.

Stone pillars marked the entrance to the Westmont. Reis drove through them and up the winding driveway, then pulled up in front of the clubhouse. The parking valet opened the door for the judge then went around to the driver's door. Reis was already out of the car. He gave the valet the keys to the Cadillac. He had a second set in his pocket, which he would use later.

As Grant and Reis walked toward the main dining room, Burton Rommel walked up to them.

"We have to talk about Tim," Rommel said. "I'm hearing rumors that he's in trouble. This could affect our decision to have him run for Harold's seat."

"I'm having dinner with Tim and Bill, Burt. I'll straighten everything out."

"Good."

"Call me tomorrow and I'll tell you what happened."

"I will. This is something that we have to do right now," Rommel said emphatically.

"I agree completely. It won't do to wait around and let events take their course."

"Glad we're on the same wavelength."

The Kerrigans walked in a minute after Rommel walked away.

"I've arranged for us to eat in one of the private dining rooms," Grant said.

A narrow hall led to the back of the Westmont, where there were three private rooms. The one in which they were meeting had been swept for bugs shortly before the judge arrived. When they were all inside, Grant closed the door.

"I'm going to insist that Victor check you for listening devices before we talk."

William stiffened, but Tim laid a restraining hand on his forearm.

"It's okay, Dad. Let him frisk us so we can get down to business."

Reis was quick but thorough. When he was done, he shook his head.

"Victor, will you please wait outside and make sure that we're not disturbed."

"How are you feeling, Tim?" Grant asked as soon as the door closed behind Reis.

"Maria was acting on your orders, Harvey," Tim answered, "so you can cut the shit."

Grant stopped smiling. "What is it you want?"

"Your assurance that Cindy, Megan, and my father won't be hurt if I keep my mouth shut."

As soon as he closed the door of the private dining room, Victor Reis left the building and asked the valet for the keys to the car in which he was interested, and the number of the space in which it was parked. He also asked for the space where

Grant's Cadillac was parked. The valet gave Reis the keys and the information without asking any questions.

The Westmont's parking garage was a short distance from the main building. Reis was wary as he walked across a small outdoor lot to the garage. Two other members were waiting for their cars but Reis knew them. There were no strange cars or trucks within view.

Grant's Cadillac was on the second floor. Reis checked the garage before taking the carton out of the trunk. No one was on the floor. The other car was parked nearby. Reis carried the carton to the car and put it in the trunk. A minute later, he gave the keys back to the valet and returned to wait outside the private dining room.

Half an hour later, Reis drove Grant home. The judge's cell phone rang when they were almost to his gate. Just then, Victor Reis noticed two cars in the rearview mirror. It was very dark, but Reis was surprised that he hadn't noticed them before.

Grant pulled out his cell phone. "Hello."

"It's me."

"Why are you calling?" Grant asked.

"The carton wasn't in the trunk."

Grant blanched. He was about to question Victor when he saw two cars parked in front of his gate. Reis braked sharply. The trailing cars hemmed in the Cadillac. J. D. Hunter stepped out of one of the cars. Several armed FBI agents got out of the other cars and surrounded Grant. Hunter pressed his identification against the driver's side window. Standing behind him was Sean McCarthy. Reis lowered the glass.

"Good evening, Judge Grant, Mr. Reis," Hunter said. "Could you please step out of the car?"

"What's this about?" Grant demanded.

"Aiding and abetting the attempted murder of Tim Kerrigan, for starters. Then there are the attempts to murder Amanda Jaffe, Frank Jaffe, and Jon Dupre. Oh, yes, I almost forgot. There's the murder of United States Senator Harold Travis. I'm sure that there will be a lot more charges, but those will do for now."

fifty-four

J. D. Hunter knew that Harvey Grant would hang tough, so he let him stew for an hour before joining the prisoner in a narrow, uncomfortably hot interrogation room. The judge knew all the tricks and made no protests about the heat or the time he'd been kept waiting. He just looked Hunter in the eye with a cool, appraising stare.

"Good evening, Judge," Hunter said as another agent wheeled a television hooked up to a VCR into the room. "You're probably expecting me to try to trick you with clever questions but I don't have any. And I've been told that we can't use rubber truncheons anymore."

Grant remained stone-faced.

"We're not doing good cop, bad cop either," Hunter continued. "Just show and tell. So sit back and relax. Any cooperation with our investigation on your part will be strictly voluntary. Personally, I hope you don't cooperate. We've got enough evidence to send you away right now and I really don't want to cut you any breaks."

A third agent entered the room and stood by the door while the agent who'd entered with Hunter made certain that the VCR was working, before inserting a cassette.

"I'm going to show you a movie, but I'd like you to meet someone first. You don't have a heart condition, do you?"

Grant didn't respond. Hunter laughed. "I knew you'd be a bitch to crack." He turned to the agent who was guarding the door and nodded. The agent opened the door and stood aside. The judge leaned forward and stared.

Ally Bennett was standing in the doorway.

"Hi, Your Honor," she said. "I can't wait to testify against you and your friends."

Hunter nodded and Ally backed out of the room. Her eyes never left Grant until the door shut.

"Miss Bennett is alive and well. It was all a setup."

The judge looked thoroughly bewildered.

"Don't feel bad about being conned. The Bureau uses a magician on occasion when we want to create an illusion. This guy is really good.

I've seen his show in Vegas and L.A. Normally, I'd never let you in on a magician's professional secrets, but this will give you something to tell the other death-row inmates on cold, winter nights."

Grant kept his jaws clamped tight, but his mind was racing. Hunter nodded, and a picture appeared on the television. It was Stan Gregaros's car following Bennett's on the night Kerrigan was supposed to have killed her. Hunter pointed at the rear of Ally's car.

"One of Ms. Bennett's rear taillights was intentionally put out of commission. We had a cop pull her over to highlight that fact. When Stan got to the park, he was following a car with one working taillight. The trick depended on that piece of misdirection."

The picture changed to a shot of Gregaros entering the park and winding along the twisting road that led to the meadow.

"Earlier in the day, our magician constructed a stage set. We planted tall hedges to block the view from the road. There were black curtains on either side. Magicians call them black art drops. The drops look solid but can be penetrated by a car. At night, it was impossible for Stan to tell that there was a set at the side of the road.

"A row of low beacons guided Ally through the

drop and behind the stage, where she parked. Also behind the stage was a specially rigged car that was identical, down to the bad taillight, to the one Ally was driving. Inside the car was a corpse dressed in clothes identical to hers. Blood packs were attached to the cadaver's clothes, and a wig was glued in place. A body harness under the clothes was secured to a magnetic latch that we installed in the driver's seatback. This held the body in place until a signal released it."

On the screen, the rigged car drove up the road toward the meadow.

"A guidance wire had been laid under the gravel road bed," Hunter explained. "It led from the stage to the meadow. A unit was installed under the front bumper, which allowed the car to be driven along the wire by remote control. The agents who operated it were in a camouflaged tree house that overlooked the meadow. The remote-control system is similar to a system that the Germans are experimenting with on the Autobahn."

A maintenance truck suddenly appeared on the screen. Its high beams turned on.

"That truck was driven by an FBI agent," Hunter said. "Stan met him the next morning. He pretended to be a maintenance worker who'd written down most of Tim Kerrigan's license number.

"Anyway, the agent blinded Stan for a moment with the headlights to distract him. In the dark and momentarily blinded, he didn't see the substitution. When he saw a car with a single taillight headed for the meadow, he assumed it was Miss Bennett's."

Now the screen showed the meadow where Gregaros had thought he'd seen Tim Kerrigan murder Ally Bennett. The pictures on this section of the cassette had been taken from overhead.

"By the time Stan reached the meadow, Tim Kerrigan was already at the window of the second car. You've probably guessed by now that he's been working with us all along."

Grant felt light-headed. His stomach clenched.

"A remote-controlled tape in the tape deck of the rigged car contained Ally's half of the conversation. Our agents turned it on and off using a remote control in the tree house. A shotgun mike recorded everything Stan said. I can play you the audio if you'd like. I'm sure your attorney will want to hear it."

On the screen, Tim Kerrigan was emptying his revolver into the cadaver.

"A small reel operated by an electric motor was

installed below the front passenger seat. A thin, transparent multifilament that's impossible to see even in daylight was drawn out of the reel and attached to the corpse's left lower jaw from inside the mouth. When Tim shot the corpse, the blood packs were set off, spraying the car with blood. Then the magnetic catch was released and the reel was activated, snapping the head and torso of the cadaver to the right and pulling it face-down across the passenger seat so its face couldn't be seen. Ally's scream was played. Tim doused the interior of the car with gasoline and tossed in a match. The front seat had already been doctored to ignite with an intense heat to prevent Stan from looking inside the car for more than a second. In that second, he saw a corpse dressed like Ally. That, the shots, the blood, and the screams convinced him that Tim had killed Miss Bennett."

Hunter nodded and the agent turned off the VCR.

"I'm sorry you had to wait so long in here, but I was performing my little dog-and-pony show for Stan. I'm going to let you sit in here for a while longer, so you can think about life and death. It's useful to have complete quiet when you're contemplating such big subjects."

Hunter started to leave when he remembered something.

"Oh, I forgot to tell you that you have a right to remain silent. If you do decide to talk to me, anything you say can and will be used against you. You have a right to an attorney. If you can't afford an attorney, one will be provided for you free of charge."

Hunter paused and silently ticked off the warnings on his fingers. Then he smiled.

"Yeah, that's it. See you later."

fifty-five

Tim Kerrigan waited as J. D. Hunter rang his father's doorbell. Behind them, several agents dressed in windbreakers with FBI stitched across the back huddled against the elements, but Tim was oblivious to the cold wind and pelting rain. He felt empty inside and sadder than he'd ever been in his life.

The door opened. William looked confused by the presence of his son and the agents. He'd dropped off Tim at home after their meeting with Harvey Grant and here he was again.

"Why aren't you home?"

"Tim is here to give you a chance, Mr. Kerrigan. It was part of our deal."

"What are you talking about?"

"Harvey and Stan are in custody, Dad. These men are here to arrest you, but Agent Hunter and

I want to talk to you first. You don't have to. You can ask for a lawyer, but I think that would be a mistake."

"We have the carton with the signed confessions," Hunter said. "The other members of your group will be in custody before dawn."

Francine appeared at the top of the stairs.

"Who's there, Bill?"

Hunter walked past William and held up his identification. Tim and the other agents followed Hunter inside.

"I'm with the FBI, Mrs. Kerrigan. I have a warrant to search your house. We'll try to be as neat as possible. An agent will have to stay with you during the search."

"What is he talking about, Bill?"

"Let them search," Kerrigan told his wife.

"Can we talk someplace private?" Hunter asked.

Several officers headed up the stairs. Francine called after her husband, but he ignored her and led Tim and Hunter down the hall to his office. Hunter closed the door, cutting off the sound of Francine's strident protests.

"Ally Bennett is alive, Dad," Tim said as soon as they were seated.

William looked bewildered. It was the first time

Tim could remember when his father did not appear to be totally in charge. William turned to Hunter.

"You told me that Tim murdered her."

"Miss Bennett's murder was staged. She's alive and well and prepared to testify. You should know that we have Detective Gregaros on audiotape and videotape at the scene of the staged murder, making very incriminating statements. We also obtained a warrant before you met with Harvey Grant at the Westmont, and we have a recording of your call to the judge telling him that the carton is not in the trunk of your car."

Hunter paused. William held his tongue.

"Aren't you going to ask us what carton we're talking about?" Hunter asked.

"I don't know anything about a carton."

"No?" Hunter said. "So this is the first time you've heard about the carton of confessions that Victor Reis took from the judge's trunk, the carton he was supposed to put in your trunk? Doesn't ring any bells?"

William Kerrigan said nothing.

"We had to trick the judge into moving the confessions, because we had no idea where they were," Tim said. "I told you that I knew about them and was going to tell the police. We knew you'd tell Harvey and he'd figure out that we'd get a search warrant. That forced him to move them immediately. He couldn't give them to anyone who had signed a confession. That eliminated everyone but the original members of your group. Wendell Hayes was dead and Pedro Aragon is in Mexico. That left you."

"We had Tim insist on meeting at the Westmont to bring you and Grant together," Hunter said. "We thought you'd take advantage of the chance to switch the evidence there and we assumed it would be moved from Grant's car to yours. Since neither of you could afford to have Tim see the transfer, we were certain that Victor Reis would do it while the three of you were talking.

"We studied your car while you were with Tim at the hospital, and got a duplicate with matching plates and a lock that would take any Mercedes key in case you gave your key to Reis. The parking valet was an FBI agent. All we had to do after that was have the valet give Reis the number of the slot where the duplicate car was parked. He put the carton in the trunk, we drove the FBI car away, and put your car in the slot we'd just vacated."

"We've been through the confessions once,"

Tim said. "Some of the names came as a real shock. It made me sick to think that I trusted these people."

"You're going to be charged with conspiracy in the murder of Harold Travis and the attempted murder of the Jaffes, Jon Dupre, and your son," Hunter said. "The murder of Senator Travis can put you on death row.

"We'd like you to work with us. It would be helpful to have one of the original members of The Vaughn Street Glee Club as a government witness. It would mean a life sentence for you. But you have to act now. We haven't started to interrogate Harvey Grant and Detective Gregaros, but they know that Ally is alive and that Tim set them up. I promised Tim we'd talk to you before we spoke to them."

"What's it going to be, Dad?"

Kerrigan glared at Tim. "I should have known you'd never have the guts to kill someone."

Tim hung his head. Even now his father could hurt him.

"Your son was very brave, Mr. Kerrigan," Hunter said, "and very insistent that we give you the first opportunity to cut a deal."

Kerrigan stared at the agent. "I have no reason

to cut a deal. I don't know what you think Harvey Grant and this detective have done, but I'm not part of it."

J. D. Hunter ordered one agent to drive Tim Kerrigan home and another agent to drive Tim's father to jail. Cindy saw the car drive up and opened the door for him.

"Are you all right?" she asked warily. Tim had not told her what was going on, but she knew something terrible was happening.

"Is Megan asleep?"

"For hours."

"We need to talk."

Tim led his wife into the living room. "I'm going to tell you everything. I want you to know that I love you." Tim looked down. "I haven't always loved you but I know I do now. You might not love me when you hear what I have to say."

"Just tell me what happened tonight," Cindy said. Her tone was neutral and Tim could see how hard it was for her to hold in her emotions.

"My father has been arrested for conspiracy to commit murder and the attempted murder of several people, including me."

Cindy stared as if she did not understand.

"Harvey Grant and several other people—some

of whom we know very well—are also in custody."

"My God. That's impossible."

"They are guilty, Cindy. They are ruthless. You have no idea."

"Did you . . . ? Were you a part of this?"

"No! I've been working with the FBI."

Tim dropped his head again. He felt like he had the weight of the world on his shoulders.

"Then what have you done?" Cindy asked.

Tim took a deep breath. He was going to confess everything, absolutely everything. Then he would accept whatever Cindy chose to do.

"I am not the person you think I am. I am a bad person."

He choked and could not go on for a moment. Then he inhaled, he looked Cindy in the eye, and he began by telling her how he had deserted Melissa Stebbins a week and a half before the Rose Bowl.

fifty-six

Kate Ross found Amanda Jaffe idly stirring a cup of coffee in a booth in the hospital cafeteria. She looked solemn and exhausted, like everyone else in the restaurant.

"How's your dad?" Kate asked as she slid into the other side of the booth.

"He's in surgery. The doctors don't think there's any permanent damage. They'll be done soon and I'll find out for sure."

"Are you okay?"

"Physically, yeah. I was lucky. But I'm . . ." She shrugged.

"I know all about it, Amanda. One part of you is thrilled that you're alive and the other guy isn't, and another part feels guilty as hell, even though you know you didn't do a damn thing wrong."

Amanda nodded. "It's something like that. I'm

trying not to think about what happened at the house. Mostly, I've been worrying about Frank."

"I've got something for you that will help take your mind off Frank for a little bit. Jack Stamm called the office. He's scheduled a hearing at two to dismiss all the charges against Dupre."

"What?"

"Daniel is going to handle it, so you don't have to worry. And there's more, and you're going to love it. Harvey Grant, Stan Gregaros, and Tim Kerrigan's father are in custody."

"The Vaughn Street Glee Club?"

"That's what I'm thinking. And there's something else. Did you hear what happened to Tim?" Kate asked.

"Someone had a newspaper in the intensive care waiting room, so I saw the headline. I can't believe that Maria Lopez tried to kill him. Does anyone know why she did it?"

"All I know is that she's under arrest. I've tried some of my sources, but either they don't know anything, or they're not talking. But whatever is going on, our client is in the clear. Daniel will call when the hearing is over. I asked him to try and find out why the charges are being dropped and if it has anything to do with these arrests.

"One more thing. A patrol car went out to Jon's

safe house after I phoned in the shooting. The basement door was wide open and the police recovered some shells and found some blood, but no bodies."

"So your friends got away."

"It looks like it."

"I think that solves the problem of what to do with the duffel bag."

"Are you going to turn it over to Jon?"

Amanda stirred her coffee and stared into space. Kate let her think.

"An awful lot of people would be hurt if those tapes got out," she said. "And maybe they deserve to be. These men are supposed to be the pillars of our society—they're the ones who are always talking about getting tough on crime—and it's all a fraud."

"I can't disagree with anything you've said, but I don't know if I want to be the one who brings everyone down," Kate said. "Maybe the best thing for all concerned would be for the contents of that bag to disappear."

Part Seven

PEDRO'S
FORTUNE

fifty-seven

Tim Kerrigan slipped his arm around Cindy's shoulders and watched Megan scamper along the beach in search of seashells. Hugh Curtin had a friend—an ex-Cardinal linebacker—who owned a condo on Maui. They'd been seaside for a week and had one week left before Tim had to return to Portland for the hearings in The Vaughn Street Glee Club case, in which he was the star witness for the government. The only thing that kept the scene from being perfect were the armed guards who accompanied the Kerrigan family everywhere they went.

Tim was on leave from the district attorney's office. There was no way that his sexual escapade with Ally Bennett could be kept secret. He would have to testify about it in open court. Tim was certain that Harvey Grant would make sure that everyone learned of his other meetings with prostitutes. Jack wouldn't be able to keep him on. He wasn't sure he wanted to stay, anyway.

Huge had been right. He had been hiding in the DA's office. Where he would go from there was another question. With his sordid past, politics was no longer an option. Burton Rommel had made that clear during a hastily called meeting a few days after the case had exploded. He wouldn't be able to do anything much for a while, anyway. Testifying for, and debriefings by, the state and federal prosecutors would keep him busy. He was actually grateful for the time off. It was helping him heal the wounds he'd inflicted on his family.

Tim had always longed for his father's approval and never received it. William had made him feel small his whole life. Now he knew that his father was a fraud, and he had finally accepted that his worth was not tied to his father's approval.

Tim's confession to Cindy had been the most difficult thing he'd ever done. He could see the disbelief and pain etched on her face as she sat in shocked silence during his recitation of his deceits. Then he'd told her about the turning point—the day he'd spent with her and Megan at the zoo.

"I had convinced myself that I could kill Ally and get away with it, but I knew it would be like committing suicide. Deserting Melissa Stebbins had almost killed me. Murdering Ally Bennett would have finished me off.

"But that's not what stopped me. It was Megan." He had choked up and had to wait before going on. "I'd betrayed you in every way possible but I was still a hero to her. When I met with Hunter I felt like I was making my ninety-yard run again, but this time on my own, with no blockers. I knew that every sin I'd committed would become public knowledge but I hoped, when she was old enough to understand, that she would think of me as . . ." He'd paused again. "Not a hero. I'll never be that. But as someone who tried to do what was right."

He and Cindy had slept apart that night, and Tim was convinced that his marriage was over. Cindy was civil but distant for the next few days. He didn't see much of her anyway, because he was at FBI headquarters, the Multnomah County district attorney's office, and the U.S. attorney's office, night and day. One evening, he'd come home late and walked past the open door to their bedroom toward the guest room where he'd been sleeping. Cindy was still awake and she'd told him to come to bed. Neither of them said much while they made love, but Tim knew that she'd taken him back and was going to give him a chance to start over.

Up ahead, Megan had found a piece of driftwood and was calling to him to come see. Cindy smiled at him and squeezed his hand. If that warm pressure was all he got back for his ordeal, Tim decided that it was more than enough.

fifty-eight

For two weeks, starting the night after she'd killed Manuel Castillo, Amanda's nightmares had been ferocious. She'd finally given in and used the pills that Ben Dodson had prescribed. The drugs made the nightmares stop, but taking them didn't feel right. She had stopped taking the pills three days ago, preferring to deal with her personal demons stone-cold sober.

Killing Castillo had been awful, but the slaying was self-defense and she was not ashamed that she'd taken his life. Castillo was a terrible person. The police had told her that she had rid Portland of a psychopath who had killed without compunction. Sean McCarthy had even read her a list of murders in which Castillo was the main suspect. What calmed her most was the certainty that Frank would be dead now if she'd hesitated.

The previous evening, Amanda had slept through the night for the first time. She had dreamed, but it was a normal dream. Today, during her weekly appointment, she'd told Dr. Dodson that she wasn't taking the pills. He was supportive, but he warned her that one good night did not mean that her problems were over. She knew she had a way to go, but she felt better than she had in months.

Frank was still recuperating at home. He thought he might try working half days starting next week. Amanda wanted to move back to her condo, but she was still camped out in her old room because she didn't want Frank to be alone. His left arm was in a sling and he was limping badly. It was hard for him to get around, and cooking was especially difficult with one arm.

A week ago, Amanda had driven to the Y for her first workout since the home invasion. By the time she walked onto the pool deck, several of the swimmers in the Master's program were in the lanes set aside for the team. She was walking to her lane when Toby got out of the water.

"Amanda!"

"Hi."

"I couldn't believe it when I saw you on TV. Are you okay?"

"Not completely, but I'm getting there. I thought I'd try to get back in my routine."

"Good idea." Brooks shook his head. "It must have been awful for you."

Amanda didn't answer. She felt uncomfortable talking about the attack on her father's home.

"I actually thought of giving you a ring to see how you were doing," Toby said. "I almost called you twice."

"Why didn't you?"

Toby shrugged. "I didn't want to hassle you. I figured you probably had enough people calling. I know if something like that happened to me I'd probably want to be by myself."

Toby hesitated. Then he looked into Amanda's eyes. "And I don't really know you. We only talked twice for a few seconds."

Amanda tried to sound calm but her heart was going as fast as it did at the end of a race.

"Next time, I could probably manage at least a minute," she said.

"How about this weekend?"

"I've got to check with my dad. He's out of the hospital, but he's still recuperating. Can I call you?"

"Yeah." Toby grinned. "This'll give me time to figure out how to recruit you for the team."

"Try bribing me. Dinner at a classy restaurant might do it."

"I'll check my bribe budget and await your call," Toby said as he slipped back into the water.

Amanda headed toward a lane. Somewhere during their talk she'd stopped feeling scared.

The maitre d' led Amanda, Toby Brooks, Kate Ross, and Daniel Ames to their table in the back of the packed restaurant. Mephisto's was Portland's latest attempt to replicate New York hip. It was noisy, crowded with trendy dressers, and Amanda figured herself for one of the oldest people in the joint. Toby had suggested the place for their second date, because the food was supposed to be good and the people-watching great.

An anorexic waitress introduced herself as their server and took their drink orders, which had to be shouted over the din.

"If I lose my hearing I'm suing you," Amanda yelled at Toby. He grinned.

"I'm going to the ladies' room," Kate shouted in Amanda's ear.

Amanda told Toby where the women were headed and followed Kate's back through the crowd. As they passed the bar, which was three deep, someone touched her arm. Amanda turned and found herself face to face with Jon Dupre.

"You here alone?" he asked.

"No. A date and friends."

"Point out the table and I'll have a bottle of champagne sent over."

"That's not necessary."

"Of course it is. If it wasn't for you, I wouldn't be here, tonight, and able to treat you."

Dupre's smiled faded and he looked serious. "You did a great job, Amanda."

"You really should be thanking Ally."

"Have you heard anything about where she is?"

"She's in the witness protection program and has a new identity. They won't tell anyone where to find her. The only thing I did hear is that she has custody of Lori Andrews's daughter."

"That's great. I hope she has a terrific life."

"She deserves one. You'd still be in jail if it weren't for her. She must have loved you a lot to risk so much for you."

Dupre looked puzzled for a moment.

"You mean romantically?" he asked.

Amanda nodded.

"You've got that all wrong."

Amanda looked confused. Dupre laughed. "You didn't know, did you?"

"Know what?"

"About Ally. It's why she took Lori's kid. She wasn't in love with me. Lori was her lover."

"But she told me that you and she . . ."

"What? That we screwed?"

Amanda nodded.

"We did, once—a threesome with Lori, actually. But it was clear that they were a lot more interested in each other than they were in me, so . . ." Jon shrugged.

But Amanda had stopped listening moments before. **Ally and Lori had been lovers**. Suddenly everything made sense.

"What's wrong?" Dupre asked.

"Ally must have been furious with you for sending Lori to Senator Travis."

"Jesus, was she ever. Ally went off the deep end when they discovered the body."

"She forgave you, though, didn't she?" Amanda asked.

"After I was busted. She came to the jail and told me she'd do anything to get me out. I guess she meant what she said."

Amanda felt so stupid. Suddenly, a heavily made-up redhead in a skintight, low-cut dress pushed through the crowd and latched onto

Dupre's arm. Amanda noticed that her pupils were the size of wagon wheels. Dupre saw her checking them, and colored.

"Who's this?" the redhead asked suspiciously.

"Maggie, meet my attorney, Amanda Jaffe."

Maggie nodded and flashed Amanda a proprietary glare.

"Nice meeting you," Amanda said. "See you around, Jon."

Kate Ross was waiting for Amanda outside the door to the restroom.

"What did Dupre want?" she asked.

"Just to say hello."

"That pencil he's with had a cocaine mustache when she left the little girls' room."

"I'm his lawyer, Kate, not his mother."

"Touché."

"I want to run something by you," Amanda said. There were no other women waiting, but she checked around her to make certain that no one could overhear them. "Jon said something that got me thinking. Did you know that Ally Bennett and Lori Andrews were lovers?"

"No shit!"

"Maybe The Vaughn Street Glee Club wasn't responsible for Senator Travis's murder. They had the motive to kill him—he was out of control and putting the conspiracy in danger—but think about the MO."

"You're right. It wasn't the same."

Amanda nodded. "The club sedated its victims to fool the police into thinking that a murder was a suicide. But there was never any question that Travis was murdered."

"And look at how he was murdered," Kate said, more to herself than to Amanda. "The person who killed Travis hated him."

Kate was quiet for a moment. "Are you thinking that Ally killed Travis to avenge Lori Andrews?"

Amanda nodded. "Carl Rittenhouse told Tim about a phone call that Travis got the night he died, telling him that Jon Dupre wanted to make it up to him for the incident at the Westmont. A police report says that a call was made from Jon's house to the senator's house that evening. We know that Ally was the only person with Jon after Joyce Hamada and Cheryl Riggio left, and Hamada said that he had passed out."

"So you think Bennett made the call, lured Travis to the A-frame, drugged him, and beat him to death?"

"It's possible. I mean, it all makes sense. Even

Wendell Hayes's attempt to murder Jon. Hayes and the others thought that Dupre had murdered one of their own. Maybe they were trying to kill him to avenge the death of a member of their secret circle."

"Wait a minute. What about the earring? Dupre's earring was found at Travis's cabin. How did it get there?"

"Ally blamed Jon for sending Lori to the senator after the way he beat her the first time. I think she doped Jon, too, then took the earring from Jon's house and planted it to frame him. But once he was arrested, she regretted what she'd done and tried to save him."

"I guess it's possible," Kate said. "But can you prove it?"

"I'm not even going to try. My job was to clear Jon. I don't have to find Travis's killer. That's a job for the police."

"And you're not going to help them, are you?"

"Travis was scum. He murdered Lori Andrews and he got what he deserved. Whether it was Jon who killed him, or The Glee Club, or Ally Bennett, it can remain a mystery, as far as I'm concerned."

"What if Grant or Kerrigan or someone else is convicted for killing Travis?"

Amanda remembered how she felt when Castillo kidnapped her and the terror that had almost paralyzed her in Frank's basement. Castillo had been acting on Grant and Kerrigan's orders. They wanted to break her, to kill her. And it wasn't just her. How many other people had they murdered? If they went to death row for a crime they didn't commit, so be it. Justice would be served when The Vaughn Street Glee Club failed to exist.

fifty-nine

Pedro Aragon was sunning himself on the patio of his hacienda when one of his men brought him the phone. A nubile, brown-skinned woman in a thong was lying beside Pedro. The woman looked a lot like the fantasy woman in the dream that he'd awakened to on the day he met Harvey Grant, Wendell Hayes, and William Kerrigan so many years ago.

"It's Señor Kerrigan."

Pedro had been expecting the call but he had hoped it would never come. He was sad that Bill had made it.

"There's a lot going on, Pedro."

"I know. I get the papers here. Poor Harvey and Stan. It doesn't look so good for them. How are you doing?"

"I'm sweating bullets. So far, they haven't given

me up. Neither has Maria. You did a good job raising her. She's a great kid."

"Thank you, Bill."

Pedro waited. He knew that his old friend would get to the point soon. He could hear the strain in his voice.

"We should get together, fast," Kerrigan said.

"Sure. When can you come down?"

"I was thinking that you'd come up here."

Pedro wondered who was forcing Bill to make the call. Was it the FBI, or the DEA, or the Portland police?

"It's all rain and gloom in Oregon, but the sun is shining down here. Visit me, **amigo**."

"That will be difficult."

"I have a lovely young woman with me, Bill. She makes the best margaritas. I'll get one for you, too. You want a redhead, a blonde? Whatever you want."

"It wouldn't be smart to meet down there. After what happened with Manuel, there's got to be a million eyes on you. Come up here, but we have to move. I'm not under suspicion for the moment, but that could change fast."

The woman lying beside Pedro shifted from her belly to her back, giving Pedro a lovely view of her breasts. He especially liked her nipples, which stood up nice and straight.

"What's that you said?" asked Pedro, who had been distracted by the nipples and had missed Kerrigan's last sentence.

"I said you could fly up in your private plane. Use the landing strip in Sisters. We'll talk in my fishing cabin in Camp Sherman. No one will be watching it."

"Good thinking. Let me check and get back to you."

"When do you think you'll know?"

"We got to move fast, right?"

"Very."

"Then I'll be back to you soon. Take care."

Pedro hung up. He smiled sadly. Fucking Bill Kerrigan. There was no honor among thieves. Blood, that was a different story. Maria was holding up. Pedro stopped smiling. He worried about her. The lawyers said her case was tough, but they weren't giving up. Maybe they'd cut a deal.

Pedro sighed. He stood up and walked to the edge of the patio. There was a swath of lawn, a large pool, more lawn, and then the jungle. Armed guards walked the perimeter.

Pedro watched the guards for a moment before

losing interest. He turned away. There were those breasts again. He felt himself getting hard. Better do something about that, he thought. He patted the woman on the rump and whispered in her ear. She giggled and got off her lounge chair. As Pedro followed her inside, he felt a moment of melancholy. The Vaughn Street Glee Club was no more.

Then he cheered up. It had lasted longer than he ever thought it would—much longer. He felt sorry for Harvey and Wendell and Bill, but Pedro was a big fan of Darwin. Survival was for the fittest, no? He was the sole survivor and he was going to get laid as befitted the leader of the pack. He felt like he would live forever.

Miss Sunny Day was peeling off her G-string on the main stage of the Jungle Club while its owner, Martin Breach, sat in his office at the back of the strip joint, waxing philosophical. The recipient of his musings was his only friend and chief enforcer, Art Prochaska, a giant with a bald, bullet-shaped head and no conscience.

"I was at that Chinese restaurant on eighty-second yesterday, Arty. You know the one."

"The Jade something."

"Yeah."

Breach handed a narrow slip of paper across the desk to his friend.

"I got that in my fortune cookie. See what it says?"

"'While we stop to think, we often miss our opportunity,'" Prochaska read slowly.

"Exactly. That fortune got me thinking about how life can give us surprise opportunities, like the Jaffes, for instance. I do a favor for Frank, now his kid does one for us by chopping up Manuel Castillo. Such a nice kid, too. Who'd of thought she had it in her?"

"That was sure a surprise, Marty; a girl making hamburger out of Castillo."

"With Pedro's muscle off the street we're seeing a little anarchy in the drug business," Breach continued.

Prochaska only had a dim idea of the definition of "anarchy," so he just nodded and hoped that Breach wouldn't ask him about it.

"Aragon is weak right now, what with all the judges and lawyers and cops who are connected to him being arrested." Breach paused and fixed his beady eyes on his friend. "Do you see where I'm going with this, Arty? Opportunity is knocking. Like the cookie said, we'll miss it if we don't do something fast. What do you think?"

Prochaska's brow furrowed for a moment while he contemplated the opportunity about which his friend spoke. Then he remembered that the gist of Marty's fortune-cookie message was that thinking too much could screw up everything. Thinking had never been Prochaska's long suit anyway. He was a man of action.

"What's that anarchy mean?" Prochaska asked.

"Everybody running around doing what they want. No order or nothing."

"Order is good, right?"

"Sure. Especially if the right guy is giving the orders."

"Pedro's not just going to give us his territory, Marty. He'll make trouble."

"Yeah," Breach said thoughtfully. "He's the type of guy who'd say we'd have to take it over his dead body."

Prochaska grinned and Breach stared at the wall in rapt concentration.

"Anthony speaks Spanish, right?" Breach asked.

"I think so."

"Think he'd like to go to Mexico?"

acknowledgments

I depend on the advice of experts in various fields to make my novels as realistic as possible. Special thanks goes to Dr. Jim Boehnlein, Dr. Karen Gunson, Sgt. Mary Linstrand, Ed Pritchard, Ken Lerner, Norm Frink, and Dr. Don Girard. If it sounds like I know everything it's because of these folks. All errors are mine.

Thank-yous to Nikola Scott, Laurie Shertz, Jerry, Judy, Joe, Eleonore, Doreen, and Daniel Margolin, Helen and Norman Stamm, Pam Webb, and Jay Margulies for taking the time to give various drafts of this book a critical read. My daughter, Ami, usually helps out but she's out of the country in the Peace Corps.

Dan Conaway, my editor, came up with several excellent ideas that make **Ties That Bind** significantly better than when he first read it. He is a pleasure to work with, as are all the people at HarperCollins.

I always thank Jean Naggar and everyone at her literary agency. There is a reason for that. They are the best.

And a final acknowledgment for a good friend and fellow writer, Vince Kohler, who provided expert advice on firearms whenever I nagged him for it, and who took time from his work and writing schedule to read my first drafts. Vince passed away and I miss him.